'Bold, evocative and brave – *Gulliver's Wife* is a revelation
in story-telling. I am in awe of Lauren Chater's talent.
Gulliver's Wife had my heart from the opening line and didn't
let go until long after I finished the final page.
An exquisitely told tale of love, loss and the magic of life.'
TESS WOODS, AUTHOR OF *LOVE AT FIRST FLIGHT*

'Wise, tender and heartening ... Chater shows a deft hand in authentically
recreating the challenges and injustices faced by the spirited
women in her novel so that their setbacks and triumphs felt like my own.'
SALLY PIPER, AUTHOR OF *THE GEOGRAPHY OF FRIENDSHIP*

'Filled with evocative details of life in early 1700s London,
Gulliver's Wife is an enthralling reimagining of the lives of the women
around Lemuel Gulliver, and an invitation to consider the untold
stories of women throughout the history of literature.'
SARAH ARMSTRONG, AUTHOR OF *HIS OTHER HOUSE*

'A beautifully written novel that maintains a page-turning
pace, heightened suspense and literal wonder on every page.'
CASS MORIARTY, AUTHOR OF *THE PROMISE SEED*

'*Gulliver's Wife* is exquisite, empathetic and engrossing
storytelling from an extraordinarily gifted writer.'
WENDY J. DUNN

GULLIVER'S
WIFE

Also by Lauren Chater

The Lace Weaver
Well Read Cookies

GULLIVER'S WIFE

Lauren Chater

SIMON &
SCHUSTER
London · New York · Sydney · Toronto · New Delhi
A CBS COMPANY

GULLIVER'S WIFE
First published in Australia in 2020 by
Simon & Schuster (Australia) Pty Limited
Suite 19A, Level 1, Building C, 450 Miller Street, Cammeray, NSW 2062

10 9 8 7 6 5 4 3 2 1

A CBS Company
Sydney New York London Toronto New Delhi
Visit our website at www.simonandschuster.com.au

© Lauren Chater 2020

All rights reserved. No part of this publication may be reproduced, stored in a retrieval system, or transmitted in any form or by any means, electronic, mechanical, photocopying, recording or otherwise, without prior permission of the publisher.

 A catalogue record for this book is available from the National Library of Australia

Cover design: Christabella Designs
Cover image: Magdalena Wasiczek/Trevillion Images
Typeset by Midland Typesetters, Australia
Printed and bound in Australia by Griffin Press

 The paper this book is printed on is certified against the Forest Stewardship Council® Standards. Griffin Press holds FSC® chain of custody certification SGS-COC-005088. FSC® promotes environmentally responsible, socially beneficial and economically viable management of the world's forests.

*For my mother, who taught me
about the wonders of life and death
and everything in between*

'It is an inexpressible pleasure for travellers, when after many traverses and tossings too and again, they return quietly home to their studies and rememorates all the unexpected pleasure that they encountered with upon the one coast, and the horrible vexations and confusions that they had upon another.'
The Ten Pleasures of Marriage, Aphra Behn, 1682

'. . . a wife should be always a reasonable and agreeable companion, because she cannot always be young.'
Gulliver's Travels, Jonathan Swift, 1726

Prologue

The sea has given birth to a man.

He dreams on a bed of sand and his dreams are slippery. They beat a gentle cadence: the soft whisper of plumage, teasing his mind with tokens of the past. His first fight as a student at the local grammar school, the fizz of blood in his veins, the taste of copper. His opponent's face – he cannot recall the boy's name – crumpling beneath his fist, features vanishing in a glossy oil painting of skin and teeth. He sees his mother's thin body hunched over the writing desk, begging Uncle John for funds to send him to Cambridge college. Most of all, he dreams of the river, its start in Trewsbury Mead and then its course through the centre of London. He remembers a poem once read to him by his tutor, a few paragraphs of shambling script the man wrote himself. The work was badly formed, but one phrase stuck, one image: the Thames was the river of time, his tutor said. Between its currents we were born and within its muddy borders we must expect to expire.

The water of this Indian Ocean is so different from the Thames, though.

He lifts himself, or tries to, first one leg and then the other. They will not turn to account; his legs appear stuck fast, bonded to the sand with ropes of kelp. His guts cramp. He jerks his head upwards. A patch of hair near his forehead rips free of its moorings and beneath the searing pain, he feels blood pool in the cradle of his ear.

God save me.

Gulls wheel overhead, pale wraiths against the fading light. Their raucous cries split the air and raise goose pimples on his bare skin. When he set out from Bristol with the rest of the crew – a lifetime ago, it seems – two crows tore each other to shreds in the sky above the mast and a maelstrom of feathers and guts rained down across the deck.

'An omen,' someone said, and the others laughed. Did he laugh with them? He cannot remember, but the shrill noise of the gulls now fills him with a sickening dread and he can see himself as they see him, looking down from a great height. There is his hair, the colour of wet sand, fanned out against the shore and there his arms, hands clenched by his sides.

Struggle as he might, he is caught, fastened like some ancient sacrifice. It's useless to fight. He would do better to rest and conserve his energy for the struggle ahead, for whoever has him ensnared will surely return. There is no magic, after all. He, Lemuel Gulliver, is a man of logic and science. No room for pagan belief, omens or imaginings. When his opponent returns, he will take his chances and then, somehow, he will find his way home.

The sun is beginning to sink on the horizon, just visible if he gazes down past the bridge of his nose. Water tickles his feet. The incoming tide.

Each surge brings a spate of foam rushing up his legs, the sound muffled through the blood clogging his ear. Although he should be tense, he finds his muscles relaxing. He allows his head to fall back until he is floating, weightless. The water is warm. This is the end, he thinks, and the thought no longer seems troubling. There are worse ways to go. Laid out on an operating table beside his organs, or waiting for his guts to strangle him to death like Jimsy and the others whose bodies now rest at the bottom of the sea. It proved beyond him to help those men, but perhaps he can help himself. He can free his mind of its bonds, help cut away the extraneous fetters that tie him to this life. One by one, he sets them loose: his daughter, his son, his maps. His wife.

A blast echoes, like the bugle cry of a horn, and his eyes fly open. Darkness. Water is everywhere, waves splashing up his cheeks. He is pulled in every direction, rolled into the surf. His mouth opens wide in surprise, allowing a glut of seawater to surge in. Unable to surface, he drinks, and as the water fills his lungs, imagines he is drinking the ocean dry. There will be nothing left but brittle coral and the pearly bones of dead men.

Dizziness spins his head. He spits out a mouthful of bitter brine. Now seemingly unbound, he claws the current with his hands, legs kicking. Exhilaration swoops through his body, inflating his limbs as he breaks the surface. Water slaps his chest, his toes grip the sea bed. Each breath is a bellows, a furnace sparking fire in his chest.

The shore within grasp, he lunges out and falls headfirst, flailing, into the wash. Spent, he lets the small waves caress his face.

Only then does he hear the voices.

1

Wapping, London
April, 1702

'Widow Gulliver, is it true your husband once saw a monster?'

Everybody turns and Mary's cheeks grow hot under the hawkish scrutiny of a dozen pairs of eyes. The confinement room above Stewart's bakery seethes with gossips. Some are Sal Stewart's neighbours, but others hail from further afield – Sal's sister, for instance, who has travelled from Dorset on the coach. Ranged about on sofas and chairs, they are waiting, expectant, wine glasses half-raised to parted lips.

Mary frowns at the bed where she is knuckle-deep in Sal's privities. The presence of gossips is an unfortunate necessity. Should Sal's infant die, their testimony will protect her from whispers of murder and witchcraft. Mary is so used to performing her tasks in front of an audience that the intrusion of voices doesn't often bother her. Today she wonders if the benefit is worth the fuss.

'Perhaps,' she mutters. 'I cannot say. I wasn't there.'

The gossips explode, all of them talking at once, reminding her of a fire that broke out six months ago at the builders' yard. How swiftly that single column of flame multiplied, flaring over and over, until every man was hacking at the burning rigs in their timber cradles to save the ships before they burned. The women toss questions at her: How big was the monster? What did it look like? How did he fight it off?

'I don't know,' she says, or, 'I can't presume.'

When they tire of the subject, talk turns to other things: Queen Anne's impending coronation, the Spanish war, the treacherous French, the soaring cost of sugar. Poor Sal, sweltering on the bed, is all but forgotten.

'How are you faring?' Mary says. Beneath her hands, Sal's body shudders. Sweat slicks her face and neck. She wears a man's knee-length cotton shirt, her breasts splayed beneath the thin fabric, nudged aside by her belly's heaving swell. 'Not long now.' Mary smears the blood and mucus from her fingers onto a clean clout.

Sal struggles onto her elbows. 'You felt it? The child?'

'Yes, he's a good head of hair on him. I hope you've trimmed enough bonnets.'

Sal's face breaks open in a smile before the pain begins to build and she must succumb to the spasmodic urges of her body. Mary tracks her movements with a sharp eye. This is the second child Mary has helped Sal birth; she remembers the first, a white-skinned poppet who, despite Mary's fervent ministrations, never opened her eyes in this life. Sal's grief-struck keening haunted her for weeks afterwards. She couldn't help thinking of her own lost souls back in the early days of her marriage, their clotted endings in the chamber pot after a night of cramps. Many physicians (and even some midwives) consider a lifeless child a gross aberration, but Mary has never thought it so. Each child, however tiny, however imperfectly formed, is human in her eyes; each worthy of its mother's love.

Sal's groans intensify. 'Lord help me,' she mutters, bunching her husband's shirt in her hand. From downstairs comes the rhythmic thump of fists pummelling dough and the yeasty smell of bread loaves rising in a hot oven. The gossips have quietened. Someone passes sweetmeats, but the platter of candied fruits and marchpane revolves twice before returning to the table, untouched. Everyone has lost their appetite for both conjecture and comestibles; their attention is riveted, at last, on the struggle taking place at the edge of the bed, where Mary has propped the baker's wife on her knees. The close air in the room is charged. All the women feel it, though they won't admit the truth even to themselves: low-down tugging, the sympathetic contraction and stretch of uterine walls.

With much encouragement, the baby's crown appears, an ellipsis of dark matted hair, vanishing and reappearing. Each surge brings Sal's infant closer to the moment of separation, the slippage between two existences. Mary dangles the eaglestone near Sal's buttocks. The small geode belonged to her mother, who used it to tempt little imps out of their cosy wombs.

On the cusp of this precipice, Sal's body flags.

'I can't!' she wails, after another half an hour of pushing has passed. 'I'm done!' She pounds the mattress with her fists and writhes, possessed. The women step back; even Kat, a ruddy country wife who birthed six of her own, looks sorrowful and cannot summon the right words to help.

Mary leans down, whispering encouragement, pleading, promising, until Sal's spirit reignites and she roars.

The child slips out into Mary's hands: greasy, shivery blue, sprouting black hairs on his head as soft as thistledown. Apoplectic cries tremble his body; his legs jerk like a frog's. Mary cuts the navel cord and hands him to his mother, who collapses back on the bed, pulling him to her chest. The room fills with the sound of contented suckling. Kat opens the shutters, warm sunlight flooding in as mother and infant observe each other, the baby's lids already at half-mast.

Mary, bundling up the afterbirth, notes the tender way Sal cradles her dimpled deity. In all the years she's been helping women birth their babies, this first meeting between mother and child still strikes her as nothing short of sacred. Life is hard for Mary's clients, not just its inception but its continuity. A bout of illness, a lean winter, wars fought in distant lands: any one of these things can tip the balance. She knows, better than most, how fortunes can tumble, how luck, good or ill, can mean the difference between plenty and poverty. Infants under her care are always expiring because their very grasp on this life is fragile as the roots of a primula. When Mary was a girl, she used to pester her mother, demanding to know why death claimed some and spared others. Over many years, she's come to accept that there are no answers, no talismans or potions which can halt death in its tracks, but knowing she has played her part in the triumph of these living births is its own reward.

George Stewart appears in the doorway, twisting his apron nervously, his dark hair floured winter-white. Mary shows him how to make a cradle with his arms.

'Why, he weighs no more than a loaf of rye,' he says, blinking down in wonder. The infant purses his cupid lips, dreaming of milk, milk and more milk. George's forehead creases, no doubt thinking of the little girl, resting under the grassy hump in

Bonehill. Mary blows gently over the newborn's face until he crinkles his nose and flutters his dark lashes.

'He's beautiful, George,' she says, her smile full and warm. 'A healthy boy. He intends to stay.'

'Aye,' George says, bestowing clumsy kisses upon the small fingers welded tight to his own. 'Aye, Mary, you're right.'

On the step of Stewart's bakery, Mary swelters in the afternoon heat, clasping an enormous basket of loaves and cakes. A warm breeze teases the folds of her red midwife's cloak and billows the loose stomacher and wide grey sleeves; the flexible fabric allows her to catch slippery babies with ease or wield a mattock into the hard earth of the garden. Around her, women depart the bakery in groups of twos and threes, complaining of the heat.

'Farewell, Missus Gulliver!' calls Elsie Burr.

'Good luck,' Mary calls back. 'God be with you!'

Elsie grins and pats her belly. Only a few weeks stand between this day and her own confinement, although since she lives upriver, she falls under Midwife Hopkins's care. Her hatless hair gleams as she strides away, arm in arm with her mother. They pass a hog rooting through a pile of steaming refuse; alerted, it lifts its head and charges. The older woman screams but Elsie, clutching her stomach, chases after it. For a woman approaching confinement, she is remarkably spry, but then Mary has known pregnant women threatened by danger to summon the combined strength of four or five men. She's seen one mother face down a rabid dog and yet another mount a burning staircase to drag her children to safety.

The frightened hog veers left and Elsie pursues it all the way to the corner, shouting obscenities. When it disappears, she returns, red-faced, and the two women resume their slow perambulation.

'That one will have no trouble in the confinement room.'

Mary turns to find one of Sal's many cousins standing nearby, clutching a worn travelling case. The woman's face is tanned and freckled under the broad brim of her hat. Even here in Wapping – an East London melting pot of impoverished dockland families, nomadic sailors and enterprising businessmen – the woman's old-fashioned dress and way of speaking marks her as other. She is, perhaps, the wife of a farmer who works the fields beyond greater London.

'I'm bound for Bell's Inn,' the woman says. 'There's no room here at Sal's. Kat has crammed everyone in the parlour, sleeping head to toe. She is bossier than a shepherdess with a wayward flock and I would rather spend the night with a stranger than listen to her scold.' She peers into the basket George has filled with loaves and cakes. 'Will you need help eating all those?'

Mary smiles. 'My daughter Bess is always hungry.'

The woman clucks. 'I hope you will enjoy some yourself. You deserve it. I've no babies of my own, but if I did I would pray for a midwife like you. It was your encouragement made the difference to her today. I noticed, even if others didn't.'

Mary flushes. 'Sal would have done it herself,' she says. 'With or without my encouragement. Women sometimes do not know what they are capable of.'

The woman eyes her, curious. 'How long you been a midwife?'

'Forever, it feels like. It's a long story. Too long for me to go into now . . . My mother taught me the trade, but she died when I was young. I didn't practise again for years, until my late husband went to sea.'

Sal's cousin nods, taking in her words. 'Your husband, the storyteller?'

'Late husband.'

'Ah, yes. I'm mighty sorry for your loss.'

She shrugs off the woman's polite platitude. It's been three years now since Lemuel left on the *Antelope*, two and a half since a lad from the dry docks came to tell her that his ship had sunk off the coast of Sumatra. The funeral was held in Nottingham. She'd watched the men carry his empty coffin into the family crypt, expecting at any moment to see him spring out of the congregation and announce it was all a hoax. When the last of the mourners left, she approached the coffin to say her final goodbyes, a chill creeping up through the dank earth to numb her legs.

Her grief was complex, a mystery even to herself. Letters had begun to arrive before they'd left London for the funeral – invoices demanding payment for credit accounts held in her husband's name. One missive contained a sum so staggeringly large the shock sent her, trembling, to her knees. Flicking through the invoices was like perusing a directory of London's most popular amusement halls. Names swam before her eyes – the Green Grasshopper, the Cheshire Cheese, the Rose and Lamb. Places she'd never even heard of, much less set foot in. Domestic mysteries unravelled as she remembered how each time Lemuel had returned from sea, he'd handed over a paltry amount of coins 'for your keeping and that of the children' and then the next day begged money from her purse, which she forfeited to keep the peace. All along, he'd been racking up more debts, out of her sight. In the crypt, there was no body to direct her anger towards, only an empty timber casket. She remembers leaving without a backwards glance, thinking that although the debts would need to be paid, there was some relief in knowing he would never again walk into their lives, bringing trouble with him like a swarm of fleas.

Mary points Sal's cousin in the direction of the inn and the woman says her goodbyes. The last of the gossips sidles past her on the step with a muttered, 'Good day,' and then the bakery is empty, at least until George thumps back downstairs to reopen.

Mary's house is only three streets away, but the heat and the basket impede her progress. Four men jog past, resplendent in fine livery, hefting an empty sedan chair between them. She imagines hailing them, the exquisite sensation of airy weightlessness, but she can't afford to waste coins on such luxury. She turns down a narrow walkway clogged with pedestrians and livestock, cradling the basket to shield its contents from the rough elbows of passing labourers and the unwanted attentions of bare-footed cress girls brandishing limp produce on oilskin trays. Despite her blithe reply to Sal's cousin, the loaves and cakes in her basket are sorely needed. When she gets home, she will divide the cakes into eighths, wrap them in thick layers of muslin and place them in the cool buttery to ward off the mould. The prized white bread (not their usual coarse brown, stamped with the despised H for housewife) will be safely stored in its basket. Each day, Alice – their maid – will slice off a hunk and crumble it onto a plate to be eaten with their supper broth, and in the inventory book Mary will scratch her nib through *One slice of Mister Stewart's bread* and place the ledger back on its shelf. Thus their happy windfall will not be greedily gobbled but added to the pool of victuals that account for their monthly food expenses.

A door nearby opens and Mirabel Pearce emerges, a rolled-up hearthrug tucked under one arm. She shakes the rug, unleashing a thick cloud of soot that sticks in Mary's throat. Mirabel is all apology, her face streaked with smuts. 'Let me fetch you a cup of ale, Missus Midwife,' she says. 'Step inside and see the twins.'

Mary thanks her but waves the woman off.

'Shall I send Dora down later with some jellies?' Mirabel persists. 'She's fixing some for Mister Pearce. His ship came in yesterday, praise God. We're so thankful to have him back. I fairly fell at his feet, such a relief it was to see his blessed face.'

She waits for Mary to walk on before resuming her violent drubbing. What a strange beast marriage is, Mary thinks. Only last month, Mirabel was lamenting her lot and confiding the morbid conviction that her husband would meet his end at the hands of cannibals or mutineers. Thank God for Mary's own freedom – for the ability to work and enjoy the fruits of her own hard-won self-sufficiency. Her children, praise be, are well fed and their material needs met. Johnny, at the grammar school in the north, is a little too far away for her liking, but with time and luck, she will accrue the funds to move him to a London institution nearer home. Her eldest child, Bess, has a lively intelligence and an aptitude for letters and book-learning many would envy.

Life as a working woman without a husband has its blessings – not that she would ever admit as much to Mirabel Pearce for fear of causing a scandal. She is proud of her frugality, her ability to cope with disaster – disaster, after all, has been her constant companion, always waiting until she falls asleep to show her images of debtors' prison or whisper threats of ruined reputations. When, six years ago, they lost the surgery and had to move across the water from London to Southwark, she'd barely been able to sit still for worrying. She'd flitted like a bee trapped inside a bottle, pausing only long enough to scribble notes to anyone who owed them money. At night, her chest pained her, a phantom corset crushing her ribs, strangling her breath. She pictured their possessions carted off, cold ashes blowing in the grate, even the fire taken from them. The courts took a dim view of those who could not pay their debts. As a girl, she'd spent long hours in Newgate Prison, helping her Mam deliver the infants of labouring women who'd pled their bellies in exchange for a few more weeks or months of life. Dying in childbed seemed an infinitely better prospect than enduring the lewd attentions of the guards, the strippings and beatings.

'I know a man,' Lemuel had said, rubbing his hands together. 'Owes me a favour. We shall turn it round, you'll see. Have faith in me, Mary, for the love of God.'

But she'd lost faith in her husband years ago.

Their destination – the Needle in Wapping, the house where they now reside – was let to them by a friend of Lemuel's uncle and Mary had to admit it was better than what their last savings would have netted them elsewhere. At least the beams were dry, the planking solid. A freshly painted signboard, etched with needle and thread, hung over the door. The previous tenants – a merchant and his bride – had moved upriver and left some good pieces of furniture behind: a timber bedstead, a china cabinet, oak chairs bearing hardly a scratch. Best of all, they had drained the soil in the vast back garden and planted fruit trees, planning for a crop of figs and limes. It was not difficult for Mary to integrate her own cuttings and herbs. Lemuel left for sea soon after they moved in, promising vaguely that he would send money back when he could. A few months later, when nothing had arrived, Mary learned from a sailor's wife that no money ever would come since an advance had already been paid against projected profits. Lemuel had simply not given her a penny of it. She would have laughed if she'd had the strength. What else was his deceit but confirmation of what she already knew? If she and her children were to survive, she would have to take on the responsibility herself.

That very day, she had marched down to Anne Clifton's house and asked to be trained as a midwife. Six years' experience has taught her discipline. It has given her a sense of identity and completion she could never have achieved when she was a young mother, running Lemuel's surgery in Fetter Lane, spreading straw over the bloodstains.

At least she need not rely on anyone but herself.

2

Inside the Needle, Mary is immediately assailed by voices, one sharp, the other soft, coming from the kitchen – Alice, instructing Bess how to cook a haunch. Mary imagines her maid's wide face, scalded red with steam from the hob and Bess's sulky one, hair frizzed by the heat. Loosening the ties on her midwife's mantle, she hangs the crimson cloak on the row of hooks, a sense of warm contentment washing through her. The hallway is filled with dappled golden light. There are just enough hours left in the day for her to dig out a new plot for the borage, presuming she can resolve the domestic discord in the kitchen, where raised voices climb in frustration as the pots continue to boil.

''Tis ruined.' Grim-faced, Alice tilts the pan so that Mary might better observe the burned butter. 'A white sauce is not tricky, missus, but it does require watching. I turned my back on her for one second. What's to be done? That was the last of the butter. Now the mutton will be dry as kindling.' The maid darts an accusing glance at Bess, who slouches against the cabinet, arms folded over her stained smock.

''Twasn't my fault,' Bess mutters. She turns towards the plates, refusing to look at the maid who, at twenty-one, is seven years her senior. 'I was only doing what you asked. The sauce ruined itself.'

Alice grips a brush and begins to scrape the bristles over the blackened pan. 'If you had been paying attention,' she grumbles, 'instead of ruminating over that pamphlet –'

'What pamphlet?' Mary says at once.

Bess squirms against the dresser, her hand creeping into a bulging pocket. 'It's nothing,' she protests but her hesitance as she digs out the forbidden pages and places them in Mary's outstretched palm suggests the resigned demeanour of a shoplifter caught with the proceeds of her crime.

Mary scans the pamphlet, the relevant information highlighted in bold letters. *Murder* is one word; *hanging*, another. The date of the forthcoming execution is stamped indelibly in lampblack.

'Bess,' she says, disappointment battling dismay. 'Where on earth did you find this?' The question is rhetorical; Bess is a magpie, always seizing on small cast-offs and scraps of ephemera dropped near the market by careless hands. Pamphlets are popular all over London, especially amongst the lower classes who lack the distraction of playhouses and pleasure gardens. After years of working and living in Wapping, Mary sees no distinction between her own family and those born poor, although she won't stoop to buying the pamphlets, Jeremiah Grape, the parish constable, prints in his horrid shop to sell to the masses gathered on hanging days.

Mary avoids Execution Dock when she can. As if the rough crowds and deafening noise are not bad enough, the grim reality of the killing strikes her as particularly callous. Are there not enough ways already for a person to die? And if the law decrees they must, would it not be better for the act to take place in private? Wouldn't God desire his subjects be treated with dignity and compassion, whatever their sins? Of course, she's never voiced her opinions, anticipating their unwelcome reception from neighbours like Missus Pearce, who, for all the charitable work she performs on behalf of Wapping's orphans, will happily recount the gruesome details of the hanging of the notorious pirate, Captain Kidd, to anyone who asks: 'When the first rope broke, there were some as declared he ought to be pardoned but the next noose did the job and he was good and dead after that. You can still see his body, hanging in its gibbet at Tilbury Point. I hope it will be there when the twins are grown, so that they might learn where the path of wickedness leads.'

Mary has never taken Bess to Tilbury. At fourteen, the girl is still prone to occasional nightmares. They don't distress her the way they did following her father's death, but Mary still hears her sometimes, muttering in her sleep, fighting the bedclothes. Since her withdrawal from Missus Priest's Ladies' School three years ago, she's been directionless, helping in a haphazard way with household chores but often sneaking off to her bedroom or to Lemuel's old study, leaving Alice to perform the bulk of the work. Although Mary starts each day with the best of intentions, determined to impress upon her eldest child the merits of duty and responsibility – the two creeds which have governed her entire existence – there's always some crisis demanding her attention, a medical emergency or a plant which needs harvesting. Each day ends with her crawling, exhausted, into bed while in the next room Bess remains blissfully unchastised.

Crossing to the hearth, Mary balls the pamphlet in her fist and throws it into the flames.

'Since you can't be trusted to help with supper, Bess, you'd better go up and straighten your room. And no more of this hanging business, it's unbecoming. People will talk.'

Bess holds her gaze for a long moment, pink-cheeked and defiant, before she stalks out.

A relieved silence wells in her absence. Alice, abandoning the pan to prod the sizzling haunch, nods approvingly to herself.

'This come for you,' she says, wiping her hands on her apron and handing Mary a cream envelope inscribed with her name.

Mary takes the letter but does not open it. Instead, she says, 'Missus White will surely spare us some butter. Nip down the street and ask her, will you, Alice? I'll remake the sauce when you return.'

She waits for Alice to leave. The letter is from Richard, her late husband's cousin – a short note, advising of his imminent return and enquiring after the family's health. As she unfolds the last crease, a small sprig of dried hyacinth falls into her lap. The faded racemes have lost a little of their brilliant purple lustre but the remaining scent, sweet and heady, brings a tired smile. Richard often sends such jewelled tokens of his regard, a reminder of the early days of their friendship. She pictures him in his lawyer's chambers in Fleet Street, carefully extracting the dried bloom from the pages of a legal tome.

Tucking the sprig into her hair, she busies herself at the hob, pinching the stubborn haunch with the tongs until it rolls, exposing a flank of pale, uncooked flesh. She shakes back her wide sleeves, heat melting on her hands and cheeks. Perhaps one day . . . But she will not allow herself to think of their joint households yet. Work and children come first, as Richard knows. Her duty to her clients, forged on an unimpeachable reputation, is more important than any girlish desire to be touched or loved. There's no urgency, is there? *Nothing should be done in haste but the gripping of a flea* – that's how the proverb goes.

They have all the time in the world.

The third time she spoke to Lemuel Gulliver, aged seventeen, he told her she was as beautiful as the sun. Well, that is no great compliment, Mary thought, pragmatic even at her tender age. To look upon the sun is blinding and its heat, in summer, intolerable. Unless he means *I'm constant and never changing?* Pa always absented himself when Mister Gulliver and his cousin arrived. Muttering apologies, he hastened off for an appointment with a pin man in Ludgate or to cast his eye over a shipment of silk newly arrived from the East. Mary longed to go with him to visit the family of Huguenot weavers who made the hair ribbons they stocked in the shop, silky lengths of spruce green and starry violet and cherry pink. But no; she must stay and help the gentlemen with their selections.

On her eighteenth birthday, Lemuel visited the shop alone and gave her a silver locket with his portrait inside and told her he was going away.

'Oh,' she said, crestfallen, for by then she'd begun to look forward to their company – Lemuel, fair and fine-mannered, and Richard, shy and dark and always sporting a rash of pimples across his cheek or neck. If Lemuel was going away, that meant Richard would be, too.

The cousins were like twins born to different mothers. Whether it was watching men wrestle a crocodile at the Hand

and Dial, chasing salubrious breezes in the city's pleasure gardens or braving the wild rapids near London Bridge, the cousins were inseparable. Lemuel's booming voice filled the shop with their adventures, Richard chiming in every now and then to correct a detail, but more often content to stand back and let his cousin do the talking for them both. Their company was a welcome alternative to the fussy old gentlemen who patronised Burton's Hosiery, or worse, their valets, who stank of wet wool and horseshit and pressed themselves against her when she turned around to unlock the samples.

But Richard was already away – called north to visit his ailing grandfather – and Lemuel could not say for certain when or indeed if he'd return. Mary's stomach swooped each time she thought of Richard seeking her gaze and chatting with her quietly while Lem admired his legs in the fly-spotted looking glass. Knowing her interest in plants, Richard always brought her a cutting, the stem wrapped in damp muslin. She kept them in saucers ranged about her chamber and pressed them between the leaves of her heaviest books to trap their redolent perfume which, to her, was the scent of hope.

'Will you be gone long?' she said, distracted. 'When will you return?'

'You are so sweet, my dear, to be concerned for my welfare,' Lemuel said, placing his hand over hers on the counter. 'I'm away to Leiden to learn physic and complete my studies. Two years I will be gone. When I return to London, I plan to open my own surgery.'

'A surgeon? Then you'll want much finer hose than Burton's can supply, sir. We will have nothing to tempt you.'

'On the contrary,' he said, lowering his voice and brushing her ungloved fingers with his own. His hands were thinner than hers, the fingers long with squared-off tips. The silver locket – later lost in the move between houses – twinkled hopefully on its linked chain, a heart-shaped promise she dared not touch. 'It's my fervent hope I will have something to tempt you. We can be married before I go. I've spoken to your father, who has given his blessing.'

He meant to be kind, but she would have snatched her hand back if she were not so afraid of offending him. How she wished it were Richard making this offer. Perhaps, Mary reflected miserably, she'd mistaken Richard's intentions. Had he tired of her company and this was his way of avoiding an embarrassing confrontation?

Swallowing her disappointment, she tried to imagine what life might be like, married to a man like Lemuel. She saw herself stranded on a bobbing flotilla of ice, cast away from everything she'd ever known, only her husband for company. Was it nerves or a portent of some darker future? She did not love him; of that she was fairly certain. But could she? Did it matter, if she were well provided for? At least she would no longer need to endure the attention of the pinch-bottoms in the hosiery shop. And would marrying him mean giving up her tantalising dream of joining the midwife's trade? Despite all the things she'd witnessed assisting her mother in the birthing chamber – women spitting and clawing like lunatics, privities so torn and bruised they made pissing an unbearable agony, small, still bundles carried past a knot of silent siblings – she missed the excitement, the thrill of new life squirming in her bloodied hands. When her father died, his trade would die with him, so her choices were either to marry or apply for a licence to train as a midwife. If Mam had survived, Mary would have begged her for advice. As it was, there was nobody to ask except for Pa.

'You are a fool if you refuse him,' her father had said, his embroidery needle quivering. 'You will get no better offers.

He is training to be a surgeon, you know. You could do worse – his cousin will only be a solicitor, little better than a parson without a parsonage. I have set something aside for a marriage portion but it is not enough to live on comfortably unless your husband has money of his own. If your mother were alive she would say the very same: marry and forget the midwife's trade. Please your husband and give over any thoughts of your own industry. 'Tis unbecoming in a woman. Gentlemen prefer a wife to think solely of them.'

He'd rubbed his eyes with a scarred knuckle, his sight already troubling. How many more years did they have before it gave out completely? Since Mam's death, it was just the two of them. How could she expect her father to care for himself while she took up a midwife's apprenticeship? There was a part of her that resented Pa – and Lemuel, too – for forcing this choice on her but another part whispered that there was no choice; there was only survival or poverty, family or isolation. When viewed this way, her marriage could be seen as an investment, a fortification against misfortune. And perhaps, in time, Lemuel might encourage her to seek her own path of learning, so she could help women the way her mother had taught her.

They were married the Sunday before Lemuel's departure, in full view of the Church. She would have preferred a quiet day, the better to quell the speculative whispers and knowing winks of the congregation, but Lemuel wanted to show her off. After the exchange of rings, he led her past his smirking friends and the raucous revellers followed them all the way to their lodgings in the Old Jewry, Lemuel laughing at each man's vulgar catcall, showering the crowd with glittering pennies. At every street corner, Mary searched in vain for a glimpse of Richard's face. His conspicuous absence felt like a reinforcement of his disinterest in her future. When she put the question of his whereabouts to Lemuel, he merely shrugged and said he was not his cousin's keeper. If Richard chose not to attend the nuptials when he had been dutifully informed, that was his decision.

Mary's bridesmaids, hired by Lemuel, were mercenary shopgirls who pecked off her bridal dress while they chattered like barnyard hens. Shivering in her thin shift under the bedclothes, she waited for the last of the gallants to leave, for her bridegroom to find his way upstairs and seal their transaction. But when he joined her, dressed in a nightshirt that barely covered his hairy knees, he was surrounded by men she did not recognise and so drunk he could barely walk unsupported. Ignoring her squeaks, they flung back the bedclothes and deposited him, groaning, beside her.

Dawn found her still a virgin, the hot spear she had anticipated revealed to be nothing more than a flaccid disappointment. Hunched by the window, sipping lukewarm mutton broth, she'd watched the sky lighten from indigo blue to pallid grey, wishing with all her heart that it was Richard, not Lemuel, snoring in the bed behind her.

A week later, Lemuel was Leiden-bound, having left her to organise the furnishing of their rooms and oversee the ordering of the comforts he expected to find on his return: wine, candles, soap, coal. Hannah Woolley, the London doyenne of household instruction, advised newly minted wives not to abuse the freedom of their husband's purses, nor throw money away on trifles and luxuries. Mary had no concerns in this regard, having spent the past few years managing Pa's accounts. Thrift was her trademark. With Lemuel gone, there was nothing to do but act the role of wife as best she could. With luck, they would soon be blessed with children. God would not be so cruel as to deny her that joy when she had fulfilled her duty to her father by marrying a man she did not love.

'Married?' Richard said in astonishment, when he arrived on her doorstep a month after the wedding. Travel-weary, he clutched a wilting bouquet and his hat. Lemuel had written to him from his lodgings at Leiden and told him to look in on her at this address. Imagine his shock, to learn his cousin and Mary had joined hands without informing him! Had she not known his true intentions towards her? His hopes for their joined future?

'But the letter,' she said, prickling all over with sudden fear. 'The letter he sent, the invitation to the wedding . . .'

'What letter?'

A lump lodged in her gullet at this proof of Lemuel's deception – the first of many. As she stood there trembling, a boy from the clockmaker's at Clerkenwell arrived bearing Lemuel's wedding gift – a jewel-toned timepiece. Years later when it was sold, its absence on the mantel brought stark relief. She had come to associate it, in her mind, with that day of revelation and the dreadful moment of realising exactly what she had lost.

The front door slams. In the kitchen, Mary straightens.

'What a time you were, Alice,' she says into the dim passageway. 'Bess and I have eaten. Where on God's earth have you been?'

Alice leans against the doorframe, drawing long, ragged breaths. Pale-faced, she runs a palm over her greasy scalp, blinking in bewilderment. 'Lucy White,' she croaks. 'She's been raped, in her own home. The constable's there now, speaking to her husband. Lucy's in no fit state –' She snaps her mouth shut, as if she can keep the awful truth at bay by holding in the news.

Pushing her onto a stool, Mary fetches an ale. The maid gulps down the draught and wipes her lips with a trembling hand.

'Constable Grape asked Missus Clifton to examine her. I saw Lucy first; she didn't want to talk to anyone but me. I cleaned her up best I could.' She looks up at Mary, the whites of her eyes glimmering half-moons. 'They haven't caught him yet. Disguised himself, didn't he? Wore a handkin over his face. He might have done worse, if Robert White hadn't come home when he did. Might have murdered her where she lay.'

Her voice catches and her head droops, as if the effort of holding it erect is too much to bear. Mary squeezes her shoulder. Leaving Alice nursing the empty mug, she hurries out into the hall to check the bolts. The criminal could be anywhere – over the river or hiding in a warehouse at the docks. He could be searching the streets for another soft target – a house, perhaps, devoid of menfolk and manservants. How can two women and a young girl hope to defend themselves against such violence?

The hall blooms with dusky shadows. Dry-mouthed, she tests the chain, fingering the metal links strung across the door. She counts the bolts, rattling each one in turn over and over until she can be certain they are secure. Cold iron wards off ill luck, her mother used to say. But can it repel a violent man?

In St Gregory's parish last year, a seven-year-old girl was seized outside her parents' house, carried off right under their noses by a blackguard who poured ale down her throat and raped her in a nearby building. That man met his maker at the end of a Tyburn rope but it was the child Mary had thought of as pamphlets of the man's demise circulated. The child, who had now to live with the memories of what had befallen her as well as the physical curse he'd bestowed – a virulent case of the pox.

Thank God her Bess is safe upstairs.

3

Bess is lying on her bed, communing with her dead father's spirit and dreaming of escape when she hears the bang of the front door, followed by scurrying footsteps. The urgent noises remind her of the day news of Pa's last fateful voyage arrived – the one which split her life into two phases, 'before' and 'after'. Creeping into the corridor, she peers down the stairwell to see Alice join her mother beside the front door. The two women confer quietly, heads inclined. Bess cranes as far forward as she dares, watching her mother's agitated gestures, the emphatic flick of her wrist. What can she be saying? What has happened? There's still enough light for Bess to discern the worry lines around her mother's mouth, the way she splays her hand against the timber door as if the Needle is a fortress she must defend, an English-built Batavia ringed by trenches and canals and coconut trees stretching up into a godless sky.

A baby, Bess thinks suddenly and her interest sours. Something has gone wrong and Mam is being called out to make an urgent delivery. Nothing else could possibly inspire her mother to such a state of heightened animation. Mam thinks of nothing but babies unless she's in her garden and then it's herbs that occupy her mind. If Bess were a hollyhock, Mam might notice her for long enough to enquire about her day or take the time to encourage her hopes and dreams. But Bess is just a girl, unworthy of her mother's attention, her feelings of less value than a mewling infant's. It's not surprising Mam misunderstood her interest in the hangings. If Pa were here, he would have understood her curiosity. He understood everything.

Unwilling to linger any longer in the musty corridor, Bess retreats to the sanctuary of her bedroom. If Mam goes out, at least there will be no interruptions. Bess takes comfort in the books and curios, the empty birdcage glowing in the last strands of daylight through the shutters. She trails her hand along a japanned box left over from her days at Missus Priest's School. The timber box is black and silky smooth, beautified by layer upon layer of varnish. Bess wonders what became of the other box she started but never finished. Did some other girl complete it in her absence, one whose parents could absorb the fees set by Missus Priest, the proprietor? Bess spent two years at the school before her parents lost the surgery and with it, the means of paying. She remembers little of the school now, except how worthless the other students – the daughters of middle-class shopkeepers and clergymen and merchants – made her feel. Her only comforts were Johnny, when he was home from school, and her little bird, the absence of which still pains her. And Pa, of course.

An abundance of treasures is spread out on the bed, her late father's belongings; the objects of her ritual. Bess touches them one by one, absorbing their fraternal power. She cups a notched tortoiseshell in her left hand then sets it down and picks up a tiger-striped nautilus. Stroking the smooth spine, she lifts it to her ear, wondering if Pa's voice might somehow breach the divide and drift back to her. Nothing comes but the whispering sea.

She plucks an old tankard off the counterpane, the handle a bare-breasted mermaid, locks of yellowed ivory flowing to her waist. Bess is especially proud of this item, since she discovered it months after Pa's passing, hidden under the dresser in the kitchen. It must have rolled under there one night and miraculously escaped her mother's mass purge of anything valuable. Now it belongs to her, a reminder of her father's wild adventures. Although the liquid contents evaporated long ago, Bess fancies she can still detect the aroma of ale, her father's drink of choice if something stronger – burgundy, for example – was not available. Under its yeasty spell, his stories grew increasingly fantastical and elaborate.

Bess remembers the shadowed world of the kitchen springing to life as she sat cross-legged, staring up at him. She remembers a chair transforming into a sultan's throne, the table rumbling in her father's hands as a Lima earthquake trembled the house. She remembers Henry – her father's manservant – laughing as Pa pretended to pluck a handful of grapes off their stems and pop them into his mouth, only to spit them back out in surprise. Bess counted the grapes, gleaming in the rosy warmth of the firelight: six hard little pellets of purest gold. Treasure worth a hundred silk dresses or a fleet of ships as grand as the *Swift*.

Pa had beckoned her over, tipping the pellets into her cupped hands. 'Your treasure now,' he'd said – the last words he ever spoke to her. Before climbing into bed, she'd placed the gold carefully under the loose floorboard in her room, dreaming of all the places it would take her – India, China, the ice-cold waters of the North Sea, Jamaica, Bermuda, Bombay. Places even Pa hadn't been. They would go to sea together and share the spoils. In the morning, the gold was gone but Pa had left a note in its place, promising he would return.

The note is so fragile when she fishes it out of the cup, she's afraid it will crumble to dust as she unfolds it. But here it is, the proof she cannot let go – his promise to return. Bess chants the words to herself, an incantation of longing. Come back, she says, the sound of her own voice startling and child-like. Breath held, she strains for an echo, an answer, but there is only the house, creaking and settling like the joists of a great ship, sailing them all into the dark.

4

They bring him after sundown.

Mary hears rapid knocks and casts a worried look at Alice, who lifts both palms in warning. *Wait and see.* When the knocking is repeated – louder, insistent – they both jump.

'Missus Gulliver!' calls an unfamiliar male voice.

'Don't go,' whispers the maid, but Mary sets down the hose she has been darning and reaches for the candle. The hall is dark since they no longer light the sconces unless expecting company. Shadows flee before her, filling the spaces on the bare walls where paintings of storm-tossed ships once hung.

Mary draws the bolts and Alice's solid presence at her back lends her courage. The door judders open, ushering in the foul stench of canal waste from the gutter. The taper's greasy light falls on two men holding up a third. *Drunk*, is her first thought but they smell of brine, not liquor. Two of the men are strangers.

The third is her husband.

He staggers forward, cursing, supported by his companions, his boots scuffing the steps. 'Stand aside, Mary, for God's sake!'

Lemuel's face brightens, one brief flash before the light winks out as she drops the candle, which rolls away, hissing. Although aged, there's no mistaking its symmetry, the loose jowls and turnip nose, the ears pushed slightly forward.

In the dimness beyond the doorframe, the muttered cursing continues. She sinks to her knees, scrabbling on the varnished wood, her fingers finding only dust. Where is the blasted candle? She thinks she might be sick. The dead cannot rise; it is impossible.

Light dawns at her back and footsteps thunder on the boards. Alice reappears, bearing a fresh taper. The maid helps her to her feet and brushes her down before they turn to the waiting men. Mary supresses an unnatural desire to laugh. This is preposterous. Somewhere close by, stagehands are waiting to whisk this grim-looking man – an actor, wearing her husband's visage, a dark blue coat and knee-high boots – off to his next scene. His body is gone, lost in the currents. An empty coffin inscribed with his initials sits mouldering in the Gulliver crypt. And yet . . .

There is his florid face, bristling with ragged whiskers. He glares at her through bloodshot eyes, swaying, as if the slightest puff of wind will knock him off his feet. The question nips at her: If he has not been in Heaven, then where on God's good earth has he been?

Lemuel, clearly tired of waiting for an invitation into his own house, pushes past her, helped by his companions. They are sailors, she realises, their once-white shirts rinsed grey with sweat and seawater. Brown breeches billow around their calves. Locked together, the trio take up all available space, a many-headed monster, lurching along the passage towards the parlour. She flattens herself against the wall, allowing them to stagger past.

Inside the parlour, Alice rekindles the lamps. The men ease Lemuel into a chair. Out of habit, Mary kneels to prise off his unfamiliar boots. The grain is coarse, the leather tight. By the time she has worked his heel out of the shaft, she is sweating.

'Thank you, Mary,' he says, when the second boot stands at stiff attention beside its companion on the hearth rug. She glances up, unnerved by his gratitude. He has never before thanked her for performing her duty, never in such a gentle tone. The floor is hard under Mary's knees, cool air rising from the buttery beneath the boards. Lemuel sprawls in the armchair, stretching out his legs. She wants to ask him how – why – if she is dreaming – but his mouth is clamped tighter than a mussel shell, so they regard each other silently until Alice clatters in with a tray of ale and three cups.

'For the master,' she says, handing Mary a mug.

She raises the cup to his cracked lips. His skin is clammy, despite the warmth of the small room, the extra bodies hemmed in by the mismatched furniture. A few drops splash from the mug onto his lap. She watches them hover then sink, tiny jewelled islands consumed by a fabric sea.

One of the sailors taps her shoulder. 'Excuse me, missus.' He has removed his hat and crushed it to his chest, exposing chapped ears. 'We're grateful for the drink but we were to deliver Mister Gulliver then go straight back to the docks. If the captain catches us lurking . . .'

'Of course,' she says. 'Of course, I understand. Thank you for bringing him home.'

'Aren't you going to ask them what happened? Where he was?' Alice hisses as they follow the sailors out. Mary waits until they have waved the men off and shut out the noise and smell of the street before she replies.

'We shall have to ask him ourselves.'

He is trembling when they return, from shock or something worse, she cannot tell. Alice runs to fetch a blanket while Mary helps him shrug off the blue jacket, so stiffened by salt and sea breezes that when she throws it on the floor, it remains distended, as if it cannot forget the shape of him.

'This is Alice,' she says, when the maid returns, certain he will not remember her. Alice bobs a curtsey, unfurling the blanket over his thin body.

Hunching his shoulders up around his earlobes, Lemuel barely spares her a glance. His presence looms, casting its long shadow over them. Alice, usually so self-possessed, dithers in the doorway, as if she cannot decide whether to stay or leave.

The flickering light of the candles illuminates the soft pink cushions stuffed with duck feathers, a jar of loose buttons and darning needles resting on a stool. The room is not the dark-panelled domain it was when Lemuel lived here, the lintel lined with skulls and pipes and tokens of his travels. It is a woman's space now, designed to accommodate emergency alterations and ironings. A pile of clean clouts, stacked to knee height, waits to be shoved into the linen press, and in the armchair opposite the hearth, Mary's kitbag has toppled onto its side. Lemuel is as out of place here as a bear who has wandered into a pleasure garden, but for reasons Mary doesn't understand, it feels as if *she* is the interloper, the past three years merely illusion. One blink is all it will take to complete the reversion.

Can he really be here? She stares at him until her eyes water and his features blur. The chattering of his teeth reminds her of a child's game of chance; she hears the creamy knuckles shaken in a balled fist, the bones scattering in the dirt.

'Wh-where is Henry?' he says.

Ah, *there* he is, she thinks, relieved to discover his earlier gentleness was mere accident. Of course he asks after his manservant before enquiring about his children. 'Gone,' she says.

He arches his back. 'Gone? Where has he gone? Who sent him off? When will he return?'

The footstool scrapes across the boards. She lifts his withered legs and props them on the cushion – he will need to sleep where he sits, they cannot manage him between them. First thing tomorrow, she will send Alice across the road with a message for Tom Clements to bring his son to help them get Lemuel up the stairs. 'Henry left of his own accord, and Missus Perry has gone over water. Bess is upstairs and Johnny is at the grammar school. They will be so pleased to see you.'

He says nothing. Alice brings a cloth and a bowl swimming with oil.

'Are you comfortable?' Mary dabs at his hairline with the cloth, hesitant at the first tingling shock of contact but growing bolder, rubbing small windows of filth away from his crusted skin. The scent of lilac, thick and cloying, fills the room. He frowns; he is still thinking of Henry, his manservant, wondering, she supposes, who tempted him away. All it took was the news of the *Antelope*'s sinking. Henry did not have another situation to go to, he did not even stop to say goodbye. He merely shouldered his strongbox and left through the side gate, trampling a carpet of thyme in her precious garden.

The firelight shines on her husband's wigless scalp, skimming the uneven notches and depressions where a sailor's blade clipped too close. The stubble is quite grey now, the colour leached away.

'You must have many questions,' he says unevenly, his hands scratching under the covering.

'They can wait.' It takes every ounce of her self-control to say this, but she has been patient for three years; what's one more night? 'We can speak tomorrow, when you're rested.'

He nods, his chin wobbling, then his rheumy blue eyes bore into hers. He says, 'Could I trouble you for a sleeping draught? Just for tonight. I am afeared of sleeping. My dreams . . . they are full of strange horrors. If you only knew what I have seen. Those men who brought me, they know. I wake them at night with my screams. Why do you think they were so eager to be gone?'

'Who were they?'

'Oh . . . sailors.' His hand disturbs the air, their names motes of sunshine slipping through his fingers. 'Under the authority of . . . Captain Biddell. Please, Mary. The draught.'

His fingers have found her wrist and his grip tightens; blood throbs, constricted. Then he is sinking back against the bolster, weak again and helpless, his hand lying innocent and inert on his lap. She thinks of Bess. If her daughter remains undisturbed by Lemuel's dramatic entrance, it's possible she can be temporarily distracted until he's well. They've been here before – each time he returned from sea, it took longer for him to adjust to being home. Mary grew used to abandoning their shared bedchamber in a bid to escape involuntary muscle twitches, night terrors and blundering confusion. She did her best to keep Bess away, too, concerned she would be frightened by what she couldn't understand. If Bess has been woken, she will not want to wait to ask her father where he has been; she will demand the truth at once. Fourteen cannot wait, it longs to know everything. It is suspicious of delays.

'I can make you a draught,' she says, slowly. At least under the spell of a mild soporific, he will not wake screaming and raise the whole house.

Lemuel closes his eyes, grinding his jaw against the incessant rattling of his gums. 'Thank you, wife.'

Wife. The word comes as a shock. She hasn't considered herself a wife for two and a half years.

Leaving him in Alice's care, she goes to the stillroom, a narrow place squashed between the kitchen and the garden at the back of the house. Sheafs of drying herbs whisper against her shoulders as she opens cupboards and rummages through drawers, searching out the ingredients that will dull her husband's pain and tilt him into a soft dreamland. Borage, oil of roses, a finger of mallow root, a few yellowish petals of all-heal. From the back of a cupboard, she retrieves a jar of poppy heads, floating in syrup. The petals, dark as midnight, shimmer as she lifts them out. Snipping them in half, she tips the crescents into a bowl and sets about crushing them to a liquid pulp. The rise and fall of the pestle is soothing; it reminds her of Mam, who taught her this recipe, who showed her how to squeeze the poppy seeds against the brass bowl to spill the sap. She has done this a hundred times before, most recently to ease the agony of a dying neighbour whose infant lodged so firmly in the birth canal, even the surgeon shook his head and turned away. Mary remembers how the woman called for God. Skirts rucked up, straining against Mary's arm while her life's blood pumped from her privities. *God save me! God help me!* Her body stretched as tight as leather hide over a drying frame, then softening as the draught took hold.

The stillroom is warm and dry, thanks to the residual heat of the oven. Through the large window, her garden is a shadowy mass, the herbs dark sentinels watching the house.

Mary pushes the back of a spoon against the mush, sieving it through a cloth until the liquid pools into the clean bowl. Something moves beyond the window, a fleeting shape and she looks up, startled.

An owl, she says to herself, although her skin is curiously stippled.

In the parlour, Lemuel swallows the draught in one gulp, smacks his lips then tips his head back against the cushion and closes his eyes.

Alice stifles a yawn.

'Get some rest,' Mary tells her. 'I can manage here.'

Alice eyes the slumped figure doubtfully but at Mary's insistence, she goes, promising to lock up on her way. The bolts rattle and the stairs creak beneath her weight before a muted quiet descends.

They are alone at last. She sits in the chair opposite him, elbows on her knees, watching, waiting for him to open his eyes and accuse her of changing the parlour to suit herself, abandoning his memory so quickly. But he stays as he is. The shivering has ceased.

When he is snoring softly she goes to the desk in the corner. Squeaking open a drawer, she pulls out a piece of parchment and fills the inkwell. Her quill nib scores the parchment's surface. On her way upstairs, she props the letter against the stand, ready for the morning's penny post.

A golden band peeks under Bess's door – the girl has forgotten to extinguish her candle again. Bess's inner sanctum is a sprawling disaster of books, old maps and curious food smells that linger even when the source has been identified and removed. The shelves are littered with the detritus of her father's travels: Dutch clogs, an Indian turban, a chalk-white unicorn horn. Each time Lemuel returned, he lavished his daughter with frivolous gifts which had no practical or educational purpose. Some were downright dangerous. Mary was once forced to remove a ceremonial knife and another time a paper wasps' nest riddled with white ants before Bess could come to harm.

The forgotten tallow sizzles in its holder. Mary blows it out and Bess stirs, frowning in her sleep. Mary feels the old desire to protect her daughter rise up. This time, she will need to erect a fierce maternal barricade between Lemuel's fantastical stories and Bess's innocent beliefs. Sometimes Mary's love for her daughter frightens her; it is a huge thing, with ill-defined edges, smothering rationality. Any sensible mother would have taken her in hand long ago and pushed her into a trade or service. Since when have love and sense gone hand in hand? Mary's secret wish is for Bess to train as a midwife, but she isn't ready to let her go just yet. If she can keep her safe for a little while longer – if she can undo the damage Lemuel did when he fed her nonsense about taking her to sea – then perhaps she can prepare her daughter for the hardships she will inevitably face. She will be grown up soon enough. Soon enough, she will learn how cruel the world can be.

Mary tugs out a book tucked under the corner of Bess's bolster – Sir Robert Dudley's *Dell'Arcano del Mare*. Opened to a map of Portugal, the volume's markings are familiar: the sea monster roiling in scalloped waves, the coastline with its branching fingers reaching out into the sea. Closing the book softly, she places it on a stack of others. The gilded titles glow, as if to remind her of their wasted worth. She should have sold them – would have, if Bess hadn't begged to be allowed to keep them. God knows, they needed the coin. Now she finds herself wondering if Lemuel will want them back. Surely he cannot be so cruel? But another version inside her nods knowingly, says: *You know exactly what he is capable of.*

5

After half an hour working in her garden, Mary feels no better than when she stumbled from the house, dazed by lack of sleep and with Lemuel's preposterous claims ringing in her ears. Earlier this morning, with the help of Tom Clements's son, Charles, she'd assisted him up the stairs and pushed the boy out the door before Lem had started babbling. Now she cannot banish the young man's shocked expression nor guess how long it will take before he spreads the news of her husband's return. Bess sleeps late; Mary has at least delayed that awkward encounter.

Her back aches, her calves prickle under the layers of cotton. In one hand she grasps an iron-clad weeding spade, the blade sharpened to a lethal point; in the other, a ragged length of ivy. She gives the ivy an experimental tug, feels the weed's stubborn resistance. The twisted tendril laying siege to her mallow is only one of many surface shoots. Like a scenting hound, she has followed the runner; now only a foot or two of earth stands between her and the source.

A human creature, not above six inches high.

Plunging in the spade, she gouges the clods until the tip catches on something firm. The unearthed root ball of the ivy weed is similar to a man's heart, a complex arrangement of fibrous muscle and nodes. When struck, it bleeds a sap-like substance. Victorious, she hoists it out, lifting it by its hair, dirt scattering onto her shoes.

She sits back panting, on her haunches, waiting for the fresh air and burst of energy to calm her jangled nerves. This garden is her private sanctuary, the symmetry and geometry of the plants and trees designed to foster a deep, contemplative sense of calm. The herbs and flowers in their beds are the descendants of the seeds her mother passed on to her. Perhaps it is almost pagan to indulge in such earthly pleasure but each plant in her garden has its pleasing purpose: medicinal, gourmand, ornamental. Nothing is wasted and everything has its place. Even the bees have their role to play, always pausing first at the hollyhocks before they move on to the woodruff, some elemental compulsion propelling them from flower to flower. The ants consume the garden's dead waste, chomping through old branches and litter, stripping leaves down to their skeletal core while in the cool darkness beneath the topsoil, the earthworms dance.

Today, the garden fails to work its usual magic. Trouble is brewing – she feels it in her marrow as surely as she knows that the day will be warm. Her plants know, too. Sensing the heat, the gilliflowers have closed their petals while the white, lacy umbels of wild carrot appear singed, tobacco-stained. Afflicted by a sudden, queer sense of being watched, she turns her face up to the diamond-casement, expecting to see Lemuel in the place where, a short time ago, she stood with her back against the shutters, listening to her husband's delirious ranting.

What she learned from his strange ramblings was this: cast away with no hope of rescue, he was taken in by a race of tiny people who first imprisoned then released him, on the condition he act as emissary and broker peace between them and their warring neighbours. As recompense, they treated him like a god, even gifting him his own flock of tiny sheep. Their enthusiasm soured when he refused to subject the Blefuscudians to the Lilliputians' tyrannical demands. Escaping to the beach, he hailed a passing English vessel. The captain, fearing piracy, planned to put him off, but the testimony of his old friend Peter Williams – a lucky coincidence, his being aboard – saved him from the sharks and waves. Thus, he was delivered, although his little sheep are missing and he cannot recall where he left them.

At the conclusion of this strange narrative, he met Mary's confused silence with a bleary-eyed glare of withering disdain before rolling over to stare at the wall. The casement is empty, so he must be where she left him, sleeping off his adventures in their canopied bed.

She hears the scrunch of twigs forced back against the fence slats. By the time her visitor squeaks open the gate, she's on her feet, brushing off her smock and smoothing back her hair.

'Where is he?' Richard pants. The damp hairline verging his peruke suggests he has run all the way from his lodgings across town. Little silver clasps dangle from his unbuttoned frock coat, winking like corrupt magistrates.

'Richard,' she says, gripping the spade handle, blinking up at him against the glare. No longer the Billingsgate boy with bad skin, he has grown into a tall, good-looking man with hazel eyes and neatly trimmed black hair whose voice rises with excitement when asked his opinion on constitutional reform. If pressed by her to declare on which side of politics he falls, he is wisely democratic, confirming his love for Queen and Country while espousing the good works done by both parties and cautioning against blind allegiance. They have remained firm friends all these years, even as their lives diverged. The only thing they've ever fought about is, perhaps unsurprisingly, Lemuel. Whether intentional or not, Lem's original sin – neglecting to write to Richard and warn him of their impending nuptials – was the beginning of a silent war between the cousins, erupting in a verbal confrontation the morning Lemuel stumbled home a week after Johnny's birth. Hearing raised voices, Mary had hugged the baby to her breast and crept out to listen to Richard air a lifetime of grievances in the surgery waiting room. She'd been surprised to learn that his catalogue of hurt went as far back as childhood. What she had taken as commonalities between the men – a taste for adventure and amusement, no matter the price – had been mostly driven by Lemuel. Richard's presence was that of a help-mate, a keeper, someone to remind him when he was almost out of pennies and make sure he got home in one piece.

'I refuse to help you any longer or stand by idly while you hasten your family's end,' Richard had said. He stormed out, slamming the surgery door so hard in his wake that Mary feared she too had been banished from his good graces, that their friendship was broken beyond repair, yet another victim of her husband's thoughtlessness. A note bearing Richard's initials and a sprig of dried dogwood soon arrived to reassure her of his continued loyalty to her and the children. Mary still has it somewhere.

Reaching into his coat, Richard produces another letter now, infused with the musky scent of his toilette. She recognises her midnight summons, her own frantic scrawl.

'Is this a jest, Mary?'

She shakes her head. It would be easier, she thinks, if it were. She remembers sitting in her parents' house, listening to her mother chatter on about a Kentish woman who had given birth to a baby sheep. People travelled from miles around to see the lamb gambol about the croft on unsteady legs and suckle at the woman's pap. Mary's mam went too, returning a week later clutching a waxy clump of shorn fleece. But it had turned out to be nothing more than an elaborate hoax.

He squints up at the house, sucking his teeth. 'It's true, then.' His shock and misery so visibly mirrors her own, she almost takes his arm but catches herself in time. It will not do. The last time she saw him plagued by similar disbelief, they were standing in the churchyard, waiting for the rector to arrive so Lemuel's funeral could commence. Mary had slipped her arm through Richard's in a sisterly way, the gesture as natural as breathing. Through the crepe sleeve, she felt the warmth of him and detected the rapid, arrhythmic flutter of his heart. If it continued to thud like that he'd be taken ill, so she pressed closer, hoping his pulse might slacken. Instead, it accelerated. Sweat glittered on his neck. His body trembled. He had turned to her and whispered, 'I killed him. I told him I wished he was dead and now you see? See what I have called down?'

'No.' The fierceness in her voice had frightened her, the tone she reserved for the final stages of a woman's labour, to remind her to place her trust in God and in the power and strength of her own remarkable body. 'No,' she said again, softer. 'You were a good friend to him, Richard. Plenty of men would have walked away and never given him a moment's thought. But you're here now and he will know that, in spirit. He will know that you came back.'

He hadn't answered, but his breathing had slowed and he had touched her hand lightly and gone to take his place with the rest of the family.

'Where has he been all this time?' he says now.

'It's a matter of conjecture.'

'His or yours?'

'Both. He's . . . resting.'

Richard's frown deepens – he knows, she thinks. Through some small betrayal, she has disclosed her fear and aroused his suspicions.

'I cannot credit it,' he mutters. 'You're quite certain it's him?'

Her mouth twists in a wry smile. 'Are you suggesting I don't know my own husband? 'Tis Lemuel himself, I assure you.'

They walk together along the gravelled path to the house. Marigolds beam in bright clusters and the pink valerian thrums, its delicate panicles bowed by a seething mass of bees. Richard sneezes three times in quick succession and dabs at his nose and eyes with his balled handkin.

'You ought not to be out here,' she observes. 'The pollen is fearsome.' She hands him a clean linen square.

'In your letter, you said "fevered". Have you sent for a physician?'

'Not yet. I intend to treat him myself first, with simples.'

'Truly, Mary?' He steps in front of her. His height and broad shoulders take up so much space there's little chance of sliding past. To look up at him again will diminish her, so she sighs and turns her gaze instead to his buckled shoes. Rising out of them, his cream stockings cling to his long calves, following their graceful shape. The stitches are familiar, as is the simple embroidery of bees and flowers twined at the ankle.

Each winter she sews a pair and sends them to his lodgings, a private joke, the legacy of their hosiery shop days. Sewing them is a blasted nuisance; she would not wish it on her worst enemy. But for Richard, she makes the effort. What will happen this year, she wonders?

Dread sits on her shoulder, an invisible spectre. What does Lemuel's return mean for them both? Everything will change now. Everything she and Richard might have been to each other is gone. She has a sudden vision of the hosiery shop, the silk ribbons coiled on their spools, the stockings of varying quality spread in their sample cases. She wishes she could rewind time, reeling back to that moment when she said yes to Lemuel's proposal in order to please her father. How much are a pair of men's stockings worth now? It's been years since she stepped inside a hosier's. Pa died two winters after she was wed, the year the Thames froze. While skaters scratched an elegant script across the frosted river, she was busy arranging her father's funeral and Lemuel, back from Leiden, was busy spending the last of her bridal portion. Only Richard's company had been of any comfort.

'How long have we known each other?' he says quietly, and when she doesn't answer, he uncurls his fist and pretends to count, touching his fingers with his thumb. 'Twenty years this Martinmas. Tell me.'

'There's a hole in your stocking,' she says. Her throat is scratchy, her eyes hot. She feels feverish herself, as if she is sickening. 'Leave it with Alice, she'll see that it's mended.'

'You're evading me.'

She looks up, bristling. 'What would you have me do, Richard? Pay a quack to gawp at him before carting him off to Bedlam? Condemn him as a madman? Expose him to ridicule and neglect? And me, and the children as well?'

She shudders. Bedlam, and other asylums like it, are, in her opinion, worse than Newgate. They are prisons not only of the body but of the soul. In such places the maniacal ravings of the permanently distracted cannot be distinguished from those who might improve, were they not forced to bide together, men and women, the poor and the elderly, the criminal and the unfortunate orphan who has seen too much for one so young. Mary closes her eyes, but an image remains painted inside her eyelids. A grimed cell, a pair of chains, a woman's face, filth crusted and partially obscured by long, matted hair. When Mary tries to plait the woman's strands, they snap off her scalp like broken straw. *Mother, your hair*, she tries to say, her voice choked with dismay, but if her mother hears, she gives no sign.

'Who said anything about madness?'

Richard's words recall Mary to the present. She chews her lip, but what is the point of delaying the inevitable? Richard deserves the truth. He deserves to know what Lem said this morning, the strangest tale he has ever told. Is it real or myth? She cannot say, although instinct guides her to suspect he's dreamed the whole thing. A result of sun exposure or fever, perhaps loneliness, stranded for so long without company. In all the years of their marriage, after everything they have endured, she has never felt so adrift.

'Little people? That's new,' Richard says, when she has finished. He looks winded by the news. 'Does he mean fairies, perhaps? There was a fairy tree outside our old village. People tied wishes to its branches. My old ma used to sneak out in the mornings and rub her face with the dewy bark. She said it was better than any peddler's potions. It must have been good for something; when they laid her out, she didn't look a day over thirty-two.'

'Your mother died when she was thirty.'

'So there, you see? These fancies run in the family and you know his history. I advise you to think nothing of it.'

She shakes her head. 'It's different this time, Richard. This isn't some dog dressed as a lion or man with a tin heart. It's not a singing pig or a fox which sheds its fur during the full moon. His tale is elaborate. He seems . . . utterly convinced. And . . .' She cannot help glancing up at the diamond casement, as if her husband might appear and disprove her. 'He told me to keep it a secret, for now. He waited until Charles Clements was out of the room before confiding the story to me.'

Richard frowns. 'He instructed you not to repeat it? Well, that changes matters. If it's true, then he needs proper help. A physician, as I suggested. I know a man – name of Gaunt. Lives in Warwick Lane. He treated one of my clients last winter. I saw him two weeks ago at the assembly rooms, dancing a gavotte. Shall I write, ask him to come?'

'No,' Mary says, quickly.

'Why not?' He looks down at Mary's cat, which has detached itself from the shadows near the house and padded over to nudge against his leg. 'Hello, fish breath.'

Mary crouches, holding out her fingers. The cat sniffs them before returning to Richard and the puzzling abundance of London smells trapped in his clothing. 'Traitor,' she says, pushing herself upright. 'Why not? Because I could lose my job, if the Bishop catches word of Lem's illness. He must stay here and be cared for. I've written to your uncle and asked him to keep Johnny at the grammar school until the holidays.'

'How has Bess taken the news?'

'I haven't told her.' They have arrived at the back door. Through the crack, she can see past the stillroom into the kitchen where Alice stoops over the stove stirring the pottage, swirling her spoon through the grains to prevent them sticking to the pan. 'God's truth, I'm afraid to. You remember how she worshipped him.'

Richard nods, his gaze full of sympathy. 'I do. If Lem was in the room, the rest of us might as well be made of sticks. What will you say? About his . . . stories?'

'I'll keep them from her, if I can.'

'Is that wise? Would it not be better to warn her? She's older now, you won't keep the truth from her, so explain the gravity of the situation. Give her time to adjust. She'll see it for herself, as soon as he's awake.'

'I know that,' she snaps.

'You must enlighten her – gently,' he says. 'Banish all fancies and promises of putting to sea. She will not thank you, not at first. But you can't allow them to persist.'

The weight of his hand on her arm softens her. 'I'll tell her,' she says. 'Today before I start my rounds.' Mentally, she calculates the visits she must make – three parish women to be examined and two sickly infants who won't feed. Eliza Lacey, who gave birth three days ago, needs her sutures checked and she must remember to pack the cordial broth for Catherine Wickes to ease her windpains. The normalcy of these thoughts assuages a little of her guilt as she imagines the confrontation with her daughter. How to explain the unexplainable? And how to keep Bess safe, if Lemuel continues to rave? She wishes she could ask Richard to speak to Bess. He's always gotten along with her daughter better than she has herself, although perhaps that's because Richard makes no demands of Bess. He has no claim to discipline or instruct her, after all. He is not her father, nor even her stepfather.

Their thoughts must be circling each other, because he takes Mary's elbow before she can slip inside.

'Why didn't you marry again when I urged you to?' He wears what she has come to think of as his fiduciary look, the one reserved for his most pitiable cases. She flinches but he continues as if he hasn't noticed and she can tell from the way the words tumble rapidly that he has been rehearsing all morning. 'I could have protected you,' he says, lowering his voice. 'Nobody would have blamed you. Death in absentia. I drew up the document myself.'

A sour taste coats the back of her throat, as if she's chewed a wad of bitter lettuce. The memory of his proposal jars painfully. Six months after Lemuel's funeral, Richard arrived on the Needle's doorstep buttoned into his best suit and wearing the stockings he wears now, the ones she devoted precious hours to stitching, when she should have been helping Alice prepare supper or tear old petticoats into rags for clouts. She'd known he would ask; it was not unexpected. And yet, when the moment arrived, she found herself refusing. The timing felt wrong.

For months after the news of her husband's death, Bess had been plagued by nightmares of drowning and Johnny's school work had slipped, occasioning frequent visits back and forth to Nottingham. An influx of workers, employed by the Company of Shipwrights, had arrived in Wapping to construct a fleet of galleons. Naturally, their wives came with them. Mary's client ledger was overflowing with new bookings. Each day's work spilled into the next and she had her hands full managing the workload along with her domestic duties. Much as it pained her to refuse, she could not marry Richard. She could not chance causing Bess further distress in her fragile state, nor risk offending those neighbours who might offer up their hasty union as proof of an adulterous affair, begun months or even years before her husband's death.

Glimpsing Richard's disappointment, she'd squeezed his hands and assured him that everything had its season. Was her garden not living proof? Patience and faith, that's what every good gardener and herbalist needs. A rose can bloom inside a snow-covered hothouse. A nest of bare sticks which has lain dormant all its life can burst, unexpectedly, into flower. A plant so brown and sickly looking it is surely destined for the scrapheap can surprise you by sprouting green stems all over. Where there is life, there is hope.

Only now, it's too late. Any rights she claimed as a widow will revert to Lemuel. A husband owns his wife; she is considered femme covert. Reformers protest the unfairness of this law, which places women in the same category as lunatics, wards and outlaws. Mary Astell, advocating for the equal rights of women, asks: If all men are born free, how is it that all women are born slaves? But Mary Astell does not have two children dependent on her income. She doesn't have the responsibility of women who need protection in their most vulnerable moments, nor the burden of house repairs, servants' wages and a job which hinges on an unblemished reputation. The only real safety for some women lies in marriage. And Mary has thrown away her chance to correct the mistakes of the past. She finds herself married to the wrong man twice. Her fate is bound with Lemuel's. She tries to make light of the situation, although nothing has ever struck her as so utterly mirthless.

'Who, pray, would have me? A working woman with two children ... And where would that leave Lem? It's not his fault he was shipwrecked, no matter what came before.'

Richard refuses to be distracted. 'Mary. I'm so sorry for your troubles.'

She squirms, tugging her arm free. 'Hark, do not look so grim. In a few months' time Lem will recover. He'll grow weary of us again and return to sea. Then things can return to the way they were.'

'But how much damage can he do while he is home? And you will still be married at the end of it all.'

She makes no answer. Only yesterday she was a widow of independent means. Now she is some monstrous hybrid, a creature who has tasted freedom and knows too well how things might otherwise be. All her accomplishments – her midwife's standing, her children's welfare, her ability to employ and keep a servant – seem small and insignificant, dwarfed by the grander narrative of Lemuel's return. They are fragile achievements, at risk of being scattered by a snatch of spiteful gossip. A cruel trick, she thinks, this loss of sovereignty. She needs time to grieve the loss of her old self but time has sped up, moving too fast for her to breathe, let alone think.

The cat squeezes past her into the stillroom, swinging her wide hips and switching her tail.

'Will you at least allow a physician to examine him?' he says, softly.

'I'll consider it,' she says, hoping to placate him although she is beginning to regret writing. Their history is too complicated and Lem's return has only made things worse. If her note was a little frantic, she is almost blameless. It was late. She was in shock. 'I will think on it,' she says, then adds, 'Thank you for coming.'

'You won't.' He is buttoning his coat, struggling to pull the little hooks through the stubborn clasps. 'I know you. You've already made up your mind. Pass on my health to him, then. Let me know if you need anything. Anything at all. I am east bound tomorrow. One of my clients passed away and it seems he kept three families, all within two districts of each other;

Lord knows how they never met. The will shall take some sorting. I'll be lucky to return inside of a fortnight.'

Mary summons up a tired smile. 'Thank you, Richard.'

Instead of turning, he stares hard at her. His eyes have cleared, now that they have moved away from the clouds of pollen or perhaps, as he often says, she is his protection charm, the only thing safeguarding him from seasonal allergies. Kind eyes, the warm green-brown of alder catkins. Eyes that know her, inside and out, better than she knows herself.

'Your chin,' he says.

She lifts her hand, expecting to find a streak of viscous sap. Perhaps the ivy left its mark? But there is only the gentle swell of flesh, the small burred notch where the smallpox once departed her body. She remembers her mother, a dim shadow through the fever haze, grinding and stirring, the slosh of liquid. A caudle of stewed herbs – her mouth filling with pennyroyal and yellow doxy and warm goat's milk. The very same receipt she gave to Bess when she sickened. Praise God, her girl recovered, but Johnny has not yet suffered smallpox. It's another worry to add to her bundle. Sometimes she thinks she can feel them, her fears, bumping about in the invisible sack she hauls with her at all times. If she is graced a minute's peace at some labouring woman's bedside, she brings out her troubles and examines them, fretting particularly over those that have lain dormant for more than a few hours. Has the rent been paid? Have they enough laid by to last the winter? What chores will Bess leave unfinished? Now, she can add one more: Will her husband recover his wits or will his return ruin them all?

She is still in thought when Richard leans over and strokes his thumb along the seam where chin meets neck. She shivers.

'Oh,' she says. 'There's someone walking over my grave. What was it? A smut?'

He holds up his thumb for inspection and her initial suspicions are confirmed: in death, the ivy has had its revenge. She licks the back of her hand and rubs it along her jawbone.

'Still as smooth as a maiden's,' he says, and when she looks up, he taps his chin.

'Away with you. Go on.'

He grins and all at once, he is nineteen again and she is seventeen. They are standing in her father's shop and the adult world of children, chins, wills, weeds and troublesome husbands has ceased to exist.

6

A few hours later, Mary is mixing up a tonic for Lemuel in the stillroom when a series of knocks disturbs her. Alice is at market with Bess so there is no one to answer but herself. Her friends are waiting on the front step, their mantles rippling in the warm breeze.

'My dear,' says the tallest, pinning Mary with sharp, black eyes. 'We heard.'

'We've brought supplies.' Elinor hoists a glass carafe. Her face is stamped with the tall woman's likeness and dark colouring but she is younger, with a soft, pleasing figure. She nudges the third visitor, a plain, neatly dressed girl who mumbles a greeting before gazing over Mary's shoulder, shameless curiosity shining from every pore.

'Come inside,' she says, swinging the door wide. 'What a world we live in. News travels remarkably fast.'

'Now, Mary.' The tall woman, Anne Clifton, picks at the ties knotted at her throat. Her advanced years show on her face, the soft skin pleated with fan-like folds. The dress she wears underneath her mantle is the rich red of cherries, shot through with brilliant silver threads. 'There's no need for embarrassment. Why did you not send for us at once?'

''Tis too late now.' Anne's niece, Elinor Banks, shrugs off her own mantle. 'The whole marketplace is alive with news of his remarkable return. We would have come sooner, but we wanted to stop at Robert White's house and ask after Lucy.'

'She told us all about the villain,' Susanna says. Anne's young apprentice fluffs out the crimped waves of her ginger hair, flattened by the bonnet's flax. 'Wicked! I prayed last night for his capture.'

'They've not caught him, then?' Mary's stomach plummets, thinking of Alice and Bess at the market. But the image of a man assaulting them both during broad daylight refuses to catch; the constable will have his watchmen on guard for any disturbance.

They move into the parlour, Susanna's hungry gaze lingering on the pair of boots by the hearthrug. 'Where is the master, please, missus?'

Mary hears a noise and glances through the open door, imagining a flutter of white nightdress in the dimness of the passageway. But there is nothing. 'Mister Gulliver is abed,' she says, distracted. 'His fever is still troubling. I fear it will be a good few weeks before his convalescence is over.'

'Let me attend him.' Anne is rolling up her sleeves, the skin on her forearms loose and wrinkled like an old stocking turned inside out. 'I've some things I wish to try.'

'Simples?'

'Not precisely.' The old woman's hand flutters inside her kit, rummaging. 'I mean to say yes, there is a decoction to soothe his fever, but I've brought a tonic, too, to aid his balance. Tom Clements said he's unsteady on his legs.'

In response to Mary's raised eyebrow, she draws the bottle out and shakes it, the liquid contents roiling like a trapped ocean inside the glass. 'Sea wormwood,' she says. 'Unless you've already tried it?'

'No,' Mary says. 'He's had nothing but an elixir of poppy. You're certain the wormwood won't affect his liver? It's always been weak and gave him no end of trouble when he was a lad. I've read it can cause bleeding.' She falls silent, reluctant to say more in case Anne mistakes her professional curiosity for impudence. There are some days where she wakes up feeling no wiser than when she arrived on Anne's door six years ago to begin training as a novice midwife.

Anne's lips quirk but Mary detects a hint of pride in those sparkling dark eyes. ''Tis common wormwood you speak of,' she says, snapping her bag closed. 'Not this variety, which grows by the seaside and is nourished and cleansed by the sea air. This sort is good for expelling worms and drawing out maladies of the mind. Trust me, dear. Would I wish him harm?'

Mary tries to ignore the memory of Anne's oft-repeated threat to slip wolfsbane into Lemuel's drink if he did not put the needs of his family before his own pleasure. But what was said in jest cannot be taken seriously and Anne's reputation is more uncompromising than her own.

The oldest and most respected midwife in London, Anne's rigorous medical training at the famous charity hospital Hôtel-Dieu in Paris foreshadowed her triumphant London return. Her empire now extends all the way from the boundary stone at Stepney to the fine dwellings of Limehouse, where merchants' wives labour on pelts of rich sable and sip sweet infusions of cinnamon water proffered by dark-skinned maids. Anne's real power lies in her ability to act as an intermediary between the Bishop of London, with whom she dines once a month at Fulham, and the midwives he oversees who deliver new souls into the Protestant flock. Although rumour suggests Anne is a widow, her husband died so long ago there are those who doubt she ever married. Even Elinor, raised by Anne after the death of her parents, can't say for certain. If, one day, Anne chooses to cohabit again, it will not be for money, for she has enough wealth to last her into the next life, and her time is much occupied with the training of young midwives. Her appearance at a labouring woman's bedside precipitates not only the endowment of breads and sweetmeats, but fine tapestries and diamond pins and all manner of assets most women dream of possessing.

Mary smiles despite the nagging shame of exposing her husband's peculiarities to one of her closest friends. If anyone can soothe his nervous anxieties, it is Anne. Behind her back, the midwives refer to her as Mother Superior and the title seems apt. Any woman powerful enough to allay the Bishop's fear of birth is one worth following. For twenty years, Anne has managed the Church's expectations. A skilful negotiator, she has never given up fighting for better conditions for 'the mysterious office of women', the birthing ritual no man is permitted to witness unless he be a surgeon, and even then admitted only in emergencies.

Anne has a talent for getting her own way, which can be traced back to her training days when a fellow student, a man, began a campaign to ensure her view of the surgeon's table was blocked during lessons. Soon after, the scholar absconded from his medical studies and returned to London where he gambled away his inheritance and died in a Holborn ditch after losing his footing on a patch of ice. *Sheer bad luck*, say some. *Anne's curse*, whisper others. Mary, who once watched Anne convince the Bishop to waive the licensing fee for a midwife whose husband had lost both his hands, suspects it was a combination of Anne's persuasive nature and her iron-clad determination to succeed that decided the young man's fate. In their world, power takes a different form and must never be seen to threaten or intimidate. It must be artfully employed through small acts, invisible to the city's powerbrokers. If Mary has learned anything from Anne over the years, it's that silence can be as sharp as a rebuke and that equally, a honeyed word dripped in the right ear can mean the difference between *yes, madam* and *no*.

Anne disappears up the stairs, leaving Mary alone with Elinor and Susanna.

'This Rhenish is a present from Missus Fish,' Elinor says, her skirts sighing as she sits on the sofa. She pours the wine into three dishes.

'Her child is born, then?' Mary says.

'Aye, at last. And what a monstrous size 'twas! I think Missus Fish felt guilty for clawing me during her throes. Look.' Elinor tugs aside the lace at her neck to reveal the long red welts of Deborah Fish's distress. 'Poor woman, she would have rather preferred the rack. She is so slight. Such slender hips. But mother and babe are both well now.'

Handing Mary a dish of wine, she says, 'Go on. Have a sip of that and then you can tell us all about Lem. We are all friends here. Susanna has been sworn to secrecy. Haven't you, my pet?'

Susanna lifts a shoulder and frowns down at the wine in her dish, barely half a knuckle's worth.

'You are an apprentice,' Elinor reminds her. 'How would it look if you were soused? The Bishop might issue a fine.'

Mary suspects Susanna will argue – something about the set of her jaw reminds her of Bess – but the girl relents.

Slumping back against the sofa cushions, she begins to shred a sprig of dried rosemary in her lap, plucking despondently at each thorny stem.

'So, your husband is home,' Elinor says. 'I thought . . . the shipwreck. It's all so mysterious.'

Her keen eyes bore into Mary, who lifts the dish to escape, the Rhenish sliding down her throat and settling in her stomach. 'He washed ashore,' she says at last, touching a spot of wine on her lip. 'Onto an unknown island.'

Elinor leans forward. 'Were there cannibals?'

'Not to my knowledge.'

'Oh,' she says, looking crestfallen. 'So what happened?'

Mary hesitates. Gulliver's story sloshes in her head. He was still repeating his claims an hour ago when she looked in on him, rolling his head on the pillow as he spouted nonsense. She cannot repeat this outlandishness to her friends. This is how a lie begins, she thinks, holding her dish out for Elinor to refill; embellishing the facts that fit and hiding the ones that don't.

At least she was able to explain Lemuel's return to Bess and bundle her out of the house before the girl caught more than a glimpse of him. Bess's disbelief had quickly turned to the most intense expression of joy Mary has ever encountered. Flinging down her pottage spoon, she'd barrelled up the stairs two at a time and was standing with hand on the door when a panting Mary caught her up. *One minute*, she'd cautioned. *You remember how ill he gets. He's asleep. You don't want his illness to get worse.* She allowed them the briefest of embraces before pushing Bess back out and slamming the door. *Cruel*, her heart whispered. But what if he hurts her? Who could say whether his delusions might manifest in physical outbursts of frustration? She endured Bess's glare of hatred the way she has often endured her husband's failed promises – by picturing Johnny's soft cheeks and gentle laugh. By remembering the good times she and Bess shared before the winds of fortune changed and they lost the surgery. Rhymes by the fireside. Spinning tops constructed from gleaming acorns. When Bess asked, in a raw voice, where he had been, what he had suffered, Mary gave the same story she now imparts to Elinor and Susanna.

'Well, let me see. He lived there for two years, eating whatever he could catch. Built a little boat from the timber washed ashore and when a sailing ship passed, flying an English flag, he hailed it and rowed out to meet them. They brought him home.'

Elinor shakes her head. 'The poor man! To be all alone, for such a long time. It is beyond belief – incredible, even – that he did not go mad for lack of company.'

Mary thinks grimly of Lemuel's claims, his strong assertions that he was not alone. Abstracted, she swallows more Rhenish, praying Elinor does not press for more. Her friend is right, it is a superior vintage, the fruity tartness giving way to mineral warmth. Her limbs feel pleasantly drowsy.

'Did you hear the news about Hugh Chamberlen?' Elinor says.

Mary shakes her head. The efforts of famous surgeons like Hugh Chamberlen who hope to dominate the female-led practice of midwifery have been going on since before she was born. Allegations of sorcery and ignorance were the surgeons' earliest attempts to discredit and defame the women. When that failed, and the midwives' clients continued to trust their labours to local experts instead of surgeons and their knives, certain individuals stepped up to intensify the crusade of harassment and intimidation. One man in particular – Peter Chamberlen, Hugh's ancestor – made it his life's mission to capitalise on the London midwives' success. Less than a century ago, he petitioned the medical community for the right to be the only practitioner authorised to answer a midwife's summons when surgical instruments were called for. In exchange, he offered to train women himself and establish a College of Midwives over which, naturally, he would assume complete control. As proof of his commitment, he offered to share his family's most secret invention: iron clamps, inserted into the womb during labour to seize an infant's stubborn head and haul him into the world.

Alarmed, the midwives quickly mounted a defence. Supported by the clergy, they begged the College of Physicians to see sense. Were women not best placed, they asked, to carry out their neighbours' most intimate procedures and protect their feminine modesty? Were they not sanctioned by the Church to baptise infants who tragically expired soon after they took their first breath? It was not the responsibility of surgeons or physicians to be bothered by such trivial matters. They were busy keeping the adult population alive, administering emetics and treating burns from cooking fires. They were amputating severed limbs and extracting bladder stones and keeping scrofula from spreading. Ranked against such serious matters, wasn't childbirth best left to women? Weren't women, unenlightened as they were, better equipped to handle the messy business of birth, along with the accompanying hysterics? Babies died all the time; God would ensure they were taken care of. What good would it do to go stirring up trouble where women were concerned?

Thankfully, their ploy worked. The College of Physicians dismissed Peter Chamberlen's proposal, cautioning that his secret instrument belonged firmly in the surgical realm, while the practice of midwifery, as everyone knew, remained humbly home-based and insignificant, in the grand scheme of things. In parlours all over London, midwives toasted their secret success. But their merry-making was short-lived. Although, Chamberlen senior never succeeded in his takeover, his children have repeatedly tried to revive his beloved project. The secret instrument is hardly a secret any more, but still they refuse to share it, issuing patent lawsuits when a similar product enters the market, ensuring that they are the only ones who hold the key to its design.

'Hugh Chamberlen claims to have made improvements to the clamps that will render the services of female midwives obsolete,' Elinor says, sounding bemused rather than troubled. 'Aunt Anne says it is nothing to fear. Very likely, it is just idle talk. Those Chamberlens love to hear their own name bandied about, praised or cursed – they do not care which.'

In the pause that follows, Mary gathers her scattered thoughts. Dear me, she thinks, settling the dish of Rhenish cautiously onto the side table. If I drink any more of that I, too, will start gabbling about little people and tiny bleating sheep.

As much to test the steadiness of her voice as to contribute to the conversation, which has been rather one-sided, she says, 'Hugh Chamberlen never witnessed a birth in his life. I doubt he has ever asked for details.'

'Quite true.' Elinor smiles, all pearly false teeth. She lifts her dish to her lips with steady hands; she has no trouble holding her wine, being accustomed to such indulgences because the East India Company – in which Elinor's husband holds a high-ranking position – hosts parties each month in Leadenhall Street. For the East India Company, midwives represent something of a novelty. Unlike most working women, they are seen as professionals in an age where gold is nearest God and the new century offers myriad opportunities for expanding global trade. Mary has been only once to a company gathering – Lemuel took her, back when he was briefly captain of his own vessel, the *Swift*, a ship he won on a lucky hand of ombre. She recalls being shocked by the opulent wealth hidden by the manor house's frontage: silver platters strewn with strange, spiky fruits; striped flowers so unlike any English blooms, she imagined an artist dabbing them into oily life then reaching into the canvas to extract them whole. Everywhere, jugs of wine and pitchers of ale held by servants in immaculately pressed cuffs and collars who seemed solely employed to scrutinise guests' glasses and hurry forward to refill them.

'Do you recall what Hugh said when Aunt Anne acquainted him with a first-hand account of childbirth?' Elinor pulls down the corners of her wide mouth, affecting Chamberlen's dour, toad-like expression, her bosom swelling as she puffs out her chest. '"'Tis a monstrous violation! How will I ever make love to my wife, knowing her passage has been so ill-used?"'

Mary smiles at the accurate impersonation. Even Susanna smirks. Tossing the rosemary stem aside, the girl sits up. 'Is that why the Chamberlens are so keen on surgery?' she says. 'Because they dislike the thought of tupping their wives and mistresses after they've given birth?'

Elinor's eyebrows shoot up. 'What would you know of it, dearest? Have you been doing something you shouldn't?'

Susanna's smile fades. Picking up her dish, she swallows the thimbleful of liquid, defiant. 'Do you think me so foolish, missus, as to know how babies are born but not how they're made?'

'I'm sure *I* never told you,' says Elinor, fanning herself with her splayed hand. 'When you were my apprentice.'

'No, you didn't.' Susanna's cheeks are flushed. 'Missus Clifton filled me in some. The rest I pieced together from Jane Sharp's manual.'

'Well, you might know but you shouldn't talk about it. Where is Bess?' Elinor says, looking around.

Guilt lodges in Mary's stomach like a stone. 'Alice took her to the market earlier. They should be back soon.'

'She must be pleased to have her father returned. She always worshipped the ground he walked on. I imagine you were quite overcome with emotion, to see them reunited.'

'I –' Bess's face rises up in Mary's mind, her mask of shock melting into rapture. 'Yes,' she says, in the smallest voice she possesses. 'It was very touching.' She looks at her hands, folded in her lap. Silently, she curses herself for not explaining the situation to Bess years ago. She should never have allowed the girl's belief in her father's reckless promises to flourish unchecked. But who could ever have predicted his return? She should have been more judicious and inured herself against catastrophe. Where has all her good planning and sense led her? Although rare, it's not entirely unusual for citizens declared dead in absentia to return. Soldiers mostly, men stationed in far-flung outposts of the Empire's reach, fighting wars nobody in London has even heard of. The walking wounded are often taken for vagrants when they return, unrecognisable even to their families unless some scar or birthmark confirms their identity. These disciples of Lazarus are held up by the clergy as proof of God's miracles but as time passes they often struggle to fit into their old communities. What will Lemuel's role be, once he recovers? And hers? Mary shifts uneasily on her chair. She suspects she cannot go back to taking orders, after all these years. She can't dig out that old Mary – compliant, consoling – and dust her off, out of a sense of duty. She will not. She *cannot*.

Anne's return stirs Mary out of her dark reflections.

'Well, Mary,' she says, folding herself into a chair, gripping the upholstery with yellow-stained fingers. She looks drawn and colourless, as if the ministrations have worn her out. 'You will have your hands full, I wager.'

Mary reads no judgement in Anne's dark eyes, only sympathetic concern. 'You gauge the extent of it,' she says carefully, rubbing her hot hands along her skirt to ease the throbbing. Are they prickly with shame or simply flushed with relief that Anne knows what she is facing? Perhaps she's not as alone as she thought.

'I do. But I also have faith he will recover.' Anne touches Mary's knee. 'Let me give you my advice: feed him, water him, give him draughts if he requires them. It will take some adjusting, to be home amongst civilised people.'

'And his . . . stories?' She focuses her gaze on Anne, acutely conscious of Susanna and Elinor's scrutiny.

'Let him talk,' Anne says. 'Where is the harm? Nobody else need know. Eventually, he will sort out what is real and what is fancy. The mind takes longer to recover but once the body heals, the rest generally follows. Take heart, Mary.'

Take heart. As if it's so easy to rectify past wrongs and face up to the future. Mary hugs herself, digging her elbows into the boning of her stays. Her stomach aches. She wishes, not for the first time, that her mother was still alive. Liz Burton would be an old woman now. The strands of golden hair little Mary had loved to twist round her fingers would be threaded with grey. The hands that had soothed women in their travails and pacified newborns would be wrinkled and flecked with age. Very likely, her mouth would be all blackened gums. Hardly anyone over the age of forty retains the teeth God has given them. Mary wouldn't care. She would hug her old mother as if she smelled of sweet lavender and rose petals. She would sit her down in the kitchen and heat a brick for her feet and pour out all her troubles. Until she became a mother herself, she did not know the extent of what she'd lost. She did not appreciate the many small kindnesses her mother showed her while daughters in other families were whipped or beaten for such trifles as spilled milk or lost buttons.

The day after Bess's birth, Mary's joy had curdled as the responsibility of new life set about to crush her. She hadn't known it was possible to love something so fiercely and deeply. To be delighted and afraid in equal measure. The future was a vast universe, dark and unknowable, with no guiding stars to light the way. Staring into Bess's elfin face, she had never felt closer to her own mother. This was the bargain women made. She had split herself and this tiny, yawning baby was the result. Until she died, her heart would never be whole again. Some part of her would always be out there, beyond her reach. Johnny's birth was another chipped fragment. At least, for now, they are both safe.

The older woman runs her hands over her bright red skirt, smoothing out the wrinkles, chatting to Elinor and Susanna about parish babies as if she hasn't a care in the world. But her dark eyes return often to Mary and although she looks worried, Mary feels somehow better. Anne was born the same decade as her mother. Under her guidance, Mary completed her training and rose through the ranks, first as a deputy and then as a fully fledged midwife. It was Anne who helped her obtain the six testimonials to support the application for her midwife's licence. Anne who collected funds from the other midwives to help her pay for Lemuel's funeral. With Anne on her side, nothing seems so dreadful or dire that it cannot be righted. Let Lem rant and rave. Let Bess despise her. Let Richard chide her for her indecisiveness. She will weather the worst with dignity and courage. Draining the last of the Rhenish, she stands to collect the dishes from her friends.

The moment of peace is shattered by the sudden slamming of the front door.

They all turn as Alice whirls in, clutching the doorframe. 'I lost her!' she wails.

'Who?' says Susanna, but Mary is already on her feet.

'We were outside the bookbinder's,' Alice sobs, as Mary dashes past. 'She wanted to watch Mister Humphrey. I asked her a question and she didn't reply. Run off. I'm so sorry, madam. And a criminal at large. Oh, what if he finds her and does her an injury? I could never forgive –'

Her words vanish in the deafening noise from the street.

7

Bess runs until her lungs ache. She is a divining rod, pulled along by a fey wind, her feet carry her wither they will. The sour smell of the bookbinder's goatskin and gum vanishes as she tips her chin towards the big blue bowl of sky and mouths a silent grateful prayer for Pa's return. The memory of his warm embrace blots out the less agreeable one of Mam hovering nearby, envious as usual of their special friendship. Is it any wonder Mam looks so worried? Her reign is over now Pa is home. Everything will change – for the better. Everything will return to the way it ought to be. Balance will be restored.

Bess's heart thrums with happiness.

On the corner of Rain Street, she skids to a halt to avoid crashing into a woman in a dirty smock leading a cow to the slaughter yards. *Leading* is perhaps too generous a word. Gripping a rope tethered to a collar round the beast's neck, the woman alternates between pulling and shoving, spraying curses. The cow, a scrawny, dun-coloured thing, digs its hooves into the mud, refusing to oblige by moving either forward or back. Black eyes framed by feathery lashes regard Bess with slow-blinking indifference.

'Shift, you worthless bag of bones!' the woman screeches, delivering a stinging blow to the cow's rump with her palm. The cow lows mournfully but doesn't shift. A queue of jolting carts and wagons begins to gather and Bess's stomach swirls like laundry in a tub as she imagines Alice's firm hand clamping her shoulder. But when she looks around, the faces belong to strangers, frowning at the woman and her stubborn cow blocking the path.

Bess watches a boy set down his cart to pick up a handful of mud and fling it at the woman. It spatters – thwack! – on her apron, a dirty starburst exploding with such force she is surprised into silence and drops the tethered rope to clasp her muddied breast. The cow bellows again – Bess imagines it is a thank you. Smothering laughter, she skips around the beast, patting its bony rump. If she could speak cow, she would warn the creature to run off to the marshes edging the parish and never look back. *I know how you feel*, she would say. *I, too have spent my life enslaved to the whims of another, doomed never to experience a moment's freedom except the ones I steal for myself.* Pa says that cows speak in accents, like people, that if a Midlands cow met a London cow, they would converse in entirely different ways. Bess has never explored this theory. The furthest she has travelled is Nottingham for her father's funeral. (A sham! Pa is not dead but alive, praise God and every angel she has ever prayed to.) One day, she will travel farther. She will sail to the edge of the world and peer down into the dark abyss where sea monsters live. Really, she knows this chasm is a self-indulgent fancy, since she is not so foolish as to believe the earth is 'flat as a stove lid and that it floats on water like half of a sliced orange', as Cyrano de Bergerac writes in his famous travelogue. She cocks her head as she hurries along the road but the cow has gone quiet and a sudden eruption of wheeled traffic around her suggests the struggle is over. Poor thing.

A shadow falls across her path.

'Quills?' A peddler holds the edges of his stained coat out like the tattered wings of a crow. 'Bootlaces? Playing cards? Combs a ha'shilling. Pretty girl like you deserves a comb.' The man leers, his gaze raking her body. His tongue darts out to moisten his chapped lips.

Bess recoils. At three-quarters the man's size, she cannot hope to overpower him. If Alice were here, she'd box his ears but Bess's hands wouldn't even wrap around his filthy neck. The gazes of the people around her slide past as if she is nothing.

Sensing her helplessness, the peddler grins and lunges for her cap. 'What's under there, I wonder? Give us a look. Red or brown? I like a blonde lass, myself –'

Bess's heart slams against her ribs. A scream sticks in her throat. All she can do is point over his shoulder and widen her eyes in an approximation of terror.

'A bear!' she sputters. 'It's loose! Out for blood, God save us!' She can almost see the bear thundering towards them, its fangs dripping blood.

Releasing her, the peddler turns, squinting into the street behind. 'Eh? Are you blind, girl, or a lunatic? Ain't no bear –'

Bess hears no more. She is running up the street, grinning, flushed with pleasure at her triumph. A bear! What utter nonsense. Bears sometimes escape from the baiting rink in Bankside, but there hasn't been a bear in Wapping since

Bess can remember. Pa would be proud of her, the way she handled that.

Coming here was a risk. She's never allowed out on the streets by herself. She skips cleanly over a river of sluggish effluence. When she returns, she can tell Pa all about the foolish peddler herself. If Mam lets her see him, that is. Her mother's intrusion into her thoughts is sobering. What if the peddler is Lucy White's attacker? Mam's warning sounds in her head like a bucket clanking down a well. *Dangerous to be out alone. Stay with Alice.*

But there are always dangers. What's a world without danger? Without excitement? The alternative is being stuck all day in a house doing chores Bess cannot stand. Besides, the man's probably on a ship to the Americas by now. Would he really linger, risking discovery? Unconsciously, she tears at her thumbnail with her teeth. She wishes Johnny was still at home. Bess loves to tease him and tickle him, distracting him from his studies. She misses him when he goes away to the school in Nottingham. With Johnny gone, there's nobody to play pirates with, only old Puss, who once raked Bess violently with her claws when she tried to jam a lace ruff around the cat's bulging neck.

Spying a shortcut, she ducks down a blackened laneway branching off the main road. Brick walls rear on either side, a few hand spans apart. Imagine if they closed around her now, like the pages of a great book . . .

Bess hurries on, trying to shrug off her of discomfort. At the very end of the lane, an intoxicating sight greets her: tall mizzenmasts and gleaming ships and churning, mustard-coloured water. Clamouring voices – scullers, watermen, sailors, dockhands – mingling with striking hammers from the builder's yard. Wapping Docks, the Thames. The edge of her world. A rat scampers amongst the broken brickwork as she passes. A clear idea is forming in Bess's head, growing sharper as she nears the end of the alley. It seems her feet have known all along where she most desires to go: Execution Docks, to see the pirates swinging in their cages. Mam forbids her to visit, especially on hanging days when riotous crowds clog the docks and spill from the taverns. Bess has always complied. But today is a red-letter day, a day worth celebrating. Pa is home. What could be better than to defy her mother and fly the victory flag of independence? Bess may have inherited her mother's hair, slender nose and soft grey eyes, but that's where the similarities end. They are as different as night and day. Sometimes, she thinks her mother must have confused her at birth with another girl.

Bess's shoes echo on the muddy cobbles. She is almost at the end of the alleyway when her neck prickles. She feels eyes on her, wet and grimy as the stonework. Is she being watched? Something scuffles nearby and she whips about, seeing the peddler's darting tongue. A rat scrabbles past, holding something slimy in its paws. No gawkers, just rats and her overactive imagination.

Sniffling, she hurries on, straightening her white cap over her hair. The bright, canary-yellow ringlets it conceals were once a source of endless embarrassment when she attended Missus Priest's School, although she grudgingly accepts them now. When she is grown, her natural curls will negate the need for those instruments of feminine torture whispered about at the girl's school: the dreaded curling papers. Nobody sees her hair, anyway. Each morning, Bess gathers up fistfuls and jams them under a frilled mob cap she found in the back of a drawer. She suspects it was left by one of the house's former occupants, the merchant's young bride. Bess imagines the woman set sail with her husband for some exciting place. By the time she realised she'd left her cap behind, it was too late to turn back. Something about the stiff, white cloth, pleated at the brim, appealed to her and the first time she wore it, Mam looked soft and approving. *It makes you look younger*, she'd said, touching her own curls wistfully. Bess had wanted to throw the cap out into the street right then and watch the iron carriage wheels crush it to pieces, but she liked the cap too well to go through with it. The linen tickles the back of her neck as she digs in a finger to unhook a ruffle. The noise and hubbub of the dry docks and the churning water of the mighty Thames is deafening. Beyond them all, down a set of timber stairs, lies her destination: the viewing platform. Taking a deep breath, she steps out into the sunshine and scurries across the road.

When Bess was eight, her father gave her a bird, a nightingale plucked from somewhere on his travels through the Levant. Philomela's feathers were as soft as smoke and her eyes shone like bright marbles set in fine filigree. Before he left for sea again, Pa showed her how to care for Philomela, how to make her balls of pasta, rolled up like snails, using a secret recipe he'd discovered in a book on Italian bird care. How to spread a little spongy moss under her brass swing and dissolve a pinch of sugar in water to keep her in good cheer.

For a short time, everything was wonderful; Philomela's presence helped to fill Pa's absence. Bess snuck her pieces of sticky marchpane and delighted in watching her hop between chair, desk and bed, inspecting each new stage with an imperious tilt of her head. When Philomela sang, unhinging her jaw as wide as an opera singer, Bess was filled with such savage joy she imagined the sound came from somewhere deep within herself.

One morning, she awoke to silence and found Philomela lying at the bottom of the cage, her claws drawn tightly to her chest. Nothing marked her; it was as if her spirit had fled unexpectedly, as if God had reached in and snatched it, mid-tune. Mam suggested she'd either died of fright or had been harbouring some hidden disease. She offered to take Bess to the bird market to choose another. Bess refused. She hated the implicit suggestion that because Philomela was diseased she deserved to die, that something sweet and rotten had existed inside her, something that could not be cured. Mam looked hurt, as if *her* bird, *her* best friend had died, not Bess's. What had her mother expected, that she could distract Bess with a replacement, buoy up her spirits with a shiny new toy? Well, she would discover that Bess's loyalty was worth more than that. Philomela's cage would sit empty, a testament to her bird's sweet temperament and Bess's intractable grief.

They buried Philomela under the climbing rose, scraping back the early spring clods, and that should have been the end of it, but it wasn't. Each morning, Bess rose in secret and went down to the garden. On her knees, she dug into the earth with her hands, flicking soil away until Philomela's body reappeared. Philomela's chestnut wings were smeared with dirt. Her glazed eyes caught the last of the dawn's starlight and in their surfaces Bess saw her own face reflected, lips parted in wonder. After a fortnight, Philomela's plumage was all but gone. A patina of blue-green mould speckled her skin. Turning the bird over, Bess felt no disgust, only searing curiosity and a desire to understand the mystery of what she held. Freed from its feathered bindings, Philomela's flesh was two separate shades: pale blue on top, dark crimson underneath where the blood had pooled. Whenever she heard Henry coming, Bess shoved the bird back into the hole. After a month of daily exhumations, the compulsion to dig up the bird vanished and she left Philomela to rest in peace. The question, however, had remained locked inside her ever since: What happens to a person's soul when they die? Where does it all go?

Bess stares up at the prisoner swaying on the gibbet at Wapping Stairs, struck by the old stirrings of curiosity. The man's flesh is pulpy, strips peeling off his bones like flaking paint. He's been dead at least a week, although it's possible that partial submersion (his thighs are just visible, waterlogged by the tide), along with the unseasonable heat, has hastened decay. Two determined crows peck at the corpse's torso through the iron bars of the cage. At first, Bess thinks they are unravelling his clothes, plucking at the seams of his sodden waistcoat and breeches, until one of the birds emerges with a fleshy streamer dangling from its beak. Bess's nail creeps into her mouth; she chews, the taste of her own skin a familiar comfort. A soupy smell of putrefaction swims between the dead man and herself. She is sharply aware of the breath trapped inside her nose and mouth, the tiny gulps that leave her lungs aching and unsatisfied, but keep the bile from rising. Her skin feels all-over greasy, as if she has rolled in tallow fat, and a hot cinder burns inside her stomach, spreading waves of rippling heat. She feels corrupted, as if death has crept up her toes and legs, setting in like rigor mortis. A dead man, she reflects, is not the same as Philomela, a little bird who never did anything but sing sweet songs to try and cheer her.

Following the sweeping curve of the river, silted water moves sluggishly past the corpse and floods the stairs on which Bess stands. She steps away, nauseated, wishing she had never come.

'Hung for a pirate.'

She whirls about, startled. Believing, for a moment, it was the corpse who spoke.

The boy sits a few steps above her, crunching his way through the crisp outer skin of an apple. How long has he been watching her? Bess narrows her eyes and bunches her fist, in case she needs to box his ears to escape. She senses this boy won't believe her, even if a bear was snarling right behind him.

'Let me pass,' she says, willing her voice to stay even. 'Let me pass or I shall make you.'

The boy grins at the threat and trots down the stairs until they are standing side by side on the viewing platform. She surmises he is sixteen, perhaps a touch older. He has a square, clean-shaven face, framed by chestnut hair secured at his back by a navy ribbon. He wiggles a finger through the cage but his gaze is turned on her, not the corpse.

'You were staring at him hard enough,' he says. His accent is elastic, both strange and unfamiliar, the vowels stretched apart like strands of toffee. 'I'm surprised he didn't spring to life or reach out and catch you and drag you down to Hell. It's been known to happen.'

A smile curves his lips and Bess's wariness shifts into dislike. How dare he laugh at her!

'Did you follow me?' she says.

His blue eyes crinkle with amusement. 'Why would I do that?'

'How should I know? Perhaps it's a nasty habit of yours, sneaking about.'

'A poor sneak it is who calls attention to himself by speaking first. Someone told me this is where they hang the pirates. I thought I'd come and take a look.'

'You're a sailor,' she says, having observed enough of them to know. His clothes are in a better state than some others she's seen. A handsome black jacket, replete with matching bone buttons, camel-coloured breeches tucked into gleaming boots. 'Thinking of changing careers?'

He laughs and leans back, surveying her. 'Yes, I'm a sailor. Waiting for my master to issue my next assignment. Which do you think holds better prospects: sailor or pirate?'

Bess is silent, unused to being asked her opinion on anything, even in jest. 'I suppose it depends,' she says, at last. The gibbet creaks. She feels the dead man's stare, the magnetic pull of his eyeless sockets, but she refuses to look. She is glad not to be alone with only the dead for company. And it is far more pleasing to concentrate all her energies on this curious stranger. He is, she realises, devastatingly handsome, though there is a self-awareness in the way he moves and speaks that suggests he is well acquainted with this fact.

'What did he do?' she says. 'The buccaneer?'

The boy leans closer, as if they are old friends. 'According to the builder I asked, he was the son of a Scottish minister who took to sea and was pressed into service after failing to salute a Navy vessel. It warped his mind. He had great ambitions to catch pirates but instead became one himself. When a Navy officer demanded he hand over his crew, he clubbed the man to death and sailed off to save his friends from the press gang. Eventually, he was caught and strung up here to serve as a warning. Do you think his sins were very awful?'

Bess considers. 'Not really,' she says, before hurrying on: 'What I mean to say is that it's possible for anyone to sin, no matter what circumstances they are born into. But did he? Sin, I mean? If he was acting for the greater good of his friends, then can he be blamed for disobeying a rule that would likely have been the cause of their deaths? My father told me about the press gangs.' Her back tingles; she hears Pa decrying the cruelty of the whip, the raw, wounded flesh swabbed with oil of squills to halt infection; imagines the groans of sailors facedown on their hammocks, nursed by the rocking ship into fitful dreams. 'God will search his soul for sin. I don't know that any man should be punished for following his heart. Or any woman, either.'

She stops, painfully aware that she is chattering. She's hardly surprised to find the boy's attention diverted; he is looking out over the river, nibbling his apple. Up close, it looks less like an apple and more like an onion, white pleats armoured by a bronze carapace.

'What is that you're eating?' she says.

'This? A tulip. Want one?'

'No, thank you.'

He brings it out anyway, retrieving the bulb from his pocket, making a great show of withholding it before tipping it into her hand. 'They used to be priceless. Now my master gives me a bag each time we set out. He says I have hollow legs.'

The bulb is smooth, a green mast rising from the stem. Bess lifts it to her nose; it smells of ripe earth and sweet herbs and salty brine.

'Go on,' he says, 'give it a try.'

Bess stares at the little bulb but resists clamping it between her teeth. 'Don't they belong in the ground?' she says, weighing it uncertainly.

He laughs. 'True, they do. But why waste good food? And when you are at sea for months on end, you crave something tastier than dried sea-biscuit.'

Drawing back his arm, he flings the chewed tulip stem into the water. Bess watches it toss about in the foamy wake of a barge, one of many dotting the river's surface, crowded with working men heading home. The fading light makes halos of their dusty hair and tired faces. The barges knock together and the bargemen jab with poles to break them apart, their low growls echoing up the bank, increasingly saturnine. A sleepy, end-of-day pall has descended over the wayward crafts.

'Casper de Vries. Dutchman, if you couldn't tell from the accent.' He holds out his hand.

Bess stares at it, uncertain how to respond. She's never held a man's hand before, except for Pa's. After a moment's hesitation, she takes it. 'Bess Gulliver.'

Casper's skin is rough, lumpy with calluses that have burst and healed. She holds on, daring, determined not to break first, and is rewarded by a rush of pleasure as his fingers press urgently into her palm.

'Unusual name. Your father is never Captain Gulliver?'

Of course it is her father who has caught his interest.

'He is, in fact.' She extracts her hand, which now feels numb and tingly, as if it belongs to someone else. Perhaps it does. Standing in front of the corpse, staring at his bloated face, she'd never felt so heavy, as if last winter's cough was still crackling in her lungs. Now she feels renewed. Who would have guessed today would turn out so grand? Pa's incredible return and a conversation with a handsome boy. Later, she will replay their conversation to herself, inventing ripostes she would never be bold enough to say aloud. At least it will be a way to fill the boredom of her solitary punishment.

For there will be punishment; of that, she is certain. Mam won't be pleased to learn she's run off, especially after the attack on Missus White. She won't listen to sense and Pa is too exhausted yet to defend her. Mam will ply her with extra chores, like she always does. She's too soft to use the cane. Bess worked out years ago that her mother doesn't approve of striking children. If she's visiting a client who does, she'll drop hints about broken spirits and encourage a system of rewards and incentives over physical chastisement. *We must set the strong example we want our children to emulate*, Bess has heard her say. And she's always quoting that snobby old matron Hannah *something*, dispensing snippets of advice that make Bess want to roll her eyes back in her head. What punishment will it be today? Sewing bonnets for the poor foundlings or weeding her mother's garden? At least she's done what she came to do: she's seen a dead man with her own eyes. It wasn't so horrifying, after all. She might come again, with Pa next time. Maybe Casper will be hanging around and Bess can introduce them.

'I should be getting back,' she says. 'It was nice to chat. And thank you for the tulip. I shall remember your advice about them, when I go to sea.'

Casper's pleasant expression becomes mystified. 'I'm sorry – *when* you go to sea?'

Bess lifts her chin. 'That's right. Pa is going to take me, when he is rested from his latest journey. He promised years ago. He said –' She breaks off, suddenly blushing.

An uncomfortable silence follows, punctured only by the screech of gulls and the tide slapping against the steps. Bess's skin tingles uncomfortably. She wishes Casper would say something – anything – but he is oddly mute, as if waiting for her to laugh.

She has never voiced her secret desire aloud to anyone except Pa. She has never even confided the extent of it to Johnny. The idea of sailing off to work as her father's assistant belongs exclusively to Pa and herself. Bess can't remember a time before the plans existed nor a time when she was not ruminating over a better route or wondering aloud whether it might be preferable for them to pack a skillet or a pot, depending on what utilities the galley cook supplied. Each time her father returned from sea, his remarkable stories were accompanied by reassurances that one day, they would both be sitting on a beach, listening to the wind thrash through palm trees and reflecting on the wonders they had witnessed, the strange animals and odd languages, the improving nature of travel. She remembers tracing her finger down the curved spine of New Holland on one of his maps while Pa sat nearby, eating an apple and tossing out suggestions of other islands they could visit on the way. Death should have put an end to all these musings. Instead, they are what Bess remembers most vividly about her father. *Travellers have more power than a king*, he was always saying. *The King has to stay with his people. Travellers can follow the wind.*

Did he mean all travellers, though, or just some? Bess never questioned it. She was eleven when Pa's ship sank. Too young to disagree with anything he told her. Now, having spoken her yearnings aloud, she feels foolish. Women on ships are exceptions, rarer than white peacocks. They are hardly ever permitted aboard unless some strong reason can be argued for their going. A century ago, Queen Henrietta Maria sailed back and forth between Holland and France, trying to pawn the crown jewels to save her husband King Charles from the axe. But she was a queen and Bess is just a commoner; how did she expect to get on board without anyone questioning her sex? It's the kind of childish oversight which makes her long for the safety of home.

Casper is watching her, though, and she can't allow him to see how unsure she feels. When Pa's health is better, she can ask him herself. Perhaps he's always harboured some secret plan to smuggle her aboard? He's been at sea long enough to ingratiate himself with ship owners and the men who dispense employment amongst the sailors. There may be a way. This hopeful thought eases a little of her discomfort. She pastes on a crooked smile, trying to ignore the worry nagging at her belly.

'He said we'll discuss it later. When he is recovered from his journey.'

'I see.' Casper frowns. 'How old are you?' he says, as if the thought has only just occurred. 'Where is your chaperone?'

Bess swallows. This part is always her undoing. She can never know which of many signals betrays her when she lies. Is it her voice? Her eyes?

'Seventeen,' she says, lifting a careless shoulder the way she has seen older girls do. 'I sent my chaperone home. She was complaining of a stomach ailment.'

Casper's lip curls. He doesn't believe her, not even for a second. But he doesn't pursue this line of questioning. Instead, he bows low. 'Well, may our paths cross again, Miss Gulliver. Soon.'

8

Bess turns away from his grinning, teasing face – her head held high, dignity personified – and climbs the stairs, mentally preparing herself for the noisy assault of the dry docks. Although the working day has ended for some, the boardwalk, twelve feet wide, still seethes with frenzied activity, crammed with crates and kegs of all sizes, yoked together by tarred ropes. A shoal of men streams past: storm-weathered sailors shouldering sacks; traders in leather jerkins, crouching to inspect the goods winched off waiting ships. A dockhand tips a sheaf of tobacco into an overseer's arms, as tender as a lover; the man inhales, as if the bushells impart a fragrant bouquet sweeter than ambergris.

Bess is transfixed. In all her fourteen years, she's never been to the docks alone. When Pa used to bring her down here, the industry of the place never failed to inspire. High up on her father's shoulders, safe as an eagle chick in its eyrie, she had surveyed the bustling trade with wide eyes. She remembers tightening her arms around Pa's neck as he plucked a shrivelled pod off a barrel and cracked it in his palm. Bending her nose to the split seed, she'd inhaled the smell of loamy earth, faintly spiced like the soil in her mother's garden after a night of spring rain. The scent has stayed with her all this time; if she closes her eyes, she can still conjure it along with the sense of wonder. What can't men do, when they join hands together? This is the beating heart of London – of life, really. Men like her father are the lynchpin on which the world turns. Without them, everything will grind to a shuddering halt. They are like the Titans Pa told her about, like Cronus or Hyperion or mighty Oceanus, gods of sea and of land. Mam and her friends consider their midwife's work indispensable but Bess knows it is men like Pa who ensure London's children have a future. Men keep them all afloat.

Still thinking of Pa, she starts off in the direction of home, pushing past the dockhands moving back and forth between the warehouses and the floating galleons. An arm knocks heavily against her shoulder. Turning, she leaps aside to avoid being knocked down by a tall man, bare-armed and barrel-chested, hefting a stone slab upon his shoulders. Someone shoves her aside – unbalanced, she stumbles forward, the timber edge of a crate biting sharply through her skirt and stocking. She cries out then sucks in a breath.

From nearby comes rippling laughter.

'You lost, sweetheart?'

The woman's shimmering salmon-coloured dress draws Bess's eye.

She shakes her head. 'No, missus. I know where home is. But I've hurt my knee and . . .' She trails off, distracted by the sudden presence of two more ladies, one dressed in emerald green, the other blue, sidling out of the crowd to stand beside the first. In their bright silks, they are gaudy parrots surrounded by common hedge-sparrows. Bess relaxes a little. Dangerous, indeed! She wishes Mam were here, to observe these women's bravery. Not all women are afraid to be seen out of doors.

'Did you find a daisy in the dust, Belle?' The woman in the green dress turns her eyes on Bess and the girl's skin crawls as the woman's feline gaze pins her into place. That look reminds her too well of the peddler's glance, hot and syrupy with desire. But what could a woman want from her? If anything, it's Bess that needs help. A kind shoulder to lean on, a little assistance hobbling home. The throbbing in her knee is growing worse. She lifts the hem of her skirt to inspect the damage – a deep gash oozing blood through a ripped hole in her stocking. She's about to ask Belle if she might borrow a handkin when the woman speaks.

'Could be a carnation,' Belle says. 'With a splash of colour.' Her stays creak as she bends, cupping Bess's face. Over the tightly laced bodice, Bess can see the woman's breasts, powder-soft like fresh milkbuns squashed in a pan. 'How old are you, my love?'

Bess tries to answer but finds she can't. Belle's hypnotic eyes remind her of fish scales glimmering in a reed-filled pond. The thick scent of gaudy violets tickles her nose.

'Good stems,' the girl in the blue dress says, quietly. 'Well fed. Fourteen or fifteen, I'd reckon. She'd be too much trouble, I dare say. Bet she's never even laced herself. Look at her smock. Looser than a nun's habit. Let her be.'

'It's not your place to say, Meg.' Belle turns her fish-scale eyes to the girl in blue, who flashes Bess an unreadable look before lowering her eyes.

Their talk pounds in time with Bess's pulsing knee. Daisies, carnations, stems. Are the women flower-sellers? She looks them over again, expecting to see baskets filled with wilting blossoms hooked around their arms. But they are free of adornment, save for the furled fans on their elbows which swing cheerily in the breeze blowing in off the Thames.

The truth dawns and Bess, flushing, bends her head to hide her embarrassment.

Cupping her injured knee, she tugs her skirt down so hard she hears a seam rip. Wrenching her chin out of Belle's grasp, she straightens as much as her injury will allow. Belle purses her pink lips and for one fearful moment, Bess imagines a sly hand circling her wrist, clenching tight as a hangman's noose. But the women break apart as she limps past them and when she dares a glance over her shoulder, their bright dresses have been swallowed by the throng.

Tears press against her eyes. Where is Pa when she needs him? If she can only reach the wall that runs beside the warehouse frontage, she can pull herself along and put some distance between the women and herself. She sees Mister Fisher, one of her father's old friends, standing outside the doors of his warehouse, conversing with a merchant. He has always been kind to her.

'Mister Fisher!' she calls, but her voice is lost in the thunder of feet. Something slams into her shoulder, buffeting her to one side. Her foot buckles painfully and she goes down, landing hard in a stringy pile of fish guts. Nobody stops to help, the sailors simply swirl around her, surging forward, an endless parade of breeches and feet. If she raises her hand, will anyone come to aid her? Will they even hear her over the din? She thinks, ridiculously, of Casper, wondering if he followed her. Someone treads hard on her fingers. Snatching them up, she cradles them, throbbing, in her lap. Mister Fisher is all but invisible from down here. Bess cannot even see the wall, and there is certainly no sign of her father or even

Casper. She might as well be at the bottom of the ocean, at the mercy of the fish and sharks. Perhaps the souls of pirates haunt the sea, too; they must go somewhere.

A great sob heaves its way up through her body, but nobody hears.

'Elisabeth Grace?'

Mam's voice is shrill, splicing through the discord. Bess would know it anywhere.

'Here!' she shouts, trying to lift herself. 'Here I am!'

Some sailors shift aside, grumbling, and Mam's face materialises. Bess has never been so glad to see her mother in all her life.

'Oh, God be praised.' Mam embraces her. Her hair is a golden riot, curls tickling Bess's nose. She is radiant, lit from within like a pane of coloured glass. An angel of goodness. Together, they limp across to the wall.

'Where were you?' Mam says. Her eyes are swimming. She wipes them with the hem of her mantle. 'I thought – I was so afraid.'

'I told Alice I was going to peep at the dead man,' Bess says, reasoning that Mam might forgive this transgression quicker than her running off. 'She must not have heard me.'

Mam pauses and her grip tightens on Bess's hand, just hard enough for the girl to detect the tough cushions of flesh. Mam's hands are unusual: strong and sinewy from her time spent in the garden, yet soft from all the butter and duck fat she rubs into them for the birthings. 'Bess, are you telling me the truth?'

'Of course.' Bess won't meet her mother's eyes. The day's events weigh on her, the good (Pa, Casper) and the bad (the creepy peddler and the callous bawds). She wants to be alone with her thoughts so she can consider them properly. The last thing she needs is for her mother to look at her the way she's looking at her now, slightly mistrustful. She hobbles along, grateful for the sudden distraction of Mister Fisher who comes forward to greet them. Mister Fisher is an elderly widower who dresses in fashions some years past their prime. Casper, Bess imagines, would not be caught wearing such a pilled and faded fustian. She catches herself. Why should it matter a jot what Casper de Vries wears? She knows next to nothing about him. He will be gone tomorrow, very likely. She will never see him again.

This thought makes her turn to glance back the way they have come. The crowd has thinned now. Afternoon sunlight melts over the tall masts of ships and the gleaming gundecks. She can just see the top of the gibbet, the rope disappearing into darkness. The bawds are gone, off to ply their wares elsewhere or perhaps some man has secured their services. Pa would never go with women like that. Strange, that she never noticed their presence at the docks when she was a lass, looking down on the world from her father's shoulders. Alice always clutches her close when bawds pass them on the street, as if their sinfulness is contagious, like head lice or an attack of ague. Not Mam, though. She inclines her head as if the women are her equals, and sometimes sends Bess and Johnny's old, ill-fitting clothes down to the shanties for their children. 'Those children are not to blame for their mothers' desperate circumstances,' Bess once heard her say, after Alice returned from the market clutching a pamphlet circulated by The Society for The Reformation of Manners. 'They are damned, no matter what they do. If the authors of such tracts looked beyond their own self-righteousness, if they saw those newborn babes for what they are – sinless and in dire need of charity – they would better serve the parish and the poor women they claim to help.' Bess did not catch Alice's reply because Mam noticed her eavesdropping and closed the door between them. She found the pamphlet later in the kitchen hearth, scorched letters fanned out over the coals as if somebody had torn the paper to bits before throwing it in.

Mam bids goodbye to Mister Fisher, who urges her to pass on his best wishes for Pa's recovery. Mam's expression clouds and as they shuffle off Bess hears her mutter darkly about the 'prodigious spread of gossip'. At least Pa will be waiting when they get back. If his fever has died down, Mam might let her sit with him. Bess thinks of all the things she has to tell him, the little tales of interest she has stored in his absence. To have him returned is the best present she could possibly ask for. She wonders how Johnny will take the news. He was only eight when Pa left and always shy of the Great Man, as Henry referred to him.

Another thrill: Henry won't be here to monopolise her father. It will just be the two of them again, and Johnny, when he returns home. Bess will need to show Johnny the right way to behave around Pa. How to read his moods, something Mam was never very good at doing. With some encouragement, she's sure Johnny will find their father a kind and generous ally. Of course, she'll need to ask Pa about their travel plans but her confidence in her father is so watertight she cannot conceive any act of failure on his part. Even her knee hurts less, the heat abated. Her whole body vibrates, a plucked string waiting to be heard.

When they arrive home, Mam orders Alice to take Bess straight to her room and bind her knee and, when that is done, to find her in the kitchen where she will take over the preparation of supper.

Alice is filled with an endless supply of hurt, reproachful looks; she casts one every time she looks up from daubing herbal paste onto Bess's cut. Her fingers tremble and she manages, quite without meaning to, to smear the mixture onto the faded coverlet and the cuffs of her sleeves.

'Thank you, Alice,' Bess says. Propped up in the bed, she is cushioned by bolsters, legs stretched in front of her on the counterpane.

Alice pins her bottom lip with her teeth. 'Why'd you run off? Your mother left me in charge and it was my duty to guard you. I would not be surprised if she turned me out, not surprised at all. After all she's done for me.' She pauses in her ministrations to fix Bess with a baleful stare.

Bess flushes. 'I'm sorry,' she mumbles, uncomfortably aware that Alice deserves better treatment. Three years ago, right before Pa went to sea, Missus Perry hired her to be their scullery maid. Months later, Missus Perry was gone, along with Pa's manservant Henry, and young as she was, Bess knew it had something to do with money. Things started to disappear. A pair of brass candlesticks from the dresser. Mam's best Holland sheets out of the linen press. Pa's spyglass and his silver compass, nothing left but the dusty imprint where they had rested on the lintel. Mam's face grew more pinched each time Bess saw her, her eyes more sunken. Although their family had never been wealthy, that summer was the worst. Cold pottage for every meal, congealed in its own milky juices. The worried squeak of the floorboard in the master bedroom as Mam paced, Bess's dreams swelling with dark waves. Spluttering awake, she would scream for Pa through a raw throat, but it was Mam who came.

Each day while Mam worked, a different neighbourhood family took care of her, the Gibsons or the Tooleys or the Kendall-Greens. Most had children Bess's age, but Bess found they shared little in common. The girls were good and quiet and sat darning their piecework or trotting along after their mothers while the boys helped their fathers in the workshops. Bess longed for Johnny to keep her company, but he was back at the grammar school, under the thumb of their stern Uncle John. Once, when she tried to initiate a game of pirates, her playmate's mother coldly suggested that it might be better if Bess was kept home or sent to the charity school in Shadwell, instead of pestering hardworking families. It went on like this for a little while, Bess being passed from house to house and family to family until she felt grubby and ill-used and utterly dispirited, like a threadbare handkin nobody wanted to touch.

Then Mam announced that Alice would be their new maid-of-all-work. She would be something like a housekeeper and a nurse and a scullery maid, all rolled into one. She'd be in charge of the cooking and the cleaning and Bess would help her. It was an arrangement which suited Bess at first, since she feared the charity school where poor children were caned for wearing shabby clothes. As if they had a choice! But over time the house became a prison. Now Alice is more like a warden than a nurse, always coming to find her and draw attention to what she should be doing. And yet, the woman's loyalty can't be faulted.

She is both relieved and ashamed when Alice sets the paste down, squeezes her shoulder and retreats to the hallway, still sniffing. Through her bedroom window, Bess sees birds circle the shipyard, and the evening sky shimmers pink and gold. She leans back, taking a sip of the milk Alice left. Mam is right, her room *is* a disaster. Nests of discarded clothing, books strewn haphazardly like crumbling tombstones. She can't be expected to clean now, though; she is injured. Shutting her eyes against the mess, she allows her mind to wander.

One day in particular stands out in her memory. Bess isn't sure how old she was but she remembers stretching her neck to look up at her father, admiring the shine of his brass coat buttons. She remembers the spyglass in her hand making rainbow circles on the study walls and Pa's hand descending to stroke the curls Mam had done her best to comb. Pa's hand still caught though, his fingers tangling in the knots as he boomed out laughter. Pa's surgeon's chest hulked in the corner, a big brown trunk full of bottles and potions and surgical instruments Mam had forbidden her to touch. But Mam wasn't there, was she? She was working. She was always working. So Bess dug down into the chest, shifting the lancets and the pipkins, the bladders bulging with bitter wormwood. Uncorking bottles to sniff their contents and screwing up her nose to make Pa smile. With the study door closed, it was almost like the two of them were on their own private vessel. Too bad Pa had lost the *Swift* before she'd had a chance to set foot on it. She imagined it was like that, full of maps and old atlases, feathers and bones. The scent of salt and tobacco and sweat. A place of wonder and limitless possibility where wood-panelled wainscotting hugged the walls and the dark beams of the vaulted ceiling met together like hands in prayer.

'Bess? Are you awake?'

She sits up, stirred out of her reverie. Mam slides the tray onto the side table and removes the items: a bowl of broth – stringy, as usual – and, delight of delights, a whole shortcake, doused in a sticky, sugary glaze. One of Mister Stewart's specialties.

'We need to talk,' Mam says. 'We did not have much chance this morning.'

Bess puts out her hand for the shortcake but Mam moves the pastry out of reach, determined, it seems, to force a conversation before handing over the reward.

'You should never have run off, Bess,' Mam says. 'It was a wicked thing to do. A cruel trick. You could have been crushed to death by a crate or the victim of a very heinous and terrible crime. The consequences of which you – an innocent – cannot even imagine. Think of Lucy White – a girl's virtue is a prize worth protecting and worse sufferings exist than unwanted children or infections. What on God's earth were you thinking? You could have been kidnapped or put on a ship, enslaved.' Mam pauses to puff air from her pink cheeks. Bess can tell she is warming to her theme, that there are more recriminations and reprobations to come.

To speed things up, she mumbles a hasty apology. Of course she should not have taken to her heels so thoughtlessly, but she did so want to see the man swinging on his gibbet and Alice had no inclination to take her. She is very sorry and will never do it again.

There, she thinks. That's an end to it. To her surprise, Mam doesn't relax into compassionate and forgiving smiles, as she usually does. She twists her gold wedding ring around her finger fretfully, the metal twinkling in the afternoon light streaming through the shutters. Bess supposes she continued to wear it as a symbol of her loyalty towards Pa, even after his death. Perhaps she should have been a trifle nicer to him when he was alive.

'I expect you want to see your father properly,' Mam says at last. 'I expect you are . . . confused and this reckless rebellion is your method of coping. I lay the blame at my own feet. I should have spent more time with you. Taken the trouble to explain, offered more comfort. I wish your brother lived closer. You must miss him.'

Bess nods slowly and her mother continues. 'You have, I'm sure, divined certain truths about your father in the long years of his absence. We need not speak of them directly. You know to what I am referring.' She flicks Bess a hopeful, nervous glance before dropping her gaze back to the ring.

Bess watches the gilded band spin, mesmerised by its fluid shine. Her thoughts have drifted to Casper. She wonders, idly, what he is about. What do sailors do when they are not at sea? How do they amuse themselves? Belle's swishing salmon gown and creamy skin slide coyly into her mind and she wriggles up against the bolster, frowning.

'Bess? Are you listening?' Mam places her hand over Bess's slight one. Her voice is soft, her eyes large and luminous. Warm from all her fiddling, the ring burns against Bess's knuckle like a hot kiss. 'I said, do we understand each other? Can you forgive me for not telling you sooner?'

Telling me what? Bess tries to concentrate but her mother's meaning eludes her limited understanding. Mam's hand trembles. Slowly, it dawns on Bess that her mother has wronged her somehow and is now asking for forgiveness. A surge of power leaps in her veins. The thought occurs that she could hurt her mother badly by refusing. But what good would that do? If she complains, Mam will simply reproach her and this surprising power, which has appeared out of nowhere, will drain away, diminishing her capacity to negotiate. Far better to wait and see what can be leveraged.

Whatever Mam's done, it can't be too dreadful, so she nods slowly then reaches past her mother for the shortcake.

'Consequences,' Mam says. She seems relieved, patting Bess's hand before tucking her own neatly into her lap. 'Every action has consequences. Some irreversible. I want you to understand, I had your best interests at heart. I desired only to protect you. I was afraid it might come as a shock, if you knew how things truly were.'

Bess lifts a shoulder, half-listening. Something the bawds said earlier beats its wings inside her head.

'I need a new dress, Mam,' she says, around a mouthful of crumbs. She takes a gulp of milk. 'Please. And a . . . a proper stomacher.'

Mam frowns. 'What's wrong with the dresses you have now? Are they too short? Have you grown again? Shall I ask Alice to lower the hems?'

A flake of pastry sticks in Bess's throat and she coughs to clear it. Is her mother in her right mind? Are those grey eyes incapable of seeing what is so very clearly in front of them? Or does it simply suit her to keep Bess small and shrunken, silenced by bland dresses? Was it Bess's monthly bleeding? Did her mother read something frightening in those dark blotches of impending womanhood and believe she could stave off the future by keeping Bess trapped in the past?

'Lower the hems? Look at me!' She indicates the dull smock, worn thin through many washes, and the shapeless brown sack-dress underneath.

Her mother blinks, assessing Bess's arms, legs and torso like an undertaker in his workshop. 'Bess, I fail to see –'

Bess bites her lip hard and shuts her eyes. Lace patterns dance in the darkness, filigree swirls of black and red. Frustration ripples through her. Why should she be the one to say it aloud? Perhaps the words will come easier if she doesn't have to face her mother. 'I'm not a child, but you dress me like one. You make me wear these smocks and dresses, as if I'm six. Folks aren't stupid, Mam. Everyone can see I'm a young woman, in shape if not in name, everyone but you.'

Breathing hard, she hopes Mam cannot see how close she has come to crying, the embarrassment of such an admission making her speak more forcefully than she intended. Perhaps it's better they both confront this uncomfortable truth.

Her mother says nothing. Bess waits for her to argue or scoff. Mam's gaze is lowered and Bess can't tell whether she is angry or upset or ashamed.

'You're right,' Mam says. 'Forgive me. I simply can't accept . . . I did not realise. It's difficult, to see your children grow up. I'll take your dress measurements to Missus Sparrow tomorrow. Would that suit you?'

Bess gapes. To have her feelings confirmed is unbalancing but a new dress is a delight. Not a childish smock, but one that will enhance her growing figure. She doesn't trust herself to speak so she nods numbly.

'Good. In return,' her mother says, 'you must do me a favour. No visiting your father without supervision. If you want to see him, either Alice or myself will sit in, as we used to, you remember? He needs rest, in order to put his sufferings behind him. I must ask you not to disturb him until I tell you he's fit to be seen.'

Bess frowns, but what good would it do to argue? Pa will soon heal. They have days, weeks, months stretching ahead of them in which to speak before he inevitably returns to sea. She nibbles the shortcake, to show her mother she can be calm and rational, but her mother has more to say.

'There is another condition. You must promise not to wander the streets, not even with Alice, until the attacker is caught and punished. Church and home. That's where you can be kept safe.'

'But then, what am I to *do*? Remember Missus Priest's?' Bess is satisfied to see Mam flinch. She knows Mam feels guilty for withdrawing her, although if truth be told, Bess could hardly stand the place any longer. All those wasted hours spent japanning boxes, gluing seashells onto bits of paste . . . 'When you took me out of there, you said I didn't need a school to teach me how to be a skilled gentlewoman,' she says, deliberately reproachful.

Her mother's hand creeps to the back of her flushed neck. 'That's true. But you have me. Johnny will be home soon for the summer. And of course, when your father recovers you may visit with him.' She brightens. 'I could ask Missus Clifton to let you come with me to the birthings. Unofficially, of course. You wouldn't be allowed to do more than hold my things.'

Bess wrinkles her nose. She has only been to one birthing, but found it so tedious she vowed never to return. She remembers sitting for hours in the warm fug of the confinement chamber, listening to fussy gossips describe their own violent birthings as if they were soldiers returned from French battlefields. Their stories weren't half so interesting as Pa's and she did not understand how they endured the waiting so patiently, content to chat while the woman's labour dragged on and her screams grew louder. 'No, Mam. Best not,' she says.

'Well, in that case, there are the usual duties. Alice dearly needs help with the housekeeping and I need an assistant gardener – and there are all those bonnets to be sewn for the parish poor. It's time you learned, I suppose, to keep your own house, for you will one day have need of the skill.' Bess scowls but Mam busies herself plumping the bolster, as if she hasn't noticed. 'So, there, it is settled. I will speak to Missus Sparrow about some new dresses and you have promised not to go wandering.' She pats Bess's thigh, as if the whole conversation has been mutually cordial and the outcome to her liking.

Mam leaves the room and moments later Bess hears her moving around next door. She hears low voices: her father, asking questions. She cannot hear Mam's muffled responses. How Bess longs to go to him. To be trapped at home, with her father only steps away but forbidden to speak with him is cruel. A sly little voice whispers: *But you never promised not to visit him. All you need do is wait for the right moment, then you can go in and see him yourself.*

Swinging her legs over the bed, she hitches up her skirts and squats over the chamber pot. When she stands, she is grieved to find crimson moons staining the porcelain. Of course. She clenches her teeth and, wincing, goes to the stash of clean clouts she keeps in a box on the shelf. She shoves one into place and pulls on a red petticoat, arranging the folds as best she can to hide any stains. Although her courses started a year ago, there is no rhythm to their arrival, no way of knowing how many weeks of relief she will be spared the crippling pain. Mam is always kind to her on the bad days, always sympathetic. If she calls out, she knows Mam will send Alice to heat the water and bring her a scented rag so she can dab at the blood streaking her thighs. Alice blames Eve for cursing them all with this womanly affliction; when she talks about her own monthly blood, she gets a hard look on her face, an angry look, as if she might forget herself and spit into the hearth.

But the commencement of Bess's courses did not anger her; in fact, she was elated. She'd imagined, somehow, that the crimson stain would make her an ally to Mam and Alice. How wrong she'd been. She'd sat up late that first night, waiting for them to invite her down to talk over all the secret women's business that hitherto remained shrouded. But they never did and nothing has changed. Only Pa's presence ever made a spot of difference. Mam avoided confrontation when Pa was home, so all Bess had to do was please herself.

Smoothing down her smock, she limps across to the bed, wishing Mam would walk in with a sprig of parsley for her to chew or a heated warming pan for her belly. Why am I like this? she thinks. What is wrong with me? It's as if there are two Besses trapped within one body. One version is kind and helpful, endlessly obedient, the one who follows her mother's good example, the daughter Mam deserves. The other is an aberration, intent on thwarting everyone around her. This second Bess is ugly, twisted like one of those stunted wilding apple trees that blights the edges of the parish. Monstrous conceptions, vastly different to their companions, they bear nothing but sour, bitter fruit. Even the birds do not savour their offerings but leave the pulpy corpses to rot in ditches and burst in porous clouds when they are trampled by horses' hooves.

Bess lies on the counterpane, rubbing her stomach. Something knobby digs into the back of her knee. Poking about in her skirt, she pulls it out. The forgotten tulip fits snugly in her curled fist and she squeezes it tightly, her hard little comfort. Pa says the fields of Holland are filled with such promises. In springtime they burst into blossom, pushing up through the soil in dazzling rows of snow white, pale yellow and ribbon pink. She wonders what kind this is, whether, if planted, it will grow, or remain forever stunted. Raising the bulb to her mouth, she bites down hard. Juice explodes on her tongue and she gags, the flooding taste – bitter, overwhelmingly vegetative – not at all what she expected. She spits the chunk into her hand and Casper's gift sits there, broken and glistening, further proof of her failure. What a disgrace she is, incapable of even choking down a tulip bulb.

Groaning, she curls on her side and wishes that Philomela was swinging over her bed of moss, pouring out her song.

9

Mary wakes to the sound of whispering. She peers through the pre-dawn light, searching out her husband's shape in the four-poster bed. He is asleep, but dreaming.

She pushes herself up from the trundle bed and pads softly to the bedside. The whispers have separated now into their individual strands. Names she doesn't recognise, places and events that hold no meaning. Sometimes his prison is an island, other times a ship. Often he curses, or beats his head against the bolster, muttering about something called a *flimnap*. Touching his shoulder, she says his name, repeating it until at last he stirs and opens his eyes.

''S'matter?' he slurs. His cheeks are paunchy, grizzled and unshaven. 'Are you here with a message from Peter Williams?'

She hesitates. That name again. 'No. You were talking in your sleep. I thought you might prefer to be woken.'

He doesn't thank her for waking him, but rolls away. A moment later, she hears him snore. The trundle bed is cold when she slips back under the coverlet. She moves, trying to get comfortable on the prickly chaff. At last, she gives up and carefully crosses the room to ease open the door.

In the silent kitchen, she pours some milk into a mug. A hundred times better than Rhenish, she thinks wryly, as she sips. Milk is something she refuses to skimp on. She feeds it to her children and encourages her clients to drink it, if they can absorb the cost. Donkey milk is better than cow; it tastes closest to breast and a smear of it on a minor abrasion works wonders. Her favourite beast is a sweet little jenny called Koko, who is led from door to door each week by an Islington milkmaid with sleepy eyes and patched skirts. Today is not a milking day, but oh, how Mary dearly wishes it was. She craves the comforting feel of Koko's long, bristled ears, her mild, docile manner, her intelligent, dark eyes blinking slowly in the shaded yard. Koko can be trusted not to nibble Mary's precious herbs; she is the best-behaved animal Mary has ever met. If ever Mary is blessed with unexpected riches, she will buy Koko and fatten her up on a diet of plums and barley straw. It's a ridiculous fantasy but one she cannot seem to be rid of. Surely the animal is tired of being dragged from house to house? In Mary's garden, her life would be immeasurably improved, her milk shared amongst Mary's weaker clients, to fortify them during their pregnancies and build their strength. If more women were granted access to nutritious food and drink, they would be better equipped to manage the rigours of childbed. The donkey could even help Mary facilitate the birthings; her kit could easily be strapped to Koko's back to save her own energies for the long hours of labour.

The house shifts and settles. A nightjar calls and Mary, half-dozing, imagines she hears the clop of hooves and a soft, punctilious bray.

'Up early?' Alice shuffles in, wiping the grit from her eyes. 'The master, again? Nightmare, was it?'

Mary downs the last of the milk before she answers. 'He can hardly be held accountable, I suppose.'

Alice pumps the bellows, reviving the dwindled fire. 'I dreamed I was back in my father's house.'

'Oh, Alice. You didn't.' Mary comes to help her. Together they toss handfuls of fresh coal from the scuttle into the hearth, the old nuggets crumbling, spilling their red-hot marrow.

'I did.' Alice wipes her dusty hands on her apron. 'I dreamed I was back there and he was standing over me, holding his whip, shouting at me to get my lazy arse out of bed. Then he was kicking me. I felt his boot here –' She touches her sternum. 'Here –' She fingers a bulge at her back. 'There was a sour taste in my mouth, as though I'd swallowed poison. Thought I was going to die.'

Mary winds an arm around the woman's shoulders. 'You are safe here,' she says. 'Remember what I told you?'

Alice nods. Thick hanks of dark hair hang limply down her back under her work cap and Mary resists the urge to gather them together and comb them with her fingers, then pin them up out of the way. She is protective of Alice even though she knows this is a source of jealousy where Bess is concerned. Bess, compared to Alice, has been raised in relative comfort. Yes, Lem has mistreated her in his own way – all his stories, his visions of taking her to sea with him. (In what world would this ever be possible?) And Mary herself has clearly sheltered her too long from the dangers of the adult world. For that, she must atone and she has, at least, started the process. A few dresses are a small price to pay to accommodate her daughter's wounded feelings. Bess has never known violence – has never experienced it nor seen its brutal consequences on another woman's body. Of course, there are other marks men leave on their wives and daughters, unseen and invisible, known only to the victims themselves. Lemuel's posthumous debts, for instance, which beggared them all, including the servants. As things grew dire, she'd offered them a choice – stay and forfeit their wages for a month until she could pay them or seek employment elsewhere. Henry left at once – his loyalty had always been to Lemuel – and Missus Perry packed her things the very next week to work with her daughter for a well-off family in Red-Lyon Square. The loss was crippling. Forced to manage the housework as well as her duties as a midwife, Mary felt herself floundering.

'You'll be off too, Alice, I suppose.' The scullery maid was a recent acquisition, hired to do the jobs Missus Perry felt were beneath her before Lemuel took to sea on his last doomed voyage: the hauling of coal, the draining of the cesspit when the nightsoil men neglected their duties. Mary was astonished when Alice dropped to her knees, hands clasped.

'Don't put me out, missus. For the love of all that's holy, let me stay. I'll work for nothing, just bed and board. I'll do anything you ask. Please. My father works at the tannery ... I can't be going back to him.'

'Why ever not?'

Grimly, Alice had lifted her blouse to show the faded bruises purpling her stomach. Mary knew then she could not in good conscience send the girl home to her lout of a father. Not even if the scant stock of food in the pantry had to be shared between them and they went to bed with hollow stomachs. They would make do. When at last, through a combination of frugality and hard work and selling what they could, she managed to pay off Lem's outstanding debts, she paid Alice double what she owed her and they feasted on parboiled oysters and Norfolk fool to celebrate, Bess helping Alice stir the cream and scrape the sugar off its cone onto the glistening dates.

'St George's Day tomorrow.' Alice sweeps the broom across the hearth, gathering the ashes. 'And the Queen's coronation. We're almost out of candles. Best stock up.'

Mary stretches, rubbing the ache out of her spine. In all the fuss over her husband, she has quite forgotten that tomorrow is the Queen's day. If they don't buy their victuals today, prices will soar. 'I'd better see the chandler myself, since I've rounds to do.'

The maid nods her agreement and shuttles ashes towards the back door. Mary washes out her mug and sets it to dry beside the blue-patterned jug that holds the last of Koko's weekly largesse. After checking her kit is well equipped for the morning's examinations, she helps Alice empty the chamber pots, slopping the night's leavings onto the cesspit, the thick stench an engulfing fog.

At ten in the morning, Wapping's market square is already clogged with shoppers and vendors plying their wares. Damp cress, river water for those who cannot access a street pump, salted haddock; all manner of things bought and exchanged for a sum. Most of the parishes have their own market, though like Wapping's the range of goods is not as varied as that found in Leadenhall or Billingsgate. Wapping's market square is unsheltered, affording no protection from an unlucky downpour, but it suits Mary's purpose today for she threads easily between shoppers, and the open air provides a little respite from the stench of ripe vegetables and sour meat. At the chandler's stall, she's surprised to find Mister Grillett in attendance.

He pastes on a smile as Mary approaches. She's heard him say that midwives are his favourite clientele, after link boys, stationers and whores – anyone who needs a light to work.

'Missus Gulliver,' he says. He is a large man who stinks of old bones and tallow fat and has pinned a rose to his shirt, in preparation for St George's Day. The ragged bloom has already wilted; as he swats at the flies, another petal peels away, settling upon a yellow wax cylinder like a spot of blood.

'Away from your factory today, Mister Grillett,' she observes.

'Aye. Missus Grillett is poorly. Suffering an ague, brought on by toothache.' He bares his own rotten ones.

The candles are set out in soldierly rows, the cheaper ones at the front, finer quality at the back where Mister Grillett can protect them from would-be thieves. When she tells him what she wants, and how many, he bundles them together and names a price.

'That's twice what we paid last week,' she says, gripping her purse tightly. 'I suppose you will lower it again after tomorrow's celebrations are done with?'

The greasy man shrugs. 'Unlikely. It's a permanent price rise and out of my hands, madam. Times are hard. Taxes are on the rise again. What with the Queen's new war on France and Spain, Missus Grillett says we must conserve what little we have in case England runs out of candles. Naturally, this increases the value of the ones we are willing to sell. And you must have heard about Missus White; folks want to keep their houses lit, they are afeared of what lurks in the dark.'

Mary steps backwards, repulsed. The nerve of him, using poor Lucy as a means to sell his shoddy wares! It turns her stomach. 'Folks could always learn to make their own candles,' she says.

His smile transforms into a petulant frown. 'If that's how you feel, Mother Midnight, perhaps you ought to try your hand at it? I suppose there's little difference between us – I butcher animals for their fat and you butcher women.'

She almost drops her purse. 'I do not butcher women!'

'That's not what I heard.' With his free hand, he fingers his chin, the skin there disrupted by throbbing pustules. 'I heard you told the surgeon to cut Charlotte Woollet's baby out of her dead body.'

Mary tries to swallow. All the air seems to have evacuated her lungs. She hears the coins rattle in her shaking hands. 'That baby would have died if we had not acted so swiftly.'

'Perhaps,' he concedes. 'But now it has no mother, so it might well have been better off. To defy God's will is surely a sin of some kind, Missus Gulliver. It will weigh against you when the day of judgement comes, mark my –'

She walks away. Trembling all over, she is hardly conscious of the direction her feet are marching her. The noise of the marketplace is muffled by the heavy throb of blood pounding in her ears. With each step, she hears the word 'butcher'. The bag bumps against her thigh, lightweight, insubstantial, a jumble of tools and phials and herbal tinctures. The kind of thing a child might carry, a toy stamped with the impression of a real medical kit. *Butcher.* Is that what people really think of her? Most people in the parish treat her with respect, but what people say and what they think are two entirely separate things, as well she knows.

A whistling woman and a crowing hen; neither are fit for God or men.

She's heard the saying thrown about but until today she has never considered it could refer to herself. She knows too much; that is the problem. Although the surgeons are derided for their greed, they are still afforded their high status, their superior knowledge. But a woman who thinks and acts with speed to save a life . . .

They still need candles so Mary searches out a hawker she has seen before who sells old ones melted down and reshaped. As she hands the coins over to the man, she hopes she is not contributing to the thriving trade run by thieving servants who sell their masters' half-used stubs. She puts the lumpy, foul-smelling tallows in her basket, frowning as a trace of blackened wick sticks to her thumb. Although the candles are cheaper than Mister Grillett's, she can't forget his words nor their import. Since the King's war ended in '97, Londoners have experienced something of a reprieve in taxes. But this new war with France and Spain could not have come at a worse time for her or for many of her clients. Violent riots and protests are what they have to look forward to, along with poor folk slipping further down the ladder until they tumble out of sight altogether.

As Mary bids the hawker goodbye, she finds a line of customers waiting their turn behind her. Clearly, she is not the only person who cannot afford Mister Grillett's tallows. Her chest tightens with the ever-present fear of penury. After the purchase of the candles, Mary has just five shillings left in her purse to last them the week. Bess's dresses are a luxury they can barely afford, but she has promised.

Abigail Sparrow, her third client of the morning, lives above the haberdasher's shop bordering the square. On the doorstep Mary pauses, gathering her professional focus before she goes upstairs to greet Abigail.

Slipping open her bag, she eyes the contents, mentally naming the herbs and tonics, a practice that usually calms her agitation. Today, the names of the herbs escape her.

As she moves a jar aside, she realises with a shock that her wedding ring is gone. It must have slipped off her finger and dropped into the bottom of the bag. She jams in her hand but her desperate search turns up nothing. Tracing her steps back, she scans the ground for a glint of gold. Nothing. Her stomach drops. Is it a sign or just another bit of rotten luck? After Lem's disappearance, she continued to wear the ring to remind parish folk of her protected status as a widow. *My poor husband*, she said, when men and women expressed doubts about the decency of her living alone. *He would have wanted me to keep working.* What was the point of keeping up that charade, she thinks bitterly, when the opinions of men like Elias Grillett hold more weight than her own? She should have sold the thing when she had the chance.

A wedding ring is clearly a flimsy excuse for protection anyway, for it cannot ward off ignorant spite. Will they have to rely on Lemuel now to protect them? Perhaps his manly presence in her home will satisfy the naysayers. If his past actions are anything to go by, he will be of little use to her as an ally. When Mary informed him six years ago of her plans to join the midwives' trade to supplement the failing surgery, he'd laughed and then, realising she was serious, asked why she felt the need to embarrass him. *Belittling* was the word he used, if she remembers right. It was *belittling* for a gentlewoman to work. Proof, some might suggest, that he was not man enough to support his own family. As a surgeon, he had his pride (she doubted that but let it pass by without argument since there were more important things to fret over). If one of them didn't start earning, they would soon be out on the streets or at the almshouse. He tolerated her trade for the money it brought in. But if forced to choose between his loyalty to her or the surgeon's guild, Mary knew who he would support.

Will he try to stop her from practising, once his wits are restored? The thought makes her squirm. Elias Grillett will be pleased. Picturing the chandler's greasy face, the swollen lumps on his chin and cheeks, she wishes she knew a real curse. *May he be forever blighted by adolescent pimpling; may his candles set his own wretched factory aflame.*

All through Abigail's examination, Mary is distracted. She measures the woman's progress with her hands then promptly forgets the figure before she has had time to jot it down. The fortifying potion she worked so carefully to decoct this morning erupts when she prises off the stopper, leaking its contents into the rug and rendering good herbs and wine useless.

'I'm sorry,' she says when, for the hundredth time, her notebook slips from her grasp and flutters to the floor. 'I'm all at odds, today.'

''Tis no trouble, missus. I'll fetch it.' Agnes Sparrow, Bess's age, puts down the ribbon she has been slipping through the hem of a petticoat and slides her hand under the sofa to retrieve the notebook. Mary thanks her and the girl ducks her head before resuming her seat beside her sisters. The five girls range from nine to nineteen. All have their mother's mouse-brown hair and thick eyebrows, as well as her talent with a needle. In the light-filled room above the haberdasher's shop, they are like bright little birds, working industriously under their mother's supervision to stitch mantuas and cravats and undergarments, cut from the bolts of silk and linen lining their father's shop.

Abigail, reclining on the other lounge as Mary completes her examination, smiles fondly at them. 'Are they not good girls, Mary?'

Mary agrees that they are. 'Have you experienced any more dizziness? Any black spots?' she says, helping the woman to sit.

Abigail shakes her head. Darting a look at her girls, she lowers her voice. 'I've bled a little, though. Just a drop, here and there. Nothing like the other times. I'm tired, too. When I rise, I feel like climbing straight back onto my tick. Do you think that a troubling sign?'

Mary lays her hand on the woman's bulging stomach. Under her palms, she can feel Abigail's baby turning somersaults in its watery cell as gracefully as a jongleur. She smiles. 'Not at all. If anything, I would expect you to be doing even less than you do at present. For instance, is it necessary to keep up such a rigorous routine? Can't your girls help you with the cleaning?' When Mary walked in, the woman was on her hands and knees scrubbing the floor, her big belly brushing the boards.

Abigail lifts her shoulders. 'I like a tidy workshop,' she says. 'And the girls are busy enough finishing off all the orders for the Queen's day. Thank the Lord, they'll be done by tonight. They do help with the cleaning, when they can. Winnifred is always bringing me thoughtful little gifts. Teacups of mutton broth and milk rolls. She is such a sweetheart. I'll miss her, when she leaves us to be married.' She glances lovingly at the eldest girl, whose fingers are a blur of movement above the silk petticoat she is hemming.

'Is she to be married then?' Mary asks, tidying away her examination implements.

Abigail's smile wavers. 'Not yet. A gentleman has been courting her, but the terms have not been agreed upon. Thomas has been putting money aside these past years. I'm afraid, though, that it will not be enough. The cost of living seems only to spiral. These new taxes are greatly vexing. I hope Winnifred's gentleman will be patient. It would break my heart to see her lose her chance at happiness.'

The woman dabs at her face with her handkin. Cupping her belly, she says, 'I only hope this next little wonder is a boy. Thomas is certain he will be. Thomas gave up meat before we conceived. A physician advised him so. The man has eight sons, all living, so he must know something about it. Not that my girls are a burden,' she adds, her eyes flashing as if daring Mary to contradict her. 'Not a whit. They're the finest little seamstresses this side of the water. What I'd do if any harm were to come to them, I cannot imagine. Since the attack on Missus White, I've kept them indoors. Kept them busy. Imagine if they were spoiled.'

She shudders and Mary, seized with sympathy, squeezes her arm. In addition to the fear of attack, five girls equates to five bridal portions. How can any family hope to have enough to send their girls off to make their own way in the world? She can well imagine the relief a boy might bring to this family. Women are not encouraged to follow in their family trades. If they hope to better their situation through marriage, they should be like some of the daughters who attend Missus Priest's School, girls whose only role in life is mere ornamentation.

And then there are those men – fathers – who consider boys to be the only sex worth raising. Thomas Sparrow doesn't strike Mary as one of them, but you can never tell what a person's marriage is really like from the outside. If Johnny had not been born a boy, she wonders, would Lemuel have lambasted her or accused her of conspiring against him to give him only girls? Yes, he took a shine to Bess when she started walking and talking and following him about, but before that he had precious little to do with her. He barely ever held her but of course, Bess does not remember that. His interest could be attributed more to Bess's persistence – always hanging around him, waiting for him to notice her – than his own energy. He showed more enthusiasm for Johnny, taking him up to Nottingham after his birth to show the boy off to his family. Poor Bess, forced to stay behind with a family friend. At Johnny's breeching ceremony, her husband's elation inspired him to buy ten rounds of drinks at the Black Bull tavern. Mary had to go down the day afterwards and hand over most of her pay to cover it.

To deny this world is made for sons not daughters would be foolish, so Mary can't begrudge Abigail's hopes. Life is hard enough for boys. For girls, it can be a wretched punishment. Even queens are not exempt, if the rumours Mary had heard flying about in the marketplace this morning are anything to go by. Everywhere she went, gossips whispered about the Queen's inability to carry a child to term, attributing the losses she has weathered over the years to her habit of prodigious overeating and neglectful duty to the court. They did not add that the Queen spent most of her life under the thumb of her brother-in-law, King William. The Glorious Revolution where 'not a drop of English blood was spilled' was glorious in name only. In reality, the King raised English taxes to pay off all the dukes and lords who played peacemaker when he arrived and allowed him to walk in, without protest. How the Queen must have shaken with anger when she discovered that her brother-in-law had arranged an injunction to ensure that when her sister Mary died, he could claim the throne for himself. Eight years, the Queen waited, for the monarch's death to augur her own ascension – eight years of begging access to her own money like a pauper to pay for her servants.

If that's how things are at the top, what chance do Abigail's daughters stand? What chance does Bess?

Mary fidgets awkwardly. 'Missus Sparrow, I must ask you for a favour. I need a dress. Two, in fact. For Bess. It seems that fashions have changed and she's in need of some clothes to suit her. She's growing so fast I can scarce keep up. I have her measurements with me. But I must ask you for second-hand gowns. We cannot afford new. Something wholesome, but not homespun.'

Abigail's sad expression transforms into one of sheer delight. 'Dresses for your daughter. How wonderful!' Clapping her hands, she gathers up her skirts and struggles to her feet, the girls rushing to help her. Mary feels almost forgotten as they start to plan. Pushed to the edge of the room, she clutches her kitbag, listening to their bright chatter.

'I'll go down and find that taffeta Pa was keeping for Martinmas!' Agnes cries, thumping down the stairs.

'And the tabby with the lace collar!' calls Winnifred.

Watching Abigail's face, animated by the sheer pleasure of dresses, Mary wishes she took more of an interest in clothing. Then perhaps she wouldn't have failed to notice her daughter's changing shape. Love is blind, as they say. There is nothing she would not do to protect her daughter, nothing she would not give her if it was within her capacity to supply. But no matter how hard she wishes, there are some things she must admit she cannot change. A good dress, or two, will have to serve as a peace offering. Whatever other mistakes she has made today, Mary's heart feels lighter for granting her daughter's wishes. By the time she leaves the Sparrows', she's too preoccupied imagining the look of gratitude on Bess's face to worry about Mister Grillett's dire words.

*

The biting odour of vinegar and wood ash stings her nose as soon as she walks through the Needle's door. She finds Bess kneeling in the kitchen, rag in hand, dabbing gingerly at a blackened pot. A dish of ashes and the jar of salt Alice uses for scouring stubborn stains off the copper cooking pots sit nearby. Her daughter's hands are slicked with brown vinegar. Alice, elbow-deep in a sudsy bucket, is clearly holding down her frustration with both hands; the kitchen is her domain and she dislikes anyone disrupting her system of cleaning and cooking. It would be fine, of course, if Bess were a different sort of girl. The kind of girl who follows instructions without needing to know why she must do something in a particular order. Never satisfied by a simple *Because I say so*, she can be infuriating to the point of madness. Mary's heart gives a guilty twist and she recalls the one time she took Bess to a birthing. The girl asked so many questions and sighed with such evident boredom that Mary, flustered, sent her down to the water pump just so she could get on with her business. No wonder Alice looks so cross. Bess is not an ideal pupil. She scowls up at her mother and Mary feels her smile slip. Nevertheless, she aims for brightness.

'Good news,' she says. 'I've spoken with Missus Sparrow and chosen your new dresses. Missus Sparrow is altering them. When they arrive, Alice will have to show you how to put them on. Or shall I help you?'

'I want Alice,' Bess says at once and Mary, stung by this swift rejection, looks away.

'How was the market?' Alice says, her strong arms quivering as she heaves a pan into the suds.

Mary offers a half-hearted explanation and goes into the hall to put the cheap tallows away in their box. She would like to confide to Alice her worries about the taxes, about Mister

Grillett's dire predictions and the mysterious displacement of her wedding band but Bess's presence makes this impossible, so she keeps all this troubling knowledge to herself.

A letter from Richard waits on the hall table. Mary rips it open, her heart swelling with hope. *So, I am not altogether alone.* The letter is filled with Richard's usual effusive sentiments, with questions about the children and Lem's health. Mary frowns. Strange, to see her husband's name printed there after so many years' absence. Even her relationship with Richard feels tainted now. The clean sweet scent of dried Angelica from the cutting he has folded into the envelope cannot banish her fear. What if Lemuel drags them all down with him into debts she cannot repay?

Behind her, Alice clangs a pan. Mary pockets the letter quickly and goes upstairs. She finds her husband half-dressed, rummaging through the linen press. At the sound of her step, he turns.

'What are you doing?' she says, genuinely surprised.

Annoyance absorbs his features. 'Nothing,' he says, jerking back his hand. 'I fancied I would take a walk and look in on an old friend. I was searching for my waistcoat.'

'In the press?'

'Well, where else would it be?' he snaps. 'Everything here is topsy turvy, you've gone and changed it all. This house is like a puzzle box. Do you find it amusing, to hide my things from me? Because I can assure you, madam, it is not.'

'Nobody has hidden anything. Are you feeling well enough to go visiting?' Slightly panicked, she eyes his grizzled chin and creased shirt. There has been no more talk of little people, but how can she be sure he will rein himself in once the drink flows? 'Perhaps you ought to wait,' she says. 'I can send for Tom Clements to help you with your toilette.'

'No need.' He swats his hand in the direction of the master bedroom. 'You are here now; you can help.'

He stands back, blocking the hall with his broad bulk, leaving her no choice but to enter the bedroom first. As she shuffles past, he falls into step behind and huffs out an impatient sigh. Deliberately, she slows. His breath mists the back of her neck. The audacity of the man – the brazen cheek! – to assume she has nothing better to do than attend to him. As if it isn't enough that his presence makes the house feel cramped, he must lay claim to the very air she breathes, stealing her energy like smoke drawn through a flue. She would like to duck under his arm and flee to the comfort of the kitchen, a place he doesn't visit much unless driven there by thirst or hunger. But if she helps him now, he may heed her suggestion to stay in. Sacrifices must be made to safeguard his future – and, by proxy, her own.

Inside the bedroom, she creaks open the casement, letting sweet air pour in to replace stale and to vanquish the lingering scent of illness and medicants. At her bidding, he sits on the bed, watching her search through the drawer for a dull-edged razor. The tortoiseshell handle gleams under a fine layer of dust, smooth save for the inscription of her husband's initials. Most of the items from his toilette were sold off, but she saved this, supposing that Johnny might want it one day when he is grown. Thinking of the animal who gave its life for the gift, it's entirely possible her son might refuse. She knows Johnny inside and out and he is a sensitive child, attuned to the plight of animals and the needs of others. Raised mostly by women, he has a gentle, soft-spoken manner. He cried so little as a baby that she sometimes woke, gripped by the certainty he had died in his sleep. Even now, with miles of green fields and roads stretching between them, they are connected by something she has not the words nor the power to express properly. She might say it's the same as that dizzy feeling she gets when she looks up too quickly at the night sky on her way home from a birth and the stars all bleed together, or when a newborn she has just helped birth opens its eyes for the very first time. A little glimpse of something greater than her own fleeting earth-bound existence.

'I wish Henry were here.' Lemuel plucks at the coverlet, frowning. The manservant's absence is like a wound he cannot stop worrying at. For Mary, Henry had one important use: he kept her husband at a distance. When Lem was home, he and Henry were off at once to avail themselves of all the pleasures London had to offer. At least with Henry around, she didn't need to see to Lem's daily needs, helping him dress, running his bath, dealing with his travel arrangements whenever he decided to visit his family up north. She can't recall what year it was that Lem hired him without consulting her. She'd simply arrived home one day to find Henry stamping about in her garden, carrying linen from the house out to the toolshed, where he planned to sleep. When Lem went to sea, Henry pottered in the garden, watering plants and tilling soil. The little contribution he made towards the household chores hardly justified keeping him on. She would have put him off long ago if she'd not been afraid of Lem's wrathful response when he discovered his manservant's dismissal.

Watching her husband run a shaking hand over his bristled chin, she wonders if he's lonely, whether Henry was employed to fill the void Richard left. Pity creeps into her heart, insidious as a weed. Despite the separateness of their lives, they share children and a difficult past. Together with Richard, he has known her for most of her adult life. And he is still powerful, she reminds herself. Painful though the truth might be, he is still within his rights to put her out on the streets, if he wishes, or have her locked in Bridewell with the female lunatics. Her children smuggled off and hidden somewhere she will never find them. No protection exists which can prevent Lemuel exerting his rights, if he's of a mind to do so. How can love flourish under such conditions? Or trust? It makes no sense to her. A husband's power is absolute and unshakable. Even in death, they have the advantage. If a man kills his spouse, he's granted a quick death at the end of a rope.

A woman who does the same is burned alive.

'If Henry were here,' she says, unable to resist a little provocation, 'he would warn you not to exert yourself by stepping out before you are fully recovered.'

She fills a basin with water from the pitcher, lathers his skin with a sliver of soap and scrapes the edge of the blade down his cheek. Each tentative sweep of her hand succeeds in scything away a smattering of grey hairs. How did Henry do this? The concentration required hurts her head. It's the opposite of gardening, where it's still possible to gain knowledge by stumbling your way through and learning as you go. One mistake here is a bloody catastrophe. She draws in a breath as the razor snags against an old scar near his ear, a spot of blood welling up like a sharp little ruby.

'Sorry,' she mumbles, dabbing at the droplet with her thumb.

'Alice tells me you're still working as a midwife,' he says. She circumnavigates the curve of his lip, scraping gently as he continues. 'You did not write to my Uncle John to ask for a widow's allowance, I take it.'

'I did,' she says, a trifle bitterly. 'He refused.'

Lem's jaw tightens. 'He always hated me. It is his fault I lost my livelihood. If he had paid for me to extend my studies at medical school, I could have trained as a royal physician. I would have been physician to the King.'

The blade rasps over the cleft in his chin. The silence stretches as he waits for her to agree with him. The truth sits between them, unspoken. It was Lem's carelessness, combined with the rising taxes to support the King's war, that lost them the surgery. Mismanagement and overspending on her husband's part, but of course, she cannot say this aloud. He'll only deny the imputation.

'Yes,' she says, at last. 'You're right. Uncle John's to blame.'

He relaxes visibly. How pleasant it must be, she thinks, as she scrapes the blade along his jawbone, to have your every thought and opinion confirmed. To be unacquainted with doubt.

Perhaps she's assumed too much, for he frowns. 'You believe me, don't you, Mary? About the island.'

Her thoughts churn. Confirming the existence of his island and his little people is not the same as agreeing with his reasons surrounding the loss of the surgery. If she says yes, does that mean he will expect her to stand by him in public when he recovers, and support his impossible claims?

A cold dribble of soapy lather slips down her wrist, making her shiver. Time. She needs time to investigate. Those sailors who brought him are surely long gone by now but there must be others, people who know him or sailed with him. This Peter Williams, for example – she would dearly like to know where he lives. Gulliver mentions the name so often she supposes he nurtures a strong bond.

'If you believe it,' she says, slowly, 'then I cannot dissuade you.'

She knows at once it is not the answer he seeks. His tanned face stiffens under her hand, his bottom lip pushing out like a petulant child's.

'What are you suggesting?' He grips her wrist and the razor splashes from her hand into the basin, a seeping wound of cloudy soap and wispy blood.

'Lem,' she says, quietly, 'you're hurting me.'

Glassy-eyed, he sets her free and she rubs at her wrist. 'I don't suggest anything,' she says, 'except for you to stay here until your malady has passed and you feel more like yourself.'

For a moment, she thinks he will comply. His hand creeps under the counterpane as if he might fling it back and take refuge in the safety of the bedclothes but her heart pitches as he pulls out a crumpled fustian waistcoat from under the folds. Glaring at her, he shrugs it on.

'Where are you going?' she says.

'Out to see a friend. I told you.'

'But –'

He grunts in exasperation, a sound she remembers from the many times she returned home at midnight to find Bess still awake, fetching drinks for Lemuel and Henry when their glasses ran dry. 'Leave off, woman,' he says. 'Look to your own troubles.'

The irony of this statement is both amusing and painful. Watching him tuck his shirt into his breeches and jam on the dusty hat hanging near the dresser, she imagines crossing the room and swinging the door closed, bolting it from the outside and sealing him in. But it will not do. She has no authority to lock him in his room against his will nor can she bind him to her by anything outside English law. Decency and duty are invisible bars he can melt through at any moment he chooses.

As he shuffles into the hall and lopes down the stairs, she hisses a warning: 'Be careful!'

He disappears, leaving no clue whether he has heard.

10

On the morning of the Queen's coronation, Bess wakes to the sweet song of a hundred joyful bells, their chorus a jumble of patriotic phrases: *God save the Queen* and *I am for England*. After so long under the reign of the Dutch Stadholder, England seems to be disrobing, throwing off a mantle of heavy, fusty old brocade in favour of light sprigged muslin, apricot silk and fine London lace.

Lying in bed, still drowsing, Bess imagines the crowd gathered down at the docks, the swell of people, coloured banners snapping in the breeze. She imagines she is the new queen. No, not the Queen – who would want to be haunted by all those baby ghosts and saddled with an ugly husband? Or wait until she is past her prime to inherit the throne from her brother-in-law? No, she is William Dampier, returned to England after rounding the Cape of Good Hope. She is Sir Francis Drake, triumphant after his defeat of the Spanish. She is Pa, a surgeon and the captain of the *Swift*. Now men and women scream her name and shout her praises all the way from the Tyne to the Thames. They shout, 'Elisabeth!' just as they once did a hundred years ago, when the old queen showed her fearless white face at the prow.

Something warm and heavy traverses the length of her body, needling the coverlet with claws. Yellow eyes flash, and a pressure settles on her chest, solid and immovable. As the cat pins Bess like an insect to a specimen board, the monotony of the previous days comes flooding back in all its tedious misery.

Bess groans, shoving at the cat until she jumps off the bed and stalks out, indignant. So, she is trapped here. No running off, no exploring, no adventures to be had except those within the garden. Her hands throb; she lifts them out from under the covers and sees a speckled rash spreading from her fingertips to the heels of her palms. Alice's potash. She is scarred, her hands will never recover. She rubs them together, observing with interest the rasping sound they make.

Bess throws the covers aside. Another day with Alice. Another day of scrubbing, cleaning, needlework. It's not the work itself she minds so much, only that she seems to make no useful contribution. Everything she touches is a disaster, and Alice is quickly losing patience.

In the room next door, she hears Pa muttering to himself. She dresses quickly, dragging on her petticoat and her old smock. Outside her parents' bedroom door, she puts her ear to the wood and listens. All she can make out is Pa's sleepy ramblings, words strung together without thought or meaning. Her chest is wound tight with despair. She heard him stumble in last night, clattering up the stairs and then the muffled thud of the bedroom door. If only Mam were not so stubborn. It occurs to Bess now that perhaps the stories her mother told her about Pa being ill when he returned from sea might be true. When she complained about not being let in to see him she'd supposed that Mam was just being overprotective. Assumed that her mother just enjoyed having some power over him, too. When Pa recovered, he always took charge, demanding to see the household ledger, eating whatever he was hungry for, taking Bess out when he felt like a walk down to the docks, not caring if she left her chores unfinished.

A blue-eyed wink was all it had ever taken to secure Bess's loyalty. A wink and a warning. *Don't tell your mother.* She never did. She obeyed Pa's every order and every instruction. He was their captain, wasn't he? Head of the household. Her mother was just a worrier who liked to flaunt her authority whenever he was away. Bess had enjoyed watching Mam grow flustered as Pa ordered her about. She loved to watch her pa scoop handfuls of coins and traders' tokens out of the teapot in the parlour while Mam was at work. The china teapot had belonged to Mam's mother, Bess's grandmother. It was one of the only things Mam owned which had belonged to her and Mam kept it filled with farthings and pennies *for emergencies only*. Not that the notion ever stopped her father. Munching on a pilfered shortcake, Bess had watched with glee as her father breathed new life into their stale existences and upended her mother's carefully ordered world.

But now . . .

From somewhere far off comes the sound of bells ringing out over the river. Bess counts them. *One . . . two . . . three . . .* She feels clammy, as if her father's fever has reached out and touched her through the door. Maybe she's the one who is mad. Maybe everything she thinks is real only exists because she wills it to. If that were so, though – if she could grant her own wishes – wouldn't she be able to make her mother change? Wouldn't she feel some assurance that what she most desires – to sail off on her own and have adventures like her father – is bound to happen? Instead, there's a dull buzzing in her head like thrumming bee song and her mouth tastes faintly metallic. The truth swims in and out of sight, a faint mirage. The shapes are there – the lines drawn, like the contours on a map – but she can't quite see the whole. She hears her mother's quick footsteps on the other side of the door and flings herself down the hallway, taking the stairs two at a time.

Alice exclaims and curses under her breath when Bess displays her ruined hands, spreading her raw fingers like a glover's mannequin.

'Did you not coat your hands first in duck fat, as I told you?'

'Of course.' Bess lowers her eyes, the lie dripping effortlessly from her lips. 'Do you think you might have put the wrong solution in the tub?'

Alice chews her lip. 'I suppose so, yes. It's possible.'

'My hands hurt. And they're so itchy.'

After rummaging in the stillroom, Alice brings out a balm that smells only faintly better than the potash. 'You'd better rest your hands today,' she says. 'Light duties only.' She squints up at the blue sky beyond the kitchen door. 'You can care for your mam's plants, make sure you keep the water to them. It's sure to be warm again, and Lord knows I don't have time. The cesspit overflowed again. It needs draining.'

Bess, only half-listening, massages the greasy balm into her knuckles and watches Alice scoop up ashes and fling them through the kitchen door. 'Couldn't we go down and watch the celebrations, Alice? Just for a short while? It's not every day a princess becomes a queen; even an old one. There'll be river games and prizes and races. Iced cakes. Fireworks! It will be better than the fair.'

Alice, hauling herself to her knees, clatters the dustpan back into its spidery corner. 'I'm afraid not, Bess. There's too much to do, with your pa home. And your mam don't have the coin to waste. Some of us have work to do,' she finishes tartly.

'I could go by myself.' Bess picks at a crumb of skin clinging to her reddened thumb.

Alice frowns. 'Nay. Your mam says you are not to roam about by yourself and you're not to bother your pa unless I have a spare moment, which I do not.'

'But –'

'Need I remind you what happened to Lucy? Maybe your mam thinks you're too young to know what really happened but mark me, Bess, a man who does that to a gentlewoman will have no qualms about taking advantage of a young girl. Your mother is too soft by halves. Let me tell you – a woman loses more than just her virtue when she is raped. What would you do with a great lump of a baby you didn't ask for? Haven't you heard enough of your mam's stories to be afraid of childbirth? If not, you should be. If the childbearing doesn't kill you, you'll die slow of sheer exhaustion. You're lucky to have a mother who cares enough to worry about your well-being. An afternoon of fun today is tomorrow's regret. Now, out you go to water the garden and then you can come and sort the pantry. The mice have chewed through the grains again. You must have forgot to put the lid back on the jar when you poured them in last week.'

Planting her hands on her wide hips, Alice fixes Bess with a stare. The maid reminds her of a pitcher they once owned, solid and unbending, a flare of blue skirt skimming her curves to taper around shiny boots. Alice's obsession with cleanliness extends beyond the house to her person. Bess has never known anyone to wash so often. At market, the maid spends half her weekly earnings at the soapmaker's stall, buying hard slabs of grainy castile which she uses to scrub her hands and neck, working up a vigorous lather. As a result, her skin is always dry and peeling, flaking off in patches around her nose and mouth. When Bess once asked why she didn't just sponge like everyone else, Alice's bitter laughter surprised her. *Six years*, she'd said, slapping her rag across the table. *Six years, and I still can't get the stink out.*

Bess glances away. What's the use of arguing? It will do her no good to remind Alice that there's been no sign of the attacker, nor any proof that he's still in Wapping. When the maid gets into one of her rare dark moods, there's no shifting her out of it. Slipping the balm into her skirt pocket, Bess goes to collect one of the buckets filled with rainwater clustered at the side of the house. Heaving the bucket up, she trudges over to the pink blossoms her mother is always fussing over. Mam's words ring in her head: *Any sudden change in climate, any unexpected downpour can damage the roots.*

Bess isn't sure what these flowers are called but their thin pastel petals remind her of Belle's silken skirts. She wonders what kind of dresses Mam has bought her. Homespun, no doubt. High-collared with long sleeves to cover every inch of skin and dyed black, like the Puritans wear.

A breeze tugs at Bess's smock and ripples the pink flowers on their stems. They're so fine and delicately translucent she can see the dark fretwork of veins standing out in each petal. When rubbed between finger and thumb, the plant gives off a sweet apple fragrance. Bess sniffs, unwilling to admit how pleasant it is. No wonder her mam prefers the garden to London's stinking streets. No wonder she comes out here as soon as she returns home, to weed and bask in the perfumed loveliness. If Bess wasn't so hot and angry at her – and Alice – for denying her a glorious day of celebration, she might be tempted to sit out here, too, enjoying the peaceful sight of the plants stirring in the wind.

'Orders are orders,' she tells the plants, dumping a heavy shower over the blossoms. The stalks shiver and bend under the weight. One of the blossoms detaches itself and flutters down like a swooning girl as Bess shakes the last of the droplets out onto the soil.

The bells are still chiming across the river when she wanders back out into the garden three hours later to repeat the process. Their joyful pealing does nothing to improve her sour mood. Bess lets the warm water trickle through her fingers, relishing the burn on her damaged skin. The herbs give off their usual powerful scent, thickening her throat, watering her eyes. Medicinal, they always remind her of past illnesses and of Mam, sitting at the foot of her bed, watching her struggle through a fever. Smallpox, it must have been, for she remembers the bright swathes of red fabric tacked about the room to draw out infection. Hallucinations broken by moments of clarity where pain clustered so sharp behind her eyes she heard herself screaming for Pa to help. It was Mam who sat by her though, who stirred a paste to spread over her chest and pressed a poultice to her raging throat. She never left Bess's side, or if she did, Bess didn't see her go. Pa came once – Bess remembers him lurking in the doorway in his nightdress, a shivering candle held aloft – but he must have been called away on urgent business because it was her mother whose loving presence remained unwavering. Sometimes she lay down and Bess would feel her chafed hand stroking the back of her prickly skin, over and over, as she murmured soft words of comfort. Sometimes, Bess dreamed that she was stranded on an island – Sumatra, perhaps. She saw a beach the colour of cinnamon and a grove of quivering date palms. She smelled ripe, sticky fruit and heard the gentle crash of waves beating the shoreline.

Tell me about Sumatra, she would ask her mother through swollen glands. But Mam never could. Mam had never left England, so how would she know? Instead, Mam told her about babies. How they grow inside their mother's belly, expanding from the size of a kidney bean until they are big as a melon. How when they are first born, their tiny faces are all crumpled, like balled handkins in need of a shake. Bess learned about the seeds her grandmother gave her mother, how Mam's herbs were descendants of the little garden behind the hosiery shop in Newgate Street. The botany Mam taught herself, back in the heady days of early marriage, was drawn from the interest in plants and herbs her own mother had fed her. As a belated wedding gift, Uncle Richard had given Mam a book, a thick slab of a thing. *Theatrium Botanicum, The Theatre of Plants*. Before she had to sell it to make ends meet, Mam had committed all the pages to memory, so she could describe them to Bess in vivid words: the gnarled tree trunks, the herbs in their ordered rows, the winged cherubs, blessing the garden with bursts of rain and sun.

When Pa returned from sea, her mother's stories faded from Bess's mind along with the illness. How could her lessons compete with his, or with the shells he brought back, the words he'd gleaned from other places and cultures? Babies and botany were hardly as exciting as pirates and cannibals and adventures on the high seas. Birthing might fulfil her mother's ambitions but Bess always felt she was destined for more; she was determined not to settle for a mediocre life as a midwife, at the beck and call of other women. Unbidden, Casper floats into her thoughts, full of smirking disbelief. If what Bess suspects – but doesn't wish to confirm – is true, if there is no way to get her on board a ship and the vision she shared with Pa is merely a fever dream like those she experienced during the smallpox epidemic, then why has Mam never spoken to her about the impossibility of sailing away? Why has she let Bess carry on believing? Anger flushes through her. I am going backwards, she thinks, her palms tingling in alarm. I am shrinking; soon I will be ten then six then four and then I will disappear altogether, winking out like a falling star.

'Elisabeth Gulliver.' The voice comes out of nowhere, making her jump.

'Who be that?' She squints into the shadowy hedgerows beside the house.

Casper de Vries is slouching against the wall, wearing the same clothes he was dressed in the day they met, slightly more rumpled. When she waves him forward, he slinks across and dangles his long arms over the gate, staring at her with his cool, assessing eyes.

'What are you doing here?' She looks up at the house, but the windows reflect only the sky. 'How did you find out where I live?'

'The sea's becalmed, no trade winds, so we're stuck here. I thought I might see you at the docks, celebrating the Queen's day but you weren't there, so I came to pay you a visit. It's not easy to find people to talk to; not everyone is so friendly. Most English people are wary of us Hollanders.'

Bess digests this slowly. When Pa and Henry drank late, she often heard them sniggering about 'the Boglanders', claiming they were the descendants of frogs, that they liked to eat their young and tup their grandmothers. The seas are a battleground where Dutch and English traders strive for dominance, and the enmity between the two nations is exacerbated by the spread of vicious rumours. Bess sneaks a glance at Casper, wondering if he senses this nationalistic betrayal. But the boy seems resigned.

'We're staying at Bell's Tavern,' he says. 'It wasn't hard to find your house. Everybody knows Captain Gulliver. You know they have a saying about him, down at the inn? "As true a thing as if Captain Gulliver said it."' He grins. 'Did he really see a monster? Not everyone is convinced that he did.'

Bess flattens her lips in disapproval but doesn't stick her fingers in her ears because such childish acts are beneath her. Doubts about the veracity of her father's stories have always swirled around the parish and Bess has always chosen to ignore them. 'I'm not supposed to talk to strangers.' She snaps off a twig of hawthorn. The stem is bright green with tightly furled buds, and its scent – sweet, musky – together with Casper's presence makes her feel slightly giddy, as if she might drift up, up, and float clean away. Spring fever, her mother calls it; baby-making month, when hedgesparrows and wrens preen their feathers and vie for each other's affections and zigzag in wild arcs across the garden, oblivious to everything but their own amorous pursuit.

'Why do you think I didn't knock at the front door? Was that your mother I saw leaving earlier? She looks stern.'

'Yes, that's her. She's worried about Pa, that's why she looks so grim.'

'Why is your house called the Needle?' Casper says. 'Is your mother a seamstress?'

She laughs. 'Not at all. She's a midwife. Mam hates sewing, although she's good at it. It's good practice, she says, for stitching up women's privities after birth.'

She regrets the sentence as soon as it's out, repeating the words to herself in the uncomfortable silence that follows. Birth? Privities? Her cheeks are on fire. Did she really just say that? Tossing the strip of hawthorn away, she picks small flakes of bark off her greasy palms to cover her embarrassment. The itching has eased a little thanks to the balm, the welts fading from angry red to mottled puce.

'Does your mother work?' she says.

A pause. 'I don't know,' he says. 'I haven't set eyes on her for years. She ran off when I was ten and left me in a workhouse in The Hague.'

Bess's mouth falls open. She can't imagine going a day without seeing her mother, let alone years. There's something unnatural about the idea that makes her stomach twitch as if she's swallowed a wriggling worm. Isn't it a mother's duty to stay with her young, no matter what? Can there really be women out there who abandon their children? Men leave. They go to sea or find work elsewhere, travelling wherever their work takes them. Sometimes they don't come back. She's always assumed that foundlings lose their mothers through death or accident. Surely, it's a sin, as a woman, to disregard your children's welfare? Wouldn't such an act of motherly rejection leave some mark? She stares hard at Casper but apart from a flinty look in his eyes, he seems unchanged.

'I ran away,' he says, breaking his own stick from the hawthorn, 'as soon as I was old enough.'

'To sea?'

'Where else?' He rubs the shoot between his palms, crushing the buds. 'A Dutchman's heart belongs to the sea.'

'And your father?'

This time his face is blank, betraying nothing. 'Never knew him. My mother would never say. I follow my master now.'

Bess clucks her tongue and frames her face into what she hopes is an expression of sympathy. She wants to squeeze his hand but such a bold gesture would not be seemly. Instead, she says, 'Is he kind to you?'

He laughs. 'What do you mean, kind?'

She thinks of Pa, always encouraging her to go to sea, never treating her as if she deserved to be anything less than a sea captain, like him. Golden grapes and the promise of further riches. A blue-eyed wink. 'Does he treat you well?'

'When the winds are good.' His teeth flash. 'Yes, he is a good man. He comes from Texel, an island in the north. He taught me to read and write a little. He can be demanding but he finds work for both of us on the ships and he takes care of me.' His tone hardens. 'Better than my mother ever did or those who ran the workhouse.'

Bess says nothing. There's a workhouse in Clerkenwell. She visited years ago, when Mam went to help a poor vagrant woman through her labour throes. Bess remembers watching stick-thin children scoop pease-porridge into their mouths with stale crusts; the shuffle and scrape of wool as they spun the flax. They were too tired to talk to her, she remembers that. When she asked them to play, they just stared at her, hollow-eyed. It was only later she understood that the concept of playing was foreign to them. When Mam emerged from the sick chamber, she looked downcast and her eyes were red-rimmed with exhaustion. Bess overheard her telling the churchwarden that the woman needed milk and meat to fortify her so the baby would live. The churchwarden said he would do what he could but insisted the woman was lucky to have given birth in a safe, warm place. Most parishes shuttle labouring women back and forth, hounding them past the parish boundaries, forcing them to birth their babies in the street. Those women and their children are like ghosts, belonging nowhere. Many children end up back in the workhouse when their mothers abandon them.

Looking at Casper, she wonders whether he chose a life at sea to escape this cycle of rejection. When she suggests this, he looks surprised and then thoughtful.

'I've never thought about it. I suppose so . . . perhaps.' He inspects her with renewed interest, as a bird might eye a fallen plum. 'How old are you really, Elisabeth Gulliver? You aren't seventeen.'

'You're right,' she says and when he grins in a self-satisfied way, she says, 'I'm twenty-one. And it's Bess, not Elisabeth. Bess, like the good old Queen. I bet old Bess wanted to be an explorer, too, when she was a girl. I bet she wanted to go to sea, same as me, but she had to learn how to behave gracefully and queenly. So she sent Francis Drake and Walter Raleigh off to do it for her. I bet she read everything she could, waiting for her chance to go. That's where we're different – I'm not going to wait. As soon as Pa is recovered and he says the word, we will go together.'

'He's ill, then?'

Bess frowns, searching Casper's face for traces of mockery. Finding none, she confides, 'A temporary ailment. His mind is confused. He finds it difficult to tell sometimes what is real and what is the past. I'm sure he will soon be well and then he can buy another ship; his old one was lost, you know. Then we'll sail off and leave this place – England, that is – behind.'

She stops, aware that her words have run away with her again. Doubt flares inside her like an ember and she folds her arms, braced for his retort. Casper doesn't challenge her claims, though. He grins as if nothing she's said is at all impossible and after a long moment, she finds herself grinning back stupidly, relaxing her shoulder into the hedgerow, lost in a heady waft of fragrance.

'I should be going,' she says at last, pulling herself erect. 'They'll come looking. Chores, you know. I scrubbed the floor so hard yesterday, my hands bled. Look.'

She holds them out to show him, quietly thrilled when he looks impressed and forces a low whistle through pursed lips. His breath is a warm zephyr tickling her fingers and it makes her think of trade winds, oscillating north to south, driven by mysterious forces, the push and pull of magnetic tides which will one day carry them both away.

When Casper flicks straw-coloured hair out of his eyes, Bess's heart tumbles in rapid somersaults. She wishes this moment could last forever. This must be how Columbus felt when he made landfall after so many months at sea, dreaming of the fabled shore. The same febrile awakening, the same exquisite torment; wanting to stay on the beach, to bask in triumphant pleasure but, in the same instant, desiring to know what lay over the snaking hills, hidden in the shaded darkness beyond the trees.

Bess's skin is still warm when she walks back into the kitchen. Tingling hands thrust deep into her pockets, she fingers the lumpy tulip bulb Casper has given her to replace the one she couldn't eat, along with a promise to call again if the winds remain unchanged. Tonight, she will pray for stillness.

Alice glances up from the scarred table where she's preparing dinner. Her round face is pale and sweaty and she scowls as Bess saunters past.

'Decided to join us, have you?'

Bess halts beside the dresser, startled. Until a moment ago, she was thinking about the girls at Missus Priest's School, the ones similarly cursed with curly hair, wondering how their maids managed to brush it smooth and pin it up until it sat stiffly like a giant bow waiting to be unwrapped. What secrets did they know? She wishes she had paid more attention but their gossip always bored her. Now Alice is glaring at her as if she has eaten a month's worth of food in one sitting.

'Us?' She looks down in confusion at the trussed pike on its dish, gobbling its own tail. Oh no, she thinks, is it fish day?

'Yes, Bess. *Us*. Me and your pa. I've been waiting for you to come back in so you could help me with supper while I check on him. Believe it or not, you aren't the only person in this household.'

A basin of herbs and macerated dates sits near Alice's elbow. Grasping a handful of stuffing, she rams it into the pike's belly, the slit leering open like a pale pink mouth. Taken aback by the fishy odour and Alice's aggression, a hint of nausea swells inside Bess's stomach like a cold wave. Ever since she was small, she's been unable to stand the taste or texture of fish. The very smell of it wafting through the house makes her gag. Something about its slippery saltiness stoppers her throat and no matter how it's cooked, she can't choke it down. Now on Sundays, while the rest of the family dine on mackerel or haddock, Alice helps Bess stir together a simple broth to eat with thin slices of cheese and bread. But this afternoon the hob is bare; no victuals save for that ghastly lacquered fish staring at her through cold, milky eyes.

'I can't eat that,' she blurts. 'I'll be sick.'

Alice throws up her hands, spraying breadcrumbs across the table. 'Then by all means, starve.'

'Alice!'

Twitching a black plait over her shoulder, Alice stabs her fishy finger in Bess's direction. 'I saw you.'

Bess steps away, almost tripping over the cat, who has been lurking, hoping for scraps. The cat yelps then runs away.

'I saw you with that boy,' Alice says, her voice rising. 'Standing by the gate, lounging about, no decency at all. Is that how your mam raised you? Who is he?'

'He's . . . a friend.'

Alice glares at her, shaking her head. 'A *friend*? A friend who does not even use the front door or introduce himself?' She shoves another handful of stuffing into the fish, and Bess winces at the rough treatment. 'And after your mam warned you about strangers and everything I said earlier about Lucy White. The danger! And this is how you repay us?'

'Don't tell Mam.' Her throat is raw and scratchy. She leans across the table and grips Alice's forearms. 'Please, Alice. Don't say a word. It was nothing – I – he's just a friend, I swear. He came to tell me about the Queen's coronation. I promise: no more talking at the gate. I'll tell him to come to the door and you can meet him yourself. Mam, too, and Pa. He's harmless, not even from around here. He's lonely. His mother left him in an orphanage when he was just a boy and he has no family to speak of . . .'

The words unspool thoughtlessly, but it appears her brute honesty has succeeded, because Alice, tight-lipped, gently shakes her off and says, 'Very well. I won't say a word. But you should tell your mother. You can trust her. She understands more than you think.'

'I can't.' Bess brings her hands to her face. Mam will never understand. She wouldn't even speak to Casper if he came to the door. A Dutch sailor with no family to speak of or recommend him? Bess knows exactly what her mother would say. *The wrong sort of friend for you, Elisabeth.* No one will ever be good enough for her darling Bess. Bess will be alone forever. There's no point saying this to Alice so Bess concocts a more acceptable story.

'She'll be so angry. I can't, don't you see? All the fuss with Pa being home . . . I don't want to worry her. Here.' She picks up the apron hanging on the back of a chair and ties it on. 'Let me dress the fish while you check on Pa. It's very likely Casper will go back to sea soon. I won't see him again.'

Alice's frown deepens at the boy's name but she slings the breadcrumbs back into the bowl and dries her hands. 'A sailor. Of all the boys. Fine, then. I won't tell her. But it's on your conscience, Bess, not mine. I know your mother would rest easier knowing what you're about.'

Stripping off her apron, she fills a mug with ale, puts it on a tray and carries it out into the hallway. Bess, screwing up her courage, crams more stuffing into the spliced fish, wondering how close she has come to disaster, to punishment that might restrict her movements further. Might Mam forbid her to leave the house at all, not even to venture into the garden?

'Too bad for you,' she tells the pike, settling a crown of parsley over his oily head. 'You think your troubles are over? They're just beginning. Wait till Puss sees you all dressed up in your finery. He'll suck the flesh from your bones.'

II

'Mister Grape is here.'

The light from Alice's taper reveals the grooves of her exhaustion and Mary spears her darning needle through the hose. The Queen's coronation is over. Outside, the revelries can still be heard echoing up and down the Thames but inside the Needle, the women are darning by the feeble light of a single candle, getting on with the work as best they can.

'What can the constable be wanting,' Mary says, 'at this late hour?'

Alice smothers a yawn. 'He didn't say. Should I show him into the parlour?'

'No. I'll see to it. Can you pull the linens out of the soak? I'll be there to help when Mister Grape leaves.'

Nodding sleepily, Alice thrusts her the candle and stumps off to the kitchen, her white cap shrinking in the dark. Mary watches wistfully, wishing she, too, could retreat. She aches from her crown to her toes; she crossed the parish six times today, in addition to one emergency visit to aid a woman who drank a dangerous decoction of herbs, hoping to bring on her labours. Whispers about Lem followed her wherever she went but only a few clients mentioned seeing him outright. The rest watched cautiously, smiling over-bright if she caught them mid-stare. The would-be rapist has slipped into the background; Lemuel is the one people want to know about. She could have sworn it was her husband's name she heard on every street corner, the stories of his exploits vanishing when she slid past. Whatever mischief he has been concocting, he's left little evidence for her to find, a trail of breadcrumbs grown soggy in an unexpected downpour.

Anticipating his secret need for funds, she's transferred a goodly portion of the teapot savings to a discreet porcelain pitcher in the china dresser. What little remained has already disappeared, along with a few items of value – a bone-handled spoon, an embroidered bedsheet. Where is he getting the money to pay for his wine and entertainments now? she wonders. Has the sale of those goods funded his nightly exploits? Or – a darker thought – her wedding ring? She has no doubt he's been drinking. He often comes home soused, rambling as he did the first night. He barely picks at his supper tray. Wherever he's eating, it's not at home with them.

When she returned this evening, she found him agitated, pacing the bedchamber with the windows thrown wide, mumbling to himself about winds and tides. Calling down to Alice, she'd managed to wrestle him back into bed before Bess noticed and when at last he seemed placated, she descended to a cold supper of mutton pottage and an even frostier atmosphere. The mutinous glares Bess cast her mother were so acute, it was a wonder the girl didn't cut herself. Alice, meanwhile, tapped her spoon on the table with such force the cat mistook it for a summons and jumped onto the table, upsetting the milk jug so a sour river of milk and mutton broth poured into Mary's lap. It seemed a fitting end to the day she'd had. At least that's an end of it, she'd thought, helping Alice mop the puddle as Bess banged her bowl into the water bucket and stalked upstairs. Nothing else could possibly go wrong. She hadn't reckoned, of course, on Jeremiah Grape.

The scent of his person is detectable from the hallway, a curious miasma of bitter turpentine, lampblack and the cotton he uses to clean the tokens of his printing press after each use. Through the hairline crack of the door, she sees Jeremiah drop to his haunches, a meaty hand on the notched doorframe. He seems to be examining it, running his hand up and down the warped edges, frowning as he fingers the chips broken off by former tenants carting their furniture in and out. He is a thickset man, a pugilist crossed with a bloodhound, shirtsleeves pinned up over thick, white forearms matted with coarse orange hairs. A printer, a stationer, a constable; he is all these things, but first and foremost, he is a Grape, like his father, which means Mary knows she must watch herself. Old Mister Grape was a notorious spy and he has raised his son in his mould.

'Mice,' she says, drawing back the door, catching Jeremiah off guard so that he sways and almost tumbles. 'The vermin around here chew everything, Mister Grape. They have voracious appetites. You'd think this house was made of gingerbread, the way they gnaw its beams.'

He recovers quickly, straightening up and rearranging his features so his dislike is mostly concealed. Still, Mary feels herself bristling. This is her house, after all.

'Missus Gulliver. God give you good day. Or good night, as it stands.' His gaze drifts over her shoulder. 'I hear your circumstances have altered, madam. Your husband has returned.'

'Indeed,' she says, speaking forcefully to smother the tremor in her voice.

Jeremiah frowns. Since the untimely death of his sister in childbed, he has treated all midwives, herself included, like potential criminals. Two years ago, he tried to have Midwife Bickerstaffe of Leicester charged with murder. Although the woman was exonerated by her good record and the indisputable fact that nobody, not even a surgeon, could have saved Jeremiah's sister from such a mighty haemorrhage, the loss has poisoned him. More than once, Mary has heard him in the market square airing his loud opinions on the immorality of the female 'cunt-doctors' to whomever will listen. Each time, she pretended she had not heard. Men like Jeremiah are beyond reasoning with and best avoided unless they force a confrontation.

'And your own household changes,' she says, affecting a veneer of pleasantness. 'I hear you have recently wed. My congratulations to you both.'

'Your absence was noted when the wedding banns were read.'

She spreads her hands in supplication. 'I'm truly sorry. Missus Bell had started her confinement and her labour was long and difficult. Babies are a blessed inconvenience; they don't care for schedules and they certainly don't care for weddings. But you had better come inside. I'm sure you don't wish to stand here speaking in the dark.'

He follows her into the parlour, his boots echoing down the hallway. Refusing her offer of a seat, he chooses to stand near the window, facing her, arms folded against his chest.

'Is there any trouble?' she says.

He leans forward, unsmiling. 'Have you done something wrong?'

If I had, I would not confide in you.

He holds his mouth in a little moue, waiting for a confession that does not come. At last, he says, 'You heard about Lucy White. There's been another attack. Margaret Somerset was assaulted this evening while her husband was at the tavern. I've just come from their house.'

Mary's heart thuds painfully as her hand flies to her throat. She pictures Margaret's youthful, good-natured face, the little silver fishbone scar on her cheek, evidence of a childhood accident when she toppled off her father's wagon. Margaret's cousin gave birth only last year. Was that when Mary last saw her? In the birthing chamber? Shutting her eyes, she sways in her chair, hearing Margaret's joyful cries, seeing her gallop in an undignified way around the room. *I'm an auntie*, she'd crowed, too delighted to take any notice of the older gossips shaking their disapproving heads. And now? Mary opens her eyes to find Jeremiah watching her.

'Is she alive?'

He nods, slowly. 'Yes. Beaten but . . . alive.' He frowns, as if the outcome is an undesirable one, and Mary understands, with a jolt of disgust, that a dead woman cannot make a fuss but one who survives presents the authorities with myriad problems. She grips her handkin, winding it between her fingers. Anger bubbles in her chest as she imagines poor Margaret's shock, the shame and guilt and confusion, the same reaction she has observed countless times during her years of service. Nobody warned her before she took up the midwife's trade that she would be called upon to assist the courts in their persecution of sexual criminals. Her mother kept the ugly truth hidden, although she would doubtless have confided it when Mary was older. On Mary's first day in London's Court Sessions, she had to testify against a man accused of 'ravishing' his eleven-year-old stepdaughter. Her voice cracked as she described the girl's wounds, the stains which led the child's mother to her suspicions. After delivering her evidence, Mary's legs shook so hard, she needed to be helped from the witness stand. The things she has seen and heard, the women she has held, stroking their heads in her lap, before gently, gently lifting their skirts to record the damage. Venereal distemper, oozing pox, torn lips; it is enough, she often says to Alice, to make you swear off men altogether. What rankles most is the futility of it all, the lack of successful convictions in the face of overwhelming evidence. Most rapists are acquitted of their crimes because girls Bess's age and older are considered capable of giving consent. What's a young woman's word against a man's?

Mary is so choked with such seething, bubbling rage on Margaret's behalf, she can barely bring herself to ask the constable for further details.

'He wore a mask over his face and cut off a lock of her hair before he ran. Some macabre souvenir. I've asked Missus Clifton to examine Margaret. She's there now and we will use anything she can tell us as evidence when the criminal is caught.'

'Good. Anne will comfort her.'

Jeremiah shrugs. Comfort is women's business; his concern is judicial.

'Did you come to warn us?' she says.

He opens his mouth, then hesitates before his jaws shut like a steel trap. 'No,' he says, eventually.

'Do you think it was a stranger? Or someone local?'

He looks up at the smoke-blackened ceiling. 'I should like to question your husband, to know where he was when Missus White and Missus Somerset were assaulted.'

Mary straightens, her whole body tingling. The idea of Lem hurting Lucy is laughable. *Suspect.* The word thrums in her head. She hardly trusts herself to speak but she must answer. She must reply, or the horrible man will take her shocked silence as proof.

'You surely cannot think Lem was involved in those crimes? He's practically incapacitated.'

Jeremiah pauses to sneer down at her. 'Is he? Mayhap you're protecting him. Why did he return? Where has he been? Nobody seems able to say for certain and his presence in the tavern would suggest he is not as ill as you suggest. It wouldn't be the first time a man's gone native and come back, would it, Missus Gulliver? Nor will it be the last.' He fingers a stain on his cuff. 'I imagine some men find such life a paradise. I myself have never left England, but one of my wife's cousins travelled to Calcutta with the company. He went missing. Nobody heard from him again until the news of his death reached England. Married a local girl and sired five sons, all called James. Who can say what kind of depravities those men enjoy? Perhaps your husband desired to slake his animal lust on unsuspecting English victims.'

Although his words concern her husband, Jeremiah's disgust seems directed at Mary herself. She can't let him bully her, though. She won't. Whatever he may believe, Jeremiah is not the first to try and intimidate her. Six years as a midwife has enlightened her to the methods used by men to achieve their aims. Defensive husbands, hostile landlords, even wretched stallholders like Elias Grillett. They are all the same, when it comes to coercion. *Never show them how afraid you are,* she hears Anne Clifton whisper.

Mary strides over to Jeremiah until they are only a handspan apart. Inside, she trembles but outwardly her body is as hard and unyielding as fossilised stone. She has to tip her chin to stare up at him but her stance is so implacable, he retreats.

'Your insinuation is offensive,' she says. 'Missus Clifton has examined Mister Gulliver. She can tell you all you need to know. Mister Richard Sympson, lawyer, of Fleet Street, will vouch for his character.'

Jeremiah's expression grows sullen. 'He's not fit to be interviewed, then?'

She licks her dry lips, hoping the man can be swayed. 'He's not fit for anything much, until he's completely healed. Although he's left the house once or twice to visit friends, he returns exhausted and can barely use the chamber pot unassisted. If you've nothing further to ask, I would like you to leave.'

He grips the back of a chair, stubbornly persistent.

'Please remove your hands from my furniture before they cause a stain,' she says. At last, he goes, not without casting a long look up the darkened stairwell.

At the front door, he pauses. 'You should know that both Missus Somerset and Missus White are quite certain the criminal stank of the opium den.'

Mary's mouth is dry. Something tugs at the edges of her understanding. The crux of an enigma, waiting these past weeks for her to seize it and bring it forth. She forces her face into a mask of blandness. 'Then I suggest you direct your attentions there, Mister Grape.'

A bright figure streaks past the closing door, startling them both.

'Your cat?' he says, watching with narrowed eyes as the animal lopes down the hallway. 'I thought you said you had an infestation of mice.'

'She's old.' Mary glances into the street where a group of carousing gentlemen are taking advantage of the last few hours of revelry in the Queen's name. Dear God, will the man never leave? 'A hopeless mouser.'

Jeremiah draws himself up. 'You should be rid of her. A cat who cannot mouse is not worth a shilling.'

'I will remember that.'

She shuts the door and stands with her back to it, a hand knotted against her stomach. Then she returns to the parlour where she sinks into a chair. Alice creeps out from her hiding place in the kitchen, her face blanched. She clutches Mary's hand. Mary squeezes back.

'I heard it all,' she says. 'Margaret Somerset. Awful. Will you tell Bess?'

Mary considers. 'I don't want to frighten her.'

Alice frowns. 'In my opinion, madam, you ought to tell her. Bess can be headstrong. She needs a firm hand to guide her, not further protection. The master's state of mind being what it is, would it not be best to prepare her for the worst?'

Mary rubs at her temples. 'None of us know what's coming,' she says. 'I'll speak to Bess when I judge the time is right. Not tonight; in a few days perhaps, after church. We must make sure the bolts are tightly locked. We cannot afford to be lax on security.'

'I suppose it's a blessing the master is home, now,' Alice says, carrying the candle into the hallway. 'For protection.'

Mary follows the fluttering flame, glancing up at the ceiling boards as if they might suddenly peel away to reveal her husband in his bed. The man she has been treating these past days is flesh and bone but his inner thoughts remain closed to her and the ones he does disclose are a confusion of nonsense. Could he have hurt Margaret? He did not have the opportunity to do so, surely, unless he slipped out this afternoon before she came in, when they were all otherwise occupied. For all his faults, he has never threatened her, nor their children, with violence. But has he threatened other women? She has no knowledge of that. He was always civil to his female clients, albeit dismissive of the suspicions they confided about the source of their pain. His desire for her dried up years ago, after John was born, and yet she cannot imagine him taking out his – what did Jeremiah call it? – his *animal lust* on defenceless women. His fear of the pox was always acute, so it's unlikely he would take his chances on a woman, even a gentlewoman, if he could not confirm her health. A man can change, though. A man can fall. A tremor runs through her.

The upper bolt clunks as Alice rises onto her toes to slide it home. Gathering herself, Mary squats to attend to the lower bolt only to find she cannot manage it. The wretched bolt refuses to catch, no matter how hard she tugs. Her hands are hot and slippery after Jeremiah's confrontation and her slim fingers, so deft at identifying an infant's spine or buttocks during a client's examination, shake uncontrollably. Tears blur the edges of her vision. A small choking sob escapes.

'Here, missus.' Gentle hands prise her clumsy fingers away. 'You go on to bed, now. Take the candle.'

A satisfying click and then a heavy silence neither of them has the courage to break.

12

There's no need for Mary to fret over telling Bess the troubling news. At St Paul's church on Monday morning, they have barely stepped inside before Bess is waylaid by her friend Rebecca Morton. Ensconced in a pew at the back, they are soon busy exchanging horrified glances, leaving Mary and Alice to find their way through the heaving congregation to an empty pew.

'Why is it so crowded?' Mary says, dismayed by the throng. Monday is often quiet, which is why she chooses to visit on this day each week.

'Safety in numbers,' Alice declares. 'Nobody wants to be left alone after what happened to Margaret. Or perhaps it's overindulgence, after the Queen's day. Look, there's Mister Rose. Is he still soused, d'you think? Or just sleepy?'

They watch the man in his rumpled coat weave between the wooden pews, stumbling over a woman's skirt before dropping into a free seat, sighing audibly in relief. In every corner, housewives gather in knotted groups, their troubled voices echoing off the dark wood panels and the vaulted ceiling with its watchful cupids and whipped clouds. The children are unnaturally quiet. Normally they fidget or tease their siblings, pulling hair and pinching skin until a sharp rebuke from their mother recalls them. Today they stay close, the youngest pushing scrubbed-clean faces into their mothers' skirts, sensing the adults' sombre mood. Mary sees Abigail Sparrow and her five daughters huddled in a circle, their arms linked protectively. A few pews over, Anne Clifton chatters quietly to Elinor and Susanna. Catching Mary's eye, Anne raises her gloved hand and jabs a finger at the oak doors, as if to say: *We will speak afterwards.*

The keenest sinners have arrayed themselves at the front of the church where God's light shines especially bright and, so hunched, they wait for the rector's judgement to fall. Mary wonders if the rapist is amongst them. Is he kneeling, praying for forgiveness? Is he a son, a father, a brother? An acquaintance? The idea is abhorrent and yet, she knows what men are capable of. She has seen their handiwork too many times to count. The way some men behave in private is not the persona they present to the world. Lemuel, for example, would have it known he is a gentle Christian but today he is worshipping at the altar of slothfulness. Too many spirits, or some worse substance, have numbed his speech. He only grunted when she looked in on him earlier to ask if he was joining them. Perhaps it's best he stayed at home.

'There's Mister Grape and his new wife.' Alice points, and Mary sees the constable picking his way to the front, dressed in his customary black to hide the ink stains. He holds himself stiffly, looking through the parishioners he considers beneath his notice and greeting the worthy with a small nod. His wife follows close, afraid of being left behind in the crush. Being an outsider from beyond the parish borders, she would, on a normal day, be the subject of intense scrutiny and interest. But like Mary's husband, she has been forgotten in the more immediate drama of the rapist.

'I heard her father is an actor in Covent Garden,' Alice whispers. 'They say the girl has renounced her whole family for their sinfulness. Jeremiah is all she has now. Imagine abandoning your family for the likes of him.'

Mary shares a look of mutual disgust with her before a spreading hush alerts them to the rector's presence. The rector is a thin man with a long, lugubrious face and wisps of hair clinging to his spotted scalp. He fingers his spotless collar before gazing mournfully out at the gathered hopefuls, as if they are children who have already disappointed him. The crowd falls silent as he clears his throat.

'Why do Christians suffer?' he intones, stroking the wooden edges of the pulpit. 'Why does God allow bad things to hurt us? Heretics will tell you to turn your face away from God. They will tell you a modest and holy man is as much at risk of disaster as a wicked one. Think you on the words of Job's wife, a woman sent to test his faith. She said to him: "Curse God, and die." She said to him: "Do you hold onto your integrity, do you think you are exempt from secret wickedness?" Remember, she was a woman who had lost her children, one by one, through disease or accident. She was angry, but instead of turning to God to ease her sufferings, instead of drinking the waters of life, she grew sour. Job's answer? "You are talking like a foolish woman. Shall we accept good from God, and not trouble?" He was protecting her, as you must protect your own families. God has graced us with a new queen, a woman. She would want you to look to your wives and teach them. Help them pray. They need you to guide them.'

The congregation murmurs in assent and Jeremiah Grape's wife sits up straighter in her pew, her head tipped back in adoration.

'There is wickedness in our midst,' the rector bleats. 'It is your duty as husbands to protect your families but especially your women. What can you do to protect them? You must encourage your wives to hide their beauty, lest they tempt sin. Encourage them to be pious and holy, lest they catch sin's eye. Instruct your daughters to be modest in their dress, their speech, their very attitudes. Tempt them not towards vanity. Mothers, this falls to you also. The lascivious makes beauty his object. In thought, in act, in deed.'

He looks around his rapt congregation, his eyes resting briefly on the faces of women in the front pews. 'Modesty, always. Only in chastity and domesticity will beauty find safe harbour. Lead her there, parents. It is God's will.'

Released from the church's confines, parishioners spill down the steps into the market square, stretching stiff limbs. Conversations ebb and flow more easily now that warning, punishment and its absolution have been bestowed. Mary looks around to see Bess at the back of the congregation, still engaged in deep conversation. Alice goes to retrieve her while Mary waits on the step, shivering slightly in the breeze. Looking down Wapping's high street, she wonders whether it was wise after all to leave Lemuel alone. His fevers come and go like the tide. One moment, he is calm, the next raving. Remembering Jeremiah's words, she left the poppy out of Lem's sleeping draught so he was more alert. She hopes she has done right. The College of Physicians calls opium a powerful panacea. Addictive.

'Missus Gulliver?' Abigail Sparrow's dress ripples in the breeze, blowing around the swell of her belly. She clutches her daughter's arm for support, breathless. 'Your dresses are ready for collection. Do you think you could come this afternoon and fetch them?'

'This afternoon?' Mary says, dismayed. Yesterday she promised Bess she would help her select some flowers from the garden to press between the pages of her books, ready for embroidering on pieces of card. Mary conjures her daughter's disappointment, the darkened scowl. 'Alice will come,' she says.

Abigail chews her lip, glancing around at the people streaming past. In the sombre light outside the church, her complexion is pallid. 'Could you come, Mary? I would have your counsel. Little signs, again. Some bleeding. Possibly, it is nothing. All the same, I'd appreciate your professional opinion.'

Alice appears over Abigail's shoulder, shuffling Bess along. Catching Mary's warning glance, Alice leads Bess down the steps to wait in the little garden next to the rectory.

'I will come,' she says, touching the woman's hand to reassure her. Work is work. Bess will understand.

Abigail's forehead clears. 'Thank you, Mary. You'll be pleased with the gowns. They're fitting for a young woman. Pretty but nothing too ostentatious, as per your instructions. I know what young women are like. All the fine lace and all the ruffles.'

Mary smiles, grateful for this shared intimacy. 'Shall I come now?' she says. 'I'll need to fetch my kit.'

'Could we say four? I have Missus Harwood and Missus Lisle coming for fittings. I would delay them but we can't afford to lose their custom.' She moves off, assisted by her daughters and husband.

The rector's garden is simple compared to Mary's own, a few straggling daisies edging the lawn. By far its best feature is an ancient oak which spills its gnarled roots over the path. Anne Clifton, leaning against it, bangs her cane down into the soil so dirt flies up around the stopper.

'My leg has turned to water,' she explains when Mary joins her. 'This morning, I could barely move from my bed. I've been dragging it around all day.'

'You should have stayed in bed,' says Elinor, pressing her lips together. 'Why did you insist on coming? Sitting for so long would not have improved it.'

'I thought the extra prayer might help,' Anne says. 'And I did not want to be left by myself, at the mercy of a lunatic rapist.'

'How's Margaret?' Mary says, eyeing Bess, who is at the far end of the garden, peering into a wooden dovecote.

Anne shakes her head but doesn't reply. The women are silent, perhaps thinking of the latest victim's generous smile, her youth and vivacity, ripped away in a single selfish act. 'I sent Susanna to find a sedan chair. Where can she have got to?'

'In this crowd, you'll be lucky to find one,' says Alice, joining them. 'I don't remember the last time I saw St Paul's so full.'

Anne grimaces, shifting her weight onto her strong leg. 'Mary, I've been meaning to speak with you. Your maid tells me Elisabeth has been running off on her own. Is that true?'

Mary turns to Alice, surprised, and the maid shrugs, looking both guilty and defiant.

'It was just that once,' she says. 'The day of the Rhenish.' How long ago that day seems now.

'I understand your way of thinking,' Anne says, drawing herself up. 'Remember, I helped raise Elinor up when my sister passed. But a girl is not a bird. She should not be kept prisoner in a cage. It will only make her more determined to leave. Better she's kept busy and safe under a watchful eye, than bothering your housemaid or putting herself in danger. From what you've told me, and what I've seen with my own eyes, Elisabeth is a bright, intelligent young woman destined for far greater things than service or husbandry. It's as I told you last year when I made my offer: a girl needs a purpose.'

Bess has been picking daisies from the rector's garden, building a posy of straggling flowers. Now she drifts back, having heard her name.

'What offer?' she says, squeezing the ragged daisies in her fist. She looks awkward in that dress. Strained across her swollen chest, the smock looks like something a foundling from the poorhouse has dragged on, having none other available. How did Mary miss the signs? *You saw what you wanted to see*, she chides. *A little girl, the one you hoped to keep safe.*

Anne clenches her hand around the cane, her knuckles whitening. When the leg cramp has passed, she reopens her eyes and fixes them on Bess, lifting her chin imperiously. 'You shall be my new apprentice.'

In the shocked silence, Mary's first instinct is to refuse. When Anne made her offer last year, she did it in the privacy of her own house and suggested Mary consider the matter overnight before advising her yes or no. Mary did consider it. But thinking of Bess's first unsuccessful exposure to the birthing chamber, she decided her daughter was too inexperienced to make the most of such an opportunity. Now, the offer has been made public, in front of Alice and Elinor and Susanna, who has stumbled into the garden, breathing heavily with flushed cheeks. Now it's less an offer, more a command.

The women turn to gauge Mary's reaction. Mary looks at the sky, at the trees, at the wilted daisies in Bess's damaged hands, which although healing, are still red and peeling. She looks anywhere except at her daughter's face. Once, she let her husband take charge of Bess's future and look what happened. The fantasy he fed her has taken years to unravel. This time, she won't stand by and let her daughter founder. Lemuel can rant and rave all he likes. Bess will no longer be around to hear.

On the street, four men heft a sedan chair between them. 'You can't take her on, missus,' Susanna says. 'You have me.'

'Who's to say I can't have two apprentices?' Anne counters. 'The Bishop dare not argue. Elinor, you're in agreement. Mary?'

Her voice brooks no refusal and Mary doesn't offer one.

'Bess will be paid a pound a month in recompense; the same as you, Susanna, and she can start tomorrow. It will keep her out of trouble and she'll be safe with me. Next year, she can apply for a deputy position, and with a bit more training, can take her midwife's oath. I've a list of clients as long as my shift; I can't treat them all without extra assistance.' Catching sight of the sedan chair, she raises a thin arm and the men jog over, jostling the seat between them. 'Goodbye, Mary,' she says. 'Bring her first thing tomorrow. Come, Elinor, Susanna.'

The men grunt as they swing the chair up. Like chattel horses, they match each other's rhythm, the old dowager balanced between them. Mary watches Elinor and Susanna follow in their wake, but not before the latter has thrown Bess such a fierce look of hatred, her daughter's face pales under its smattering of freckles.

'Bess?' Alice says, cautious. 'Are you well?'

Bess ignores her. Slowly, she turns to her mother. Mary sees her bottom lip quiver and the ghostly imprint of younger Bess – eight, perhaps nine – peeping out of the older girl's visage.

'How could you just stand there?' she says, her voice dull. 'How could you stand there, saying nothing, letting that old woman decide my fate?'

A warm breeze shivers over them, fluttering the daisies in Bess's scrunched fist and creaking the branches of the old oak tree. Bess hugs herself.

'Bess,' Mary says. 'Be reasonable. This is a – a fine offer. A very generous offer on Missus Clifton's behalf. She's a wonderful midwife, and a strong teacher. I agree, she should have consulted us privately, but –'

'There was no offer!' Bess shrills.

The remaining parishioners look over, attracted by the unexpected sound. In the stillness that follows, Mary tries to place her arm around Bess's shoulder but her daughter is as stiff as a wax effigy.

'Let me go,' Bess says, and although her voice is soft, her eyes are cold and hard, shiny pebbles drenched in last night's rain.

'We can talk about this at home,' Mary says, straightening. 'When you're less upset.'

'Why bother? It's already been decided. I know how much my opinion is worth: a pound a month. I suppose it never occurred to you that I have my own plans and none of them involve babies. I wish Pa would take me to sea now. I wish he would wake up and tell me we could leave tomorrow so I might never see you again.'

Alice gasps. Mary's own breath is trapped inside her chest.

'Take you to sea?' she croaks. She can sense Alice moving to shield them from the passing onlookers. For the first time in her life, Mary finds she does not care at all about the opinion of others. Dear God, she would not even notice if they gathered to point at her and whisper that she's just as foolish as her foolish husband. Bess's face shines with misplaced conviction, with the hope Mary must now extinguish for a second time.

'We spoke of this,' she says slowly. 'Last week. I told you your father's stories were a fantasy and you nodded and said you knew. I promised you those new dresses. I offered you my apology. I thought we had an – an understanding. You must know your father could never take you to sea with him. It's impossible. Whatever he told you, it was said in humourless jest, as an amusement. I don't believe he ever considered you might take his word for truth, but you must trust me when I say that any further pursuit of that fantasy can only end in disappointment.'

Bess's eyes widen in disbelief. Mary tastes her daughter's awareness, the wash of acrid disappointment swelling her throat. She sees the girl Bess was, tiny and vulnerable, sitting at her father's feet. How she looked up to Lem as if he shone brighter than the very sun.

Before she can offer comfort, Bess unhooks her arms and walks quickly in the direction of the Needle, head down as if striding into a heavy wind. Mary's body vibrates painfully. She feels more alone than she ever has in her life and if it were not for Alice and the danger of Bess walking unguarded and unaccompanied, she might stay in the rector's garden forever, letting the roots and vines consume her as they please.

Bess continues her silence until they reach home, where she flatly declares she will not join them for supper – she isn't hungry and very likely will never be hungry again. The stairs thunder under her feet and the muffled slam of the door shatters the last of Mary's frail resolve. Crumpling into an armchair, she drops her aching head into her hands. Where did it all go wrong? All the subtle hints in the world, the gentlest encouragement, would not have made any difference to Bess, she realises now. Somehow, incredibly, the girl still believes her father's old promises. They have stuck to her like gum, tainting all the possibilities of happiness she could have found in the pursuit of other adventures. My own fault, she thinks. I should have been more forceful and exposed the fantasies as the fraudulent falsehoods they are. Time did not do the work I'd hoped it would. Instead of shrinking, Bess's fantasies have expanded, feeding on her own childish insecurities of being left behind, her natural unwillingness to bend.

Miserably, Mary worries at her thumbnail before remembering her appointment with Abigail Sparrow. Not good to bring sharp nails into the birthing chamber in case she damages her client's privities. She should talk to Bess, but lately it feels as though all the words she says are wrong, as if they're speaking two different languages. Perhaps some time away from the house is precisely what Bess needs. From way back, Mary recalls a childhood argument where a friend's mother offered to take her to Lincoln's Field to see a play but Mary's own mam insisted she accompany her to a difficult birth. How unfair it all seemed, the weight of responsibility like a millstone around her neck. *Why?* she'd demanded. *Why must I?* A fierce flame of self-righteous anger burning up her spine. Unchecked, that flame could grow and spread, consuming everything she was: a good girl, a considerate neighbour, an obedient daughter. It could burn her from the inside out and lead her down the path to ruin. That flame of resistance contained a power all of its own. It was her mother's words which broke the spell. *Because this woman needs you.* Just like that, the heat went out. Instead of going to the playhouse, Mary spent the night at Mam's side, fetching herbs, heating water and staunching blood. At dawn, just as milky stars were beginning to fade, the baby was born, feet first. Mam wrapped it in a swaddling sheet while she helped the mother and Mary, bleary with tiredness, peered down into the infant's sweet little face. At that moment she *knew*, for certain, her purpose. What she wants for Bess is the peace which comes from knowing you have made a difference to someone's life. It's time to give her daughter the chance to try.

Rousing herself, she goes to the kitchen where the sun is making its slow creep across the boards. Stretching a hand towards the milk jug, she freezes.

A mouse has lost its head. Its small skull lies abandoned in the middle of the kitchen, teeth bared, its neck a ragged stump leading nowhere. Puss watches over the prize from her perch on the cooled hob, looking mildly astonished as if cognisant of how rare it is for her to make a catch these days. Mary shoos her out and bends to scoop up the mess, folding the bloodstained fragment inside an old rag. It weighs less than a coin. Somewhere in the walls, tiny feet are scuffling. Years ago, the mice were not such a problem but now they are like difficult tenants, impossible to evict. Even as one family is caught and released, another arrives to take its place. Before Puss grew old she enjoyed making sport of entire nests, devouring whole generations in one go and scattering them through the house as gifts for Mary to find.

In the garden, Mary unravels the rag onto the scrapheap where the contents joins old peelings and apple cores and cabbage leaves so mouldy they cannot even be turned into soup. To stop Puss finding it, she tugs a slimy, black-tinged leaf over the mouse's velvet head like a shroud, her nose filling with the ripe, wet scent of decay.

In the upper windows, she sees a white shape pressed against the glass, ghostly, and raises her hand without thinking. Lemuel simply stares down at her until she goes inside, unable to abide the smell of the scrapheap any longer. As she passes the hall table, a grubby square of a letter catches her eye. Unfolding it, she inhales the scent of ink and rain and the spray of sea campion tucked inside.

The letter from Richard is full of enquiries – about Lemuel, Bess, and Mary herself. Mary hears his voice in every neatly written word. Richard is the only person she has ever met who worries more than she does. He's always fretting over his clients' wills and bequests, dashing off to ascertain the truth of something so the evidence can be used in court. A lawyer's mind must be an attic crammed full of other people's memories, all the forgotten detritus of their messy lives.

Reluctantly, a smile tweaks her lips. Faithful Richard, reliable as a ticking clock. But has she ever truly deserved him? According to Bess, she is a cold, unfeeling viper. Would Richard have stayed friends with her if this were true? Would he have asked her to wed, and kept returning to visit even after she refused? Love is blind. She shakes herself, hard. A foolish notion. Whatever exists between them now cannot be called love. Call it friendship, companionship, the camaraderie of soldiers who have been through a dozen bloody wars together and somehow survived. Never love. Love is for children and milkmaids, for painters and their muses, for birds so caught up in the warm flush of spring fever they lose sight of everything but their own desire. Unlike Lemuel, Richard has always prized duty above all else. He is similar to her in that way, he knows duty is the only armour which repels gossip and therefore, ruin.

At the bottom, he has written:

As my journey took me through Nottingham, I looked in on Johnny for you. The lad is well, he misses you and Bess and sends on his love to you both. He's unsure of what to make of his father's return. We ate in the inn near the trading post, I explained his father's condition. Nothing alarming, only that he must prepare himself for a shock if Lem's condition worsens. When I left, he seemed less afraid. I hope I have done the right thing and have not disrupted your plans for his homecoming. I shall be back in London within the week and come to visit you when I return. I remain yours, etc.

Mary lowers the letter. So Richard has done what she cannot. He has taken her son in hand and spoken to him, warned him that his father may be different, may be changed. The ugly scene with Bess rises like a bruise. Bess is right. She neglected her duty to her own daughter out of – what? Fear? Or pride? If Bess knows the truth about Lemuel, won't it follow that she will turn to Mary and ask her what role she played in the years leading up to this moment? All her mistakes exposed for Bess to see.

She spends the next hour with Alice in the stillroom, pulling dusty jars and half-empty bottles out of cupboards, ready for the soak. Above their heads, the ceiling creaks, her husband's heavy footsteps sifting dust down between the floorboards onto their heads. The stairs groan and a moment later, they hear noises in the kitchen next door – the chime of the teapot lid, the scrape of fingernails on porcelain. Alice looks askance – should they move, give some sign they know he's there? Mary shakes her head. She holds her breath, waiting for him to call out, demanding to know where she has squirrelled her wages. Animals in their burrow, she thinks, hugging her elbows.

Balanced on her haunches, Alice worries the edge of her apron. The stillroom has never felt this cramped before. A tall shadow encroaches across the floorboards under the stillroom curtain before she hears a cursing, a creak, the sound of him ascending the stairs. Slowly, Mary relaxes and follows Alice out into the kitchen where she finds the teapot slightly askew, the lid tipped on a jaunty angle. She sets it to rights, avoiding the maid's knowing eye.

Alice speaks anyway. 'Madam, perhaps I shouldn't tell you this, but he made me give him half a week's worth of victuals yesterday. A haunch of meat from the meat safe, a whole nutcake. Is he eating them himself? He's still as scrawny as an old tomcat.'

'I don't know.' She touches the handle of the teapot.

'We must do something,' Alice mutters. Privately, Mary agrees. But what?

A sudden hammering at the door makes them jump. Thomas Sparrow waits on the doorstep, a frayed measuring tape looped around his neck.

'Missus Gulliver?' he says, looking past Alice into the shadowy hall. 'I been asked to fetch you, quick. Abigail – Missus Sparrow, that is – she says that she's lost it.'

Mary stares at him. 'Lost what?' For some reason, she thinks of the ribbons in Pa's old shop. Cherry-red, enamel-blue, taffeta smooth, sliding through her childish fingers. All gone now.

Thomas Sparrow drops his gaze to his shoes. His lips move, as if he is rehearsing what he plans to say. He has always been soft spoken, or perhaps he has simply never learned to raise his voice loud enough to be heard over his gaggle of daughters and his confident wife.

Mary leans forward to catch his words.

'The baby,' he says.

13

Bess paces furiously in her room until she hears Mam ascend the stairs to consult with Alice in the corridor. She pauses long enough to learn, from their hushed words, that Alice is to watch over Bess until Mam returns from some emergency at the Sparrows'. She hears the words 'master' and 'ill', and the repeated instruction that he and Bess are not to be left alone under any circumstances. Bess's cheeks flame. She kicks a stack of books, the volumes skittering over the floorboards. Loose maps spill like autumn leaves. She tamps down the desire to crush her father's paper promises under her heels. All a lie, if her mother is to be believed. Bess conjures Mam's face, her lips framing the painful words: a humourless jest, an amusement. She stamps her feet and covers her ears, wishing to be rid of the words, but they continue to emit a dull poison she cannot extract.

Something about Mam's expression haunts her – something she missed, too focused on the sentiment of what Mam was saying. *Fear.* Mam is afraid. Of what? Of Bess herself?

She almost laughs. Can't her mother see how powerless she is, trapped inside six feet of floor and four bare walls? She needs to see Pa; she won't believe – can't – until she has stood in front of him and demanded the truth.

The bars of Philomela's cage cast spindly shadows against the wall. From her window she watches Alice emerge into the garden. Afternoon sunlight falls over the maid's shoulders as she plucks herbs to flavour their supper, a golden river washing everything in a clear saffron light. Bess feels strangely clear-headed, as if she has emerged from illness, as if her mother, by deciding her fate for her, has thrown everything into stark relief.

She slips swift-footed into the hallway, stealing across to Pa's room. She knows she has only moments before Alice returns. As she edges inside, her breath catches in her chest. Someone has drawn the shutters half-closed, permitting a narrow wedge of light to fall across the bed. Keeping to the walls, she tiptoes past Mam's dresser and the baskets brimming with darning linen, her gaze fixed on the bed. Humped beneath the blankets, the figure does not stir. His face is turned away, showing only a scrawny neck and the back of a skull shadowed in stubble. As she creeps closer, small blood blisters materialise, and she shivers with horror before reminding herself that this shape is Pa. Pa, with his big strong hands scooping under her armpits to toss her up on his shoulders and march through the docks, pausing to sniff at a barrel of shrivelled dates.

She touches his head, grazing her fingers over the bumps and lumps, the shallow dips and bloodstained notches. Some of the longer hanks of hair stick out. Maybe whoever shaved him was too scared to cut too close to the blisters in case they burst, so they edged around the scabs and left them bristling like fat caterpillars.

'Pa,' she whispers. 'Wake up.'

The jutting curve of his shoulder blade protrudes through the bedsheet. She watches it draw back, grinding against other bones in his back, his ribs. Rounding the bed, she straightens her cap and her skirts, determined to impress.

The giant in the bed sits up, yawning. Looming above her, he flexes his shoulders, stretches out arms and legs. The tousled bedclothes peel back to reveal a scabby foot, the blackened toenails chipped and peeling. Bess stares at it, then at the mottled chest peeking out through his nightshirt, grey hairs poking over the collar. He fixes her with cold blue eyes, as if she were a stranger. The distance stretches between them and Bess hesitates, uncertain how to proceed. Can this really be Pa? She snatches off her white cap, hoping it will help him recognise her.

'Pa,' she says, uncertain. 'It's me, Bess –'

With a bellow, he lunges at her, his bloodshot eyes wide and unseeing, his mouth an open pit reeking foul air.

Bess screams and ducks away, stumbling to the door as Pa's nonsense words ring in her ears. Time slows to a trickle. Each breath quills her heart, sharp and unrelenting. She feels a giant hand clap down on her shoulder but she breaks free, surges for the door. When she looks back from the sanctuary of the corridor, there is just a dormant mountain humped under the counterpane.

'Where are you off to?' Alice shouts a few minutes later as Bess hurtles past her through the kitchen. In the garden she keeps on running, stirring up pebbles until at last she reaches the tangled boundary of hedgerows bordering their neighbour's yard. Stooping, she tries to force the breath back into her lungs but it's as if she is a fish thrown onto land – no matter how much air she gulps, it's not enough.

Crushing despair anchors her to the ground, drowning out the drone of bees and the smell of Mam's herbs soaking up the last of the daylight.

She sees Alice emerge from the back of the house, shading her face with her hand, searching her out. Does Alice know how sick Pa is? Has her mother kept them all in the dark?

Alice cups her hands around her mouth and calls Bess's name. A scrim of greenery divides them, the herbs rising on their stalks to shield her. Bess sinks down to her haunches. Her guts cramp. This is beyond anything she could have imagined. Her mind returns to that last time she sat on her knees in his study, before he disappeared, a map spread in front of her while Pa sat nearby, drumming his fingers on his desk, nursing a headache and waiting for Henry to return from an errand. A Saturday, a washday, and she had taken refuge with him. She had to be quiet, which was difficult because she wanted to wriggle and ask questions. Which star was Ursa Major and which was Polaris and how could you tell the difference?

'Do you miss me when you're away?' she'd asked at last, unable to keep silent any longer but certain of his effusive flattery. Instead, his reply astonished her.

'I do not think of you at all.'

Hurt coursed through her. Flinging down the map, she ran to the door but had barely reached it before his sharp voice recalled her.

'Come here, missy.'

It was a command she dared not disobey, and when she slunk back, he pointed at the rug, indicating she should sit.

'When a person goes to sea, he leaves himself behind. It's impossible for him to be a husband or a father. He is so far removed from his old life that he cannot afford to remember. You'll understand one day, when I take you.'

'Will we see monsters?'

'Of course. But we will fight them off, you and I.'

She bit her thumbnail. 'Can Johnny come, too?'

Her father lifted a careless shoulder, his gaze still fixed on the open doorway. Laundry sounds drifted through it, the slosh of water, the soggy thump of sheets and Missus Perry's voice, imperious, ordering their new scullery maid about. 'If he likes,' Pa said, scratching the back of his neck. 'Where on earth has Henry got to, devil fetch him?'

Bess was too busy making plans to care about Henry. 'As soon as you return,' she said, 'we'll stock our ship and sail out. That's right, isn't it, Pa?'

Yet he had never come back, until now. And it is too late, his thoughts have scattered and she cannot rein them in, cannot guide him to shore. A sob works its way up her body.

A bee drifts past, and then another. Bess closes her eyes, waiting for the needle pressure of a sting to release her pent-up despair. Nothing comes. She plunges her hands into her pocket, as if she can reach inside herself and revive the parts still smouldering. Her pockets bulge with talismans: one of Philomela's feathers, a crenulated shell from Pa's collection and a dried pink rose on a card from Uncle Richard, a gift on her thirteenth birthday. And now, Casper's tulip bulb. She touches them one by one, letting her fingers rest at last on the bulb until her heart begins to slow and her breath returns to close to normal.

She walks unsteadily back to the house, through the disordered path of pebbles she kicked earlier. By the time she reaches the scrapheap, she feels calmer. An idea is forming, rising up like dough left to prove in the warm kitchen. If she can find Henry, he can help restore her father's health. Henry will cheer him, the way he always did. How to find him? That's the challenge. She can't ask Alice. The maid wouldn't have the faintest idea where Henry went. Bess doubts they even exchanged two words. So who else was he friendly with, this side of town? Only Mister Heath at the apothecary. Henry was always visiting to fill the supplies needed for Pa's medical chest. Mister Heath thought well of Pa since Pa spent a lot of his wages there, procuring the tonics and draughts required for treating sailors on long sea journeys.

'There you are,' Alice says. She looks relieved, her fingers glistening with yolk as she bastes the pie. Eyeing Bess's hair, she says, 'What happened? Did the birds carry off your cap?'

'No,' Bess says, unable to resist feeling slightly sorry for herself. 'I think I outgrew it.'

Ignoring Alice's puzzled look, she crosses to the honey crock, dips in her finger and sucks it slowly.

'I'm glad to see your appetite returning,' Alice remarks.

'Hmm,' Bess says and then, as if the thought has just occurred, 'Alice, has Mam been to Mister Heath to ask him for a tincture of Peruvian bark?'

Alice frowns. 'Peruvian bark?'

The honey on Bess's tongue is liquid sunshine. 'Mister Heath told me last month he was expecting a shipment. It's good for fevers. I only wondered if it might help Pa. Perhaps Mam has been to Mister Heath already.'

Alice smears a glob of egg white onto a clout. 'I doubt it, Bess. She's been far too occupied.'

'Perhaps I should go, then.'

'Would not be wise, Bess. Your ma wouldn't like it.' Alice studies her pie, angling her head and Bess smells the fragrant herbs she has rolled into the crust, designed to take away the bitter tang of cheap flour and old butter.

'Not even for just a few moments? I could be there and back before your pie is baked. It's only round the corner. I could ask Charles Clements to come with me. Nobody would do me any harm with Big Charlie around.' Leaning her elbows on the table, she picks up a curlicue of leftover pastry and pops it into her mouth. The butter sticks to the roof of Bess's mouth and forms a hard lump at the back of her throat. Somehow, she forces it down.

Alice's resolve wavers. 'Well, well – go ask Charlie and come back quick. No wandering near Barbary!'

Bess doesn't wait for her to change her mind. Clattering down the back steps, she shoves open the garden gate and runs through, trailing her hands along the hedgerows, careless of the way they catch at her skin, sharp as a small bird's talons.

Mister Clement shakes his head when Bess reaches the workshop.

'Lad's over water.' The ropemaker frowns as he dips a length of hemp into a pot of tar.

The acrid stench of tar and the dusty hemp fibres make Bess's lungs feel itchy. Pressing a hand to her throat, she says, 'When will he return?'

Tom Clements shifts a coiled rope aside with his boot. 'You can wait for him if you've a mind but he might not be back till late.' He points at an upturned barrel he uses as a seat but Bess thanks him and walks away. Opposite, she can see the Needle's attic and, below it, the bedroom where Pa is resting. He needs her, doesn't he? She can't just wait for things to improve. Mister Heath's apothecary is only a few streets away, although it backs onto the Ratcliffe Highway, a pitted stretch of the most unsavoury taverns and coffee houses this side of the water. Mam and Alice call the place Little Barbary, naming it for the dangerous coastline where pirates and merchants squabble over rich spoils of cargo. Duels are won or lost in the narrow maze of streets leading from the taverns down to the river and the pungent, meaty smell of old carcasses lingers; whether human or butcher's beast, she cannot say. Fear sparks through her. I'll stick to the front road, she thinks. And stay with the crowd. I'll make myself invisible, a shadow girl. She still has her white cap in her pocket. Tying it over her hair, she tucks away the wisps and sets off.

Their street is a mire of sticky horse leavings churned up by the creatures' giant hooves, the canal overflowing with brown muck, the smell of refuse and rotten things. Bess jumps the canal, her boots sending up a spray of mud. The houses tower over her as she walks in the direction of Mister Heath's, their sooty eaves jutting forward like cocked ears. An old man shuffling past stares and she quickens her pace, avoiding his eye.

When she arrives at the apothecary, the door is barred. A sign in the window reports that Mister Heath has been taken ill along with his apprentice so the shop will remain closed until further notice. Pressing her face against the shutters, Bess can just make out the dim shape of the guardian crocodile suspended over the potions and bottles, its ivory rictus a gleaming threat in the semi-dark. Perhaps it's laughing at her despair. I have the worst luck in the world, she thinks, resting her forehead on the timber. What to do now?

Feeling herself watched, she turns to scan the street but the faces of the throng are impassive, save for a vagrant woman in a tattered dress who asks Bess if she's seen her daughter and then says she must be off because the Queen is expecting her for supper. Her incoherent mumblings remind Bess of Pa and she shrinks into her dress. On the other side of the street, a cobbler is locking up, pulling down the shutters. His cheerful whistling makes Bess think of Philomela. Now she is all alone and the dark is gathering swifter than she would like, spilling across the street. She thinks about the hermits who lived here in Wapping hundreds of years before she was born. One man, John Ingram, built his cell near St Katherine's Church, so the monks would care for him if he sickened. Bess pictures his matted hair and hungry eyes, the rattling of his alms cup.

Her heart gives a great heave when someone touches her elbow. Fashioning her fingers into claws, she swings about.

'Here! Here!' Her attacker shields his head with his hands.

She stops, the fight fizzling out of her, her stomach suddenly hollowed by the evaporation of adrenalin.

'Don't ever do that,' she says, hugging her elbows, breathing hard.

Casper straightens, touching his cheek where the ragged end of her nail has opened an old wound, almost healed. He looks at the blood curiously, then touches his finger to his lips, sucking it away. 'You scratched me,' he says.

'You deserved it.' Despite her fighting talk, Bess is so glad to see him she almost apologises. 'You are like a fox, Casper de Vries, always sneaking around. Were you following me again? You do realise there is a criminal in Wapping, one you could easily be mistaken for? They might string you up and quarter you in his place.'

'And if they did, would you come to my rescue? Would you tell them it wasn't me?' He holds his thumb to the wound, pulling it away to check the progress until it dries.

Bess scoffs. 'As if anyone would listen to anything I have to say.' She glances down the street. 'Why did you come creeping? How did you know I'd be here?'

'Well, since you ask . . .' He digs into his coat, pulling out a pamphlet. 'I thought you might be interested. I was hanging around outside your house, waiting to give this to you. I was going to pretend to bump into you, if you walked out with your mother, and push it into your pocket. Why are you out here by yourself? Has anyone ever told you you walk as quickly as a man? I almost lost you at the corner.'

She flashes a grin. 'This is London. If you aren't fast someone will flatten you with a cart. What's this?'

She spreads the pamphlet out, smoothing the wrinkles with the heel of her palm.

To be seen at the Louse, Little Wapping. A Living Skeleton, taken from a Venetian Galley, from a Turkish vessel in the Archipelago. This Fairy Child, supposedly born of Hungarian parents, not exceeding a foot and a half high. The legs, thighs and arms are so very small that they scarce exceed the bigness of a man's thumb and the face no bigger than the palm of one's hand. You may see the whole anatomy of its body by setting it against the sun. It never speaks and has no teeth but is the hungriest creature in all the world, devouring more victuals than the stoutest man in England.

'I thought you might want to go one day,' he says. 'With me. As friends.'

Bess stares at him. 'You did *see* my mother, didn't you? I did mention she was stern?'

Casper folds his arms against his chest. 'Yet she lets you wander to the apothecary on your own.'

Bess fingers her cap. 'She didn't exactly give her permission.'

'I see.' He looks impressed.

She thrusts the paper back at him. 'Anyway, I can't. I won't have time. I'm starting a trade tomorrow. This is my last night of freedom.'

The truth of this strikes at the heart of her. It is, she thinks soberly, my last night before I am pressed into my mother's mould. Forced to do a job I have no talent for and will surely hate. Misery smothers her like a blanket and tears ooze between her eyelashes. Hurriedly, she wipes them away, hoping Casper has been distracted by the trundling progress of a cart crammed with books, the volumes bound together by ropes, spines glimmering like watchful eyes. But when she has blinked the last salty traces away, she looks up to find him still watching her with a look of pity and amusement. She is too wrung out by the day's events to care.

'We could go now,' he suggests.

Bess releases a soft snort into her handkin. 'I told you, I need to get back.'

'Won't take long. Do you know the Louse?'

'Of course I do,' she lies. 'Live in Little Wapping, don't I?'

His mouth quirks. 'Then you know we could be there and back at the Needle before your mother returns. What do you say?'

Bess folds her handkin into squares, a refusal already forming on her tongue. But something – perhaps the thought of returning to the house with nothing to show for her troubles – makes her hesitate. Why shouldn't she go? She's already in trouble; if Mam isn't yet home she soon will be, and Alice will have to confess to letting her go. She will need to take full responsibility when she gets back. What will Mam do? Punish her again, keep her housebound? She saw the hungry look in Mam's eyes when Missus Clifton mentioned paying her. Mam wants her to be a workhorse; she wants her to end up a dried old husk, starved of entertainment and amusement.

'Your last night of freedom,' he reminds her. 'You may as well enjoy it.'

Before she is aware of it, she is nodding and they have turned from the Needle and started towards the docks. Another cart trundles past and Casper steps aside to make way, his arm nudging hers, heavy and solid. Bess pulls away, her tongue thick and lifeless in her dry mouth. It pains her to think she has no idea what to say. Thankfully, Casper does his best to fill the void; as people shove past them, he chatters on about the places he has been – Majorca, Japan, the North Sea. Conjured by his stories, places she has only seen on maps spring suddenly to life: hills swell, oceans flood, exotic parrots in brindled trees abound with song. For someone so young, he has crossed the ocean as many times as her father.

She finds her speech returning when Casper asks her about the apprenticeship her mother has secured. The words come slowly at first but they begin to flow as she relaxes. For once, the stories she's telling are her own. They ring with truth the way Pa's never did when she tried to repeat them. In her mouth, his incredible tales always sounded false, the borrowed riches of another person's experience. They didn't make her feel warm and expansive as these stories do, as if by sharing them with Casper, she has escaped the boundaries of her own body and offered him a peek at her soul.

Bess tells him about Missus Clifton. She tells him about how the sight of blood doesn't bother her but that she's afraid of looking foolish in front of a group of strangers. What does she know about birthing babies? What if they squirm so much that she drops them? What if they latch onto her in the mistaken belief she is their mother, and won't let go?

Casper laughs. Bess hesitates, worrying she has said too much. But – 'It's true,' she insists, unable to suppress her conviction. 'You should see them, the way their little fingers cling. So strong!'

'Your mother obviously disagrees.'

'Well, but she's old,' Bess says, tossing her head dismissively. 'You ought to see the way women come up to her, always showing off their babies as if they're fine bits of jewellery. Not paste, either. Real diamonds.'

'But she cares about you,' he says, smiling. 'You're lucky to have a family.'

He sounds so wistful she bites back a reply. She would sail away at a moment's notice, if she could. Of course, she would write to Mam once she was safely launched – she's not completely heartless. There's a part of her that loves Mam and dreads disappointing her, the part that remembers all Mam's kindnesses, the sweets she saved, little cakes and dusted marchpane, gifts from clients she saved for Bess when thin soup was all they could afford. Those hungry days seem a distant memory now, thanks to her mother's hard work and sacrifice.

They reach the docks in silence, water sloshing against the pylons. At the far end, a group of coffee houses clusters against brickwork as dark as cocoa beans. Dockworkers lounge idly outside, their stillness a surprise to her. So this is where men come when their work is finished. Bess hears rough laughter. Pipe smoke stings her nose, sweet and cloying. She presses closer to Casper, wary of strangers. They make their way through the loitering men until they arrive at a signboard at the end of the row. Brightness glows within the tavern and dark forms shift behind the bubbled glass. From the doorway spill men's voices and the greasy stench of burnt coffee beans.

'I can't go in there,' Bess says. 'They'll throw me out, dressed like a girl.'

Casper pauses, considering. 'You're right,' he says. Then, before she can say another word, he removes his frock coat and shakes it at her.

She slides her arms into it. The coat swims on her body, the lining pungent with sweat and salt and vegetable matter. One pocket weighs more than the other; the one with the tulip bulbs. She waits with her arms outstretched while Casper inspects her and adjusts the seams. Under the frock coat, he wears an open-necked shirt. A circular plaque shines on a chain around his throat, stamped with two brightly coloured birds.

He sees her looking and touches it with his fingers. 'It's a hex charm,' he says. 'For luck. *Distelfinks* – thistlebirds – they eat the seeds and carry them from shore to shore. My master gave it to me.'

'It's lovely.' She wishes she was bold enough to lean closer. Will it be cool to the touch or warm from his skin? The hem of the frock coat brushes her shins. She bunches her skirts around her legs and tucks the overhang into her thick stockings, buttoning the coat over the lot. It's like playacting, she thinks. She walks a little way along the boardwalk, adopting a man's swagger. She feels remarkably free. When she plants her legs wide, knuckles resting on hips, her father's heroic pose, Casper's laughter fills her with such dizzy joy she thinks she would gladly spend the rest of the night standing here, entertaining him. But he's come to see a fairy, hasn't he? Not watch her fool around. Before they go in, there's one last thing she must do.

Untying the laces of her white cap, she tugs it off and runs her hands through her hair. *Disobedient*, she hears an exasperated Alice exclaim in her head. *How am I supposed to manage it? When you brush it one way, the other side crimps up!* The weight of all those tousled curls on her shoulders should be startling and uncomfortable but inexplicably, it feels natural as breathing. Perhaps the young bride who left her mobcap behind felt this way; perhaps she left the cap on purpose.

Casper coughs on the tobacco fumes drifting through the open doorway, a hand pressed across his mouth. Bess waits patiently for him to finish, her scalp tingling under the cool breeze. Plenty of men wear their hair long. They have wigs made for that very purpose.

Removing his hat, Casper squashes it onto her head, tugging the brim down so that the leather cuts into her sightline, the world reduced to legs. Standing back, he grins.

'Perfect,' he says.

The floor of the Louse is sticky, years of soot and ale-spills caught between the boards. Shuddering, Bess pinches the back of Casper's shirt, desperate not to lose him in the crush.

'Upstairs,' a woman says, when they reach the scratched and dirty counter and ask to see the fairy. Her rheumy eyes scan their faces and Bess tugs her hat lower, anticipating the dreadful shame of her unmasking. But a moment later, the old barmaid turns away to intervene in some dispute. Bess grins at Casper, giddy with triumph.

They take the stairs two at a time. The corridor above is dimly lit. An open door emits flickering candlelight and Bess and Casper move towards it, fearful and excited.

'Two pennies, gents,' squeaks a voice from the shadows. As the boy's shape coalesces, Bess's heart lurches in panic – she has not thought to bring any money. Casper fishes in his pocket, producing two coins. He pushes them into the box the boy holds out and then tugs at her sleeve, pulling her into the room after him.

Inside, shelves littered with curios and bric-a-brac give the impression they have entered a giant cabinet of wonders. Sconces flicker on the peeling walls. Raised on a plinth is the 'fairy', which turns out, as they edge closer, to be nothing more than a bundle of rags held together by a length of scruffy wool. The antlers branching from its lumpish head have clearly been glued on and its stocking wings, stretched out towards the yellowed ceiling, are torn in several places. The shoddy workmanship is further evinced by a rent in the fairy's ribcage, dried chaff spilling from a half-stitched seam.

Casper scoffs, disgusted. 'This is their famous fairy? I should demand my money back!'

'Don't waste your breath,' Bess sighs, her voice betraying disappointment. She clutches her elbows and bends to examine a grinning cat skull as Casper heads back into the hallway. Bess hears him complain to the boy, the ebb and flow of his Dutch accent an invisible moat circling the boy's guttural English. When he rejoins her a moment later, he wears a satisfied smile. Bess sees the boy hovering, still clutching the money box.

'Come,' Casper says. 'The lad says there is a better exhibit below.'

'Nobody's even seen it yet,' the boy pipes up. 'You'll be the first, sirs.'

He leads them back down into the smoke-filled taproom and points to a second set of stairs.

'Tell Piet that Billy sent you,' he says, as Bess peers into the oily darkness and takes a hesitant step. The stairs are slippery; she clutches the cool wall for support.

'Careful.' Casper's hand finds hers and she grasps it, grateful for its comforting warmth.

14

By the time Mary is ready to leave the Sparrows', it's growing dark. Thomas Sparrow, avoiding her gaze, thanks her quietly for coming and turns away to usher his daughters upstairs. The girls are silent and solemn-faced, their brown eyes hollowed by what they have witnessed. Mary wishes she had something to give them, a bit of marchpane or a boiled sweet, something to improve their sombre spirits and lighten the dense atmosphere of melancholy. She has never known the Sparrows' haberdashery to be so quiet before.

Winnifred Sparrow walks her to the door, pausing to retrieve a parcel from a basket. 'Bess's gowns,' she says, holding them out. 'Mother says to bring them back tomorrow and she'll hem them, if the measurements are wrong. Of course, that was before –' She blinks rapidly at the low beams. Following her gaze, Mary recalls the small, doll-like form in its bloodstained wrappings. Abigail's distress, the sobbing cries she tried to muffle, afraid of alarming the younger girls huddled into the workshop, watching disaster unfold. Heavy-hearted,

Mary had ushered them out, all except for Winnie, who stayed to comfort her weeping mother.

'Your mother will have other children,' Mary tells the eldest Sparrow girl now. 'It might not feel that way at present, but you wait and see.'

Winnifred's lips quiver and she dashes at her eyes with the heel of her hand. 'I hope you are right, Missus Gulliver. Thank you for your kindness.'

As Mary opens the door, a soft touch at her elbow makes her turn.

'Your husband, missus,' Winnie whispers, glancing around to ensure they are unobserved. 'My sweetheart's father owns the pawnbroker's in Whitehall. He says Captain Gulliver was there last week, pawning a wedding ring.'

'A wedding ring?' Mary repeats.

Winnifred nods. 'Dan's father gave him ten shillings for it. Thought you ought to know.'

She scurries back inside and shuts the door, leaving Mary on the doorstep to digest this puzzling news alone. There's no doubt in her mind now that the wedding ring is her own, purloined by her husband to pay for his pleasures. Shame creeps up her neck, a mottled rash. How many others know their situation? What are people saying? First the wedding ring and the spoon and pillow, then the coins from the teapot. And then what? The candlesticks, the chairs, the very bed he sleeps on? What can she do? If she confronts him, he will only insist the funds are needed to stop his bad dreams, which bleed into daylight hours. She needs to offer him concrete proof of his illness. She needs to make him see sense that this dangerous game he is playing affects them all.

Outside, sunset smears the sky above the shadowed houses. Mary's skin contracts as she contemplates the narrow roads leading back to the Needle and all the places a man could hide himself. She cannot bear to ask Thomas Sparrow to walk her home, so she hails a passing link boy, his torch a burning halo.

'Sixpence for you, Madam Midwife,' he yawns, scratching at his greasy wig with his free hand. 'And if any footpads go for you, I'll hold 'em off while you run. Almost killed a man who tried to rob me last month. Broke both his legs. Did it clean, though, so they'll heal. I'm not without mercy.'

'Is that so?'

'You don't believe me?' The boy squares his shoulders and stands straighter. Even at his fullest height, the top of his head barely reaches her chin. But some company is better than none and she's too tired to haggle so they set off, the boy holding his torch at arms-length as if it's a burning spear. He leads her through the market square, the stalls uninhabited save for squeaking rats and shadowy felines combing mounds of refuse for spoils. As her hem brushes against one matted creature it arcs around, hissing, and scrabbles furiously at her skirt and boots. She cries out.

The boy swings around to see.

'Away!' He thrusts the sizzling torch forward. 'Begone!'

The air is filled with burning fur.

'I've saved you,' the boy remarks, sounding surprised.

They near a crowded tavern, windows ablaze, men lounging in the doorway, watching them pass. She keeps her eyes down, trying to make herself inconspicuous but nobody approaches and they walk on without incident. In the next street, a trio of passing sailors fresh off a sloop weaves around them. One grabs the hem of her fluttering mantle while the others hoot with laughter, clutching their bellies and panting like labouring women.

Forced to stop, Mary tries to tug the fabric back but the man's grip is like an iron trap.

'Leave off!' the link boy shouts and the men turn on him like wild things, jeering insults.

Released, Mary stumbles back, her disoriented steps taking her close to the yawning mouth of an alleyway. Beyond the brickwork the darkness is absolute, thicker than a peatbog. Two seconds is all it would take for a person to pull her from this world and into his. Her pulse hammers in her throat as she hurries back to the link boy's smoking light. The sailors are shoving him roughly between them. One snatches the wig off his head and tosses it away while another grabs his torch, crowing with mirth as the boy lunges for it, teetering. The lad is close to tears.

'Your mothers would be ashamed of you!' Mary cries.

More laughter.

'Here, what's going on?' A watchman's frowning face appears, glowing in the light of his lantern. Mary recognises him as one of Jeremiah's local men. Usually, she cannot abide the way Jeremiah's posse strut around as if they own the place but tonight she's so glad to see the watchman she locks away her dislike.

Still grinning, the mariners hand the boy back his torch, before patting his head and melting away into the dark.

She thanks the watchman.

'You should not be out so late,' he counters, unsmiling. 'Only rogues and bawds stay out past dark. And a rapist at large. Ought to have more common sense, woman.'

Bristling, she draws her mantle close around her shoulders. Surely, he can't have missed it? 'I had no choice,' she says, her voice cold. 'I was visiting a client.'

He eyes the crimson cloak. 'You are Midwife Gulliver, are you not? If so, I've a message for you from the constable. Was on my way to the Needle to deliver it.'

He hands her a folded and sealed note.

Madam Gulliver,
Your services are required for the examination of a possible third victim – name unrecorded. She claims a man assaulted her earlier this evening and clipped her hair. She can generally be found at the shanties but says she will not return there until tomorrow in case he comes back. You are to visit her at your earliest convenience and make report of any injuries.
Yours etc.

A third victim. Gripped with dread, she is too aware of the watchman's scrutiny to reveal the extent of her anxiety. Nothing can be done until daybreak, so she focuses her attention on the boy. Dusting off his coat, he blows his nose into a dirty handkin and when she scoops up the wig and holds it out, he takes it without looking up, too embarrassed to meet her gaze.

'Thank you, missus.' The wig is overlarge; when he slips it on the curls slide down to cover his eyebrows. 'It belonged to my brother,' he explains, pushing the curls back with one hand. 'This used to be his patch, but he left it to me when he died last month. Along with his hair.'

After checking his torch for damage, he starts off again and she follows closely, as if the boy and his glowing orb of firelight offer any protection from devils lurking in the road. What an odd existence these lamp boys lead, she thinks, to distract herself from her worry. Up all night ferrying strangers between one address and the next, their day beginning just as the sun bids farewell to the sky. Like her, they must hold the shape of the city inside their head like an invisible map. They must learn which streets are rife with footpads, which lined with houses of ill-repute offering every kind of fleshly service. Knowledge is currency in his world, as it is in hers. It is the difference between life and death.

A thought strikes her. She taps the boy's shoulder and when he turns to her, puzzled, she says, 'Do you know a man called Peter Williams?'

The boy frowns.

'I heard he could be found at the docks,' she prompts. He will say no, she thinks. He will say: no man exists with that name. Her husband's fancies are insubstantial as mist, provoked by his physical illness. But she must ask. Somehow, she must ascertain the truth.

The boy's troubled expression clears. 'You mean Piet? Piet Willems? *Him* I've heard of. He's at the docks, when he's not at sea. There's a place where the sailors sleep. The Sign of the Louse. If he's anywhere, it's there.'

Light burns the edges of her vision. Piet, not Peter.

'Can you take me there?' she says.

Glancing up at the signboard, Mary shudders. It hangs low over the darkened shopfront, engraved with the image of a louse. Ballooned to biblical proportions, the insect is a peruke-maker's nightmare, four times as large as the beast in Hooke's *Micrographia*. Vicious claws extend from its thorax, hooks to hold and puncture the flesh. In the flickering light, the fleecy joints appear to move, inciting the creature to some blood orgy.

Underneath the sign, through a half-open doorway, Mary spies a sour-smelling taproom lit by smoking sconces. Sailors cluster around tables, laughing off their adventures. Her courage shrinks and she casts around for her friend the link boy, but he is already gone, swallowed up by the night. Come on, Mary, she goads herself. What would Anne Clifton do? The idea of Anne wandering the streets and about to set foot into this nest of masculinity while a rapist is on the loose is laughable. Anne would have interrogated Lemuel long ago and divined the truth for herself. God, she might very well have healed him and ordered him back to sea already and set things straight with Bess and Johnny. But Mary is not Anne, much as she envies the woman's courage.

Pushing open the door, she starts to make her way to the counter where an old woman wearing a stained and ancient-looking mantua is serving.

She squints at Mary through the tallow haze. 'What do you want? Here for the fairy, I suppose.' She jerks her chin at a set of stairs. 'Up the stairs, first door on your right. Pay at the door. All proceeds support poor orphaned foundlings at the workhouse in Clerkenwell.'

The woman's words muddy Mary's thoughts. 'What fairy?'

'The fairy. A wonder of the world?' The woman regards her as if she is an imbecile. 'A blessed miracle? The greatest freak this side of the water? Don't tell me you ain't heard of it.' Sighing, the woman nudges a mug of ale towards a grizzled sailor near Mary's elbow. 'Bert here has been up to see it twice, ain't you, Bert?'

The man grunts and drops his gaze to his mug.

'He is convinced it is a gen-u-ine oddity and he's been to Africa, so he would know.'

'I didn't come about any oddities,' Mary says, her impatience rising. 'I'm looking for a man. His name is Piet Willems. Do you know where I might find him?'

The old woman squints. 'Piet? What do you want with him?'

'That's my business.'

The old barmaid holds her gaze for a long moment then presses her lips together and slaps a rag onto the sticky counter, sopping up a brown puddle near Mary's elbow. Oh God, she thinks. I've offended her, and now she will say no more. Relief battles curiosity. She could turn now and walk away, convince herself that she has done her best to find the man. She could hail another link boy and soon be home, ensconced in the warmth and safety of her own house. But how can she return home when the answer to Lem's illness lies so tantalisingly within her grasp? One appeal to this Piet to explain her husband's story could put an end to the gossip and rumours circulating the neighbourhood since his return. *Butcher* – Elias Grillett's word repeats in her head, a reminder of her own tenuous reputation, one black mark away from sliding them all into debtor's prison. Piet knows something of her husband's illness and whatever it is, she must be the one to find out.

'Below.' Squeezing the rag into a bucket, the woman fixes Mary with a piercing stare she cannot decipher. 'He's below stairs, last room on the left. Don't blame me if he sends you away – last we spoke, the exhibit wasn't ready. He wouldn't give me a clue what he's got planned.'

'Got planned?' Mary echoes, utterly bewildered. She has the strangest sense she has walked in halfway through a conversation. Is Piet planning something for Lem? Can that be what the crone means? What is the nature of her husband's relationship with this man? Lemuel never spoke of him before when he returned from his travels. Does he mean their family harm?

The woman hunches her back, dismissive, leaving Mary to thread between the patrons to the narrow staircase. The stairs leading down are in worse repair than the ones going up. The warped treads are in need of scouring and splinters flake off under her boot. Clearly, the above rooms are intended for clientele of gentler means who have come to view the 'oddities': fairies, alligators, mermaids, monsters, Dutch cabinets of wonder, filled with shells and specimens floating in bell-shaped jars. Lemuel brought her a few times to such places. He must have sensed her reluctance, though, for he stopped asking. Wonders can't be bought and traded, in her opinion. They are gifts, not currency.

At the bottom of the stairs is an empty parlour where a low fire hisses in a rough grate. Two sagging chairs frown at each other from opposite corners. Carved faces on the wooden feet have bubbled and warped in the salt-laden atmosphere, their features distorted into expressions of misery. A painting hangs above the plain lintel. As she edges closer, the composition shifts suddenly into an eviscerated cow, all pearly bones and stringy sinew, the red tissue exposed like pulpy fruit. Sickened, she pulls away. Through a door lies a dim hallway; she spies the men's living quarters. Hesitantly, she moves along the corridor. Her legs and arms tingle, every cell demanding she turn and run. Where walls and floors meet, the wood has buckled, nails bursting through the twisted panels like rows of iron teeth. Some of the doors are open. Wooden bunks press into corners, men lying in languid repose. Caught up in exhaustion, they hardly glance at her. A thick smell wends along the corridor, ripe and sweet, making her stomach roil.

How many of these sailors have never returned home? How many cannot face their families after what they have done and seen? Is it possible Lem never went to Sumatra at all, but holed up in a place like this with a pipe for comfort? Did the years slip by in a whisper? Did they pass in a fever dream, while somebody – a woman, perhaps – milked the last of his coins from his purse, transmuting gold into smoke rings?

At the end of the hallway, she finds the closed door the woman spoke of.

'Mister Willems?' she calls, rapping softly. 'It is Mary Gulliver to see you. I believe you know my husband?'

The door swings slowly open. Her first thought is that fog has rolled in off the sea, as it is wont to do in summer, seeping into houses and lungs, breeding clouds of biting insects, reminding the human residents of Wapping's marshland origins. But fog doesn't localise in one place. Rich tar hits her nostrils; opium's earthy undercurrent. Blinking away the bitter sting, she looks around the sparsely furnished room, taking in the bed, the chairs, the desk. A sailor in a rumpled shirt occupies the nearest chair, pale hair fanned out, loose and uncombed, as if he has just rolled out of bed. His feet are bare. Between his stained fingers, he pinches an ivory pipe.

'Missus Gulliver,' he says, in an accent she cannot place. '*Goed om je te zien*. A welcome surprise. I'm Piet. Will you sit?' He gestures at an empty chair.

The other chair is occupied by a boy. He looks down at the floor, reluctant to expose his face. She wonders if he is Piet's younger brother; they have the same pale colouring.

'I didn't realise you would be entertaining company,' she says. 'I can return another time, if it's inconvenient.' Her head swims, hazy with fumes. She clutches the back of a chair for support.

'No, no,' Piet says. 'This is most excellent timing.' His gaze dissects her carefully, each slow blink a different body part. 'So you are Missus Mary Gulliver. Here on behalf of Lemuel, I suppose?'

'Yes,' she says.

'Yes,' he repeats. 'Lemuel, my friend, my very *trusting* friend.'

'How –' She coughs suddenly. 'How is it you know each other?'

He grins with half his mouth. 'Lem and me? Oh, we have known each other for years, crossed paths a dozen times on our travels. Fate threw us together again six months ago, as it has thrown you and I together now. And my accomplices, here to curtail my reckless behaviour.' Inclining his head, he taps the pipe, depositing a small mountain of ash on the chair arm. 'You don't mind if I smoke, do you, missus?'

She coughs again as he exhales a hissing stream of vapour. 'I wish you wouldn't.'

'If wishes were fishes . . .' He lets the rest of the thought trail away, his glittering eyes pinning her.

A movement at the back of the room catches her eye. Someone shifts in the shadows, someone lurking who does not wish to be noticed. Goose pimples rise on her arms. Is this a trap? In coming here to prove her husband's fancies baseless, has she ensnared herself? No. Don't be ridiculous. This is merely an addict's bolt hole, a pathetic one at that. Still, she cannot shake the feeling of enclosure, the thick smog rising like an unscalable wall.

'I'm glad you're here,' she says. 'I have questions about my husband's past I hope you can answer.'

Piet's smile widens. 'I, too, am glad. I've something, you see, which belongs to Lemuel. His property, entrusted to me, his dearest friend.' Bunching his fist, Piet gallops it across the scarred tabletop, his eyes never leaving hers. His knuckles, she notices, are covered in scratches and mottled with weeping sores. 'But first, let's speak. For years, I have wondered what you look like.'

His words send a shiver across her skin. 'He has mentioned me, then,' she says. 'I admit, I'm surprised. If he really is your friend, you'll tell me what I need to know.'

Piet unclenches his fist. 'He told me all about your special friend. Mister Sympson, isn't it?' He coughs into his hand to cover his smirk and Mary's cheeks blaze hot. 'So yes, we keep each other's secrets. Didn't I vouch for him when Captain Biddell pulled him aboard after he was shipwrecked? Those sailors would have tossed him back into the sea, sure as eggs. I didn't want them to bring him home to you. I would have brought him here, if it were not for those other men. Let his family look after him, they said. Lem didn't trust them with his belongings. He didn't trust you. He trusted *me*, and I kept his things safe. I am his one and only true friend. Didn't the rest abandon him when his raving started? Not me. Not Piet. Out together, home together, I am with him always and he with me.'

He warbles the last line, a mirthless tune. Mary's throat closes. It feels like a second betrayal, this long-held friendship her husband has never spoken of. Worse, it confirms Lemuel's story. There is much she does not understand in Piet's ramblings, but certain parts of it reek with the truth. It explains so much about Lem's preference of a life at sea over one at home. She wants to leave but her feet are rooted to the warped boards.

Piet waves away a puff of smoke. 'It's all water under the bridge, anyway. Before we go and fetch Lemuel's miraculous miracles, I would like to introduce you to Mister C. de Vries and Mister E. Gulliver, two of the handsomest lads I've ever met, although I confess: Mister Gulliver is more to my taste.' He gestures at the stranger in the far corner. 'Come here, sir, I command you.'

'Mister Gulliver?' Is it Lem? she thinks, peering through the haze. Has Lem come down here?

The figure shrinks back, stumbling over a pile of books, dust rising in a shimmering cloud, loose pages papering the blackened floor. In his efforts to escape, he is so clumsy he almost overturns a footstool. It catches him unguarded and he falls to his knees with a grunt. Piet marches across the room and the stranger squeaks as he is dragged back into the circle of burnished candlelight.

The other boy, silent until now, leaps up. 'Take your hands off her,' he says. 'You hear me?'

As Piet's victim gives a great twist, his hat topples to the floor. Mary bends to pick it up and dust it off. They meet halfway, the boy's fingers reaching for the hat Mary holds out, clutching the brim. At first, she thinks the opium has stupefied her. Bess cannot be here because she is at home, safe at home with Alice, her favourite books fanned out around her. Bess is in the kitchen, sucking on a piece of gingerbread, oblivious to the crumbs carpeting the floorboards, tempting night mice.

'Mam, I'm sorry,' the boy says. 'You aren't supposed to be here.'

It dawns on Mary that Bess is speaking, taking the proffered hat – whose hat? – passing it to the other boy – the real boy – who jams it onto his head. Mary wants to look at him, but her gaze is fixed on Bess, who tugs at the hem of the black jacket, yanking it down over her stockinged knees. She hasn't taken in a word Bess has been saying and the girl, at last, falls silent. Her companion puts his hand on her shoulder and squeezes reassuringly but she shrugs him off.

'Mam?' she says. 'Say something. Please.'

Mary tries and fails to summon a response. Somewhere in the room behind them, she hears Piet cough quietly, a wet hacking sound which brings her back to herself. A slow-burning fury kindles in the base of her stomach, burning a path up her core. Bess's calves are visible, her dainty ankles. She has tucked her skirt into her stockings, the fabric billowing over the back of her knees. Twin spots dance on her cheeks and she plucks nervously at her lip.

Mary clears her throat. 'Take off that jacket,' she says. 'Now.'

Bess blanches but does as she is bid, fumbling with the clasps. Shrugging the jacket off, she hands it to the boy, who bundles it up but stays close and shoots anxious looks at Mary, as if he fears she might grasp Bess by the hair or slap her face. He can't know how much she longs to do both, nor that the desire to pull her daughter into a tight embrace ignites an ache of longing. Bess has disobeyed her in the worst possible way. Why on earth is she here?

Returned to herself, Bess looks smaller than her fourteen years. She hugs her arms to her chest, chastened, her skirt stained and rumpled.

'You should go,' Bess mutters to the boy, but he only shuffles closer to her, protective. 'Go,' she repeats. He whispers something and then with a last look at Mary, departs.

Piet calls out to him as he passes, faintly mocking. 'Don't get lost, boy. I don't want to fish you out of a barrel in a year's time.'

Taking another sip of his pipe, he lounges back in his chair, and Mary sees how he has coordinated their drama for his own amusement and is enjoying the spectacle from behind half-lidded eyes. Her fear of him sharpens.

'Mister Willems,' she says. 'You said you have access to my husband's goods. If you take me to them – right now, no more games – I will give you everything in my purse, every last farthing, and then I will take my daughter home. I would ask that you do not trouble yourself about our business any longer, mine or Mister Gulliver's. You are freed from all responsibility towards him. Your duty is over.'

As expected, he sits up, alert to the clink of coins – those she has hidden from Lemuel – in the purse she has withdrawn from her kitbag. How much puff can he buy with them? she thinks. But as he holds out his hand, she moves the purse out of his grasp.

'First, the goods.'

'Yes,' he says. '*Prachtig*. Wonderful. This way, madam and miss. Permit me to lead you to your husband's treasures.'

She wants to tell Bess to stay put but there is nothing about this place she trusts and the idea of leaving her daughter to imbibe the thick opium fumes horrifies her. How much already swirls in her system?

Piet leads them back into the dusty passageway, pausing beside a door. He jams a key into the lock, muttering curses. 'Salt everything,' he says. 'Everything here rusts.' The key finally clicks, and Piet exhales and puts his hand on the latch, his gaze sweeping over her to linger on Bess. Mary moves to shield her and Piet grins.

'Before we enter, a warning,' he says. 'I last fed them this morning, so they may be jumpy. They like to bite, you see?' He holds up his fist, covered in tiny bite marks.

Mary's skin crawls and Bess recoils. The man's craziness is contagious. Surely, this is just a bad dream they will soon wake from? She digs her nails hard into her palms, willing herself to wake. But Piet is still rambling and the brutal stench of him clings to her nose.

'You must be careful not to crush them. You must be very quiet and stand very still. They're skittish things and might well attack you.'

'Skittish? They are alive, then?'

'Quite alive.' He is no longer smiling, and she feels his instability wash over her. From beyond the door comes the sound of scrabbling feet. What can they be? At Southwark Fair with Lem, she saw a variety of exotic creatures. Great prodigies of nature. A sleek eel circling a tank, a mangy lion pacing its cage. Once a dodo, although the man who took their coin claimed it was an ostrich. Surely, this is something of a similar nature, an accident of breeding.

'You will be pleased, Missus Gulliver,' Piet says. 'Your husband has brought you a bounty. I've never seen a sheep so small.' Piet pinches the air between forefinger and thumb. 'Small but fair, they are. They have the softest fleece, too; light as cloud. They will fetch such a handsome sum.'

Mary stares at him, horror dawning. What if Lem has been telling the truth? This evidence she so readily discounted – is it about to be tipped into her hands? His madness dispelled by a wonder she cannot understand?

The storeroom is airless, filled with timber crates and the pungent tang of rat droppings. The corners of the room are dark, no window or light to lift the shadows. She warns Bess to stay close. Her daughter's breathing is a steady rhythm. Piet leads them to the back of the room, the candle flame guttering, casting shadows upon the dank walls. A square box rests upon a makeshift table of crates, covered by an old moth-eaten blanket. From beneath the stained linen, a series of small sounds: scratchings and rustlings, the pattering of tiny padded feet. And very faintly, a soft, high-pitched murmur. Her pulse quickens, drumming hot in her ears.

Piet raises his candle, and in its glow his eyes are as round as saucers, their colour all but extinguished by black pupils. Sweat films his skin. 'We will be famous, myself and Mister Gulliver, when we exhibit these little wonders. A flock of tiny sheep? Who would not want such a thing? It will make our fortunes.'

He pulls the sheet away and thrusts the tallow at the cage.

All is pandemonium, a frenzy of movement, black tails lashing the air. Mary hears Bess gasp as rats pour across the crates, escaping the light, racing for the safety of the shadows. Piet howls and jumps back as the creatures scurry across his unshod feet. His light falls relentlessly upon the cage, illuminating the sticks of broken straw and the mess of fur and blood within. Bess retches and Mary slings an arm around her, her only thought that they must find their way upstairs. Their path is blocked by Piet, now pacing back and forth before the door, upbraiding himself as he clutches his head in both hands.

'Stupid! Stupid!' he shouts, the sound rebounding off the walls. Hugging her daughter close, Mary tries to edge past him, but her foot knocks against a crate. He whips around, eyes wild.

'Where do you think you're going?' he barks. 'Who said you could leave?'

Mary swallows, choking down her fear. Blindly, she fumbles for her purse and throws it down, Piet staring hard before dropping to his knees to snatch it up.

Seizing the candle and shielding Bess with her arm, she spirits her along the passageway. The sleepy men, aroused by the commotion, call out as they pass. Animal sounds, bayings, gruntings, bleatings, a wild cacophony of noise. Gorge rises in the back of her throat. She swallows it down. Through the smoky parlour, the painting looms, red gore smeared over oily bones. At last, they emerge in the taproom where faces turn to them. The old crone at the bar shouts something Mary cannot decipher over the roar of blood in her head. Get out, she thinks. Keep running. They burst into the docks, gasping. After the thick tang of opium, the fishy odour of the docks has never smelled so sweet.

15

Mary has often daydreamed about taking Bess with her to births, imparting all the useful knowledge gleaned from years of experience, first fostered by her own mother. She sees the two of them walking hand in hand along the dirty roads, visiting clients, untangling thorny problems – what to do when a baby's foot protrudes instead of its crown, or how to soothe a dying woman's panic. She sees the world fall away, the ugliness of the streets diminished by warm companionship. It never crossed her mind that it might be like this, the two of them walking in silence, too wounded by the horrifying revelations of the night before to exchange anything but stiff queries about sleep and the weather. What they really need to say to each other churns under every coldly civil sentence. Each silence stretches a little longer, deepening mistrust. If Bess were a client, Mary would gain her confidence by sharing a little about her garden or asking questions about her physical well-being. She would ask: what did you eat this morning? How are you feeling? What can I do to help you? But confidence goes both ways and Bess, shuffling along in her new mantua – a brown-striped tabby with blue laces criss-crossing the stomacher – seems to have taken a vow of silence. When Mary's third attempt to draw her out results in nothing but a blank stare, she gives up and strides on, skirting around a boy trundling a barrow of steaming hog's manure destined for the market.

Wapping, if it ever sleeps, is waking. Men and women push their carts along the rutted lanes, and geese girls usher honking flocks through the canal, spraying brackish water. Everything looks as it always does, the buildings drab and unchanging, the people industrious, determined to make a profit and earn their daily bread. Last night Mary saw a side of Wapping she tries her best to avoid. The fact that Bess saw it, too – that she knows now something of what goes on after dark – fills Mary with sour dread. All her notions of easing Bess into adulthood have lifted. Seeing Bess surrounded by danger in that awful place – with a strange boy, no less – has completely unbalanced her, as if the world has tipped upside down, sky and sea reversed.

'Bess,' she calls sharply, when her daughter falls behind again, distracted by something in a shop window. 'Do you want to be late?'

The girl stares at her mutinously, then slowly picks up her skirts.

As they pass the apothecary's shop, Bess sends a look of longing in the direction of the glittering Aladdin's cave of herbs and tinctures. She doesn't dare ask, though, and Mary is glad. Delivering two scoldings in less than twenty-four hours would make her feel worse than she already does. It would make her feel like the worst mother in the world, which is what Bess told her she was last night when they finally arrived home and all the pain and hurt came bubbling out, like black poison. It had been nearing ten o'clock by the time Mary managed to get them back to the Needle, Bess sobbing all the way. Her tears dried when they reached her room. Affronted by Mary's questions, she defended herself against what she clearly felt was an ambush and interrogation.

'You must be so pleased,' she'd said. 'All your suspicions confirmed, your hatred of Pa, what he is, who he is. You've always resented us.'

'I don't resent you!' Mary had almost shouted.

'He is *my* father,' Bess said, quietly. 'You have always been jealous.'

'Jealous?' Mary's own temper had risen then before she could catch it, a bitter laugh escaping. 'Jealous of what, Bess? Of a man who cannot keep two pounds in his purse for longer than a few hours? A man whose only supporters are those he pays or impressionable children who can't see him for what he is? A – a man who is never satisfied with what he has but is convinced that he must go in search of better? Do you understand what happened tonight? What it means? Your father is a – a degenerate. His mind and will are weak, that's why I am trying to –'

'How can you?' Bess's face worked. 'How can you speak about him like that? Pa would never have allowed me to be sold into bondage the way you did with Missus Clifton. You didn't even give me a choice. You think you know everything because you have book learning and you know how to grow plants and you know how to bring out a baby but what do you really know, Mam? Where have you been? How have you broadened yourself, stuck here in London? What experience have you gained? The truth is, you know nothing and what's worse, you have no ambition to try.'

Mary was glad Alice was downstairs in the kitchen. She was shaking with anger and could not be certain that what came out would be either civil or appropriate. 'I am your mother,' she managed to say, at last. 'You would do well to remember that, Bess. You are here in this house because I allow it. Who was that boy you were with? Perhaps you can tell me, since you seem so eager to show me how well you understand the world.'

Bess had pressed her lips together tightly.

'You realise he could have hurt you,' Mary went on. 'Whoever he is, he led you into danger. He may look innocent but that is how girls are ruined, Bess. Trust me. You are a fool if you believe him. Whatever his stated intentions, he clearly cares nothing for your safety and I forbid you to see him ever again. Let me hear you say it. Then we can put this behind us and start afresh tomorrow.'

Bess's eyes glittered with unconcealed rage. 'I hate you,' she said slowly, and in that dreadful moment, Mary had felt her heart pause as if it, too, were listening, as if it could not believe the cruelty Bess was willing to inflict.

Hollow and numb, she had wobbled out of Bess's room, shutting the door. Lemuel was asleep when she went in to collect her things, the mattress and bolster, the bedclothes. Unable to bear the thought of sharing the same room with him, breathing the same air, she went to the attic, where she set up a makeshift bed next to Alice and then lay down and closed her throbbing eyes. Some mothers would reject their daughters for such ingratitude. They would beat their backs and flay their skin. They would throw them into the streets and force them to make their own way. When Mary's exhaustion tipped her, at last, into sleep, she dreamed she was helping at a birth, kneeling between a woman's knees as screams filled the room. When the baby slid into her hands, it was boneless, just thin membrane stretched over bluish organs and blood. No skull, no ribcage, the eyes and mouth fused shut. The woman sat up, reaching for it and Mary, in confusion, saw that the new mother wore Bess's stricken face, wrinkled by poor diet and hard living. *Give me my baby*, the Bess Woman said and Mary, afraid, hugged the poor, lifeless creature against her chest, a gross penance for relinquishing all faith in her daughter. When she woke, tears stained her cheeks.

They are passing St Paul's. Bess halts at the edge of the rectory garden to run her hands through straggling daisy stalks. Watching her, Mary is startled again by how tall her daughter seems, how suddenly grown-up without her white cap. Exhaustion has sharpened her cheekbones. She looks pale and fragile in her new gown but there is something about the determined set of her jaw that makes Mary wonder if anything she said last night made any difference. How she wishes she could go back and unsay the things she said and say others in their place. She would peel back the hurt like rotting floorboards and lay bare all the things she should have told Bess years ago. Now, time is against them. The breach is so impossibly wide neither can hope to mend it. She hears Bess say again: what is your experience worth? And the answer: nothing. She has learned nothing about her daughter's nature, nothing about how to impress upon her that a girl with a trade is not beholden to her husband. If Bess can secure a licence, there is a chance she will be free – free from the burden of relying on a man to make ends meet. But that pales in significance to the things Bess has accused her of: keeping Pa locked up, concealing Pa's true condition, treating her like chattel, forcing her to begin this apprenticeship.

Anne's house is a fine dwelling with panes of rich, honey-coloured glass in the front windows. On the doorstep, Mary pauses to straighten the trim on Bess's tabby suit. Bess is so pale that dark veins pulse visibly under her skin.

'Alice will come for you later,' she says, gently. 'Are you nervous?' She tries to think of fortifying phrases that might prop Bess up, encourage her. What did her own mother used to say? But after last night's disruption, her memories of her mam are all jumbled. Now she is just a sleeve, wooden buttons, a caudle of herbs. 'You'll be fine.'

Bess scowls. She hunches away from her mother and raps on the door.

Susanna answers. When she sees Bess, she lifts her chin. The two girls eye each other and Mary feels invisible, as if she were watching animals circling, each searching out the other's weaknesses.

'Missus Clifton is still feeling poorly,' Susanna says. 'She's in the parlour with Missus Elinor. You're to come in and help me strip sheets until she's better.' She beckons Bess forward and the girl, looking suddenly vulnerable, hesitates before following her up the stairs and out of sight.

'Is that you, Mary?' Elinor calls. Hanging up her mantle, Mary steps into the hallway. She finds Elinor inside the parlour, a ledger propped on her lap. Today her dress is a dark blue confection, the hem whispering against the boards as she rises to place the book on the table.

'Bess has arrived, then?' says Anne. The older woman reclines on the damask sofa, her outstretched legs concealed by a blanket. A bowl of medicants rests on the ground nearby along with a clean chamberpot. Although unwell, she is still regal.

'Susanna has taken her upstairs,' Mary says. 'I'm sorry to hear that you're ill.'

'It's nothing,' Anne says, lowering the poultice that had been resting on her forehead. 'A headache, brought on by the pain in my leg. First the leg, now the head. It feels like wires cutting into my skull. This is the third time my leg has given out this year. I should cut it off and replace it with a wooden one.' She thumps her thigh, wincing. Her skin is the colour of pottage. When Mary touches her hand, it is cold.

'I can take Bess home,' she offers.

'I wouldn't hear of it.' Anne glances at her kindly before slapping the poultice back into place. 'I meant what I said yesterday, Mary. This is the best place for her. When I'm better, I shall need their help. And there's something I'd like to discuss with you, also. Elinor, go upstairs and make sure those girls aren't amusing themselves instead of working.'

Elinor opens her mouth as if to protest but then gathers up her things.

When they are alone, Anne pats the sofa, indicating Mary should sit beside her.

'How is your husband?' she says, one glittering eye fixed on her, the other closed.

Mary shakes her head. 'Unchanged.' She feels a sudden yearning to confide more deeply in Anne, to tell her about last night, the horror of her discovery. Piet's claims about Lem – his insinuation of their intimacy, their long-held friendship – are so sharp but still so shrouded in mystery and confusion. When she tried to speak to him about it this morning, he would not listen. He shrugged himself away, still muttering about his 'little flock', and she did not have the heart to argue. She knows the truth of his 'little sheep'; her husband's cargo was not sheep at all. Through the horror of the moment in that dirty room, she'd seen that their remains were too much like those of the miniature possums she once saw exhibited at the Bartholomew Fair. Those animals, too, had been ravaged almost beyond recognition, a mastiff hound ripping into them while their owner shrieked. Bess hasn't said a word about them, but Mary guesses she privately agrees and this has probably added to the girl's upset.

'I need to ask you something,' Anne says, recalling her. 'A favour.'

'Mister Grape has already asked me to visit the shanties. I plan to go as soon as I'm done here.'

''Tisn't that.' Anne heaves a sigh. 'Although it does worry me, the vulnerability of these women, nobody to shield them. No, Mary. I need someone to be our representative, to visit the Bishop and assure him all is well. There are rumblings of dissent amongst the surgeons.'

'You mean Hugh Chamberlen?' She thinks back to the conversation with Elinor.

'That family has ever been trouble. Pretending they are allies, when really they would like us to tear ourselves apart and make way for the surgeons and their ilk.' Anne lowers the poultice. 'I want you to take over the management of the Bishop for me, Mary. His protection is vital to us now that the Chamberlens are trying once again to distribute their forceps to every surgeon in town.'

'Me?' She cannot disguise her shock.

'I'm too unwell to meet with him, and I can't have him brought here – any sniff of weakness and we risk losing everything we've worked so hard to gain. No, you will have to go and charm him. I know you have it in you.'

Mary bites back a laugh. 'Charm? Are you thinking clearly?'

'You can be utterly charming when required, Mary.'

'Can't you send Elinor?'

'Elinor is as cold as a haddock. She's my niece and I raised her, so I can say it. She doesn't care about the other midwives, only herself and her own place in the group. But *you* care, I know you do. I saw it in you the moment we met.'

'You could wait until your health improves,' Mary suggests.

'I could,' Anne concedes. 'But I won't. We need to speak to the Bishop now before Hugh Chamberlen can work his way into the man's good graces.'

'This is a temporary arrangement, is it not?' Mary says, slowly. 'Your health will improve, I'm certain.'

'Of course it will.' Anne winces as she adjusts herself under the blanket. 'Absolutely. But I cannot allow the Chamberlens to ingratiate themselves while I'm weakened. There's a bonus in it for you, if you accept the role. Six pounds a year the Bishop pays me, to liaise with the midwives and save him the trouble of listening to their issues. What do you say?'

Mary considers. Six pounds! The extra will be useful; it might help them stave off the increase in taxes. It could bring her a little closer to enrolling Johnny in a London school. But the Bishop is a powerful man. She has never spoken to him directly. She has only seen him on visitation days, moving through the midwives who have gathered to listen to novices swear their midwife's oaths, promising to uphold the professional standards set out by the Church. Can she trust herself to speak to him without faltering? What if he thinks she is stupid, an ignorant harridan? *You know nothing.* Bess's words haunt her. What authority does she possess?

She thinks of the recent confrontation with Jeremiah Grape. He left, didn't he, when she told him to? She only needs to recall that incident to give herself strength. She is entirely capable, as capable as Elinor or any of the other midwives Anne might have asked to go in her place. And perhaps Bess will see this, once her anger has softened. She will understand her assumptions about her mother's lack of ambition were wrong.

'I will speak to him for you,' Mary says.

Anne nods. 'I'm glad to hear it. 'Tis a weight off my mind. I'll ask Elinor to make the arrangements. You'll report back, won't you? Let me know what he says.'

From somewhere above them, raised voices can be heard and both women look up at the scrolled ceiling.

'Bess will be good for Susanna,' Anne declares, reclining against the sofa. 'A little healthy competition never hurt.'

Mary leaves her to rest and goes out into the hallway. She looks longingly up the staircase, wanting desperately to say goodbye, to wish Bess well. Recalling her daughter's resentful face, she thinks better of it and slips away, unnoticed.

The houses in the shanties always remind her of crowded teeth, pushed together in crooked rows, the roofs all pitched at strange, jutting angles. Every now and then, a square of scorched earth appears, the vacant site of a pulled tooth, a burnt and blacked-out husk where nothing moves and nothing grows. Each row circles back around, so unless you know what you are looking for, you could spend your whole life pushing piles of stinking refuse aside with your boot, ploughing past women nursing babies in open doorways, dogs gnawing on chalk-white bones and children stumbling along paths with their eyes half-closed dreaming of the sleep awaiting them or wishing they had caught more.

'Hello, missus.'

Mary takes her eyes off the uneven ground to peer through the gloom.

'It's Bridget Maloney.' A shadow shifts, breaking away from the dimmer recesses of a shack.

'Missus Maloney. God give you good day.'

'And yourself, there.' Bridget Maloney's long face is just visible. 'Saw your mantle.'

'You have keen eyes,' Mary says.

'Need them, don't I? To watch the bairns.' She turns her head as a child in a dirty smock appears on the darkened stoop to ogle them, and a thin wail lifts inside the shack. 'Back inside with you, Maire.' Bridget Maloney jerks her head. 'Go on, now. And see to your sister.'

Mary watches the little figure retreat, the baby's wails petering out.

'She's grown fast.'

'That she has.' Bridget twitches the edges of a tattered shawl over her shoulders. 'What brings you down here? A birth?'

'No.' Mary tells her about the task Jeremiah has given her.

As she listens, Bridget's face tightens. ''Tis true enough,' she says. 'But only the women hereabouts know, and a few menfolk. That constable you mentioned, he sent a man down here to take notes, but the man didn't stay long enough even to ask what happened. Once he learned about the woman's profession, he took off. What a scarecrow.'

Mary frowns. 'The constable wants a midwife to examine her.'

'Good.' Bridget Maloney sniffs. 'Someone needs to. Someone needs to protect the girls and women in this place. A madman it is, who does these things. He cut her hair off, did the constable mention? Hacked it off at the roots.'

'You know her, then.'

'None too well. My Samuel doesn't like me associating with ... them kind. But of course, when he's at sea, what he doesn't know can't hurt him. She's a newcomer, been here a few months. We traded a few things when she first arrived. Lives down that way, on the row.'

Mary thanks her.

'Oh, missus.' Bridget's fingers catch at her sleeve. 'You'll be around in a few weeks, won't you?' She flutters a hand over her midsection. Beneath the thin folds of the shawl, the swell of the woman's belly strains the fabric. Another baby, Mary thinks, her heart dropping, and the last not yet weaned. 'I heard about Mister Gulliver. I hope he is recovering and that you will stay in Wapping, now he's home.'

'Where else would we go?'

Bridget shrugs. 'I thought, perhaps, a better parish. On two incomes, you might afford it.'

The baby's cry pierces the air again, sharp and insistent, dissatisfied with Maire's attentions. Milk spots darken Bridget's bodice and she flicks the shawl over them, embarrassed.

'When the time comes, I'll help you,' Mary says. 'Mister Gulliver is, thank you, much better than when he first arrived.'

'Ah, he was always one for a story. You must believe in miracles, now, after God showed such mercy in delivering him back to you.'

Miracles. The word snags in Mary's mind like a bur between yarn paddles. *Miracles*. Like tiny horses ridden by tiny people? A tiny coach and four? A race of people so dependent on her husband's height and strength they bow at his feet?

Maire trots out, patting the crying baby in her arms and Bridget scoops her up. Mary watches her shoo the child back inside the dark shack.

*

The woman squats in a patch of sunshine filtering down between the eaves, brown stubble glinting on her skull. Grey skirts puddle around dirty shoes, the leather so patched her slender toes are visible, pushed against the grain. She looks up as Mary approaches, slanting her eyes against the sun, rubbing her hand across her scalp.

'God give you good day,' Mary says.

The woman's mouth twists. 'He ain't given me much else.'

'I understand you've been sorely used.'

The woman nods slowly, her gaze drifting to the shack behind them. From the outside, it seems even more ramshackle than the Maloneys', a thin curtain pegged across the doorframe.

'The constable would like you to be examined.'

'So, he sent you? Thought you was the baby lady. Mother Midnight.' Standing up, the woman shakes out her skirts. 'I've already cleaned myself up.'

'Then I'll just record the damage I can see, in case the court requires it.' She pauses. 'I'm so sorry you've been hurt. You did not deserve such rough treatment. My name is Mary Gulliver.'

'Thea.'

Mary waits, but there is no family name. Some women do not like their family names to be known, especially if they are mistresses favoured by the sailors; problematic if the wives identify them. There is safety in just a first name.

The woman scratches her head. Whoever has shaved it, he's done a proper job, not like the half-hearted shave she gave Lemuel a week ago.

'It's Althea,' she says. 'Like the poem. "Stone walls do not a prison make, nor iron bars a cage."'

'You know Lovelace?' Mary says, surprised. Richard is the poetry lover, not her.

'Does that surprise you?'

'Not at all.' It does, though, to know Thea has her letters. How far has she fallen? Has the increase in taxes already claimed its first victims, the helpless poor who cannot climb out of penury? Perhaps she overheard the poem some other way.

Thea seems to know what she is about, since her smile widens knowingly.

'You all right, Thea?' a woman calls from a house across the way. Dressed in a sky-blue gown and a powdered wig, she looks as if she is heading off to court, not walking the dirty Wapping streets.

'Yes,' Thea says. 'Yes, Meg, I'm all right. Come on in, then, missus. Let's get this over with.'

Dragging back the curtain, she sweeps into the dim interior. A candle flickers to life and Mary smells sweet beeswax which reminds her of her garden, how a hard day's digging in the beds always empties her to the point of exhaustion. She wishes she were back in her garden, her sanctuary, with her hands deep in the warm earth, instead of here, forced to witness the brutal evidence of Thea's ill-used flesh, the very opposite of love freely given.

'I didn't steal it, if that's what you're thinking.' Thea tilts the little candle, causing honey wax to slip down and puddle in the dish. 'It was a gift from my mistress. Indentured, I was, to a man and his wife in St James, gentlefolk. My mistress read me her Lovelace and the man taught me letters. I trusted them but perhaps I was too naïve, for the fever carried them off last year. I – forgive me – started taking clients to save myself from starvation. I had a bad feeling about that man; should have known, when he wouldn't remove the handkin. But I thought he might not want me to see his face. Some men are particular about that.' She scratches the nape of her neck and runs her hand forward over the stubble. 'I should have said no but he seemed gentle and he offered me a pound. When he got me alone, he turned. He was like a wild animal. I stopped wriggling when I realised what he was about. Didn't want my throat cut, but I wish he hadn't taken all my hair with him. I could have sold it myself to the wigmaker, worth more than what he paid me for a few minutes of thrusting.'

Thea lifts her skirts, and Mary forces herself to look closely at the woman's privities. They are unmarked by outward signs of violence, just the usual puffed flesh, a few bruises. Pulling the fabric down, Mary straightens up.

'Do you remember anything else about him? Was he tall? Short?'

Thea shrugs. 'He was of middling height. No taller than you.'

'What did he smell like?'

'Smell like? Like all men around here: like he'd rolled in a dirt bath twenty years ago and never cleaned himself.' Thea smiles grimly. 'Look, he was unremarkable, missus, except that he did whiff a bit of the poppy. When he shaved me, he went about it carefully, as though he were afraid of damage. It's probably the hair he cared about. I thought about not reporting it, but Meg said I ought. In case the hair shows up some place.'

Mary gathers up the examination things. 'I'll pass my findings on to the constable.'

'They won't catch him.'

'They hope to. If you recall anything else, you can find me at the Needle.'

'I have remembered something.' Thea lifts a finger to twist an invisible curl, then frowns and drops her hand. 'Not sure if it's useful. After he shaved me, he said my hair was fine as fleece. Light as a cloud.'

Back home, Alice waits for her on the doorstep.

'Missus Thompson is here,' she whispers, holding out her hand for Mary's cloak and kit bag. 'She's in the parlour – with her husband.'

There is a warning in her voice Mary cannot decipher but she doesn't have to wait long to discover its source. Mister Thompson moves to greet her as she enters the parlour, clutching his hat to his chest. 'Missus Gulliver.' Above his grey suit, the schoolmaster's face is pale and pinched. His wife stands further back, nearer the fireplace, cradling her full belly.

'Good day to you both,' Mary says, peering around him to address her client. 'How are you feeling, Isabel? Well, I hope? The tonic I gave you last week – it did not disagree?'

Isabel shakes her head. 'Not at all, Mary. In fact, the nausea is all but gone.'

'I'm pleased to hear it. And the wind pains?'

Isabel opens her mouth to reply but at a stern look from her husband, falls silent and looks down at the threadbare rug spread across the boards.

'I'm afraid we no longer require your services, Missus Gulliver.'

'Oh?' Mary summons a small smile although she has never felt less like smiling.

The schoolmaster touches the edge of his spotless collar and Mary thinks of poor Isabel's hands, red-raw from all the potato peelings required to clean it each week. 'When my wife's time comes, I've made arrangements for another midwife to attend her. She lives over in Spitalfields, a pious woman, as is her husband. God-fearing, both of them and keep the best company, even if they are Quakers and she only recently deputised.'

The insinuation rests uncomfortably between them. To her embarrassment, Lemuel chooses that moment to arrive home, slamming the front door shut and casting imperiously about, as if he expects a gaggle of servants to dash out and attend him. Alice hurries forward to escort him into the kitchen before he can interrupt. Mary hears him ask her whereabouts, then demand a draught to soothe his aching head. The heat, he says, but she has her suspicions. It seems Mister Thompson, too, is not convinced, his thin lips pressed tight.

'Well,' she says at last, into the awkward silence. 'There seems nothing to say except good luck. And to wish you an easy birth, Missus Thompson.'

Isabel's face breaks into a genuine smile which she hides quickly from her husband. 'Thank you, Mary.'

She follows him out, her elbow tucked into his arm and Mary watches from the stoop as they are swallowed up by the crowds. They will not be the last, she thinks, choking down her dismay. There will be others, if her husband's stories continue to spread. Perhaps this new position with the Bishop offers a sliver of safety – but it could go either way. If the Bishop catches word of Lem's tall tales – if she cannot convince him to believe Lemuel's delusions are just a passing phase – then more of her clients will turn her away. Everything she has worked for is in danger of being crushed under her husband's reckless boots. It's enough to make one laugh – or would be, if she did not feel like crying. In the kitchen, she finds him nursing his head, a drink at his elbow. Alice has left the back door open, presumably to clear out the stale taproom air infusing his clothing. Mary can see the maid in the garden, tossing damp clouts over the branches of a tree.

A bloodshot eye appears though a crack between Lem's fingers. 'Mary? Who was that? Why didn't you come?'

Too angry to reply, she strides past him into the stillroom and drags the curtain across the door. Heavy in her hands, the mortar she pulls towards her is a solid, comforting weight and she tries to banish the self-important face of Mister Thompson by pounding sticks of mallow root to a pulpy paste. Lined on the shelf, the bottles she and Alice cleaned yesterday wait to be refilled. When this receipt is finished, she will pour it into the bronze, square-necked bottle she reserves only for draughts of poppy, since confusing the soporific with something else during a woman's labour might be fatal. A less experienced midwife could easily make such a mistake – something Mister Thompson could not appreciate.

Rummaging through the cupboard, she finds the space where the poppy vial is stored empty. She sets down the pestle and wipes her slick hands on a clout. Where is the thing? Perhaps she pushed it to the back of the cupboard in her haste to get at something else. But the back of the cupboard is bare. *Am I going mad?* she thinks, dropping to her knees, sliding her hand under the bench in case it's rolled away.

A sharp sting on her finger makes her gasp. Withdrawing her hand, she squints into the semi-dark. There is the jar – what remains of it, shards of shattered brown glass glinting amongst the dust. Of the poppy it once contained, there is no sign.

16

'Pass me those hart's-tongue leaves, Bess, and then the pennyroyal,' Missus Clifton says, flicking her fingers with the impatience Bess has come to expect since she's begun her training. A strong smell of larch rises as she stirs the cauldron, the iron base licked by ruby flames. The stench waters Bess's eyes and stings her throat. She inhales deeply through her mouth, brushing damp strands off her face, and turns her attention to the sheaves of bundled herbs on the tabletop. There are at least a dozen kinds, some freshly plucked and still beaded with dew, others so old and dry they are brittle corpses, flaking to bits in her hands. Which one is a hart's-tongue? She tries to concentrate, to recall the diagram in Missus Clifton's botany book. Is hart's-tongue a fern? Or does it grow on green leafy stalks, like shepherd's purse? Why didn't she pay attention when Mam tried to teach her the names? Instead, she has had a rushed education. She has had Susanna thrusting books at her while Missus Clifton is watching, then snatching them away as soon as she falls asleep. She has had brief moments of calm in the garden, digging in the soil, unearthing flowers and roots. But what is the point if she cannot even identify the plant Missus Clifton wants? Her hand hovers above a clump of waxy green leaves, almost certain.

'Quick, now,' Missus Clifton says as Bess hesitates. She has recovered well enough to sit on her stool in the kitchen and order them both about. 'If this stews much longer it won't be fit for anyone but the dog.'

'Not that one,' Susanna snaps, flicking her hand away. 'That's tansy. Do you want the woman to lose her child? Here, missus.' Susanna grasps the bundle on Bess's left and thrusts it into Missus Clifton's hands, before casting Bess a superior look. 'Don't you even know tansy when you see it? I thought your mother was a prodigious herbalist.'

'She is,' Bess says, her temper flaring.

The two girls glare at each other as Missus Clifton tosses the hart's-tongue into the pot. 'Right. Feverfew next.'

Bess quickly assesses the strewn herbs. At the edge of the table, she spies a wilted cutting. The white-ringed flower heads have been lopped away, perhaps to be put to some other use, but she recognises the leaves, shaped a little like those of the parsley plant. Before Susanna has a chance, she snatches up the cutting and holds it out for Missus Clifton. The old woman tosses it, stems and all, into the bubbling broth.

'Thank you, Elisabeth,' she says, and Bess holds herself taller. She waits for Missus Clifton to reel off more herbs, but the old woman instructs them to wash their hands at the pump and then come back when the brew has finished stewing.

'I hear your father's mad.' Susanna hardly waits for Bess to step out into the street after her before she opens her mouth.

Bess, for once, ignores the jibe. Three weeks at Missus Clifton's has taught her how to hold onto her anger, to delay it. Where before she might have snapped a pithy retort, she now nurses a quiet resentment, aware of the power her own silence commands. She has Mam to thank for teaching her that. Since the night at the Louse, interactions with her mother have grown increasingly fraught and frosty. Whole conversations have now been reduced to single words and clipped syllables. There is dignity in silence, in ignoring Susanna's pokings and proddings. It's much more satisfying to see the older girl working herself up into a state, her face growing redder while Bess maintains her calm.

The street is busy, lined with sellers. Holding her skirts away from the filthy gutter, Bess passes a hawker selling Colchester oysters, the scalloped shells and tongue-like flesh glistening wetly in the morning sun. Her stomach squeezes a little at the ripe stench. Who buys oysters in the height of summer? she thinks. The man hefts a dripping creel, his voice chasing after them, 'Fish, fish, fisho! Best belly-timber this side of the water!' Outside a goldsmith's sign, two gentlemen in lace-trimmed frock coats are arguing, their raised voices like a swarm of angry bees, attracting the notice of the shopkeep, who emerges, still wearing his fine, spotless gloves, to shoo them away.

'My father took me to Moorfields to see the lunatics,' Susanna hisses over Bess's shoulder. 'We had to walk under an arch stamped with the likeness of three chained madmen. I saw a woman inside who beat an imaginary dog, and another man who talked to pixies. The porter said for a shilling more he would show us a man in a cell who thought he was a monkey, but Pa said the man was an actor who goes home every night to his bed in Cheapside and the porter should not take advantage of good folks and try to cheat them of their money.'

Bess's head pounds but she refuses to answer. The image of her father rising out of his sickbed returns to her and she feels again the shock of it, like an illness in her bones. Since that dreadful night, she has seen her father a handful of times. His health has improved now, his tremors gone. He is almost back to the way he was before he left, except . . . except he shows no interest in her now. Not that she has much time to see him, thanks to Mam. Bess glowers down at her shoes. He always sleeps late – that hasn't changed – and by the time she gets home, he has already left the house. She hears him return, opens one eye as the candlelight passes under her door. The few times she has managed to catch him alone, he seems distracted, lost in his own world. Avoiding her gaze, he will ask her whether she's come across old belongings, things Mam sold off years ago to pay the household debts. She always shakes her head, but has noticed, with a pang of loss, the disappearance of certain items from her bedroom, including the nautilus shell and the carved-ivory tankard. She comforts herself with the thought that it is better to have him home. Those things never belonged to her, if Pa was alive. She was just keeping them safe for him and now they are back in his possession, where they belong. Best to stay silent, rather than risk Pa's unpredictable moods. No amount of prompting can shift him from his introspection. On a few occasions, she has heard him talking to himself, muttering about scandalous rumours of a liaison between himself and a Lady of the Court, the wife of a tiny Treasurer.

'A violent affection,' he sometimes says, looking disgusted. 'As if she were not six inches high and I a man.' Wisely, Bess said nothing. She knows what shape his fancies take, now. She has been unable to dissuade him of them and ease him back into the routine she used to so enjoy: trips to the docks, stories beside the fire, the resurrection of her favourite fantasy.

At the street pump, she scoops up water from the stone basin and rubs it over her neck and hands, aware of Susanna beside her doing the same. A cluster of stone crows watches from the basin's edge, their cool eyes and sharp beaks intended to deter mice and frogs from jumping in and contaminating the well. Crows are said to remember faces, to have a knack for recalling anyone who has ever thrown a stone or shown them kindness by giving them food. As Bess scrubs herself, she wonders if these little statues have seen Casper pass by. Perhaps he has washed himself at this very basin, running a rag down his neck, squeezing the droplets onto the murky ground while the stone crows gaze impassively at him.

She casts a look of longing down towards the docks. She has seen neither hide nor hair of him since the night of the Louse, but it doesn't mean she hasn't thought of him. Is he still around or has he returned to sea? Remembering the argument with Mam – *forbidden*, she is *forbidden* from seeing him, as if he is a bit of marchpane she is not allowed to touch – she feels her resolve harden. It's my fault, she thinks, that Mam blames him; the danger my idea. She can still feel the imprint of his hand now as she turns hers over, the callused fingers pressed against her skin.

When she can, she will slip down to the docks on her way home and try to see him. So far, she has not had a chance to get away. Mam insists on sending Alice to collect her after her lessons with Missus Clifton are over. Surely Alice won't accompany her back every single day?

Susanna scrubs her hands methodically, rolling up the sleeves of her dress so they don't drag. Under a light sheen of sweat, her skin is milky. Orange hair, frizzier even than Bess's, is crushed under the bonnet she wears everywhere. She would be pretty, if she wasn't so awful. The older girl made it clear from the first hour that she resented having Bess as her competition. She's always ordering Bess about, refusing to show her how things are done and then blaming her when she asks a question. Trapped inside Missus Clifton's house this past week, Bess has often conjured fantasies of watching Susanna fall under the spell of a mysterious malady nobody can cure her of. She brings the image out now to punish Susanna for mentioning Pa, a grin spreading over her face as she pictures Susanna's red curls matted damply to her forehead, her creamy skin disfigured by an eruption of pustules.

'Hurry up,' someone grumbles and Bess, shaken from her reverie, is startled to see a queue snaking behind her, women carrying empty pots and chipped vessels, men wishing to divest themselves of the various stains and filmy powders coating their skin and clothes.

Apologising, she dabs her wet hands on her apron and shuffles out of their way.

'You won't survive long as an apprentice if you don't pay attention, Elisabeth,' Susanna says, adjusting her bonnet and tucking flame-coloured wisps of hair up under its brim.

Bess's patience finally snaps. Rounding on the older girl, she says, 'If I were interested in soliciting the opinions of a notable midwife's apprentice, I wouldn't be seeking them from you, Susanna. From what I hear, you've been a grand disappointment. Why else do you think Missus Clifton hasn't deputised you yet? Why else do you think Elinor handed you to Missus Clifton last May? Nobody else wants you.'

Susanna stares at her, rosebud lips parted in a little O of surprise. Bess pushes past her, wiping her wet palms on her fabric sleeves, making her way back up the street to Missus Clifton's house. A girl selling fruit steps into her path, brandishing a tray of plump orange slices, the jewelled wheels swimming in their sticky juices. Bess's mouth floods as she imagines sucking the orange globes away from the rind. Reaching into the purse hidden in her skirt, she pulls out the shilling Mam gave her in case of trouble. In case of guilt, more like.

'Seville orchards,' the grocery girl says, handing over two slices, wrapped in a twist of paper. 'That's where these are grown.'

Bess doubts very much the girl has any idea where Seville is – she's probably never even seen a map – but she bobs a curtsey anyway and tucks the sweetmeat into her pocket.

Lifting her head, she sees Susanna standing some way down the street, where she left her. The girl's shoulders are slumped, her bonnet dipped forward, the perfect embodiment of abject melancholy.

Bess is tempted to abandon Susanna to her fate, before she remembers that awful night at the Louse, how ashamed she was, how embarrassed. Really, is Susanna any different to those girls at Missus Priest's School, all eager to show off and impress, hoping someone will notice them? Bess found their antics laughable, but these past few weeks have shown her why they behaved the way they did. Their parents did not encourage them to search for meaning beyond a good marriage or a gentlewoman's position in a rich household. Barred from learning about the world outside their own sheltered bubble of London, their smallness of mind tainted every action and every word they spoke, crippling their individuality until they resembled nothing more than a row of poppets all painted by the same dollmaker.

She is about to walk back to Susanna and beg her pardon when the sound of marching comes swiftly up the street. Susanna looks up, confusion writ on her features. The thud of marching boots seems to come from everywhere, surrounding them. The sellers scramble for cover, snatching up their belongings and melting away.

'What's happening?' she asks the grocery girl.

'It's the bakers' guild,' she says. 'The increase in flour prices. They've started early, probably hoping to stop the brigadiers catching word of it.'

'What increase?'

The girl rolls her eyes. 'The Queen's war with the French. They are protesting the soaring cost of flour. Are you daft? Don't you know anything? You should clear out, in case the brigadiers come to put a stop to it. Anyone who lingers will be arrested, or worse.'

Bess hurries back to Susanna, who stands frozen by indecision. She turns a pale, panicked face to Bess. 'What should we do?'

Bess's heart races. To calm herself, she puts her hand into her pocket where she still carries her little talismans. Her mind returns to that day at the docks when she evaded the peddler and Belle's salacious attentions. Stories won't work now, but they can shelter somewhere, wait for the violence to be over.

'We need to hide,' she says. At the end of the street, a plume of dust rises. An army of men appears, blocking the path to Missus Clifton's. Even at this distance, their aprons are visible, as are their weapons – rolling pins and chopping blocks and knives, dazzlingly bright.

Seizing Susanna's hand, Bess drags her down a side street, both of them gagging on the ripe stench of sewage from the open canal. The thunder of feet draws closer and Bess hears mingled voices, shouts. A rat scampers towards them and Susanna shrieks, grasping Bess around the waist, almost toppling her. At the entrance of the alley, Bess sees a bright flash of red streak past; the crimson red of the Queen's brigadiers. Someone has alerted them. Now the sounds of thudding violence and clashing weapons can be heard, shrieks of pain like the screech of gulls over the water.

Bess wheels around. Her stomach contracts. She runs up the alleyway, searching for an open door, an alcove, somewhere they can take shelter until the fight is over. The first door she hammers on is locked, the second too, but the third gives when she applies her weight. Tumbling inside, Bess shouts for Susanna. Together, they heave the door shut and sit against it, breathing in ragged gasps. Bess crouches then stands, pressing her ear against the door to listen to the muffled fighting.

'Missus Clifton will be worried,' Susanna says. 'She would never have let us out if she'd known. What is this place?'

'She hasn't exactly been well,' Bess says. 'I wouldn't blame her if she forgot.' Looking around the dim interior of the room, she says, 'I think it's an old shop.'

Stairs lead down to the recessed shop floor. Old display cabinets hold dusty cushions and blackened sconces protrude from the walls.

Susanna trots down the stairs to join her and smears dirt from a broken cabinet. 'What did they sell here, I wonder?'

'Hosiery.' Bess lifts a wrinkled stocking with one finger, the heel black with mould spores.

Susanna's mouth twists in distaste. 'How long do you think we'll have to stay here?'

'I don't know. I don't want to be arrested. Do you?'

Bess's stomach gives a low rumble. Leaning against a cabinet, she takes out the slices of orange and pierces the rind of one with a thumb, peeling the slice inside out to expose the soft segments.

'Here you are,' she says, holding the other out to Susanna. 'I haven't poisoned it.'

Susanna hesitates, then takes the gift. 'Thank you.'

The first bite is like warm summer after a hard frost. Each suck melts a little of Bess's fear. Searching out the lumps of stubborn pulp with her tongue, she swallows the tiny globes, lost in the purity of a moment's pleasure. A few pips stick to the top of her mouth; she spits them out and sees Susanna do the same.

'You look different when you smile,' Bess says.

Susanna makes a face. 'Did Missus Clifton really say that about me?'

Bess frowns, reluctant to answer. 'Even if it is true, I shouldn't have said it.'

'You don't know what it's like.' Susanna glares at the little pips. 'What if I make the wrong choice? These are real women, real babies. My sisters and I used to play midwives when we were small, but this isn't a game. I never thought it would be this difficult.'

'Surely Missus Clifton advises you?'

Susanna shakes her head. 'She always says it's up to me to learn. One day, I'll have to care for women on my own, so I have to think through each choice carefully or else I'll be risking the woman's life and must live with the consequences.'

'No decision at all is still a decision,' Bess says. 'Doing nothing might be worse than making a choice.'

Susanna's eyes slide sideways towards her. 'You seem to know a lot about it, for someone who's only ever seen one birth. Anyway.' She sniffs. 'I've already failed to impress her, so it little matters. Missus Elinor is such a shrew. My friend Catherine was apprenticed to her before she moved away to another parish; she said Missus Elinor made her scrub the floor and clear out the hearth and cook for her whole family, in addition to all her normal duties. You're lucky if Missus Clifton thinks you're worth training. You could do much worse.' She pauses, suddenly shy. 'Did – did your mam not wish to train you, though?'

'Mam doesn't take on apprentices or deputies.'

'Why not?'

Bess played with the stringy coil of peel. 'She just doesn't. Although perhaps she'll take one on, when Pa is back to full health. If he gets another ship or opens another surgery.'

They fall silent, lost in their own thoughts.

'I shouldn't have said that about your pa,' Susanna says, eventually.

Bess shrugs. 'It's only what everyone else is saying. Although it's not true, I'll have you know. He's not mad, only unwell.' Bess wonders how to divert Susanna from the uncomfortable truth. 'He'll be back to himself soon and then maybe he'll go back to being a ship's surgeon.'

Susanna nods, worldly wise although not perceptive enough to unpick Bess's lie. 'A surgeon is a more useful profession than most,' she says, gravely. 'What a shame they don't allow girls to be surgeon's apprentices.'

Pins and needles run up and down Bess's legs. 'They don't, do they?' she says. This is the truth, then. She feels the weight of it smother the last of her hope. Susanna cannot know how her words have wounded her.

Susanna's eyebrows contract. 'Of course not! Can you imagine it? Can you imagine what men would do to women on board a ship, nowhere else for them to run to?'

'Pa said I could,' she says bleakly. 'He always said I could train as his apprentice when I was old enough and then we'd go to sea.'

Susanna smiles incredulously. 'But you did not believe him?'

Bess doesn't answer.

Susanna's smile slowly fades. 'Bess, nobody could convince the guild of Barber Surgeons to allow such a thing.'

'I know that now,' Bess says quickly. 'I was young, then. I thought Pa might be able to. He's a good storyteller.' Even as she says it, Bess knows she is clutching desperately at her own myth.

Susanna shakes her head. ''Tis utterly impossible,' she says with finality.

They wait in the old shop for another hour and then cautiously emerge. Outside, the street is deserted. The sun has burned off most of last night's rain, allowing a crust to form over the shallowest puddles, mud stirred up by dozens of feet. A sticky patch of blood attracts the flies. The girls hurry back to Missus Clifton's house, where Susanna picks up a pinecone from a stack tucked discreetly outside the door and scrapes the mud off her shoes. The interior of the house is sweetly scented and Bess is glad to be back, away from the smell of blood and earth. Missus Clifton hobbles out to check on them, exclaiming over their soiled clothes and dirty faces.

'You'll have to stay here until Alice comes, Bess,' she says. 'Everyone will be indoors now, at least until the brigadiers are gone.'

She tells the girls to go upstairs and clean the examination room. Bess likes the examination room; she likes studying the tapestries on the walls depicting childbed scenes from *The Book of Common Prayer*, the way they glow warmly in the light from the big open windows. Susanna hands her a clean apron to tie over her mud-spattered skirt. It falls all the way to her hem and hides the stains.

'Missus Clifton is expecting a well-to-do client tomorrow morning,' Susanna explains. She leads Bess to the linen press and piles sweet-smelling sheets into her arms. They drape the sheets over a chaise and Susanna plumps the pillows, piling them on an armchair.

'For elevation,' she says.

'Elevating what?'

Susanna rolls her eyes, but she takes the time to explain, something she would not have done before their traded vulnerabilities. Bess is told to place the tapestry-covered footstool near the chaise for the woman to rest her feet on while the examination takes place, and Susanna flicks attar of roses into the corners of the room, the smell reminding Bess of Mam's garden. The Fuller's earth crumbles in her hands when she tips it out, a little dune of clay clinging to the lines of her palm. She scatters it across the hearth as Susanna chatters on about the confinements she has attended, difficult ones stretching through two dawns and three dusks, easy ones over and done with in less time than it takes to bring butter against the dash. Their earlier exchange has unlocked something in Susanna, who now treats Bess as worthy of conversation.

When Alice comes to collect her, Bess is surprised to find she doesn't want to go. Susanna's bright way of chattering reminds her of Johnny. As they hurry along the roads to be home before nightfall, she remembers what Susanna said about Pa, the sheer impossibility of him taking her to sea. But it's Mam, not Pa, she blames so she ignores her mother's enquiries about her day and runs upstairs to see if her father is home.

17

Standing on the threshold of Richard's offices in Fleet Street, Mary wishes she had chosen differently. She wishes she was not coming to see Richard after his return from the north to consult him about Lemuel but as a wife visiting her own beloved husband, the man who shares her hopes and dreams. Her cheeks burn as she pushes open the door of his offices, last night's dream still thrumming in her head.

For as long as she can remember, her dreams have been vivid, the day's events unravelling while she sleeps. Her mother believed in omens, portents; she viewed dreams as proof of God's wonder, an open path of communication between herself and the divine. Mary, ever practical, has long been convinced of the opposite. To her, dreams are merely a way of processing what has occurred. There is no secret meaning, no hidden message. Yet since the night of the Louse, she has been unable to shake the feeling that her dreams are more reliable than good solid earth. Each night she has dreamed of wonders. Cabinet drawers bursting with bones and old relics, exotic plants and stones whose colours shift from blue to pink to scarlet, shot through with shimmering flames. Sometimes, she dreams of sheep no bigger than her fist. They trot about her husband's heels, bleating for their mothers, the smell of greasy wool tickling her nose. One night, she dreams she is dancing with her husband's jacket, being swept around the room like a gallant with his bride, but there's nothing to hold onto so she stumbles, clutching at the sleeves, a hollow emptiness where his hands should be. There is no accounting for these dreams, except to suggest perhaps that the stain of Lem's return has driven her to a frustration she cannot display to the outside world. Hidden, her confusion plays out each evening in a series of disturbing and sometimes frightening sequences which remain so fragmented she cannot guess what they are trying to tell.

Last night, though, she experienced a dream so real it took her minutes after waking to understand where she was and how old and what had become of her life. After writing a full report of Thea's injuries for the constable, she went to bed and dreamed she was lying in the garden. It was night time, the moon a glowing orb. The air hummed with bees as if it were day time and the ants were busy at work. She heard them chewing, the rhythmic chomping as they broke down old leaves and trees for the earthworms. Strange flowers bloomed overhead, exploding white petals and yellow pollen. Everything felt new and sacred, a different world to the one that came before. Suddenly, she was aware of a presence, someone standing in the deepest shadows. For a moment, she was afraid. But then Richard was beside her, cupped by the earth and naked as a newborn. He filled her hands with his own and kissed her, his lips gently parted. Warmth spread, as if the cold moonbeams were the sun's rays, bringing her to life. When she woke, she was shaking, every inch of her more alive than she had felt in months, maybe years.

She knows what the dream meant but that doesn't mean she will act on it. She has lived her life observing the rules and to step over the boundaries of propriety would cost her everything. And yet . . .

He looks up as she blunders in, a smile slowly eclipsing his puzzled features. He is never cross to see me, she thinks. He doesn't order me away or tell me my imagination has run riot. During the weeks since she discovered the whereabouts of her missing wedding ring, Lemuel has denied all her enquiries, turning doubts into weapons he slings in her direction whenever something she says veers too close to outright accusation. Each day sees another item spirited off to some unknown location. She has hidden the most valuable things in the buttery but even the food store is not entirely safe from her husband's pilfering fingers. A man-sized mouse has crept into Mary's home to nibble at her carefully stored victuals and gnaw through her reserves. Alice says nothing during the day but each night she and Mary count the losses between them – a cake here, a few coins there, a missing lace collar Mary had hoped to save for Bess's dowry. The ledger book sees more use now than the family Bible, its margins scribbled over with handwritten notes that reflect the true state of their dwindling possessions. Richard would never subject her to such abuse. But it's not just the valuables which have brought her to Richard's door; there are other, darker shadows she cannot banish without help and Alice is too young and powerless to advise her.

'I brought you a sleeping tonic,' she tells him, lifting the bottle. 'One spoonful at night, two if your cough has worsened. Has it worsened? Oh – I'm sorry,' she says, catching sight of a young, well-dressed woman sitting in a baize chair. 'I didn't realise you had a visitor. Forgive me, I will show myself out.'

Richard rises from his desk. 'Missus Baker was just leaving.' He escorts the woman through the door, his hand nudging the small of her back to guide her. 'I'll be in touch within the month, Missus Baker. Again, you have my condolences. Your husband was a fine gentleman.'

He ushers her out into the noise and clamour of Fleet Street. Before the door closes, Mary sees a footman help the woman climb into a landau. The craft wobbles off, rolling through potholes, and Richard, turning back, strips off his peruke and tosses it onto a stand. He looks tired and weather-worn. The light shines on the grizzled flesh of his cheeks and the grey peruke has a greasy, unkempt appearance, all bedraggled shag like the coat of a dog kept outside in the rain.

Easing himself into a chair, he runs a hand along the side of his unshaved face and indicates she should take the chair opposite. She perches primly on it, unable to meet his eye, for each time she does, her cheeks flush.

'Here is the tonic, Richard,' she says, holding it out, wishing he would take it and dismiss her, although of course he will not.

'Never a greeting?' he says, pretending to pout. 'No God give you good day, dear Richard? You just burst in and get straight to business?'

'I didn't burst in,' she says, embarrassed to be caught out. 'You wrote.' After a long moment, she says, 'Missus Baker dresses very fine, for a widow.'

'You think so?' Leaning back in his chair, he stretches his arms over his head. 'I did not observe –'

'Look, she has forgotten her glove.' Mary peels it off the chair, pristine white, scented with jessamy butter. She half expects Richard to cradle it carefully when she hands it to him, but he merely slaps it in a drawer for safekeeping.

'It's good to see you,' he says, meeting her gaze over the polished timber desk. Is he aware, she wonders, of her tingling skin? 'I'm glad you came. I felt uncomfortable going straight to you. Wasn't sure how Lem would feel about it. Has he forgiven me for that last fight? Mentioned me at all?'

'He has asked after you a few times but only so that he might talk about his travels, his ... small impossibilities.' In the pause which follows, she picks at her own gloves, noting the stains and creases. So very different to Missus Baker's. She has never been able to keep her gloves clean, not in her line of work. 'I wonder what Missus Baker's washerwoman uses,' she says aloud. 'To get stains out.'

'I can ask her for you,' Richard says.

'She comes often, I imagine,' Mary says. Somehow she cannot stop herself. It's the dream, she thinks. Just the dream making you feel this way.

Richard inclines his head towards his shoulder. 'Missus Baker's husband was a merchant,' he says, slowly. 'He passed away yesterday.'

'And you accuse *me* of being business-like.'

Richard spreads his hands. 'Her father is a friend. He advised her to come since he is expecting the husband's family to contest the will and leave her nothing. Never too early for an opinion, is it? Have I done something wrong?'

She swallows down a retort. 'Not at all. How was Chichester?'

'Cold, same as always.' He pretends to shiver. 'I thought Lem might have come with you.'

'I wanted to speak to you alone. There's something I haven't told you, about his association with an unsavoury gentleman. A man I hope we will have nothing further to do with, however you know Lem. I'm concerned he has taken up . . . the poppy.'

'Poppy? Opium?'

'Yes.' She sets the elixir down on the desk between them, and it shimmers in the sunbeam, lacquered bronze like a beetle's back. 'When I went to make a draught last week, I discovered my supplies were missing. No more poppy in the house, in addition to the usual takings. He goes out for hours each night and returns home witless. I thought it was drink at first but now I wonder if it isn't something else, something worse. Whatever it is, he won't own the truth of it and so we walk around on eggshells, trying to appease his moods.'

Richard is silent. Refusing to look at him, she looks instead at the street through the window. The stationers and booksellers are plying their wares, the rise and fall of their voices a great rustling tide carried through the casement.

Rising to his feet, Richard rounds the desk and drops to his haunches so they are the same height. 'What can I do to help?' he says, regarding her with those familiar hazel eyes.

She shrugs. 'What can any of us do? I will not store any more poppy in the house.'

'You should confront him.'

She scoffs. 'When has that ever worked? He'll just deny the truth or come up with some excuse. Besides, I have no real evidence, only suspicions.'

'Shall I speak to him? Force a confession?'

'I rather think that would make things worse.'

Without warning, Richard launches to his feet. 'God, he is a fool. Everything he has – a family, a second chance – and he throws it away, for what? A few nights of bliss? Strange dreams? He was always chasing something. I thought he might settle down once he was married.' He pauses to look at her. 'It's perhaps why – why I didn't fight harder when I found out you'd married. I should have, clearly. I always wondered if he purposely forgot to invite me to the wedding or whether . . . whether it was merely an oversight, as he claimed.'

'What would you have done?' she says. 'If it wasn't?' In her mind, she is lying in her garden, his arm wound around her.

'Well, I would have . . . I would have asked him if he thought it was wise. Whether you were well suited. You barely knew each other. It was a hasty decision and I knew his family would disapprove . . .'

An uncomfortable silence spreads between them. Of course, she did not discover until later that they'd expected Lemuel to marry a woman of means who could provide him with the lifestyle to which he aspired. If Richard had married her, would they have still disapproved? A solicitor is not a surgeon, he has not the status or the financial backing. Passion and a desire to help people guided Richard to law. Lem's family have never understood why such traits may be valuable. All they've ever grasped is how to value things in pounds and pence. She is a fool, just as her father once said.

'Why did you never marry?' she says, softly. 'You had ample opportunity. Aside from the charitable offer you made me, were there others? All those journeys; you must have encountered women who were a suitable match. Why didn't you consider starting a family of your own?'

He holds her gaze for so long she cannot mistake the deep welling of emotion. 'I did,' he says at last, straightening up and glancing away. 'I did consider it. But marriage like that – well, it's just words on paper, Mary. A transaction, the illusion of love. It isn't . . . real, not unless you choose to make it so. And I have you and Bess and Johnny. I refuse to make a pretence of my feelings or risk hurting someone.'

His feelings. She realises she is shivering although the office is warm with sunshine and his unwavering loyalty.

'I brought you something,' he says, to ease the tension. 'A gift, from Chichester.' Opening a desk drawer, he passes her a thimble, small and delicate, made of porcelain, decorated with strands of painted dogwood. She rolls it on her palm, her sombre mood lifted slightly by the shared joke.

'Thought you'd appreciate it. I know how much you hate sewing. I was rather hoping to find a book on botany, though. To replace the *Theatrium Botanicum*.'

'Richard, I don't need your gifts. Besides, I memorised every page. If I close my eyes, I see the woodcuts.'

'Well, nobody *needs* gifts. But they can help, they can act as reminders that you're not alone. Sometimes we need reminding.'

Mary shifts on her seat, still rolling the thimble, its progress leaving tiny indentations over her skin. 'Missus Baker may be in need of a new husband,' she says, stumbling over the words.

'She may be, in time,' he says, carefully. 'But she will have a fight on her hands first to secure her widow's portion. I daresay that is her concern.'

'You could do far worse, Richard. With a wife like that.'

He pauses in the act of straightening his cuff. 'You doubt my honourable intentions towards Missus Baker? You, who would not even consider me as a suitor?'

'You know Bess was in a delicate frame of mind.'

Richard's gaze is like a hot blade slicing her to the core. She feels faint and insubstantial, as though the dream of warm desire is not a dream at all but a wakeful fantasy. In the heavy silence which follows, Mary's thoughts return again and again to Lemuel. He will ruin us, she thinks. Unable to bear Richard's scrutiny, she stands, ready to leave.

'Stay a little while,' Richard begs, and he looks so solemn she finds she cannot refuse. He runs out to fetch some chocolate, returning with two dishes of swirling brown liquid. They sip quietly, avoiding each other's gaze.

'We never used to be like this,' she says finally. 'We were fun. When did we stop being fun?'

'I believe it was around the time you married Lem.'

Mary looks up to find him watching her. 'That was a long time ago,' she says, gently.

'A lifetime ago,' he agrees. 'Several. I don't blame you. You weren't to know. In fact, I blame myself. Every day.'

The chocolate grounds are bitter on her tongue, the liquid still warm. She licks the excess off her lips while Richard lounges in his chair, closing his eyes against the exhaustion of travel.

'Tell me the news about town,' he says, and they move on to safer topics: the bakers' protest; the spike in taxes; the rapist gone quiet, perhaps sailed away on a ship, never to be heard of again. When she brings up the Chamberlens' iron forceps, Richard sits up, alert.

'I heard snatches of it last month at the club,' he admits. 'Chamberlen was there himself, trying to convince people of the benefits. He was laughed out of the club but I do not think that will dissuade him.'

'He is an aberration,' Mary declares. 'We must fight his ignorant claims.'

Years ago, it was the same fight but her mother took up the sword then, protesting with Anne Clifton in the streets, badgering the Bishop to protect their rights, the rights of every woman who needed access to a midwife. Wheels turn, she thinks, seasons change, babies come and go, uncurling like little fern-fronds, delighting or tormenting their parents in equal measure. But there are always men waiting to destroy what the sisterhood represents. God be praised for the Bishop. A few days ago, he sent a note asking her to come and dine with him, to officiate the handover between Anne Clifton and herself.

Draining the last of the chocolate, she pushes back her chair. At the doorway, Richard scans the street, as if looking for someone, and Mary wonders – ridiculous to be jealous – if he is hoping Missus Baker is on her way back to reclaim her glove.

But the object of his scrutiny is only a passing carriage he hails down, slipping the driver some coins before she can protest. He swings open the door, ushering her inside. She hears him speak to the driver, then his face appears in the window.

'Let me know how you get on with the Bishop,' he says. 'Keep an eye on Lem. Anything you find, anything at all suspicious, you must inform me. If he wants me to come and see him . . . well, I will. He is still my cousin, I suppose. One can't choose their family the way they choose their partners. You know, don't you,' he says, laying his hand on the windowsill, 'that I would have chosen you, if he hadn't.'

She stares at him, shocked into silence by the frank admission.

'I've spent a lifetime atoning for that journey to Nottingham,' he says, his voice low so the coachman cannot hear. 'All I can do now is offer my help. If Bess or Johnny need me, you know I will stand by them. I'll stand by you, no matter what happens.'

She cannot speak. Their hands brush, little fingers side by side. Before she can recover her wits, the carriage starts off and she has no choice but to sink into the plump cushions, a luxury she should really have fought harder to refuse.

18

'I knew your grandmother, Elisabeth.'

Bess looks up from the handful of chervil she is stripping, startled by Missus Clifton's admission. The old woman sits on the sofa, supervising the two girls as best she can under the dark cloud of a headache. Of late, she has taken to rambling, imparting stories to the young women which are, Bess must admit, as interesting as Pa's tales although they take a far more circuitous route.

'Mam never talks about her,' Bess says, impressed by the confidence Missus Clifton has shown by telling her. 'She was a midwife, too, wasn't she?'

Missus Clifton nods. She sips a tonic made of province roses and wine, the smell overwhelmingly sweet and pleasant. Bess wants to lay her head down and fall asleep. 'She was one of the best women I've ever known. Until she went mad.'

Bess's fingers still. Susanna, sitting opposite her, sits up straighter.

'Mad?' she repeats.

Missus Clifton nods. 'That's right. Not many people know what really happened to Liz Burton, except for me.'

'Please tell us, missus.' Bess sets down the stalks.

'Yes, tell us,' Susanna echoes. 'We won't tell a soul. We cross our hearts, don't we Bess?'

'Well . . .' Missus Clifton hesitates. 'I suppose it can't hurt now. Better you hear the truth of it than some gossip's embroidery of the facts. Wicked, some of the things they said about your grandmother at the time.'

Bess tries to imagine her grandmother's face but can only picture her mother. 'What did they say?'

'Well, it started in winter, the year your mam turned thirteen. Winter was always a hard time for your grandmother, because she couldn't go out in her garden. It was set behind the hosiery shop your mam was raised in. If you think your mother's garden is an eyeful, you should have seen your grandmother's. Plants were her joy. Plants and babies. That winter was cold. The birds froze in their nests.' Missus Clifton fingers the rim of the goblet, caught up in memory.

'Your grandmother fell ill. I suppose it was hardly surprising, all that running around she did, birthing babies in the middle of the night. So, she got sick and she had to stay in her room for days, weeks on end or risk it getting worse. Your mam looked after her; your mam has always been an old soul, old before her time. The healing power was strong in her, even when she was young. Anyway, Liz started talking to herself in her room. Then she died.'

Bess's stomach flips over. Death doesn't bother her, as a rule, but she feels sorry for her mother, losing Liz like that. She wonders if that's why Mam never speaks about it.

'What kind of things did she say?' Bess says, at last.

Missus Clifton looks down, afraid to meet Bess's eye.

'Oh, all sorts of things,' she says, vaguely.

'You said you would tell us.'

''Tisn't wise to speak ill of the dead.'

'Please, Missus Clifton,' says Susanna.

'Please,' Bess echoes. She imagines her mother kneeling by the bed of Grandmother Liz, the woman for whom she was named. Such a strange feeling it is, to know someone else possessed your name and died before you were even born to claim it. She imagines Mam taking Grandmother Elisabeth's hand and smoothing the hair off her forehead, the way she always does when Bess is ill.

'First it was the washstand,' Missus Clifton says, breaking the silence. 'Then it was the bolts of cloth stored in the corner, the spider weaving its web in the rafters. A china dog your Grandpa had brought her. Your mam's poppets.'

'Her dolls?'

Missus Clifton nods slowly. 'At first, she was secret about it. Your mam thought she was just talking to herself. But she wasn't. She was chattering to those objects in her room; she thought each of them had a spirit trapped inside it, the soul of a little lost baby who never had a chance to draw breath.'

'Oh, how awful!' Susanna cries, but Bess keeps her thoughts to herself. The chervil makes her palms tingle; she scratches them, nervously. What a terrible loss for Mam to suffer, watching her mother's wits disintegrate.

'What happened when Mam found out?'

'Well, it was gradual, you see. At first, your mam wanted to believe her. She tried to believe her. There are so many wondrous things in this world if we only open our eyes to them. That's something we know, as midwives. That's one of the secrets. Who knows how a baby is really made? We know the facts, of course, the unchangeable truth about men's and women's bodies, what is needed to create a child, the seed and stones. But how does God choose which souls will live and which ones will not? That, we don't have any answers to.

'It took your mam a while to figure out that Elisabeth wasn't just talking to herself. One day, your mam was outside the room when she heard Elisabeth laughing and chattering. Your mam went in, thinking she must have a friend, a visitor. But there was nobody there. That's when she knew your grandmother was more ill than she imagined. She wanted to believe, you see, that things could improve, but in that moment she realised that it wasn't just your grandmother's body that was run down. It was her mind too – weakened by that illness.'

'The illness that killed her,' Bess says, softly.

''Twasn't the illness.' Missus Clifton pressed her lips together.

Bess's eyes widen.

The silence deepens. Missus Clifton sighs. 'About six weeks after the whole business started, your mam was woken by a terrible scream. Downstairs, she found her mother – God forgive me for repeating this – entirely naked, covered in burns. She'd thrown herself into the fire.'

Bess gasps, and Missus Clifton nods, her dark eyes moist.

'Poor, poor Elisabeth. And poor Mary. She nursed her mother through the next few days but nothing could stem the infection. Your grandmother's death robbed your mother of her youth. And your grandfather was no help. He drank away his grief and then he turned to the poppy your ma stored in her apothecary chest. They call opium the milk of paradise.

I should have welcomed such sweet dreams myself at different times in my life – after my husband died – and I'm sure your mam wished she could do that after your grandmother's death, just drift away . . . but she couldn't. Somebody had to keep the shop running and ensure the bills were paid. Eventually, your grandfather got himself back together and things went on, but your mother was always different after that. She took her midwife's oath very seriously when she came to work with me. I deputised her. And you know the rest.'

Missus Clifton yawns. 'Fetch me a blanket, Susanna,' she says.

As Bess watches Susanna carry out the task, she remains outwardly calm but her thoughts spin. Now she knows why Mam is so upset by Pa's wild claims. She saw poor little Mam, younger than Bess is now, wanting to believe that everything was all right, that washstands could talk, that babies' souls could inhabit timber, porcelain, iron. Wanting to hide it all away and keep their family safe from gossip. Then tragedy had struck and proved how impossible this might be.

No wonder Ma has tried to shield Bess from Pa's strange stories! She is still haunted by her own mother's madness. But Pa needs help. It's too late for Liz but Pa can still be saved. Like her grandmother, he believes what he is saying. If Bess can prove to him, once and for all, that his grand fancies of an island where three hundred cooks slave over his every meal are just the tattered remnants of an illness . . . I must find Casper, she thinks. Find him and ask him to help. He could bring back the proof they need to convince Pa his delusions are merely fancies, a trick of the mind. But first she must convince Pa to do something for her.

*

'Your mam is dining with the Bishop tonight,' Alice tells her as they walk home through the dim twilight. Bess is glad.

Supper is quiet, just the three of them. Pa lounges on his chair at the head of the table, slurping his soup, his legs spread so wide Bess has to curl herself over her bowl to avoid touching his knee. His skin has lost its parched look, although the back of his neck is still beet red from the journey he makes to the tavern each afternoon, during the hottest part of the day. He doesn't ask her any questions, but Bess has greater troubles than her father's lack of interest in her apprenticeship. When he retires to his room, she waits for Alice to start clearing away before sneaking up after him.

'Pa?'

He pulls the door open slowly, his eyes blank, almost trance-like. Bess swallows her nerves. He has been like this all evening, staring into the middle distance, pale eyes fixed on the wall as if he can see beyond it to the sky outside.

'I need you to make a map, Pa,' she says. 'Like when I was small.'

'A map? What kind of map?'

'A map of the island,' she says. 'I could go and search for it. Prove it exists.'

Her father brightens. 'Oh, yes!' he says. 'A map. I will make one. But I must trust you, Bess, not to share it with anyone. And you must run an errand for me. 'Tis very important.'

Bess waits, reminded of the old days when he used to send her from his study on missions to sneak him food from the pantry. He glances past her down the hallway to make sure Alice isn't listening.

'I need you to deliver a message to my friend.' His breath tickles her ear, smelling of rotten things and broth.

Bess's stomach swoops. She watches him hunch over his writing desk to scribble a note and shrinks a little when he presses it eagerly into her hand. But she is a good daughter and God has brought her father home to her, so she slips downstairs into the hallway and darts across to the closet when Alice isn't looking. Pulling on her boots, she unlatches the door and runs down the street, keeping to the middle where the shadows cannot touch her.

The old woman who tends the taproom at the Louse eyes her as she enters and Bess lifts her chin, trying to stem her fear.

'Is Mister Willems here?' she says. 'I've a message for him.'

The woman's eyes run up and down her body. 'I bet you do,' she says, curling her lip. 'He's downstairs with some friends of yours.' She raises an eyebrow suggestively and Bess's heart swells. Casper, she thinks. Is it possible he's here, that she might speak to him again? She feels less afraid, thinking that he might be there to protect her.

'Let me do the talking,' he said last time. 'You stay behind.'

But Piet had seen at once through her disguise.

Awkwardly, she descends the slippery stairs into the dark parlour below.

Tonight, the space is choked with bodies. Some kind of gathering, she thinks, fear gnawing at her stomach like an animal's scrabbling claws. She is jolted to see women at the centre of the group, reclining in the sailors' laps. She recognises the bawds from her day at the docks – Belle and her friends – although tonight they are demure as cats with their claws sheathed. Bess positions herself so that she is hidden from their sight; she has no wish to speak to Belle again although if she sees the girl in blue – Meg? – she will warn her to run, too. Piet himself sits alone on one of the sagging armchairs, smoking his pipe and blowing smoke rings at the ceiling. Spying her, his eyes blaze and he pushes past the sailors until he reaches her, not bothering to disguise his hunger.

'I've been wondering when your father would send for me,' Piet says, grinning his crooked grin. 'I like you better in skirts, Miss Gulliver.' His accent is murkier than Casper's, as if he has spent so long away from his homeland he has forgotten where he came from. She shrinks back as his gaze flicks past her. Casper isn't here, she realises. She is all alone.

Bess swallows. 'Pa wanted me to give you this note.' She pulls it from her skirt pocket, overcome with a sudden longing for her old smock. The way Piet's eyes follow the shape of her body makes her uneasy.

He takes it from her, letting his fingers rest on hers until she pulls away. Laughing, he squints down at the words. 'You know what this says?' he asks her, looking up. She shakes her head. 'Didn't read it? So you are the girl your father said you were.'

'What kind of girl is that?' she says, her voice a whisper.

Piet smiles, but doesn't answer. Bess fights the urge to run.

Holding the note out, he says, 'He asks if I can send him some medicine because he is unwell.'

Bess swallows against the hard lump in her throat. If Pa wanted medicine, why didn't he just ask Mam? Why did he send her here? That sweet smell again, the opium haze. Bess jams one foot against the other, longing to be gone.

Piet glances back at his companions and then when she doesn't reach for the note, tosses it onto the floor. He touches her hair and she recoils.

Piet laughs. 'Tell your father I'm awaiting a shipment but it won't be here for another day or so. When it arrives, I'll bring him some medicine myself. The Needle, isn't it?'

'Very good, sir,' she says. She prays this is the end of their exchange, that she can go. But when she tries to leave, he steps in front of her.

'Your father tells me you'd like to go to sea, Bess. Is that true?'

Bess stares at him, confusion and disbelief battling for control. How could Pa tell her secret to this awful man? Has he been laughing at her behind her back, laughing with Piet and girls like Belle? She feels sick. Right now, she would gladly be anywhere but here. She would even take the birthing chamber, a place of blood and evil smells and pain. She has managed to avoid the place, Elinor seeing to the actual births while Missus Clifton's leg heals. But she would take it now over this foul-smelling room and the company of her father's strange friend.

'I look forward to discussing your plans with you,' he says. 'I'm sure we have more in common than you could guess.'

'Piet?' says someone and Bess's skin tightens as Belle appears, her eyes silver in the firelight. 'I know this tulip,' she says. 'Have you come to join us, sweetheart? Oh –' Her eyes flick over Bess's new gown. 'I like your dress. You look quite the little woman, now. Stay a while, why don't you? Stay and finish the job.'

Bess turns and runs, hearing their laughter ring out.

Pa is pacing in his room when she returns. 'Did you get it? Did you, sweet Bess? I've drawn your map. See? Here it is. I'll give you the map, you give me the medicine.' He presses a folded piece of parchment into her fingers. 'Now, you.'

Bess shakes her head. 'He didn't have any,' she says, wretched, still panting. 'I'm sorry, Pa.'

There is a pause and then shooting pain as Pa seizes her elbow. She cries out, trying in vain to shake him off.

'What do you mean?' he demands. 'No medicine? Are you lying, Bess? Are you hiding it?'

'No!' she shouts. The unfairness of his accusation is a stinging blow. 'Of course I didn't. Pa, how could you send me there?'

His face closes up at her demand for an explanation. She hears the splash of a pan dropping into water in the kitchen below. Pa looms above her and although she wants to look up at him, she is too focused on trying to free herself from his grasp.

'You're hurting me,' she says.

'If I am, it's all for the good,' he barks. 'You ought to learn some discipline. You ought to know not to touch things that don't belong to you. First, my books and now the medicine.'

Bess flinches. 'Pa – I didn't – I would never –'

Footsteps sound on the stairs.

'Bess?' she hears Alice call, her tone cautious. 'You up there?'

Without warning, Pa releases her. Shoving her roughly into the hallway, he slams the door in her face. Her arm is still aching as she turns to Alice, the maid's face full of concern.

'Are you well? I heard shouting.'

Bess's breath hitches and she has to clamp down her horror at Pa's betrayal. What can Alice do, if she tells her? What if Pa sends the maid from the house, banishes her? His word is the law. For the first time, she realises how Mam must have felt those times when Pa mocked her or belittled her for thwarting his demands. This is how it feels to be made small.

'Come down to the kitchen,' Alice says, still eyeing her as if she is a plate in danger of breaking. 'Come down and keep me company.'

19

On the boat journey to Fulham to see the Bishop, Mary fiddles with the collar of her dress and tries to keep her shoes clear of the mud swirling in the bottom of the boat. Dusk has fallen and a breeze shivers through the flowering horse chestnut bordering the river. Thankfully, the boatman has interpreted her wish for silence. They glide along, the man content to keep his own counsel while she stares past the prow at the darkening curve of the river. They pass Westminster and the Chelsea Physic Garden, shrouded in shadows. A breeze breaks the water's surface and shivers across her bare skin, hinting at cooler days and nights to come. At the stairs, he offers her his gnarled hand and she steps over the watery divide into the Bishop's world. It is the first time she has visited Fulham Palace. When she knocks at the servants' entrance, her body half-concealed beneath a creeping wisteria, a frowning maid in a perfectly starched cap and apron answers the door.

'Visitors to see the Bishop use the main entrance,' she scolds and Mary, more familiar with the back stairs of houses, with the darkness that leads into a stuffy bedchamber, feels foolish for assuming otherwise. The woman takes her around to the front of the house via a gravelled path and points to the door but will not go in.

Mary watches her disappear through the wisteria, half-wishing she could join her. Her nerves are singing. What if she makes a mistake? Anne has done her best to prepare her, going over the Bishop's favourite topics and the best method to approach him. *Always smile, never give him the impression you are anything but compliant. Then, if you must stand your ground, he will be less likely to disagree.* But there are so many things which she feels unprepared for, so many ways in which a conversation could go subtly wrong. Her stomach gurgles; she was too nervous earlier to risk a bite of pottage. She tries hard not to think of what might happen should the Bishop dislike her. Will he grant Hugh Chamberlen what he seeks? And what if he has heard the rumours about Lemuel and his wild stories?

Nervously, she adjusts her bodice, fiddling with the neckline so only the slightest hint of skin shows through. Abigail Sparrow, recovered from her ordeal, sewed this gown at her request, as Anne said she must be decently attired to dine with the man who controls the future of their professional lives.

'Light as air,' Abigail Sparrow said wistfully as she fitted the gown to Mary's body a few days ago and held up the looking glass. 'You are so handsome, Mary.'

The woman in the speckled glass looked like someone else and despite her lack of interest in clothing, Mary couldn't help but admit the gown suited her well. Delicate silver scrolls unfurl like scudding clouds across the taffeta skirt and matching bodice. Fine shoes, made from soft blue kid, peep beneath the skirt's hem. What if she slops food down her fine dress? What if her undignified manners give the game away? Perhaps it's foolish to think a dress can change you or your destiny. There's no magic woven into the filaments which can alter who she is: a commoner, the daughter of a cunning woman and a hosier. But can she rise above it? Hasn't all her hard work, her training and sacrifice led her here, to this fine house and the Bishop's company? Lemuel would disagree. He looked less than impressed when she knocked on his door to tell him where she was going.

'Off to butter up the Bishop?' he said, his mouth turned down, sour. He still wore the cream shirt from last night, stained down the front with splashes of wine. 'You know they will see through you. They'll never respect you. Surgeons know best, everyone agrees.'

'Not the Bishop. He is loyal to the midwives.'

'The Bishop is loyal to God. And God cannot be won over by fancy clothes. He is immune to female flattery.'

With supreme effort, she ignored the jibe – what was the use of drawing him further? – and told him she would be back late. Until then, Alice was on hand to fetch him what he wanted.

The entrance to Fulham Palace is grand, compared to what she's used to. The courtyard houses a stone fountain and the many windows are warmly lit by torches. The cost of keeping the house in beeswax candles would feed her family for a year, or more. Footmen in dark livery hold open the doors, admitting her to a well-furnished reception room. She has taken two steps inside when a door at the far end opens and a man walks out. He raises his head. Their eyes meet.

She is so surprised she steps backwards, almost tripping over the rug. Jeremiah Grape's face mirrors her shock. In his navy frock coat and cream breeches, he resembles a character that has stepped out of a play.

'What –' she says, just as he begins to speak. 'What are you doing here, Mister Grape?'

'I might ask you the same,' he says, recovering enough to regard her with his usual disgust.

She draws herself up. 'I'm here at the Bishop's request. He summoned me, a meeting has been arranged.'

Male voices rise and fall at the end of the corridor. She hears the constable's name called and after glaring at her, he turns back to the room and leaves her standing, foolish and alone. Mary's shoes pinch the soft skin of her heel. How she longs for her own worn boots, her own red mantle! She dithers, uncertain whether to turn and flee until an imperious voice floats out of the room, startling her.

'Madam Gulliver?'

Hesitantly, she makes her way to the door and peers in. Jeremiah stands with his back to her but Mary's gaze is riveted on the Bishop, a plump, genial man with iron grey hair and a neatly trimmed beard who comes forward to greet her. When he moves, the folds of his expensive black robe ripple as though a dark fountain of water moves with him, and his feet in their embroidered slippers seem barely to touch the floor.

'Madam Gulliver,' he says, smiling, his cheeks flushed with wine. 'Anne Clifton's replacement. So good of you to come. I hope you found your way here without any difficulty?'

She manages a nod.

'Good, good,' he says. 'I've brought you here so that I may better decide what course to take. I was hoping to hear your arguments separately but it seems that God has other plans.'

'Arguments, Your Grace?'

He grimaces, flexing soft hands over his broad stomach.

She remembers, too late, Anne Clifton's warning that he is a man who doesn't like to be questioned. 'I don't mean to pry, Your Grace, but if we have been brought here to give an account of ourselves, and you would like me to stay, I must humbly beg your generosity in telling me what it is you must decide.'

Her deference appears to appease him. He indicates the sofa opposite and she sits awkwardly on it, her stays biting into her ribs. 'Are you hungry? I'm afraid we have supped already but I will have my assistant bring some sweetmeats.'

Taken aback, she hesitates. Why was she invited to dinner, if they have already eaten? Is the Bishop testing her? She looks across at Jeremiah in time to catch the smirk he quickly hides. A ploy, then, to ruffle her. She will show them she is not so easily diminished.

'Thank you, Your Grace,' she says. 'I have a small appetite.'

'You don't eat?' he says, frowning slightly.

She allows herself a smile. 'A strict diet of prayer. Something I recommend to all my clients.'

Jeremiah scoffs but the Bishop beams, perhaps pleased by her image of parish women starving themselves for the greater good of the Church. Turning away, he begins to question Jeremiah about the particulars of the parish, how the new rector has settled in since his appointment last year, the upswing of church attendance and improvements to the rectory, funded by the sale of fertile land backing onto the commons. Jeremiah answers in short bursts. Shrewd as ever, he stops short of offering any lengthy commentary, instead allowing the Bishop to fill the room with self-congratulatory talk. Nobody asks Mary her opinion and she feels by turns both invisible and exposed. Ignored, she is at least free to examine the room and take in the rich tapestries and plump cushions, the chessboard in the corner where a half-played game waits. The Bishop, she learns, is a keen player and maintains a successful record against his dinner guests. Mary wonders if they let him win or whether, as he claims, he bested them with his superior intellect. The appearance of the sweetmeats is a welcome distraction and she selects a sugared almond from the tray, its unaccustomed sweetness melting on her tongue. The Bishop gobbles three bars of marchpane in a row then licks his sticky lips and says, 'I am considering, Missus Gulliver, whether to allow Mister Chamberlen the use of his extraordinary forceps in the birthing chamber, without the need for summons by a midwife.'

An assistant lumbers over carrying something concealed by a cloth which he sets down on the table. As the man tugs off the cloth, Mary's stomach tightens. The iron clamps look incongruous against the glossy wood. Her breath catches. Sliding to the edge of her seat, she fixes Jeremiah with a hard stare he pretends not to see. She wants to ask why and how the horrid clamps came to be here, but she is wary now of giving offence. It seems best to wait, since the Bishop appears to be a man who enjoys hearing himself speak.

'Mister Grape is a personal friend of the Chamberlen family,' the Bishop says. 'Hugh Chamberlen could not be here, since he is attending the birth of his own niece this night; his first, would you believe? He will be using his set of clamps on the woman. Mister Grape is here instead at my request to help me weigh the decision in my mind. There's strong support for this instrument within the surgeon's guild.'

'For good reason,' says Jeremiah. He shakes his head as the Bishop's assistant offers the tray of sweetmeats again. 'These forceps will prevent the deaths of hundreds of women, Your Grace. They are vital to the preservation of life. And is that not God's will? For us to give women more chances to multiply and to be good mothers to their offspring? The sting of death is sin and the strength of sin is the law but thanks be to God, who gives us victory through the Lord.'

'Quite so,' the Bishop says, selecting a lacquered walnut. 'And you, Missus Gulliver? What is the opinion of the midwives on this surgical advancement?'

Surgical advancement? She shudders but masks her horror by sipping the wine the Bishop's assistant has handed her. Under her skirts, her legs are shaking. To be ambushed on her first meeting – is it rotten luck or, as Jeremiah would say, God's will? The Chamberlen family and Jeremiah have united to thwart the midwives. This is our chance, she thinks. Our only chance to convince the Bishop not to endorse an instrument of evil and torture. She has heard stories about the use of the Chamberlens' instrument although she has never witnessed them used herself. She eyes them now, distrustfully. That curve must fit over the baby's cranium while the other extends down to the soft depression at the back of the neck. One incorrect placement and the baby's neck would snap in two.

She says, 'Your Grace, it is the opinion of the midwives that we cannot endorse an instrument so barbaric it would do irreparable harm to parish women if wielded by untrained hands. I know I speak for my sisters when I assure you that the best and only method, unless required in an emergency, is the traditional way of birthing.'

'You would say that, though,' Jeremiah interjects, standing up abruptly. Leaning down, he picks up the clamps and squeezes the handles together. 'You have your unofficial guild to protect, Missus Gulliver. Your motives are clear and, sadly, not impartial. Your Grace, let men decide what is best for

London's future children. Mister Chamberlen and his family have only ever served the greater good in the community and while the midwives have, no doubt, established a rapport with their clients, their methods are outdated. These clamps can deliver an infant in less time than it takes to get from one side of the Thames to the other. No longer will women suffer days of agony ending in heartbreak. Yet the midwives would refuse the surgeon's entry to the confinement chamber. How many women must die because of their refusal to step out of the past?'

'What nonsense,' Mary says, before she can stop herself. 'Mister Grape, birth is a sacred act. If intervention is needed, it is provided. But it should not be the first response. Would you risk the life of the infant and permanent damage to a woman's body, in order to speed up a process which cannot be rushed? These are women we are speaking of, not the murderers and criminals found in your gruesome pamphlets. They do not deserve to be tortured for the sake of expedience.'

'Madam Gulliver, you should guard your tone,' the Bishop says, although his voice is benign and a smile plays over his lips.

He is enjoying this, she thinks. He is enjoying pitting us against each other. She turns away, fighting to control her breath. Her gaze falls upon the chessboard, the figurines stalled on their paths, destined for defeat or victory. She supposed earlier that the Bishop's guests conceded him the pleasure of winning; now she wonders if she has underestimated him, if he is indeed a master of strategy. Perhaps he sees all of London as his own private chessboard, the parish mothers and their children pieces who must dutifully obey God's will. Certainly, he has coordinated this encounter with a skilful hand.

'I suggest a trial,' Jeremiah says. 'Equip a number of surgeons with these instruments and you will see an increase in your flock, Your Grace. London's sons will bless you for making the right choice.' Jeremiah throws a look in Mary's direction and she knows that she has lost.

The Bishop sits up straighter, smiling benignly at the fire. 'You are right,' he says, at last. 'A trial. Then we will decide.'

Seething with anger, she can only be glad that the Bishop is too concerned with his own affairs to notice her ragged breathing.

'Tell me about your husband,' the Bishop says. 'I hear he has been returned to you, praise God. A great storyteller, is he not?'

'His stories are just that,' she says briskly but politely. 'He enjoys company, and his tales always win him friends at sea.' She notices Jeremiah scowl and shake his head behind his wineglass.

'Is that so, Missus Gulliver?' Jeremiah says. 'For it's not what I have heard, which is that he believes his own –'

'He's merely unwell. He has been suffering from an ague, which will pass soon enough.'

'And in his absence, you have made your own friends,' the Bishop says. 'Missus Clifton is a formidable woman. If she hadn't told me herself she was dying, I would never have believed it.'

Mary gapes at him. Even Jeremiah blinks in confusion.

'Dying?'

The Bishop frowns. 'I take it she has not discussed the matter with you?'

'She assuredly has not,' Mary says. 'Are you certain there's no mistake? She seemed in good health when I saw her yesterday.'

'There is no mistake. She's in grave health, Madam Midwife. I had my own physician examine her and confide the truth to me, without her knowledge. A month, I'd say. Perhaps a little longer.'

Mary sets down her wineglass, reeling. It cannot be true. Anne has been off-colour, yes, she has been temporarily unwell. But she isn't dying. Nobody ever died of a bad hip and headaches. And what was all the talk, then, of not showing weakness in front of the Bishop? Has Anne really been foolish enough to use his physician and trust the man with her confidential condition? If the Bishop knows the truth, others soon will.

At once, Mary sees Anne's plan unfold before her. She sees Elinor's little kindnesses to her aunt, her frequent visits to the house, 'just to check', Anne's sly recruitment of Bess; her final apprentice. By allowing the Bishop to break the news, she has avoided doing it herself. Pity floods Mary's throat and she finds she cannot swallow.

'I see it has come as something of a shock,' the Bishop says, gently. He taps the edge of Mary's wine goblet and the assistant moves to refill it.

'I'm sorry,' she says, dashing away tears. 'I have known Missus Clifton a long time. She was friends with my mother.'

'I, too, have a long association with her,' the Bishop says, sounding mildly aggrieved, as if Anne is a favourite pet whose death presents an inconvenience. 'That's why it pains me to know she will soon depart this earth. It's difficult to replace women like Anne. But I'm certain she has chosen you for a good reason, Missus Gulliver.'

Soon after, the Bishop ushers them out, ordering his assistant to escort them down to the steps to where a barge waits to carry them back upriver.

'You do not mind travelling together,' he says, stifling a yawn. 'Better for you to be accompanied, Madam Midwife, than to brave the river alone.'

As she is helped into the barge, Mary reflects that she would rather travel with anyone in the world than Jeremiah Grape. She catches the constable's eye then turns her face to the blazing torches and ramshackle houses gliding past.

'It wouldn't have saved her,' she says. 'That instrument would have quickened her death. I pray you see sense.'

Jeremiah snorts but does not reply.

'Do you truly believe,' she goes on, 'that Louisa would have wanted her death to be the cause of so many others?'

'You don't get to say her name,' he says. In the pale light of the lantern, his skin is waxen, his knuckles white as he clutches his knees. 'I'll destroy you – you and your sisters. This time next year, you'll be out of work and the only midwives will be men of Hugh Chamberlen's choosing. You had best save your prayers for your own children, madam, for they will soon be on the street along with your degenerate husband, disgrace that he is.'

The man's vitriol is so sharp she feels it gather around her, condensing in waves. His threat about Lemuel confirms her own fears. She doesn't dare antagonise him further. Smoothing out her lovely skirt, she stares out at the river instead, longing for the comforts of home. Hot tears of anger prick her eyes and she screws them shut, unwilling to expose her weakness. At Frying Pan Stairs, the barge has barely bumped against the stonework before Jeremiah scrambles out. Ignoring her entirely, he flags down the nearest link boy. It takes some minutes of searching and asking outside the tavern before she secures another, but she is partly glad of the darkness for it hides her tears.

When at last, the boy guides her into her own street, she sees a knot of people gathered at the far end, torches blazing in their hands. A burble of sound rises and falls, the rumbling of dissent. Sweat breaks out on her skin. Oh god, what if Bess has been hurt? She runs, almost reaching the Needle's front door when somebody shouts her name.

'Madam Gulliver!'

Jeremiah looks as unhappy to see her as she does him, his cheeks suffused with violent colour, his chest heaving, as if he, too, has been running. 'You saw nothing on your return up the hill?' He looks over her shoulder, as if he suspects her of guarding someone.

'No,' she says, trying to move past him.

'You did not pass anyone suspicious?'

'No!' she shouts. 'What's this about? I must see my daughter – Bess, is she safe?'

He hesitates. 'Emma Morton's youngest was seized on her way to her grandmother's cottage and held against her will for an hour. She was raped and shaved, just like the other victims. My wife gave me the news and I gathered the watchmen.'

Mary's heart beats loudly. No, this cannot be happening. She thinks of Emma's face, screwed in grief, and poor Rebecca, the terrible abuse done to her body. 'This is unacceptable. You are meant to watch these women and girls. What have you done to protect them?'

'What have you done?' Jeremiah says, instantly defensive. 'What is your excuse? Your daughter is with your maid, your husband is away from home. Perhaps a night curfew should be enforced until this criminal is found.'

At first, she thinks he is talking about Lemuel. But as he continues, the truth dawns: it is the women who are to be kept inside.

'If women are not safe in Wapping, it is my job to see that their husband's property remains undamaged,' he says. 'If women leave their homes, they tempt the criminal. When he is found, he will be strung up or burned. I would rather like to see both.'

'What about my clients? If I cannot move about the streets at night, how will I help them?'

'What's more important?' Jeremiah snarls. 'The safety of all parish women or the childbed of a few?'

'Constable.' A man touches the constable's elbow and Mary recognises the watchman who scolded her for being out at night. 'We should check the docks again. He may be hiding.'

'You heard the news,' Alice says when Mary has bolted the doors and checked the locks. She and Bess are sitting side by side in the parlour. Mary drops into an adjacent armchair. Her whole body aches, her arms so tired she can barely be bothered to unlace her boots. What is her exhaustion, though, compared to Rebecca's pain?

'Poor Rebecca,' Bess blurts, to nobody in particular. Every few minutes, she releases a hiccupping sob and Mary touches her shoulder, trying to comfort but unsure exactly how. Bess endures her hand for a moment before shrugging it off. 'She never thought it would happen to her,' she says, quietly. 'When she told me about Margaret, she said her mother was going to put new bolts on the door. But after all, she was only walking to her grandmother's house in Stepney. She would not have expected . . .' Bess trails off and sniffs loudly.

'It's not her fault,' Mary says, softly.

Bess does not reply.

'Where is your father?' Mary says. He should be here, she thinks. He should at least be here to speak for himself, to provide Jeremiah with an account of his movements so she does not have to.

Bess shrugs but Mary notices her hand creep up to touch her elbow.

'The master went out a short time ago,' Alice says. 'Said he was off to visit a friend.'

'What friend?' Mary says. Anger thrums through her body. She knows where he has gone.

'You ought not to think so badly of Pa,' Bess says, as if she has heard Mary's thoughts. 'He's doing his best.' She speaks without her usual conviction, though, and rubs her arm compulsively. She stands up and walks out into the kitchen, Alice and Mary trailing closely. Finding herself followed, Bess scowls into her mug and returns to the parlour where she takes one of the armchairs and opens a book.

'What's that you're reading?' Mary says.

'Nothing,' she says, slamming the book face down onto the table. 'I'm going to bed. Unless you insist on following me there, too?'

Alice and Mary exchange glances. 'Of course not,' Mary says, but when Bess has gone, they go into the hallway.

'I'll go up and keep an eye to her,' Alice says. 'My own flesh, might as well be. Can't imagine how Missus Morton is feeling. I'd give my life for that girl.'

Mary touches her arm. 'I know you would.' She hesitates, then asks, 'Did the master say when he'd be home?'

'He didn't, but he's been acting queer all day. More so than usual. Talking to himself, again.' Alice pauses. 'Will he ever get better?'

Mary thinks of Piet, recalling his twisted, sardonic smile, the fug of opium in his ghastly den. 'I hope so,' she says, but when she goes upstairs to wait for Lemuel in the bedroom, her heart is heavy.

'Where have you been?' she says when Lem at last returns.

Her husband weaves on his feet, his eyes heavy-lidded.

'Are you drunk?' she says. 'Do you know what took place here earlier? While you were out enjoying yourself?'

'I presume you will tell me,' he says. He can hardly focus on her. Gripping the door frame, he steadies himself.

'A young woman was assaulted. Bess's age. And here you are, slinking in from God knows where. I hoped you would be here to protect us.'

'It doesn't suit you, Mary,' he says, in a sour tone she recalls from her old life with him. 'Acting the shrew.'

'You must be feeling better,' she says, coldly, 'if you are out with friends. No more little people, then? No more islands?'

Lemuel says nothing, simply pushes past her, slinging himself onto the bed. 'You have no idea the things I've seen,' he says. 'You would be terrified for your life, madam. I have seen monsters, the like of which –'

'Lem,' she says, too tired to argue, 'the only monster in this house is you.'

20

Bess hugs herself against a sudden breeze as she waits with her family at the turnpike for Johnny's carriage to rumble into view. The sky above is hazy with smoke from the tanneries and the drizzling rain has burned off so the ground steams lightly, as if the crust of the earth is cooking. The rain has descended with greater frequency of late, catching people unawares, filling the water tubs in the garden until they overflow. The seasons shift so gradually, Bess has found the best way to track them is through the flourishing or dying of Mam's herbs and the level in the tubs. The garden works to its own unique calendar of bulbs and blossoms.

    Bess shivers outwardly, but inside she is lit up with happiness at Johnny's impending return. Although she's fallen into something of a routine at Missus Clifton's, she misses having someone else to talk to when she gets home. She frowns, remembering how she once thought Pa would be enough. How wrong she was. Since the night he sent her to the Louse, he has been distant and curt and, as a result, she retreats more often to her room, taking solace in the books Missus Clifton lends her and puzzling over the map.

She fingers the square in her left pocket, wishing she could draw it out now and ask Pa exactly what it means, the island floating in an expanse of unnamed sea. On one side of the map, he has written *New Holland* and at the top *Sumatra* although from what she has read about those places the coordinates seem wildly contradictory. If only there were someone to ask. She could ask Johnny, but she has not decided yet whether to burden him with the knowledge of the map. He's only a little boy, a helpless little cricket. She will have to protect him. Casper would be the right person to ask but she has no idea if he's still in Wapping. Have the winds changed? How much wind does a ship need to set off?

She brings out a slim volume, something to pass the time while they wait outside the tollhouse for the vehicle to deposit Johnny back into their lives. As she tilts the book, a shaft of sunlight glances off the figure of a woman etched on the parchment, a fascinating diagram she returns to often. The woman's stomach is peeled open like the leaves of a cabbage and at the very centre an infant nestles, arms and legs like little florets, a stringy cord leading to a bulging sac. The woman's privities are shielded by a demure blossom.

'Are you reading Jane Sharp?'

Bess looks up to see Mam mouthing her shock, her head angled as she studies the diagram. Bess hugs the book, reluctant to reveal too much. She certainly has not yet forgiven Mam for what she did, handing her future over to Missus Clifton.

'I read that book when I was your age,' Mam murmurs. She is dressed in her sky-blue mantua, the frayed ribbons of her hat looped under her chin and looks – Bess would never say this to her – surprisingly lovely, as beautiful as any of those women who come and go at Missus Clifton's, leaving the waft of their perfume in the examination room. If those women are canaries, all shine and glossy feathers, then perhaps Mam is an owl, self-possessed, watchful.

Mam taps the book with her gloved finger. 'Missus Clifton knew her,' she says. 'Did she tell you? Jane Sharp was famous, the first woman to publish a book on midwifery. All the rest were men.'

'I know.' Bess can't help showing off. 'I've read them.'

Mam's face registers surprise. 'You have been busy.'

'Well, there's nothing else to do, is there? Except washing and leading women to and from the appointment couch. Missus Clifton can't walk far on her bad leg. When she recovers, she says she'll take us to a birthing. Elinor does them now.'

Her mother frowns, imagining, Bess assumes, that she should be working harder, being dragged to births she doesn't want to attend and forced to confront her reluctance. She turns away, leaving Mam with only Pa to talk to. Out of the corner of her eye, she sees her mother's hands tighten around her new purse as she returns her gaze to the street, scanning the horizon as if her father is a pane of glass. Pa doesn't seem to notice, though, too busy scratching the toe of his boot through the mud and playing with the cravat Mam tied for him before they left the house. She wishes she could resolve the mounting tension between her parents but what can she do? She's hardly ever home these days.

Johnny doesn't know what he is coming back to. She imagines him leaning against the coach window, watching green fields transform into shambling dwellings, the clay turning to mud mixed with sewage. London is London.

No use wishing it were prettier. Nottingham is the greenest place she has ever seen, abundant with meadows and shimmering rivers, a place from a summer dream. She remembers snippets of the visits she made to her Uncle John's estate, the grand Gulliver seat, row upon row of her ancestors' faces peering down from the walls. Bess remembers the funeral, watching them slide the coffin into the crypt while she wept.

'The coach is late,' Mam says, biting the tip of her glove. Doubtless, her thoughts are full of highwaymen and footpads.

Bess waits for Pa to say something comforting, but he continues to rub his boot in the mud like a child whose boredom is relieved by dirtying himself.

Across the road, people are bustling about outside Bell's Tavern, the place where Casper said he and his master are staying. Travellers clog the tavern's doorway with their comings and goings, heaving trunks and bags. The inn is a stopping place, more luggage than people, but she imagines she sees a wisp of pale hair blowing like a dandelion clock, hears the crunch of a tulip bulb.

She's thankful for the distraction of thundering hooves pounding the dirt as the coach rolls into view moments later. Dark horses stamp and froth as the driver climbs down to unlatch the door. Mam is beside him in an instant, reaching in for Johnny, ignoring the grumblings of the other passengers who push her aside, eager to leave the bone-rattling contraption behind.

Bess spies her brother's fair curls crushed against Mam's chest as she embraces then releases him. Meeting her eyes, Johnny lifts his hand in greeting and she waves back, grinning. He is thinner than she remembers and taller, more gaunt. It won't be long before he surpasses her in height. What do they feed him at that school? She always imagines the meals are sumptuous rich cakes and beef porridge, but perhaps she's wrong. Perhaps his meals are as meagre as their own usual fare, thin broth and lumpy carrots. Or perhaps he's been ill.

'Hello, Bess,' Johnny says as Mam, still covering him with kisses, walks him over to where she and Pa are standing. Mam squeezes him so hard it is a wonder he can breathe.

'Here is your father,' Mam says. Bess can tell she is nervous by the way she keeps worrying at her glove, nipping the tip of it. She would never do that to her bare nails.

Johnny looks up at Pa, his little face grave and solemn just as Bess remembers it. Pa smiles absently; does he even remember him? Johnny was only five when Pa left on the *Antelope*. Pa shakes Johnny's hand as if they were equals, and Bess feels invisible. All her pride in her own learning and trying to be a good apprentice vanishes when she sees Pa slip Johnny's hand into the crook of his elbow. She feels all alone and wishes she were brave enough to run over to Bell's Tavern and search for Casper. Instead, she hangs back, sullen and despondent, watching as Pa picks up Johnny's small case and the three of them walk back up to the Needle, Mam holding tight to her son as if afraid he will blow away.

Later that day, Bess is enticed from the sanctuary of her room by the beguiling scent of stewed capon, laced with mace and cinnamon. She sniffs appreciatively, although she can't suppress a touch of envy at this feast Alice and her mother have spent the afternoon conjuring in honour of her brother's return. When was the last time Mam made such a fuss of her? Descending the stairs, she sees her father coming in through the front door, pushing Johnny ahead of him, the boy's hair molten golden in the afternoon sunshine. They meet at the bottom of the stairs, Pa gripping his shoulder.

'Where've you been?' Bess says and Johnny shrugs, looking tired and embarrassed. His clothes reek of tobacco – he hasn't even changed since Bess helped him carry the trunk upstairs to the bedroom they will share until he returns for the next school term. Pa seized him at once and Mam was too busy helping Alice prepare the meal to take charge of his whereabouts.

'Nowhere important,' he says.

Bess eyes them with suspicion, thinking of the Louse. Clearly, Pa prefers her brother's company, which shouldn't surprise her. If her dealings with him over the past weeks have revealed anything, it's that she can't expect him to shower her with praise the way he used to when he lived here before. Somehow, she has displeased him and she cannot account for it.

'Nowhere important?' Pa says now, frowning down at Johnny's wan face. 'I didn't think you'd be so dismissive, Johnny. Nothing to be embarrassed about. Why, you should be proud. It was your card hand won us the goods!'

He claps the boy's back and her brother winces. She's about to ask for more details when her father suddenly turns and holds back the door to allow entry to two men, hoisting a chair between them, a heavy old thing pieced together from odd bits of ship's timber.

When the men ask where they should put it, her father directs them into the parlour, Bess ogling as they pass. She casts Johnny an incredulous look.

'What did you do?' she whispers.

'It was Pa,' he shoots back. 'He bet – well, don't tell Mam – he bet her old teapot. So I had to win, then, didn't I? You know she loves it. And then Pa bartered it anyway – exchanged it for that chair.'

She shakes her head but his shoulders slump so miserably, she doesn't chastise him further. Instead, she goes into the parlour where the men, at Pa's insistence, have settled the chair in the centre of the room. An ugly thing, she thinks, the scarred timber, worn away on the arms, in dire need of polishing. As the men file out, Bess watches Pa avail himself of the unexpected addition, settling his rump on the hard seat as if it's a down-filled cushion. Mam's armchair, she notices, has been pushed back to make room and her kitbag, always kept nearby in case of emergencies, relegated to a dark and dusty corner.

What will Mam think? Bess glances back at the kitchen where her mother and Alice are still banging skillets, oblivious to the presence of this unwanted furnishing which is so worn and ill-used, its next destination may very well be the woodpile.

'Come sit,' her father barks. For a moment, she feels a flush of the old pleasure at being chosen, singled out for his attention. She has taken a small step forward when Johnny moves past her. Bess's stomach plummets, the realisation – it's Johnny he wants – a dispiriting truth that seems, somehow, inevitable. She watches Pa vacate the chair so Johnny can hoist himself onto it. He holds himself stiffly on the incongruously large chair, staring at Bess miserably and clinging to the armrests like a castaway in a current. Pa fails to notice his discomfort, or perhaps he does not care.

'We will make a man of you, yet,' he says.

Johnny's lip trembles.

'Supper will be ready soon,' Bess says, taking pity, offering him her hand. 'Let's see if Alice and Mam need our help.'

21

'Johnny has bruises on his ribs. Did you notice?' Mary flattens the chaff on the trundle bed with the heel of her hand. Moonlight bathes an old tea chest and the spokes of a broken spinning wheel as she beats the bolster into softness. She lies down, then sits up again to beat it some more. I am like a dog, circling and circling until I find my comfort, she thinks.

'I noticed nothing,' Alice says. She unbraids her hair into three dark strands.

Mary props herself up on her elbow. She has removed her bed permanently to the attic, the better to avoid her husband's midnight escapades. She has conceded the bedchamber to Lemuel as she once conceded everything sacred to her: her work, her children, her sense of worth. She will not do that again, she vows. It would be better if he returned to sea altogether, if their lives could resume and she could find her way back to the way things were before.

A week has passed now since Johnny came home, but her son's presence – and the new chair – have done nothing to alleviate her husband's mood swings. He comes and goes as he always has, sometimes stumbling in from the tavern just as she is going out in the morning to make her rounds and check the progress of labouring women she's unable to attend for fear of breaking curfew. During those times, he glares at her through bleary eyes and she feels his disgust creep over her from head to foot. Inside, he shouts for Johnny and the little lad scurries down the stairs to prise off his father's boots and fetch him draughts to cool his throbbing headaches. Johnny, it seems, has become her husband's new Henry – obedient to his will, unable to refuse his requests, he hovers at the fringes of Lemuel's world, as Bess used to. Once or twice, when he has managed to rouse himself before sundown, Lemuel has taken Johnny with him to the coffee house or the tavern where men bet their goods on hands of ombre. The child has proven a slight disappointment, though, in this regard, failing to win anything like the horrid chair which now occupies prime position in her parlour. Johnny is always quiet when they return and seeks refuge in the kitchen, while Lemuel retires to his bedchamber to rest. Her son wept when he confessed what became of her mother's teapot. The news came as a crushing blow, but for his small sake, she swallowed her pain, trying to find comfort in the knowledge that the life her mother left cannot be measured in tea leaves and milky porcelain. At least her husband's threat – that he will 'make a man' of his only son – has not altogether poisoned Johnny's spirit. After returning from the tavern yesterday, her son confided that he'd been spitting his ale back in when Lemuel's head was turned and Mary, impressed by his ingenuity, embraced him tightly while Alice threw open the pantry and let him take his pick.

A few times while Lem is out, she has snuck into their bedroom and rifled through his things but so far has found no evidence of what she suspects: that his addiction to poppy has consumed him. He hasn't mentioned her sleeping arrangements, the now empty bedchamber where he reposes. She wonders if he even notices, or if he just falls face-first into the bedclothes to sleep off a night of debauchery.

The attic is snug but cosy. It's almost like old times, when Mary and Alice did not need to guard their conversation from Lem but could air their problems freely.

'They are very faint, almost healed. You would not notice if you weren't looking for them,' Mary says, chewing on her lip until she tastes blood.

'What made you look for them?'

'I don't know. A feeling.' Mary hugs her knees through her nightdress. 'Call it mother's instinct. When I asked him, he said he tripped and fell on his way to prayer a few weeks ago. But his words don't ring true. It must have been a mighty fall to bruise his ribs so badly. Of course, Lem says I am imagining it.'

'Master was out late last night,' Alice says. 'Again.'

Mary shakes her head. Something must be done. Tomorrow, she will force him to tell her the truth. She must convey how precarious their financial situation is, even with the additional money from the Bishop.

'Speaking of bruises,' Alice says, 'I had a message today. From my sister.'

'Oh, my dear.' Mary wants to comfort her friend but the night swims between them like a river of pitch.

'It's fine. But my father isn't.' She draws in a rattling breath. 'Last week he was struck by apoplexy and now his body is failing. He can barely eat nor drink unassisted. He pants like a dog and his skin's gone all grey. Hester suspects the end is close. His landlady has threatened to throw him upon the mercy of the parish but it's very likely he won't live another month. Hester asks if I'll help her see him out of this life and I said I'd need to ask you, to see if you mind.'

Mary sits up. 'Of course I don't mind. But you said you'd never go back there. Your father –'

'Is dying,' Alice says, her voice firm. 'He can't hurt me now. Hester says he cannot even lift his head or hold himself over the chamberpot. I hate to leave you with Bess and Johnny, though. And the master still at odds.'

'We will make do,' Mary says, although she is already wondering how they will get everything done. In addition to her rounds, which are now dictated by the curfew, the Bishop sends for her every week to discuss, amongst other things, the progress of the forceps trial. He has asked her to compile a list of all living children born in South London this year and the names of the midwives who delivered them. While the information is not difficult to obtain, it's a time-consuming task requiring liaison with the parish midwives and analysis of church record books. How will she get it all done?

She almost weeps with gratitude when Alice says, 'Hester says it's mostly the nights she needs help with. So, I will be here during the day. And just think – at night you'll have this cosy den all to yourself.'

From somewhere outside comes the muffled bang of the door. Lemuel returning. Mary shrugs down under her coverlet, glad to be spared his snores and the stink of the tavern.

The next morning, Alice leaves for the meat market swinging their enormous wicker basket.

'Only the freshest meat for Bess's birthday,' she says. 'A good friend of mine has married a butcher; she's promised me a sweet price and the juiciest haunch. I'll look in on Hester on my way back, if you're agreeable. She's made up a roster so that we might take shifts.'

Mary waves her off with a hollow smile, feeling more alone than she has in the three years since Lemuel's death was confirmed. In the parlour, she finds Johnny conjugating his Latin, and Bess waiting to be walked to Missus Clifton's.

'Where is Alice going?' Bess asks as they walk swiftly in the direction of Anne's house.

Mary hesitates. 'She's gone to visit the meat market and see her family. Her father is nearing the end of his life.' She takes a breath, risking a sidelong glance at Bess's face. How much should she tell her of Alice's family circumstances, the reason she left her father's house to work in service? In the wake of Rebecca's assault, there seems little point now shielding her from life's hard truths. If – when – Bess takes her midwife's oath, Mary will need to inform her anyway about the duty of testifying in court. 'Perhaps you don't know this, Bess, but Alice's father used to beat her. He knocked her out cold, more than once. That's why I let her stay with us, even when there was little to be shared. It's why she's so loyal, why she cares for you. Her younger sister, Hester, married at fourteen in order to escape their father's house. Alice blames herself for failing to protect her.'

Bess is silent, scuffing pebbles, and Mary feels guilty for not telling her sooner about Alice, but it did not feel as if it were her secret to impart. She feels as hapless as Koko, the dear little beast who delivered their weekly milk earlier this morning. When Koko looked up at her with her dark coffee bean eyes, Mary suppressed the urge to bury her face in the donkey's flanks and cry.

'When I am grown, will I have to live somewhere else, too, or could I stay on with Johnny and Pa?' Bess says in a cautious tone. She wears a troubled expression. Mary notes the conspicuous absence of her mother's name from the equation.

'When you are grown, you can do exactly as your conscience bids you,' she snaps, feeling too weary to do this dance with Bess, shuffling around the idea of blossoming independent womanhood. 'Until then, you'll have to endure my advice, I'm afraid. I have more experience than you guess at.'

Bess flinches. Then her face hardens and Mary realises, with a sinking feeling, that any opportunity for empathy and shared union has passed.

Anne is in the parlour when they arrive, chatting on the sofa to a woman some years Mary's senior. Mary recognises her as a deputy midwife from the next parish.

'This is Missus Osbert,' Anne says and the plump woman nods at Mary before immediately turning back to Anne.

'I must know, Missus Clifton, what you intend to do about the men who refuse to pay for the maintenance of their children. I have asked repeatedly for the constable to help but he insists it's the women's job to chase their husbands for welfare.'

Anne turns her dark eyes on Mary. 'Well, Mary?' she says, half-reclining, her bad leg held out in front of her.

Missus Osbert drags her gaze reluctantly to Mary's face.

'I will speak to the Bishop,' Mary says, 'and put forward your case.'

Anne nods, approving. 'Missus Gulliver will be taking over the role of liaison on a permanent basis.'

Permanent? Her courage failing, she wonders if this is how Bess felt when Anne imposed her decision upon her.

'Thank you, Missus Gulliver,' says Missus Osbert, eyeing her with newfound respect. She sails out the door, leaving Anne and Mary alone.

'Permanent?' Mary says. 'Is that true?'

Anne holds her gaze for a long moment. 'Yes, Mary. I know the Bishop told you. I'm sorry I did not have the courage but I – I was hoping I might be mistaken.'

'How long?' Mary says. She gropes for the sofa and sinks down on it. Anne can't die, she's like the Green Man or one of those spirits who exists outside of time for eternity.

'I will need you and Elinor to take over the care of the apprentices. Girls?' Anne's voice is still strong and Bess and Susanna come in, hands held meekly in front of them although Bess wears a knowing look that suggests she was listening.

'We will find new positions for you,' Mary says to them. 'You will stay here until you can be placed with other experienced midwives.' Turning back to Anne, she says, 'Is there anything else you need me to do? Any clients I can see for you?'

'Mercy Adams,' Anne says. 'Could you check? She has been on and off the past few weeks. Plenty of false starts. Her husband is due home from sea soon but he has not been there for months. The man is a brute. The last time Mercy was with child, he pushed her down the stairs. Is it any wonder some women prefer their husbands to remain at sea?'

Mary stands and shrugs on her mantle. She knows Mercy, has seen her at market, two children following in her wake. The children are always quiet and watchful, as if afraid to even speak.

As she is about to close the door, Bess slips around it. 'I'm coming, too,' she says.

Mary considers refusing her, but it's as good a time as any for Bess to see a birth.

'You do as I say, then,' she warns. 'And no running off.'

Bess bows her head, which Mary takes as a sign of obedience, and together they make their way through the twisted streets.

The Adams house is quiet when they arrive at midday, the shutters closed and bolted. Mary knocks at the front door, but when she gets no response she leads Bess down an alleyway and around the back. In the stale backyard, a scrawny chicken pecks at rubbish littering the black earth. Mary hammers on the door while Bess stands on her tiptoes, peering through a gap in the shutters.

When the door swings open, they both jump, startled. The interior of the house is as gloomy as the yard, and Mary wishes she had brought a candle to light the way. In the kitchen, they find Mercy's two children huddled together.

Mary bends down, taking in their unwashed faces and dirty clothes. 'Where's your mother?' she asks, but the children say nothing. They are both wide-eyed and glance up at the ceiling. From above comes a faint thwacking sound. It reminds her of Alice beating the bolsters of their impurities.

'Stay here, Bess,' Mary says.

Bess opens her mouth to protest but Mary interrupts her.

'Take the children outside. See if you can find something for them to eat.' She squeezes her daughter's arm and presses a coin into her hand.

The stairs creak beneath her feet. The thwacking grows louder, intensifying as she finds herself in a hallway leading to a bedchamber. On the threshold, she baulks, trying to make sense of what she is seeing.

Stephen Adams is a tall man, weather-beaten from many trips to sea. He's on the bed, straddling Mercy's helpless form, his dark clothes a contrast to her pale cotton nightgown, its taut cloth straining over her swollen belly. As Mary watches, frozen in the doorway, Mercy's husband pummels her vulnerable body, his fists a drumbeat. Her hands move to alternately protect her face and her torso as her husband delivers blow after blow, each falling on a different part of her body. A shoulder, a cheek, the nape of her neck. Mercy's eyes are clenched shut but after every blow, she whimpers and these small noises seem to incite him to new levels of violence.

Empty bottles are scattered across the floor. The room reeks of urine and tobacco.

Mercy's body stiffens as she bucks beneath her husband, shivering violently and crying out around the hand he clamps over her bloodied mouth. After a long moment, she yields, softening until she is as limp as a ragdoll, her arms dangling over the side of the bed before she stiffens again.

The truth hits Mary, as swift as a blow: the woman is in labour. Fury burns up her body.

'Mister Adams, you will desist,' she says, almost choking on the words.

The man glances up, surprised into stillness. 'Who be there?'

'It's Mary Gulliver, the parish midwife.'

'A busybody is it? You're trespassing.' He jerks his chin at the door. 'Get out, before I throw you out.'

She stands her ground. 'You must release your wife, now,' she says. 'Or you risk losing the child she is carrying.'

Lowering his face to his wife's ear, Stephen Adams sneers. 'And why should I care whether the whore's brat lives or dies?'

'You may not, but the Parish of Wapping will,' Mary says. She is shaking so hard she can barely walk across the room, stepping over the bottles, gathering her skirts to avoid tripping. 'If Constable Grape learns from me that you have killed your child, you will have the law to answer to. Twelve men. Are you prepared to chance it?' At least her voice isn't shaking.

He climbs off the bed and comes to stand in front of her, his stained shirt billowing around his breeches. 'You whores stick together, don't you?' he says, his breath a toxic wave of spoiled meat and stale liquor. 'The Bishop's harem. Bitches.' He spits in her face, a slimy glob that lands on her cheek and slides down towards her chin. She makes no move to wipe it. At the corner of her eye, she senses movement in the shadows but she doesn't dare avert her gaze, not even when Stephen Adams bends to grab an empty bottle.

Any moment he will lift his fist and bring it cracking down. She anticipates the blossoming pain in her cheek or ear, a hothouse of affliction. But Mercy has suffered much worse. Behind her, the woman lets out a howl, clutching her belly as if it might offer some protection against the rippling heat of the contraction. Rallied by her anguished cry, Mary braces herself, preparing for the onslaught. Let him hit her, if he must; she is ready.

'Well?' she says.

Stephen Adams sways, his eyes burning into her. He raises his arm but the gesture is half-hearted. She sees the fight go out of him, extinguished like a candle. Turning abruptly, he drops the bottle and stumbles out the door. She hears him in the hallway a moment later, the splash of vomit on floorboards.

Mercy weeps and her small sobs recall Mary's sense of purpose. The bottle spins dizzily as she pushes it aside with her boot and kneels beside the bed, saying Mercy's name over and over until the woman unclenches her eyes and squints up at her.

'Missus?' she says.

'It's all right now,' Mary says. 'I'm here.' Hearing a noise, she tries to rouse her fighting spirit but it seems to have fled, her body emptied of everything: bones, organs, meat, blood. Stephen Adams could topple her with his little finger now and there's nothing she could do to stop him.

When she turns to look, Bess is standing amidst the rubbish in the corner of the room.

'Did you take them out?' Mary asks her. 'The children?'

Bess nods. 'I took them to a neighbour and came straight back. Mam, I was so scared for you. But . . .' the girl says, awestruck. 'You were incredible.'

Mary's skin flushes with pleasure but then the heat flees and she feels cold and sick, disgusted by what she and her daughter have witnessed, dreading what will come.

Bess takes a few hesitant steps, but her progress is halted when she catches sight of the woman's face, all bruised and bloodied like butcher's offcuts, and the spreading pool of blood seeping out across the bedclothes. 'The baby,' she says, uncertainly. 'It will survive, won't it? You just said that to frighten him.'

Mercy groans, twisting the damp bedclothes around her. Mary clutches her hand, the woman's grip strong enough to crush bone. She squeezes and squeezes, her sounds building to a roar of pain.

Mary waits for her tightening grip to ease and then says, 'Bess, I need you to run back to Missus Clifton's and fetch Elinor. Be careful. You stay with Anne, you and Susanna, but tell her I need Elinor here.'

Bess plants her feet. 'I want to stay. I want to help. Please, Mam.'

'This is not about what you want.'

'But I could help you! I could bring Elinor back. I've read plenty of –'

Something snaps inside her. 'Bess.' Releasing Mercy's hand, she tries to push her daughter gently out into the hallway where the cloying smell of vomit makes the air feel close. Bess resists at first, then yields, turning with her arms folded.

'I understand you want to help,' Mary says, quietly. 'But you are inexperienced, no matter how many manuals you've read.'

Mercy screams, loud and long. Bess casts a frightened look over Mary's shoulder. 'But –' she says.

Mary turns, walking quickly to Mercy's bedside. Mercy's face has swollen and she fixes one puffy eye on Mary.

'Don't leave me,' she pants, her voice thick, fearful.

'Never,' Mary says. Moments later, she hears Bess's thick work shoes clumping down the stairs.

Mary arrives home before dusk, just as Lemuel is leaving and Grape's watchmen are shepherding women indoors for their own safety before the curfew begins. Lem meets her on the doorstep, and as the purple light bathes his shaved face and clean breeches, she is aware of how bedraggled she must look by comparison. Torn skirt and muddy boots, her hair a snarled birds' nest. She doesn't need to sniff at her clothes to know that the stench of shit and blood that draws the flies belongs to her. She must look like a harpy, one of those sea monsters he is always claiming to have seen: part woman, part bird, the personification of storm winds with the power to blow men off course. Didn't she do just that with Stephen Adams, with the only weapon in her arsenal – her status as a midwife, sanctified by the Church? And Mercy's baby. When it slipped into her waiting hands, small but wriggling, didn't the power surge through her, awakening her senses? Didn't she shout in triumph and then cry, for Mercy and her little girl's sake? For the victory, however slight, of life over death?

And yet, her husband is looking at her with lips pursed, as if he cannot recognise her under all the muck. She suppresses the sudden urge to berate him. If she starts, who knows where it might end? If she opens her mouth, everything she has locked away for fear of offending him will be given voice. She could lose it all: children, house, income. He has the power to snatch her life away and yet, in this moment, she really could not care. All she desires is to tell him how she feels, to speak and be heard. Heat arcs through her body and her hands and legs tremble with the effort of controlling herself.

'Mary?' he says, looking suddenly uncertain. 'Are you ill?'

She brushes past him, lifting her skirts, pushing the door open with her elbow so as not to stain the wood. The house feels desolate without Alice, in a way it never did with Lem gone. The maid has promised to send word as soon as she knows how bad her father's condition is. Mary already misses the comforting pummel of dough at the table, the wet rag-slap of her laughter.

In the kitchen, Johnny is devouring an apple, throwing pips into the fire to make them pop. After sponging her hands clean, she ruffles his hair and heaves the cauldron of soup Alice has left for her over the flames to reheat.

'Where's your sister?' she says.

Johnny points at the ceiling with his apple. 'Upstairs. She kicked me out. Said I could sleep in the hearth like the chimney boy I am. I don't have to, do I, Mam?' His pale face puckers. 'It would be mighty uncomfortable.'

'No.' Mary draws in a ragged breath. 'I'll speak to her. You can stay with me in the attic, if it's a problem.'

Bess's door is closed when she reaches the landing. All is silence, but rather than a sense of peace, the atmosphere in the upper rooms is one of tingling wakefulness, the calm before the storm. Instead of tackling it head-on, Mary hoists herself up to the attic to change out of her dirty clothes. After slipping on a new shift and a housedress, she feels almost like herself again, although she is still exhausted, still furious with Lemuel.

She knocks on Bess's door and when no answer comes, pushes it gently open.

'May I come in?'

Bess is lying on the bed, her back turned. 'You may do as you please,' she says and Mary, expecting a bitter rebuke, is surprised to hear tiredness blurring her daughter's voice. Unnerved, she scrambles for a distraction to fill the quiet.

'What's that you have there?' she says, peering over the girl's shoulder at the little scrap of paper cradled in her hands.

Bess seems to hesitate, then holds it up briefly before tucking it away. 'A map.'

'I see. Of what?'

Bess shrugs. 'Nothing. Something. Oh, I don't know. Pa drew it but . . . it makes no sense. Doesn't look like any map I've ever seen.' She sounds so dispirited Mary doesn't press the issue.

'You've tidied your room,' she observes, taking in the neat rows of books stacked on the shelves, the clothes tidied into the garderobe.

Bess pushes herself up and Mary is shocked by the sight of her pink, blotchy skin and puffy eyes. 'Why did you send me away?' she says.

'It was prudent,' Mary says softly, 'to send you back to Missus Clifton's. You're inexperienced. I did not want you to see –' She stops as Bess groans and lies back on the bed, staring sightlessly at the ceiling.

'Nothing I do is good enough,' the girl mutters. 'It's the same as the chores, isn't it? The gardening, the cooking, the sewing . . . It's the same as Missus Priest's. I try and try but get nowhere. I'll never be as good as those other girls.' She glances at Mary. 'I'll never be you.'

She sounds so helpless and despairing, Mary cannot think what to say. Never has Bess expressed a desire to be more like her. Quite the opposite.

Bess laces her hands together over her stomach, a small grimace contorting her face, and says dully, 'A whistling woman, a crowing hen. Neither are fit for God or men.'

Coming from her daughter, the proverb is startling. Mary fidgets on the stool. Where did Bess hear it? Lemuel, she thinks. Lemuel must have repeated it. Whether he meant it as a veiled threat, designed to hamper Bess's knowledge and happiness, or simply to educate her about societal expectations, Mary cannot be certain. But it has obviously impressed itself upon her conscience and a fresh wave of anger crests as she pictures his earlier look of disdain.

Bess seems to be waiting for her to speak. The candle sputters in its holder and outside in the garden, a cat projects a lament of longing into the hushed darkness.

'Did it live?'

'What?' Mary says.

Bess sniffs. 'The baby. Did it live?'

'Oh. Yes.' She hears the infant's little warring cries, her shrill protests at being dragged from warm darkness into cold daylight.

'Good.' Bess closes her eyes. 'You were right, then, to send me off. I would only have gotten in the way.'

'Bess . . .'

A tear slides down Bess's cheek. Mary leans forward to brush it off but in a brisk motion her daughter hunches onto her side again. Her thin shoulders rise and fall as muffled sobs fill the room. Mary's heart swells with pity. She hovers a hesitant hand over Bess's shoulder but the girl, sensing the movement, half-turns her head.

'Leave me be,' she says. 'Please.'

Mary drops her hand. She draws back the stool and staggers to the door, the last of her strength and control evaporating in the face of Bess's sadness. The girl looks so much older than her years, the white cap and shapeless dress now remnants of the distant past. Her plait is a gleaming rope, a lifeline Mary cannot grasp. The gulf between them has never felt so vast nor so uncrossable.

Closing the door, she leans against it, suppressing her own sobs. The hallway is dark, the only light to be found the slim bar under Bess's door and . . . another coming from her own bedchamber.

Unsteadily, she pushes open her door. She thinks back to that first night, the night Lemuel returned. Was that the night everything changed? Or have things always been like this – did Bess harbour resentments and fears of worthlessness, did Johnny struggle to confide in her? Has she just been blind to the truth all along: that Lemuel is the cause of all her troubles? He has stolen her poppy to satisfy his addiction. Things are so much worse than she feared.

Groaning, she sinks into a battered armchair and rests her aching head in her hands. In the darkness outside, a bird calls, the sound haunting. She thinks of something she has never told Bess. When her mother died young, she lost all confidence that she would ever be a good parent. She didn't realise it, not then. At fourteen, what girl imagines she will marry and have the responsibility of setting an example for her own children? The passing on of knowledge – how to teach and mould the young minds that were gifted to her. How to impress her will upon her daughter without stifling the girl's spirit. It was all so mysterious then, and it has remained mysterious, an elusive desire she both wants and is afraid of. Because what if she fails? What are the consequences? They are worse for women than for men. Any small error in judgement, any scandal . . . She has spent the better part of her life avoiding drama, but now drama has found her.

Looking around the room, she sees only evidence of her husband. Like the chair sitting incongruously in her parlour, it's as if her life has been erased by his return. She needs to find the proof of his addiction. Clothes are thrown higgledy-piggledy about, clean mixed with old. She picks up a ripe-smelling shirt and throws it on a heap. If she were Lemuel – the jacket. When she picks up the jacket, she remembers her dancing dream. The blue material still feels damp, as though she has just stripped it off him. As she shakes out the cloth, her nose fills with the briny whiff of the sea. The pockets are heavy. Feeling inside, she gasps. Her fingers unearth a bone pipe and an empty trinket box. The pipe reeks of opium. When she turns the trinket box upside down, black powder sifts out into her palm. Touching her tongue, she tastes sweetness and bitter earth. Oh god, here it is. The evidence he has done nothing to hide. She could have found it all along.

Despair sweeps through her. Closing her eyes, Mary clutches the jacket and sinks slowly onto the bed.

The other pocket touches her knee and she is startled to discover it is cold. Opening it, she discovers it is bulging with sand. Rough granules cling to her nail beds. She digs about, pushing the sand aside, gripped by a strange feeling of loss. Is this pocket of sand from Lemuel's island? Is this all the proof there is? Something hard resists her thumb. She digs it out. A shell, surely. It must be. But the angles, when she finally wiggles it free, are all wrong, the shape too cumbersome and manmade to be compared to something so organic, something smoothed by the endless caress of the tide. Carefully, she scrapes the excess sand away. Her breath catches and she has to blink several times to remind herself she isn't dreaming, but standing in her own bedchamber in the heart of London.

On her palm sits a tiny yellow shoe.

22

It's late afternoon the day after the incident at Mercy Adams' house when Bess sits down at her desk to write Casper a letter. She dips her nib in the pool of ink, then sets it against the parchment, waiting for inspiration. All that comes is the vegetable scent of tulip bulbs and a thin trace of brine.

What would she say, if he were here? She would say: Casper, you are the only one who understands me and I think we should remain friends. She would say: Thank you for showing me a side of myself I didn't know existed. She would say: Please help me prove my father wrong, so his mind can be put at ease about the things that have befallen him.

Bess replaces the quill in its holder and unlocks the desk's drawer, pulling out the little square map her father drew. Tracing her thumb along the coast of New Holland, she squints at the tiny numbers, the star-crossed lines of latitude and longitude. How did her father come by these calculations? He says his compass broke, became waterlogged when he was washed overboard. So then, how could he tell? Perhaps one of the other sailors made note of it when they picked him up, although he says the day was foggy and nobody afterwards was willing to confirm they had seen any island at all ... nobody except Piet, of course. Bess wants to remain as far away from her father's friend as possible but she wonders, if their paths do cross, whether he will confirm or deny the accuracy of the map. Better to be safe, she thinks, slipping the map into her skirt.

The door swings open and she detects a hesitant footstep squeaking on the hall boards.

'Bessie? Are you in there?'

Johnny holds an arithmetic book under his arm. Loping in, he sits on the end of her bed, blinking at her with his heavy-lidded eyes. He looks exhausted, worn out by all his attentions to Pa, and although Bess feels a pang of envy at their closeness, pity wins out.

'Could you help me with these sums?' he says. 'I can't seem to understand them.'

'Course I can,' she says, beckoning him over. 'But I'm not as good at arithmetic as Pa. Can you ask him?'

'He's not here.'

'Did he say when he'd be back?'

Johnny shakes his head.

Bess glances out the window, where the sun is beginning to set. 'I'm sure it will be soon. He promised to be here for my birthday. Alice is roasting a loin.'

The smell of it wafts up the stairs and into the bedroom, rich gravy and crackling skin turning her mouth to water. 'I'm sure he won't be long,' she says, with renewed conviction. 'Here, show me your sums. We can muddle through together.'

Drawing up another stool, she spreads the book on the desk and bids him sit beside her. Together, they attempt to decipher the answers but Bess's knowledge of arithmetic is simple. At Missus Priest's, they learned basic addition and subtraction, how to balance a household ledger, how to ensure the servants were not making off with the silver spoons. Nothing like this. Nothing that would mean the difference between charting a course for Japan and ending up in the East Indies. This kind of arithmetic is designed to help men find their way across the globe. It is intended to help them fix their position accurately, to eliminate errors through the judicious use of dead reckoning. If one can determine this point, then a landmark does not need to be seen in order to exist. Once upon a time, Bess would have delighted in such navigational rumination, but now she finds the sums are like stick insects, moving before her eyes, their answers as variegated as the plants in her mother's garden.

After thinking out loud for some moments and getting nowhere, she snaps the book shut and throws it across the room.

Johnny draws in a shocked breath and stares at her as if she has grown three heads. His expression is so comical she cannot help but laugh.

'I'm sorry,' she says. 'But much more of that and I'll go mad! Don't they have tutors to help you with these things? You surely cannot be expected to work those sums out on your own.'

Johnny sighs, looking down at his shoes. 'Some of the older boys are meant to tutor us, but they demand things in return and I –' He purses his lips suddenly.

'You what?'

He raises his chin and she is reminded of Mam staring down Stephen Adams, the same look of determination and self-assurance. 'I will not submit to their demands,' he says.

'They are braggarts, but powerful nonetheless. One of them is a magistrate's son. They like to tease me and pull my hair.' He winces at the memory and lifts his hand, fingering his curls. 'They have a name for me: Pretty Poppet. They say I'm too stupid to be anything finer than a sailor, like Pa. They say I'll be ill-used there, some captain's favourite cabin boy.'

'Oh, Johnny. That's horrible.' Bess slips an arm around him, her mouth dry.

When her hand contracts around his ribs, he lets out a sudden gasp and stumbles away from her, the stool toppling. His breath comes in shallow gasps and his eyes glimmer with moisture. 'Don't touch me,' he says.

Bess stares at him, horrified. Although she wants to help, she cannot think of what to say. How should she comfort him? What can she do to convince him she is on his side?

'Anyway,' he says, his voice still strange, high-pitched, like that of a child younger than his eleven years. 'No use complaining. I'm stuck there, aren't I? Uncle John has plans to send me to college, if I pass my prep. Otherwise it's back here in disgrace. Think of what Pa would say.'

I don't much care what Pa will say, she thinks. 'You belong here,' she says aloud. 'You should speak to Mam. Surely there are schools here in London you can go to? Then you can stay here again, with us. If you weren't around those boys, they couldn't hurt you.'

But her brother is already shaking his head, the gold curls bobbing around his red ears. 'Mam can't afford the fees without Uncle John's help. I may be slow, Bess, but I know that much.'

'She has a new position, with the Bishop,' Bess says. 'It comes with a little extra money. Don't give up. I'll speak to her –'

'No!' Johnny's fists clench at his sides. 'No,' he repeats, in a softer tone.

He crosses the room, picks up his book of sums and dusts it off. Clutching it to his chest, he goes to the door. 'Promise you won't say a word,' he says, fixing her again with his flint-eyed, determined look and Bess nods, even though her heart clamours for justice.

The sun is a faint disc on the horizon as she changes her dress, pondering how she can best help Johnny. All this time, she imagined herself alone, the only one suffering under the bondage of convention. She imagined Johnny, her mother's favourite, could do no wrong. Now that his true position is revealed, she realises with a pang of guilt how wrong she's been. She must do something to help set her brother's life back on course.

The birthday supper is to be attended only by their family and Alice, who plans to join in the celebrations before setting out for her father's house in time to meet the curfew. Mam considered inviting Elinor and Susanna but in the end, she decided to keep the occasion as small as possible. There are those in Wapping (Constable Grape amongst them) who believe birthdays should pass without note. Bess cannot remember the doctrine of the Puritan clergy who occupied London in the wake of the Civil War, but she's heard stories. The Congregationalists at their little church in Smith Street observe similar conventions, eschewing bright cloth for drab, favouring Christian prayer over Popish idolatry. Saints' days are tolerated – just – but the concept of celebrating an individual's entering the world, someone common, especially a girl – well, it is not worth advertising in case it causes disruption. But for all her rigidity, Mam loves birthdays and believes they deserve to be celebrated.

As she slips into the smoky kitchen, Bess overhears Alice telling Mam about her dying father's discomfort, his slow, steady decline. The onions she is stirring simmer softly in the pan, the smell mingling with the rich scent of roasted meat. Every few minutes the maid pauses to stifle a yawn.

'God has not granted him a swift death, missus. Instead, he is forced to endure bodily humiliations, day and night. Perhaps it is un-Christian of me but each time he cries out in distress, I think of the times he came to visit my bed at night ... and Hester, listening on the other side of the curtain, stuffing wool in her ears, and I am glad he suffers. If you could but see the agony in his face –' She stops, alert to Bess's presence near the china cabinet.

'The good plates, please,' Mam says, bent over the stove, her face beaded with sweat.

Bess frowns at the patterned china, hoping to linger and listen but the women are clearly waiting for her to leave before they continue, so she lifts the plates and carries them to the dining room.

Setting them down one by one in their places, she catches bits of her own reflection in the china. Can she really be fifteen? She doesn't feel any different. When she woke this morning to see the sun slanting through her shutters, she expected to feel smarter, or more beautiful – something other than what she was when she laid her head down to rest. The illusion melted the moment Mam shouted up that she was running late for work. Everything was the same old frenzy, throwing on her clothes, lacing her boots, walking to Missus Clifton's with Mam. Mam seemed distracted, too busy rehearsing an imaginary conversation with the Bishop to ask

Bess how she felt. At Missus Clifton's door, she'd kissed Bess's cheek swiftly before turning away and hurrying off in the direction of her first appointment, still muttering under her breath about husbands and duty and children who deserved better. Bess wanted to call her back, to ask if she could help or offer advice but the words died on her tongue so she closed the door softly instead and went to find Missus Clifton. Fifteen, it seems, is still too young to be taken seriously. Too young to know how to mend the breach of understanding between Mam and herself. Jane Sharp, in her midwifery manual, advises women to be God-fearing, faithful and respectful to everyone, but she means in a professional sense, of course. There is nothing written there – Bess should know, she has read the thing cover to cover twice already, smiling slyly with Susanna over the descriptions of male yardsticks – about how one apprentice should treat an elder midwife, especially if that midwife is her mother.

Returning to the kitchen, Bess hunts in the cutlery drawer, searching for forks that match. She finds one with an ivory handle, one wooden and three tarnished silver. They will have to do.

'Bess?' Mam is frowning over something in a pan: a cake with burned edges. Bess attempts to study it, but her mother hunches around it, protective. 'Run into the garden and fetch me some mint,' she says.

Not even a please, Bess thinks as she throws the cutlery onto the table and stalks outside into the night. The wind is tormenting the herbs, whipping the leaves into a frenzy and causing the weathervane to spin madly on the roof, loosening its arrow north, south, east, as if it cannot make up its mind. Bess is buffeted along the path, the wind lashing her skirt, teasing her hair. When she reaches the mint, she drops to her knees and yanks at the stalks until they come away, bruised, filling the air with a clean menthol scent.

'Is it your birthday?'

Bess whirls around. 'Casper?' she cries. 'Is that you?'

He steps out from behind the lime tree, the moonlight draining his clothes and face of colour.

'You're still here!' Bess's heart quivers inside her chest. She wants to fling her arms around his neck, so glad she is to see him. But the wind seems intent on separating them. Seizing his hand, she drags him through the garden beds to the little shed where her mother keeps her spades and weedhooks. She pushes him in and squeezes inside after him, closing the door so it won't bang open. They are both breathing hard and laughing.

'Listen to it howl,' Bess says, gleeful, as the wind whistles between the planks. It can't get at them here, though. It's powerless, no matter how hard it rages, thwacking the branches of the holly bush against the tin roof, burrowing under the door.

The shed smells of loam and woodsmoke. A thin shaft of light shines in through a knothole, slicing Casper's body in half. She shivers suddenly, disliking the intrusion of the macabre thought. The handle of a spade digs into her back and she shifts, dislodging it. As Casper's leg brushes her knee, she is acutely aware of how narrow the space is, of the way his breath fans her cheeks. She is aware of the heat of his body, a foreign landscape so different from her own. Into her mind pops the diagrams she has seen, the descriptions of copulation, the secrets men and women partake of in order for babies to fruit.

She tries to swallow against the raspy dryness of her throat. Thankfully, he speaks first.

'I've come to say goodbye.'

'What?'

'The wind has changed,' he says, as if that explains everything. 'And my master has found us a boat, a good vessel. *The Nightingale*. We leave for the East tomorrow. So, I've come to say my goodbyes and thank you for your friendship. It has been a pleasure to get to know you and learn about your family.'

'You can't go,' she says, cringing at her foolish words even as she speaks them.

Casper looks startled, as if it has never occurred to him that he won't. 'I must, of course. This is my life. I go where my master leads me, I follow the tide.'

She tastes salt on her lips. Why is she crying? Ridiculous, but she is as powerless to control her emotions as the wind beating its fists against the door.

'When will you be back?' she manages to say.

'A year. Two. It may be sooner. My master says the price of spice and cotton will skyrocket, with the English declaring war again on France. Don't worry,' he says, 'I'll bring you a tulip. A whole bag. Or maybe some other flower. Something your mother could plant in her garden, something rare. Then she'll have to invite me in.'

Although his face is shrouded in darkness, Bess hears the smile.

'I would like that,' she says, sniffling. She searches for her handkin inside her skirt but her fingers surprise the sharp edge of parchment. She pulls it out, unfolds it. Moonlight bathes the map. 'Pa drew this,' she says, clutching the parchment. 'It's so unlikely, but do you think . . . if you are anywhere near . . .' She sucks in a great breath. 'Could you look for it? If we could just prove to him that there's nothing there. If you could tell him there's no island . . . I think he would have no choice but to admit he was wrong.'

He takes the map from her, turning it uncertainly in his hands. Bess's hope dims – he is going to refuse. Casper holds the map up to the light, tilting it this way and that. At last, he tucks it inside his jacket. 'It's a strange request Bess. Have you ever seen a map like this? For I haven't. And I can't make any promises since it's not my ship, but I will try. I'll try for you.'

'Thank you.' She feels lighter, as if the map is a stone she has been carrying. 'There's probably nothing there. None of Pa's shipmates would even say it existed. Nobody supports his claims except Piet.'

Casper's breath catches. 'Piet Willems? You've seen Piet again? Why didn't you stay away from him?'

Bess looks away, unwilling to speak about her father's mission, his demand for medicine. She knows now, or thinks she knows, what he was asking for and it seems a betrayal of trust to confess it. When she doesn't answer, Casper gives her shoulders a slight shake.

'Listen, Bess, Piet is a bad man. I asked my master about him after what happened and he says Piet has done terrible things. He hurts people, or at least, he always seems to be around when people get hurt. Nothing has ever been proven against him in a court of law. But he is banned from the United Provinces, and no ships will take him unless they are desperate for men. You should avoid him at all costs, Bess, especially when I'm not around to protect you. It would break me, to learn you had come to any harm. I – I would not know what to do with myself.'

Bess wants to ask more, but the thrill of his words sends her spirits soaring. It would break him? Does that mean he likes her? They are close enough for him to bend his mouth to hers. She wonders what his lips might feel like – will they be rough or smooth? – and then she thinks that she doesn't mind, she will take either, if he will only kiss her.

She tilts her head up, wishing she had a candle. But perhaps it is better this way, in the dark, hiding from their old selves. His hands move from her shoulders to her back, the heat of his palms seeping through her cotton blouse, worming under her stays. Then he hesitates. She notes the bob and catch of his Adam's apple in the dim light, and in the long moment that follows, it occurs to her that he might be as scared as she is, uncertain whether to pull back or push forward.

He does not kiss her. Instead, he brushes his fingers against the back of her neck, embracing her gently. 'Bess,' he says hoarsely, his body stilling. They are at an impasse but she clings to him, unwilling to be the one to set him free.

'Where have you been?' Alice mutters when Bess walks back into the kitchen clutching the ropes of mint.

'What?'

Alice rolls her eyes. 'Your presence is required.' Hefting up the skillet of steaming onions, she tips them onto a serving platter and walks briskly into the hallway. Bess follows. Inside the dining room, she finds her mother and Johnny sitting at their places, meat cooling on their plates.

'Did I miss the carving?' she says.

'You did.' Mam's voice is clipped. She spoons glistening onions onto Johnny's plate. 'You and your father. Why were you so long?'

Bess's gaze flicks to her father's empty chair. 'The wind was banging the shed door and I went to close it. Where's Pa?'

Her mother's jaw tightens. 'Your father's whereabouts are as mysterious to me as they are to you.'

Bess takes her seat. The strange, exquisite weightlessness she experienced only moments ago in Casper's arms has morphed into a niggling worry. Somewhere in the walls, she hears scrabbling paws. A mouse, navigating the lathwork, an echo of her own fear. To distract herself, she nibbles the food on her plate. The meat is obscenely soft and falls to bits on her tongue, the honey marinade Alice lovingly applied sweet enough to make her teeth ache. Her skin feels so bruised and tender, it is a wonder no one notices. It's a miracle she is sitting here, chewing her food and swallowing, obedient, while inside her, new desires and daydreams are multiplying, possibilities stretching, limitless. She is full to the brim with them, in danger of leaping up and stripping off her clothes and running naked through the front door. Imagine the looks on the neighbours' faces! Her restlessness is like a fever, splitting her apart, curdling her like spoilt milk. Is this love? Is it love that makes her want to dance around like a wild creature? Is this how married people feel *all the time*? If so, how do they contain themselves, how do they control the urge to shout at the top of their lungs and beat their arms like wings to find out if they can, as their hearts inform them, actually fly? How do they mask it with such calm pretence? How do they stand it, pretending that they are cool and uncaring when every part of them is bursting with pure nightingale song? This cannot be how her parents feel.

'Mam, can I have some ale?' she says, for if she doesn't say something soon she is afraid she will betray herself.

Her mother sends Alice to fetch some from the kitchen. Then she brings a wrapped parcel from under the table.

'For you,' she says, handing it to Bess over the strewn remains of their meal. The parcel is tightly knotted and a sprig of purple foxglove – Bess's favourite flower – is pushed under the twine. Bess flushes and thanks her, picking at the knot with her ragged fingernails. Inside the wrapping is a cloak made of thick broadcloth, the hood pleated to fullness to protect the wearer's face. When she holds it up, the silk lining shushes against her bare arms, the folds as red as a robin's breast.

'I hope you like it,' Mam says, and Bess is both alarmed and touched to realise her mother is on the verge of tears. Mam pulls herself together, though, stiffening her spine, clearing her throat until the warble is gone. 'Missus Clifton and Elinor tell me you've been very diligent in your duties. "A great help," I believe they said. Especially considering Anne's illness and the extra work I've needed to take on with the Bishop. I'm only sorry your father is not here to wish you good tidings. But I want you to know I'm proud of you, Bess. How glad –'

The sudden bang of a door interrupts them. Wind swirls into the room, guttering the candles. Heavy footfalls and raised voices approach. Mam jumps up, her knife clattering to the floor.

'The scoundrel has always hated me,' Bess hears Pa say. 'That's why.'

He lurches into view, blinking in confusion at their tight faces, the candles ranged about the room. His overcoat is torn, the sleeve gaping open, but he doesn't seem to notice. A sharp, strange smell emanates from his hair and clothing: the smell of Piet Willem's pipe smoke. Glued to her chair, Bess watches Pa stumble to the table. He grips the edge of it as if it were a raft, the only thing between him and an unfathomable sea. Then he falls into a chair, wheezing, breathless.

Mam is on her feet, reaching for Johnny, when Piet Willems steps into the room.

'God give you good evening,' he says, grinning at them, his sharp teeth glinting in the light.

Bess is certain the house will break apart under the crushing weight of her father's fury. Tucked under the coverlet with Johnny lying on the trundle bed nearby, Bess listens to her father pace in the room next door, the trumpet blast of his voice, admonishing and accusing.

'You cannot tell me what company I may keep in my own house, woman!' Pa says.

'It's my house, too. And Bess's and Johnny's. Turn him out now and be done with it. Surely he has some other place to go? You should not be seen associating with such a man. Don't you remember how talk spreads?'

'Madam, if I were in your position, I would look to my own affairs. Your midwife's trade is an embarrassment. Who will marry Bess now, d'you think? Who will want a girl like that, now that you have poisoned her with ideas above her station and tricked her into thinking she is superior to her spouse? You've almost ruined Johnny with your soft ways. Thank God I am here – and Piet – to teach him a thing or two about being a man. When I think of the damage you've done –'

'The damage *I've* done?'

The rest of Mam's words are muffled – Bess imagines she has turned away, too furious to continue facing him. At last, everything shudders into quietness and only the wind is audible, still battering the shutters. Bess hears her brother sigh and roll over, seeking sleep. She hears feet on the attic stairs, her parents' door firmly closing and from the parlour, the sound of furniture being shifted, the squeak of wood. She shivers under her coverlet. When she is certain Johnny is asleep, she throws a shawl over her shift and sneaks out into the hallway.

A light is burning in the hall below but the landing is dark. Carefully, she climbs the stairs to the attic, hears her mother gasp and grope about for her flint and candle.

'It's just me,' she whispers. 'Bess.'

Mam lets out a groan. Bess perches on the edge of her bed.

'Bess, you shouldn't be up here,' Mam says. 'Go back to bed.'

'I can't sleep.'

Her mother says nothing. Bess hears the fretful click of teeth against nails.

'What's happening?' she says. 'Is Mister Willems staying here?'

'I sincerely hope not,' Mam says. 'Your father says he will only stay one night.'

'Even one night is too many.'

'I agree.'

They are silent, both thinking about the man dragging the furniture to and fro in the room below, making himself as comfortable as a rat in a cosy nest.

'You must convince Pa to make him leave.'

Mam snorts softly. 'Your father is beyond reasoning with.'

'He's . . . dangerous.' Bess pulls her shawl tighter, worming her fingers through the holes. 'I have it on good authority.'

'Whose authority?' Mam says, sharply.

Bess draws in a breath. The temptation to spill all her secrets to Mam – where she was earlier, who she was with – is like an ache in her stomach, a fullness she must share in order to digest what remains. 'Casper,' she says. 'He told me. He was here earlier, I spoke to him.'

Mam sits up. Although there is no candlelight, Bess senses the frown on her mother's face, her lips pursed in disapproval. 'You spoke to him, after I forbid you to?'

'I couldn't help it,' Bess says, in a small voice. The confession of her clandestine meeting does not feel as wonderful as she supposed it would. Somehow, she has mistaken her mother for Susanna. Susanna would have pressed her for details, gobbling them up like scraps of pastry. Mam does not ask for details. Indeed, she says nothing more and as the silence grows, Bess begins to panic, regretting her hasty confidence, wishing she could undo what has been said. She rises to her feet, agitated beyond words.

'Elisabeth Grace. This is intolerable.'

'We were only talking,' Bess says, but Mam, her senses honed by the confrontation with Pa, seems to perceive what truly happened as if she were there. The light flares, stark and unforgiving. In its wavering glow, every line of her mother's face is a mark set against her, every crease a miniature frown of displeasure and betrayal.

'I – This is not the problem, Mam,' Bess says, trying for evasion. 'The problem is that man downstairs. He's the one you should be worried about. What will we do about him? Casper says we must –'

'*We?* We will do nothing!' Mam explodes, shoving the candle roughly towards her and rising to her feet. Towering over her, she spreads her arms wide, her fury a wild, unstoppable force. 'What more must I do? What more must I say before you listen? I manage what happens in this house, Elisabeth. Not you. Not your friend. I am so – so –' Closing her eyes, she seems incapable of further speech and Bess, shrinking back on the bed, is too afraid to contribute. A wave of misery like a channel of cold and grimy water sluices through her.

Holding her elbows, she shivers, waiting for Mam to speak, to exonerate or condemn. She feels utterly powerless.

At last, Mam masters herself. Her shoulders slacken and she sighs wearily, waving in the direction of the door. 'Go to your room at once and stay there. Now.'

Bess waits for more but Mam angles her body towards the bed, hunching away as if Bess's very presence disgusts her. Slowly, Bess rises and walks to the door, shielding the flame with her hand. At the bottom of the attic stairs, she retches, the rich supper and the fight with her mother combining to churn her stomach. Holding in her tears, she closes the door of her room and leans against it, listening to the wind rattle the shutters and to Johnny's reassuring breathing.

23

Primed for confrontation, Mary descends the attic stairs the following morning only to discover the master bedroom unoccupied. Lemuel has already left the house, taking Piet with him. She picks her way through the mess-strewn parlour, alert to any traces of opium. Plucking fallen bedclothes off the floor, she shakes them out, frowning at a mysterious red stain on a blanket. The strong scent of roses suggests it has come from the stillroom, a rose tincture steeped in brandy to soothe the nerves. The bottle, hidden under the sofa, has been drained of every last drop. Who would drink all that in one go? She does not have to think far to come to the most probable conclusion. Her search turns up nothing else of interest. Deflated, she sits on the sofa clutching the empty tincture bottle and watches the sun slide across the floorboards.

At least the men are gone. She hears Johnny humming in the kitchen and Bess moving about upstairs. For once, Lemuel has kept his promise. The sensation of relief is strange and unsettling; she is so accustomed to disappointment where he is concerned. The image of the small shoe kindles in her mind. The shoe is harder for her to dismiss than his claims of being an emissary for a group of tiny foreign people. There must be some explanation but in her exhausted state – she barely slept, too fretful to relax her guard for more than half an hour at a time – it's hard to think clearly. Her fuzzy thoughts clump together and drift apart, refusing to make sense.

Pulling the shoe from her pocket, she turns it over on her palm, stroking the tiny wooden heel with her thumb. Feather light, it reminds her of Bess's poppets, the costumes she used to sew for them before Bess outgrew such childish notions. The memory of Bess's hurt face makes her groan aloud. Mary hadn't meant to lose her temper. Perhaps she should share the discovery of the shoe with her daughter to make amends. Together, they could formulate a plan. Closing her hand over the shoe, she tucks it away and goes back upstairs. She knocks on Bess's door and calls her name.

Although no one comes, Mary senses her daughter standing on the other side of the door, listening.

'Bess?' she says again. 'I've something to show you. Come out.'

Bess does not respond. After what seems an age, Mary gives up and goes downstairs to find Alice, returned from her father's house, spooning warm pottage into Johnny's bowl.

'I'll see to her,' Alice says, when Mary confides the situation to her in a low voice. 'Don't fret. All families have their ups and downs. She'll come around. You wait and see.'

Sensing the truth in this, she prepares herself for the day ahead. Before leaving for her rounds, she straightens the parlour and writes Richard a letter, begging him for his advice about the tiny shoe. Richard will know how to manage this unsettling discovery.

Propping it on the hall table, she snatches up her kitbag and hurries out.

She doesn't think of the shoe again until late afternoon when, after finishing a client examination at her neighbour's house, she bends to retrieve her bag and spies a small battalion of crudely carved timber soldiers arrayed on the parlour floor. Lost in thought, she observes their lumpish limbs, the block heads and badly etched faces.

'I'm sorry, Missus Gulliver,' says her client, exhaling a long-suffering sigh. 'I told Billy to pick them up before you arrived, but did he listen?'

'There's no need to apologise.' Mary touches what she supposes to be the carved blade of a bayonet. 'Who made them?'

'Billy's Pa whittled them for him. He says it keeps his mind busy when he's at sea.'

Mary's client walks her to the door and Mary nods vaguely as the woman confirms her next appointment. The wooden soldiers are so roughly constructed, she cannot imagine a sailor having the skill or the materials to make such a finely wrought thing as the tiny brocade shoe. So where, then, did it come from? And by whose hands?

Her thoughts are still chasing each other as she bids her neighbour goodbye and begins the walk home. Perhaps Richard has already sent a response? Or better yet, come himself? Her heart lifts in hope but when she enters the house, the parlour is empty and the hallstand bare. She hears Alice and Johnny laughing in the kitchen and is about to go to them when a sudden knocking at the door makes her turn.

'Bridget Maloney asks if you'll come right away, Missus Gulliver.' The messenger boy shuffles his feet, sending a light powdering of dirt to the floor.

'Is it the baby?'

The boy nods, anxiously. 'Something's wrong with it. Or with her, my ma wouldn't say. The Maloneys are our neighbours. Ma sent me to fetch you when I got back from the workhouse. I ran all the way.'

'Wait here for me to get my things,' Mary says, dashing into the kitchen for more butter to anoint her hands before the birth and lessen the risk of causing discomfort. Johnny is there, helping himself to leftovers. He has eaten constantly since he returned and she's glad to see his cheeks are fuller, the colour returning to them. Behind the curtain pegged across the stillroom's entrance, she can hear Alice wringing water, humming to herself.

'Mam, can I talk to you?' Johnny says softly.

'Not now,' she says, images of Abigail Sparrow's stillbirth echoing in her head. 'Can it wait?'

He nods, turning away from her with a bit of bread to toast in the embers of the fire. 'It's not important,' he says. 'Forget I asked.'

Maire is waiting for her at the Maloneys' shack, dancing from foot to foot, her small face a shining beacon of excitement and awe, unburdened this time by her baby sister.

'Mam says I can stay and help,' she says as Mary peers around, trying to discern Bridget's figure inside the dim interior. 'We don't really need you, I can deliver the baby myself. I hope 'tis a boy. I'd like me a brother.'

A low moan rises out of the darkness.

'Bridget?' Mary calls softly. 'It's Mary, come to help you.'

A pause before Bridget staggers into view behind her daughter, breathing heavily and leaning against the rough timber frame. 'Maire, I said you could stay as long as you keep out of Missus Gulliver's path. And here you are, standing guard like the ghost of Grace O'Malley. Get inside and light the lamp, won't you?'

Maire runs inside as Bridget stiffens, her body seized by a contraction. Mary takes in the knotted veins on her work-worn hands, the whites of her fingertips pressed against her girth. The pain must be nearing breaking point, she thinks.

Light flares in the dark room and Maire's small face reappears. Bridget coughs suddenly and wetly, tipping forward so quickly Mary is sure she will fall. Gripping the woman's forearm, she detects a flicker of heat bubbling beneath Bridget's clammy skin. Her wracking coughs turn to a long, panting wheeze before she sags back.

'You're fevered,' Mary says.

Bridget shakes her head. 'It's just a cold. The heat of childbearing flushing my skin. Tis only –'

Her words are strangled by another spasm of violent coughing. A long string of spittle flies from her mouth and spatters in the dirt.

Mary turns to the women who have slipped out of the neighbouring houses. 'Can any of you help this woman by laying on a fire and heating some herbs for me?'

'I'll help,' says a woman in a tattered shawl. Giving her name as Sarah, she takes the herbs, shooing away the sooty pigeons clustered at the entrance of her house.

Mary helps Bridget inside, easing her onto a stained mattress. Under her nightdress, Bridget's thighs and knees are hot. Mary runs her hands carefully up Bridget's body, checking for plague tokens, but she is blessedly free of boils. Just an ordinary fever, then, perhaps brought on by a bad cold. Dangerous to both mother and child, but she has seen women through worse bindings.

'Maire.' The young girl's face appears around the curtain. 'I'd like you to go and stay with Missus O'Donoghue, please.'

Maire's smile vanishes.

'Go on, now,' Mary urges. 'Your mam and I will be fine here without your help, but your sister needs you. I'll send for you as soon as I can.'

When Bridget's griping lessens, she pants, 'Why'd you send the girlie away? You think this time it will be different?'

Mary's first instinct is to reassure, but Bridget deserves the truth. 'It's possible,' she admits, uncorking a bottle of liniment. 'Birthing babies with a fever can give rise to difficulties, and I would hate to worry her. I remember when my mother took me along with her to the first birth, it scared me senseless. I could not stomach meat for weeks afterwards – probably a benefit, as we had little. But it's not a thing I'd wish children to see until they're a little older, eight or nine, at least. Of course, that cannot always be the case.'

For the next hour, she anoints Bridget with oil of lilies, dabbing her hairline, swiping the rag under her thin arms. The baby is a small, oblong lump wedged between Bridget's pelvic bones. Rudely woken from cosy hibernation, he now seems determined not to move at all, to disoblige them with his stubborn will before he is even born. Mary grips Bridget's hand tightly as waves of pain swell and recede, the woman's feet clenching in agony, toes curled over the end of the mattress.

A shadow falls on them.

'Here's those herbs you wanted,' Sarah says, thrusting the steaming mug into Mary's hand as Bridget struggles onto her elbows. The first gulp makes her gag, but with Mary's encouragement, she imbibes the vessel's contents, the syrupy smell seeping out to fill the narrow cabin.

'By God, that's sweet,' Bridget says, drawing a trembling hand over her mouth. 'You're sure it won't harm the bairn?'

'It's just simples,' Mary says. 'But with luck, it will bring down your fever.'

The fever need not be banished in its entirety, but brought down long enough to ensure the infant is less imperilled. Hot remedies should be avoided during labour, says Jane Sharp, lest they bring the woman into fever. But a woman who is already fevered must fight fire with fire; the heat must be drawn out through a baptism of sweat. There are other things Mary can do, secret ways her mother taught her to cool the bloods: damp agrimony leaves plastered over a woman's buttocks, black henbane pushed into the womb like pagan offerings. But this draught works fastest of all.

Her anxiety eases slightly when she touches Bridget's cooling leg, the flushed skin holding the impression of her pale fingertips for but a moment. The timing is fortunate. Bridget's tightenings are growing closer together, sweat soaking into the neck of her nightdress. Fluid surges from her gaping privities, spreading tributaries of pale yellow and mordant brown. Mary frowns at the murky current. She bids Sarah hold up the light. Under its merciless glare, the brown stain has a greenish cast and the sharp fecal tang is unmistakable. Mary's senses vibrate.

This baby must be born without delay.

Telling Sarah to help her, she slips her shoulder under Bridget's arm and they heave the woman up. She passes

Sarah one end of the swathing band, shows her how to pull the fabric tight across Bridget's stomach. Suspended in the cocoon, Bridget is like a great insect caught between them, her legs and arms dangling. She begins to moan, the pain gathering, condensing, her muscles tensed as if to absorb a felling blow.

She screams.

The end of the fabric in Mary's hands is as slippery as kelp. She knots it twice around her fist, ignoring the burns lacing her skin, gouged raw by the taut linen. Sarah huffs and wheezes, dragging on her own end lest it slip free and unravel. After what seems an age, Bridget's tremors pass and her legs give way. She sags, and they have no choice but to lower her gently to the floor. Head bowed, she starts to pray, her lips moving over the Lord's prayer, repeating the litany with increasing agitation. Her body heaves, seemingly without her noticing.

Drawing up Bridget's shift, Mary sees the matted boulder of the child's head.

'Bridget?' she says, running her hand down the woman's back. 'I can see your baby's head. He's almost out. Can you push again?'

Bridget snuffles but Mary isn't certain she has heard at all, the pain reaching such an intensity that she has lost all capacity for language. Insensible to their murmurs, she is locked in unrelenting agony. She is a traveller, making the perilous journey across a landscape of fear. In Mary's experience, this is the most dangerous moment of childbed. If the child sticks now, each moment that passes increases the risk that he will suffocate.

Taking Bridget's hand, she draws small circles on her flushed skin. 'You can do this, Bridget. One last push. You must keep pushing. You must fight so that he can live.'

She wills Bridget's tired body to rise, but the labouring woman remains prostrate on her hands and knees, arms and legs held tight to her sides. Then, slowly, she staggers up, the band tightening around her middle, pulled taut by Mary and Sarah.

'That's it,' Mary says, encouraging. Bridget grunts. Blood gushes onto the floor, warm and glistening. When the baby's head breaches, Mary fears Bridget will faint but she only grits her teeth and bellows louder, straining against the cloth, surrendering to some greater force.

At last, Mary spies the nub of a shoulder, then a chin, then a scrawny neck. The child – a boy – slithers out into her waiting arms, eyes crusted shut with mucus. Bridget sags, exhausted. Sarah tends to her, muttering comforts, all the while throwing worried glances at Mary, who has scooped the child up and shifted closer to the light to examine him. In her hands, the baby is small and as green as a cabbage, his skin stained with thick mucilage. Under the green, his skin is blue, laced with inky veins. Still and unmoving, he makes no protest as she turns him over, examining every inch of him, each bean-like toe, each tiny finger, each sepal lid.

'What ails him?' Bridget pants. 'Why doesn't he cry?'

The atmosphere in the room shifts. Instead of relief, there is a rising sense of disaster. Small sounds seem magnified as they strain to hear the baby's breathing, anticipating his outraged yelps. Be calm, Mary thinks, running through possibilities. Be calm. You know what this is, you have seen it a thousand times. The little boy's lungs are filled with the product of his own distress, the excrement that is the body's first voiding. To clear his airways, the fluid must be expunged. After snipping the snaking cord which connects mother and infant, she turns him carefully upside down. Pink liquid rushes out of his mouth and nose, twin streams forming a sticky puddle on the floor.

Seconds drip by like candle wax. Holding the infant, she is filled with a surge of love for Bess and Johnny. Old echoes of her own childbearing haunt the room's corners: Anne's face, her steady voice, reassuring through her labouring confusion. When Bess part-emerged with the cord wrapped around her throat like a pearl necklace, Anne had pushed her fingers inside and saved her by holding the muscular string away so she could breathe. Then when she was out, Anne had staunched the blood flow and guided Mary back through the valley of pain, back into the world of the living to meet her girl.

The gushing liquid trickles to a drip. Gently, she tips the little body up.

Please God, she prays. Please let this baby live.

More seconds pass, so slowly.

Then, finally, the little boy's eyelids flutter, his lips stir. Suddenly, he splutters a cry, expelling yet more fluid. Quickly, Mary turns him over, suspending him over her hand so the last of the poison drains away. Life pulses through him and he squirms.

'Praise God,' Sarah cries as Bridget weeps.

Mary keeps her own prayer to herself but she feels it move through her like wind stirring through branches.

'Maire will never forgive me, will she?' Mary says when, after cleaning up the room as best she can and setting aside the bloodiest linens for the pyre, she returns to check the condition of mother and infant. Both seem dazed, capable of doing nothing but blinking at each other in puzzled wonderment.

Bridget shifts her arm, slipping it free of the infant whose eyes are slowly blinking closed. 'Ah, Maire will be so pleased to see the bairn, she'll hardly remember.' She coughs quietly, her fist knotted over her mouth to muffle the sound. Outside, dusk is sifting down, the stars brightening against the dark blanket of sky.

Mary listens carefully to Bridget's rattling breath.

'I don't like the sound of that cough,' she says. 'And it's growing dark. Perhaps it's best I stay. Constable Grape and his watchmen do not look kindly on those who disobey orders.' She summons the boy who brought her and instructs him to take a message to the Needle, begging Alice to stay with the children until she returns. If he leaves now, he should catch Alice before she heads out to her father's cottage to meet the curfew.

When Maire returns, there is much gasping excitement but at last she relinquishes her brother back into her mother's arms, and agrees to let Mary share her bed. She curls into Mary's elbow, her lashes fanned against her cheeks. In her repose, Maire reminds Mary of Bess, and the pain of last night's exchange blossoms again. Bess used to lie like this, crooked in her elbow. Now she is almost grown; now she is off forming her own friendships and meeting boys. Mary closes her eyes, thinking of her marriage night, that disastrous first encounter. How naïve she was, only a few years older than Bess, with no mother to guide her. When she was a girl, her mother let slip that love could be both pleasure and pain, with the right partner. Perhaps mam's midwife's training had convinced her of this possibility – she'd met so many couples. Not all women suffered the act. Some even enjoyed it. What Mary got was a disappointment then and ever after, a coarse disregard for her mind and body that has characterised all her copulations since. If she had known it would be like that, would she have said yes? She should have married Richard, who might have given her what she still wants: a taste of carnal gratification, a deeper knowledge of her own desire, the power to unlock the mysteries of her own flesh. A man can take his pleasure where he finds it, he can hump and plough his seed into any woman who agrees or doesn't, married or otherwise. But a woman must be respectable, she must maintain the veneer of propriety or she risks losing everything: her children, her business, her status. Desire is a luxury few can afford, least of all a midwife, a woman who possesses knowledge and the power to deliver life into the world.

How Mary hopes her husband returns to sea soon, before his behaviour ruins them all. He could put an end to it all, if he wanted to. At sea, he is not bored, less easily tempted. Sailors love his stories, as Bess once loved them, and they give him the attention he needs. But on dry land he is like a fish, unable to breathe. Oh, take him back, she thinks, drowsing. If you are listening, Lady of the Sea, take him back where he belongs.

She dreams she is drowning, sinking like a stone into the cold ocean. She dreams of strong hands grasping her wrists, pulling her up, pulling her out until she falls, gasping, onto the sand. She dreams of a face looming over her, the salty tang of her rescuer's lips. He is kissing the life back into her, parting her teeth with his tongue, all warm desire and hot breath, inflating her like the rush of wind inside a bellows. Eyes wide, she searches out her saviour's features and is surprised to find her own face staring back.

*

The thin, high bleat of a sheep wakes her. Unusually, she has slept in, exhausted by the events of the past weeks and by last night's drama. Slipping free of Maire's body, she rubs her numb arm and checks Bridget's skin, as she did numerous times during the night. The fever is gone and the baby is sleeping soundly. Sarah has fallen asleep against the wall next to the Maloneys' door. She climbs slowly to her feet when Mary wakes her.

'You'll send word?' Mary says. 'If her fever worsens?'

Sarah nods, yawning. Quietly, Mary gathers her things and makes her way out into the street.

She reaches the edge of the shanties and is about to step over the boundary line when she thinks suddenly of Thea. Although the constable sent only a curt response to her letter about Thea's attacker, she had planned to come down here at some stage and let Thea know there'd been another assault.

Turning left, she heads towards the clutch of cabins where Thea lives. She passes a mangy brown dog chewing the stumpy nub of its tail and a man with his head bowed, both forearms braced against a wall, piss issuing from his loosened breeches.

The grubby walls of Thea's cabin are streaked with last night's rain. The curtain is gone and a piece of blackened wood is firmly wedged in its place. Mary peers through a tiny glassless window, the interior so dark she can make out nothing, but the faint scent of beeswax lingers.

'Thea?' she calls, rapping the door with her knuckles. 'Are you in there?'

'Thea's gone,' says a girl propped in an adjacent doorway. Thin arms and legs protrude from her cotton shift and her face is creased like a puckered apple. A snarl of pale hair crowns her head.

'Did she say where?'

The girl shrugs, then stretches her arms above her head, exposing veiny wrists. 'No clue, missus. She just up and left one day.'

Mary's stomach pitches as she thinks of Thea, tumbled from one life of bondage into something worse. Peering closer at the girl, she says, 'We have met before, haven't we? You're Meg.'

The girl draws back, wary. 'If it's about your husband, I don't know him,' she says, quickly, crossing her arms over her bony chest. Meg's body is coiled like a spring. Any moment, she will turn and bound back inside. 'Never seen him before in my life.'

'I believe you,' Mary says, gently. She forces herself to stillness, although she would like to take the girl's hand.

After a long moment, Meg relaxes and pulls her dress over her knees. 'You deliver the babies, don't you, missus?'

'Correct. I'm Missus Gulliver, at the Needle.'

Under the creases, Meg's face is wistful. Mary can scarce believe she is the same girl she met when Thea was interviewed. Without the powdered hair and blue gown and makeup, Meg is just a young girl, knock-kneed and getting by on what she can. Mary has met so many of these girls but the sight of Meg, unmasked, still saddens her.

Meg scratches her chin. 'I like babies,' she says. 'Sweet little things. I'd like to have one myself, one day. When I'm done with this business, that is. Me and Thea, we want to buy a shop near Picadilly. Course, we will need husbands to help us with the finance, but imagine if we didn't! Imagine if the two of us had our own funds. We used to talk about it all the time, before she up and dumped me. We said we'd raise our children together.'

'It's a lovely dream,' Mary says. 'I'm certain it will happen.'

'Maybe.' Meg sniffs. 'Maybe not, though. Very likely, God will punish me for getting rid of all the other babies. Sometimes I dream about them. Their fat little arms . . . toenails like rose petals.' A deep sadness creeps into her face. 'Anyway,' she says, standing up and shrugging off her melancholy. 'Time for work. If Thea comes back, I'll tell her you came asking. She left me her candle stub – suppose it was her way of saying sorry.'

She disappears behind the curtain, the scent of beeswax vanishing in her wake.

24

Bess is woken by muffled sobbing. Outside the window, a sparrow whistles a solitary tune but otherwise the house is quiet. The room is cold, the fire burned to ashes in the blackened grate. The remains of a tallow candle stand on her bedside cabinet.

'What's the matter?' she says, rolling over, blinking the sleep from her eyes. Johnny's back is to her as he lies on the trundle bed, his body shaking under the coverlet. Dawn light falls across his shoulders, turning his golden curls the shade of autumn leaves.

'Nothing,' he says, drawing in a great breath.

'It's something.' Climbing out of bed, she goes to kneel beside him. Burrowing her hand under the blanket, she finds his fingers and holds them. 'Tell me,' she says.

Johnny exhales. 'I went to speak to Pa about – that thing we talked about. Mam wouldn't listen – she was too busy yesterday. So, I asked Pa when he got home last night.'

'I didn't hear you.'

'I went down after you fell asleep. He was stumbling about his study in his underclothes, going through his papers, searching for something he'd lost. A map, I think he said.'

Bess's stomach contracts but she pushes the anxiety aside. The map's gone now. 'And so?'

'So, I – I told him.'

'What did he say?'

'He said I should be thankful it wasn't worse. He says when he went to the school, he was forced to do things he couldn't ever tell a living soul. But it made him a man. So, I must stop complaining. He says it's time for me to grow up.'

Johnny starts to cry again, and Bess turns her head away, helpless to comfort him.

'We have to find Mam and make her listen,' she says, firmly. 'Do you hear me, Johnny? Let's go up now and see her.'

Johnny pauses in his sobbing long enough to wipe his nose and say, 'She didn't come home and neither did Alice. I went to check the attic after Pa threw me out of his study.'

Bess blinks in surprise, unnerved by the news, forced to excise the image of Mam slipping downstairs in the dead of night and blowing out her candle. She looks over at the waxen stump. Who blew it out, if not Mam? The idea that somebody may have been creeping about in her room, watching her sleep, is enough to make her bladder clench.

'I'm going to see if Pa is awake,' she says. Her new mantuas are drying downstairs, the damp victims of Alice's energetic sponging, so she makes Johnny face the wall while she squeezes into one of her old smocks. The dress hardly fits now, the neck and sleeves tighter than she remembers.

Her parents' bedchamber is still in shadow, the shutters drawn to keep out the light. She makes out her father's form as she creeps towards the bed. He is lying face down, and she sees he's still wearing his clothes; he must have gone out again last night after Johnny spoke to him. Bess calls his name, softly at first then louder. Her scalp begins to prickle, fear worming up from her toes. Is he dead? But then he snores. Not dead, just sleeping.

'Pa?' she says, loud as she dares.

Pa jerks awake, lashing out blindly. The back of his hand catches her chin and she exclaims as pain flares along her jawline. Cradling her cheek in the palm of her hand, she stares at him, shocked by his unkempt beard and the cold look in his eyes, deep as inkwells pitted in his greasy face.

'What's the matter?' he slurs and she flinches. 'Who said you could come in here?'

Bess steps away, her eyes never leaving him. Excuses run through her head, but Pa is determined not to wait for any.

'How dare you come in here!' he says again, struggling to sit up. The movement unbalances him. Scrunching his eyes closed, he weaves back and forth, his lips moving wordlessly. A sour smell reaches her; the stench of urine and stale violets laid over by something sweet and cloying. The smell grows stronger, infusing her senses. It's the scent of Piet's room at the Louse, she realises, as a tide of memory sweeps back to that dreadful night. She remembers the way her heart seemed to slow and her thoughts wound down like the hands of a clock until she struggled to make sense of anything.

'I'm sorry,' she says, not knowing what else to say. 'I came to talk to you about Johnny. He –'

'Get out,' her father growls. He tries to lift himself to his feet, to push her out, she supposes. Once upon a time, she would have gone meekly, unwilling to trouble him, happy to acquiesce to his mercurial moods. But now she stands her ground, watching as he drags his legs off the bed and perches on the edge, holding his head in his hands.

'Father,' she says, but he seems not to hear her. Bending over his knees, he lifts the pot. 'I need to speak to you. Johnny and I, we need help. Neither Mam nor Alice came home last night and –'

Her father grapples with the chamber pot and the drawstring of his pants. Bess looks away, her cheeks on fire, as she hears the sound of splashing. Pa is a man, she thinks. Just a man. Not a god, not a pirate, not a dashing adventurer. There is nothing heroic about him now. When he is finished, he doesn't apologise but lies back down with his eyes closed, hoping she will disappear.

'Pa,' she says, and there is a hardness to her voice now that she has never used with him. 'You need to get up and help us find them. And we need to talk about Johnny, at school.'

Her father curses. He does not get up.

Bess's temper flares, a bright white heat. Marching to the washstand, she picks up a wet rag and returns to the bed, water dripping between her fingertips. Holding it over her father's face, she wrings out a stream.

At once he is up, shouting at her. 'Get out!' he roars. 'Out!'

Bess backs away, the cold rag gripped in her hand. A voice inside her head demands that she apologise and offer to fetch a clean rag so Pa can dry himself. The voice is childish and insistent but seems to come from far away, as if she is standing on a shoreline listening to someone shout at her across the ocean. No, she thinks. I will not apologise, nor will I run away to make Pa's life easier.

Pa's face is purple with rage. Gripping the edge of the bed, he glares at her from under his tufted eyebrows, a look of disgust that in most circumstances would make her quail.

With a jolt, Bess realises it's the look he gives her mother whenever she has done something which displeases him. Bess's chest tightens like a squeezed fist. I want my mother, she thinks. *Mam, where are you?*

She opens her mouth to ask Pa if he will not get up, but what she says instead surprises her.

'It was all a lie, wasn't it? You never planned to take me to sea, did you? You knew it was impossible. But you let me believe it wasn't. Why?' she asks, softly. 'Why, Pa?'

She expects him to tell her a story. Something which starts small and grows, encompassing all the reasons for what went wrong or how he planned to bend the rules so he could take her. She could even accept a sickbed wish; something said in desperation to comfort a child deathly ill with the smallpox. But years? That she cannot accept and she feels her heart crack like a china jug against her ribs as her father's silence grows.

Nothing he can say will make it right.

All her life, his stories have blinded her and now she sees, profoundly, who her father truly is. There is no help to be found. Perhaps she herself is guilty for inventing a perfect father out of thin air. An ideal man who brings sweet gifts and never, ever says no. The truth is, he has never really been here, not when it counts.

Bess stands clutching the wet cloth until the dripping stops and Pa, clearly sick of waiting for her to leave, turns away to face the wall, choosing to ignore her instead. When she can no longer bear his silence, she crosses the room and drags open the door. Before it closes, she catches a glimpse of her father under the rumpled coverlet, his form shrunken and helpless. Tears burn, but she refuses to let them fall.

She has just stepped onto the landing when a hissing sound emanates from the room below. At once, she thinks of Puss. The animal has cornered something – perhaps a mouse or an injured bird. She must rescue the poor creature before the cat has time to gobble it up. Clattering down the stairs, she runs across the hallway to the parlour and stops short.

It's the smell she becomes aware of first: that sharp, pungent sweetness that lingered in her father's bedchamber. When she tries to move, she finds her legs have turned to water. Horrified, she takes in the sight of Piet lounging on the sofa, his long legs sprawled out in front of him. Puss crouches nearby, her yellow eyes narrowed in his direction. Piet appears wholly untroubled by the animal's malice. Standing, he stretches both arms above his head and grins at Bess, revealing a chipped lower tooth.

'Miss Elisabeth,' he says. 'How pleasant to see you again. I trust you slept as well as I did?'

'We thought you'd left,' Bess says, hugging her arms to her chest, aware of the smock clinging tightly to her figure, the thin barrier of cotton. 'You're not supposed to be here.'

'*You're not supposed to be here.*' He throws her words back at her, still grinning. 'That boy,' he says. 'Casper de Vries. He's a friend of yours?'

'I suppose,' she says slowly, confused by this sudden shift in direction.

'Come now, I wager he is more than a friend. You can confide in me, Miss Elisabeth.' He places his hand over the place where she supposes his heart should be. 'I swear, I will keep all your secrets safe. But you must tell me if you've been intimate.'

He pauses, allowing the silence to expand until Bess's throat throbs with heat. Terrified, she swallows hard and shakes her head. His smile falters.

'Are you certain? Not even a kiss? You must be permitted to amuse yourself, especially before you marry. Isn't that right?'

'I've no call to be marrying anyone,' she manages to say. 'Not so young.'

'Fifteen,' he says, tapping his thigh. His fingers, she notices, are stained yellow as if he has dipped them into one of Mam's tinctures and forgotten to wash them. 'It's not so young. I hear your mother wed at eighteen. An old maid.' He laughs, his breath hot and sour as he leans in to her. 'In Holland, girls are married young. Before you can say *geslacht*, they have a baby right here.' Moving closer, he hovers his hand over her flat stomach. 'Then one, two, three ... many children. Sometimes ten or twelve. Imagine.'

Without warning he pins his palm against her stomach. Bess gasps and squirms free, stumbling backwards. Her insides churn. She can still feel the hot imprint of his hand through the coarse fabric. If he pursues me further, she thinks, I'll shout for Pa. But Piet makes no move to touch her; instead, he runs his fingers through his hair and continues speaking as if there has been no interruption.

'So, you plan to be a working woman, I am told, like your mother? A pity. It is unattractive in females, when they put service before their family. Clients are no substitute for your own family, Miss Elisabeth. Trust me. My mother was a wigmaker in Amsterdam, so I should know.'

Bess's breath, coming hard and fast, now catches. 'A wigmaker?'

He nods. 'That's right. She had to do it in secret, because the guild, they would not allow her to practise her art. Night and day, night and day, hair all over the place. She was obsessed with hair. She used to grow my hair very long and then she would snip it all off in one go. It made her laugh, to see those women walking around with a little boy's hair on their shoulders. She never noticed when I was ill, never fed me enough. Ah, but it is all in the past.'

'What happened to her?' Bess says, glancing at the open front door. Please, Mam, she prays. Please come home.

Piet sighs. 'All those late nights, working her fingers to the bone. Of course, she grew ill. I felt terrible for not seeing the signs. She was unwell for a long while. She died of a trembling fever. It was very frightening for a young lad like myself. So, when your father grew ill, when he was shaking and shivering, I thought, Oh, it has happened, his body is poisoned. But I was wrong. He gave me his little sheep, he told me about the island, described it in such detail that I –' He broke off to look at her. 'Well. That is why I tried to help him, gave him medicines. You want to help him, too.'

Bess shakes her head. If she runs for the front door will he pursue her? How can she leave Johnny upstairs, at his mercy? Numbing horror wells inside her. She edges her foot along the hallway, testing Piet, waiting for him to either catch her or let her run. As if to taunt her indecision, Puss springs to her haunches and streaks towards the corridor. Piet aims a kick in the cat's direction as she passes.

When he turns back, Bess is alarmed to see his demeanour has changed; the animal's bid for freedom seems to have hardened something in him and all trace of humour has vanished. Now his pupils are so wide and dark, Bess feels as though she is staring at a devil, something soulless, not a man at all.

'You are no child, Elisabeth,' he says, moistening his lips with the tip of his tongue. 'And your father owes me money for his medicine. So I will take my due.' His fingers seize one of her locks.

Shrieking, she tries to free herself but his hands are suddenly everywhere, all over her, squeezing hard. Bess screams. She writhes while he pulls her tighter, reeling her in as if she is a fish on a hook. Unable to claw at his face, she scrabbles at his hands but they are like boulders, trapping her, holding her fast. One hand creeps up to grip her breast. Bess hears a seam rip. The cry which has been building dies in her throat as cold air rushes over her bare skin. With dreadful certainty, she realises what he intends to do, how far he plans to go, and the knowledge fills her with such wild terror, she cannot move or speak. Fight back, she thinks. But it's as if her mind and her body have never met before. He pushes her against his lap, and through the layers of her skirt she feels a snaking hardness.

From far away, she hears pounding footsteps in the hallway. Her spirit soars, unlocking her stupefied voice. 'Mam!' she screams.

It's not Mam but Johnny who dashes in, holding a knife from the kitchen. In his trembling hands, the knife glints dangerously. Bess is so thankful to see her brother she hardly notices Piet release her and edge forward until he is towering over her brother.

Johnny glares up at him. 'I'll use it,' he says. 'I will. You leave my sister alone.'

Piet laughs. 'Have you ever gutted a fish, little man?' He places his wrist against the blade, rubbing gently so a thin score of blood wells up.

'I've gutted plenty of fish.' Johnny tightens his grip on the handle.

'Then you know how to kill me. I am like a fish, I bleed, I feel pain. I am lonely, nobody ever invites me to swim with them. I was hoping your sister might, but alas, your father's stories again. He said she would be ready for marriage in a few years. I was merely offering my hand, pressing my suit.'

'Go away,' Johnny says. 'Leave us alone!'

The knife trembles in his hand but Piet seems utterly unafraid of it. Stepping towards the boy, he lashes out so fast

Bess barely sees the flick of his hand. Johnny thumps to the floor, clutching the side of his face. She screams and suddenly there are footsteps at the door. Her heart leaps. Mam!

'Mary?' Alice calls.

Piet sneers and then, dropping the knife with a clatter, flees into the hallway. Bess hears Alice scream, then the sound of something heavy being shoved into the wall. The maid staggers into the room, her face white with shock. She cups her hand over her mouth and drops to her knees where Johnny lies groaning, holding his bloody cheek. When she sees Bess's clothing all torn and disarrayed she makes a strangled sound in her throat and reaches out for her with both arms. Bess falls into them, sobbing.

The three of them take refuge at Missus Clifton's, where Elinor sends for the constable. Bess has never liked Jeremiah Grape with his officious smile, but today she's glad to see him. He represents a higher authority, someone who can make sense of what has happened. When Bess mentions Pa's inebriation, that he was upstairs the entire time, Jeremiah's expression darkens.

'Parents are responsible for their children,' he says. 'It is not the parish's responsibility to ensure their safety in the home.'

Bess thinks of how sorry Pa will be when he sleeps it off, how regretful.

'Please just make sure Mister Willems is gone,' she says.

Jeremiah snorts. 'We don't take orders from children.'

In spite of this censure, he sends a watchman to the Needle and the man returns to report Piet has fled. Shortly afterwards, there comes a panicked rap on the door, and Mam flings herself into the room.

Bess has never seen her mother in such a state of disorder. Blood streaks her cheek, and her hair has fallen down over her shoulders. She looks wild.

'Bess,' she says, crossing the room to take her into her arms. Bess returns her hug stiffly. She feels so much older. Mam releases her and turns to Johnny, embracing him for so long Bess fears he will suffocate.

'That man came back.' A surge of nausea lifts in Bess's stomach as she relives the horror of his hands on her waist. 'He was there when I went down. He – he caught me –' She is sobbing now, worse than before. Susanna puts a comforting arm around her shoulders. 'He was going to – to hurt me.'

'I know,' Mam says. 'The watchman told me. Mister Grape has sent him to the Louse. They'll find him, Bess.'

'Good.' Bess turns away, allowing Susanna to soothe her. Together the two girls go into the kitchen, where Susanna heats a caudle of herbs. The brew is bitter but Bess chokes it down and allows Susanna to fold her into a chair. A hazy calm overtakes her as the herbs work their magic, softening the sharp angles of this morning's attack. She closes her eyes and rests her head against Susanna's shoulder, allowing her mind to float away.

When Mam comes into the kitchen, her eyes are red-rimmed.

'Mister Grape has more news,' she says, twisting her hands together. 'He thinks Mister Willems is the man behind all the attacks. They searched his room at the Louse and found a box of hair. All different shades.' She gulps down a sob. 'They haven't caught him but they're hopeful. People know him now, the constable's men are searching for him. He won't hurt us again.'

Bess blinks at her, still languid and sleepy. 'I want to stay here,' she says. 'With Susanna and Missus Clifton. I'm not going home.'

Her mother bows her head. 'I understand,' she says. 'Your brother –'

'He's hurt. His cheek –'

'Elinor is tending to it,' her mother says, 'it will heal. You can see him soon.'

Bess holds up her hand, which feels as though somebody has tied an iron bracelet around it. 'Not only his cheek. Those boys at his school, they tease him. They hurt him, horribly, but he was too afraid to tell you.'

Mam's expression changes to one of confusion. 'Afraid to tell me?' she says. 'But why –'

She breaks off, her eyes grown wide. No doubt she is thinking back on what was said, the moments where she might have intervened. Pity welling, Bess almost wishes she could spare her but then the memory of her brother's tear-streaked face rises in her mind and she hardens. She will not offer comfort.

'He did try to tell me,' Mam says at last, her voice breaking. 'And I didn't listen.'

Bess lolls her head back against the chair. Every part of her aches, as though she has run between Mister Heath's apothecary and home a dozen times. Into her mind floats the image of the suspended alligator, its leather skin, its cold reptilian eyes. She shudders, pulling up the blanket Susanna has draped over her. Sleep nudges at her, as demanding as a child, but she forces herself to stay awake long enough to ask, 'Where's Pa?'

Her mother's drawn and frightened face emerges from behind her shaking hands. No point hiding, Bess thinks, her thoughts woolly. No matter where you hide, the truth will find you.

'He's at home,' her mother says. 'The watchman tried to rouse him but he's confused and unwell. I've sent word to your Uncle Richard to stay with him until he recovers.'

Bess closes her eyes, but her mother's image is still visible in the cool dark behind her lids. 'I never want to see Pa again.'

25

The ordinary sounds of Wapping carry Mary home: sawing and banging from the shipbuilder's yard, the jingle of horses, sellers hawking their victuals. Their cries float, bird-like, over the street on outspread wings. Oysters, oysters! Four pence mackerel! Cherries, cherries!

At the house, she drags herself up the steps, pushes open the door.

'I knew this would happen.' Richard barely glances at her as he paces, crossing the parlour once, twice, three times, hands clasped behind his back. 'I knew something like this would happen. He's bad luck, everywhere he goes. It's always been this way.' He pauses, as if he's only just noticed her standing slumped in the hallway. A look of unbearable tenderness crosses his face, before he shakes his head and resumes his pacing, back and forth, treading a path between the furniture, which is all at odd angles.

'Where is he?' she says, forcing herself off the wall, lowering her tired body into a chair.

'Upstairs, sleeping it off. Because what else does one do, after they've destroyed their family?'

'He hasn't destroyed us,' Mary says, quietly defiant.

Richard throws her a dark look. 'Do you need reminding? He left his children in the presence of a monster.'

'It wasn't just him,' she says. 'I –'

He holds up his hand. 'If you are going to make excuses for him, I will walk out that door and never return.' Seeing her stricken expression, he softens. 'Mary, I have found a place that will help him. Not an asylum,' he says, precipitating her censure. 'A private clinic, run by a friend. I can take him there and they can help him.'

'He would not have turned to the poppy if he hadn't been shipwrecked.'

'How can you be naïve, Mary? Look at you.' He steps back, sweeping his gaze from her hair to her feet. 'You've worked hard to reach a place where you can live sufficiently without his succour. And yet you aid and abet him every time he returns.'

'They will hurt him,' she says, in a small voice. How can she explain? 'I know what they will do. He has done terrible things, he has been a bad father, a bad husband. But Mister Grape will find Piet. He is a good constable, despite his shortcomings. Bess and Johnny are safe. We can help him, Richard. We must. He needs time – Where are you going?'

Richard has snatched up his jacket. Pulling his arm through one sleeve, he perches his peruke on his head and strides out into the hallway.

'Richard!' she calls, frantic now. She catches him at the door.

'Mary.' He takes her hands, his own warm. 'I cannot help you if you refuse to listen to sense. You must make a choice. Even if he improves, you must decide what action to take.'

'What if he refuses to be helped? What if they insist on sending him somewhere worse? I've seen what they do to mad men,' she says. 'Mad women.' Her throat seizes, anger flaring before she can smother it. Hot tears burn and in the sudden blur, she sees her mother's face, the outline of ribs through thin cotton. Blackened toenails on grimy stonework, the strange contusions of her mother's bare skull. They'd shaved it, Pa told her, to stave off infection but afterwards she no longer looked like herself. Mary remembers reaching for her with both arms, her mother taking one hesitant step before the warden noticed and hurried over, wielding his brutal stick.

'She's an animal,' he warned, pushing the stick hard between her mother's breasts. 'You cannot trust her, Sir. Not near the little one. She bit me yesterday.' He held up his hand for them to see the puncture marks, the bruised flesh. 'Best you leave her now in our care. She would not want you to remember her this way.'

Mary's rage blinded her. This was Mam! Mam who had never hurt anyone. Didn't they know how many babies she'd saved, how many women? Didn't they care? But Pa nodded in agreement, and in doing so, yielded Mam up to a man who possessed greater authority than himself. Who was Pa, a simple hosier, to argue with this man who knew better? He was nobody. A small person of inferior intellect. He wouldn't fight for Mam and Mary was powerless, just a girl. What's changed? she thinks. Inside, she is still that girl, walking out of that dark chamber, abandoning her mother to her fate. Leaving her to die.

Despite what she knows of Richard, his goodness, his kind-hearted intentions, she is astonished to discover now that there is a small part of her that resists his authority and even fears him.

'I've seen it,' she says, her blood pulsing thick in her head. The sounds of the street are strangely detached and the sky above – a peerless, penetrating blue – too bright to be real. She must confess the truth; Richard must understand. She closes her eyes, draws a steadying breath. 'Before we met, I told you my mother died after the fire burnt her. Pa thought it was best we tell everyone the same. But she didn't die, not straightaway. She spent a year in the asylum. I visited her every chance I could. The men in there – they used her. The guards, the people who were supposed to protect her. They beat her with sticks when she spoke to herself. We went back once and I saw what they'd done. My own fault; I left her there. Pa was too scared to argue. So she died. Is that the kind of place you want to send Lem? Is that what he deserves, do you think, for all his faults and neglect?'

Richard is silent. His little finger strokes the back of her hand, rhythmic, soothing until her breathing slows, again. The feeling of faintness slowly pools, leaving a dull ache in her ribcage. Richard's steady gaze draws her back. Nothing to fear.

'I promise you, this place is nothing like that,' he says. 'I'm sorry for what happened to your mother. But you are a mother now. Your duty is to your children, not to Lem. Let me help him while you look to them.'

She wants to refuse, but what he says makes sense and she cannot lose him, her best friend, her only friend through the hard years. How can she let him walk away? Life without him is unimaginable, it is an endless ocean stretching on without a landmass. So, she nods, hears him expel a long breath.

'Thank you,' he says.

They get Lemuel down the stairs between them, Richard taking the bulk of his weight, slinging his semi-conscious body into a waiting carriage. The carriage is scuffed and scored all over with dents but the inside, at least, is clean. When they have heaved him in, his face still slack, Richard says, 'It's not a fancy establishment but they do good work. I have seen men recover from a variety of vices, and those who don't at least find some temporary peace. I will write to let you know his progress.'

He kisses her, his rough cheek grazing her skin. 'Good luck, Mary,' he says, preparing to hoist himself into the carriage. 'Oh, I almost forgot. The shoe you found. You still have it?'

Her fingers fly to her pocket. Yes, it is still there, the little talisman she has been carrying with her everywhere, a reminder of her husband's burden, his fantasy crossing into the realm of madness.

Digging into his pocket, Richard pulls out a card. 'I found a man, a dollmaker in St James. I thought you might take the shoe to him and ask what he knows about it. It is very likely a child's toy. But since you asked.' He presses the card into her hand.

From somewhere inside the dim carriage, Lemuel coughs. The look Richard throws him is one of tenderness mingled with exasperation, a look she has seen many times over the years. Love takes strange forms. Sometimes it is a pebble, hard and unyielding, at other times a willow birch, bending to accommodate the headlong rush of water in a stream.

'Goodbye,' Richard says.

She tries to form the word but her throat swells.

The carriage rolls away, and only then does she cry.

Mary is stamping around the kitchen, cursing Piet and herself, her footsteps shaking the plates in the china cabinet, when she hears Alice and Johnny return from Anne Clifton's in the late afternoon. She hears them climb the stairs and, a little while later, one set of footsteps descending. Alice, in her extrapolations of regret, needs soothing, and it is only when Mary has settled her beside the hearth with warm nettle tea and a slice of bread slathered in creamy butter that she finally calms down long enough to explain.

'When the boy you sent arrived, my father was on his deathbed. I knew he wouldn't last the night and I did not want Hester to be there alone so I told the master he must care for Bess and Johnny until I returned. Oh, I'm so sorry, madam. When I think what might have happened.' She shudders, clutching the mug to her, both hands cupped around it for warmth.

'It didn't happen,' Mary says. 'But I know. I feel the same.'

'Piet is the Devil, come to torment us. I knew it the moment the master brought him in.' Alice takes a bite of the bread.

Mary sips her tea, the sting of the nettles not altogether obscured by the sweetness of the lemon balm. Her lips throb. The warmth of the liquid floods her empty stomach and suffuses her tired limbs, a comfort she does not deserve. If she sits for too long, she fears she will sleep so she forces herself up. Alice has gone to help her sister arrange their father's funeral so Mary looks in on a sleeping Johnny then drifts from room to room, tidying things away but unable to settle at any task for long. Everywhere, she sees the evidence of Bess, items untidily scattered that might have bothered her before but now are sharp reminders of her daughter's absence. At last, when she can no longer stand the silence, she walks into the garden. Surveying the space, she sees that the shed door is swinging open. The wind must have got in, she thinks, barely casting a glance around the dim interior before she latches the door.

The crunch of her shoes on the pebbled path is like ice cracking beneath her heel. Bees hum past her head, curious, until she bats them away. As she looks back at the house, she notices that some of the plants near the path are struggling. Weeds have unspooled over their crucifix forms. This part of the garden is ornamental and mostly grows itself, but her neglect is obvious in the abundance of ivy snaking out over the foxgloves and snarling in the woodbine. In the shed she finds a faded apron, crusted with filth, and ties it on. After gathering her tools, she falls to her knees in the earth. She digs slowly at first and then with more determination, searching out the white cord that leads through the soil to the ivy's heart. Her back twangs and her breath circles in her lungs, emptying with each gasp as she digs deeper, unable to unearth the elusive root.

Sparrows flit overheard, chittering like laughing children, and somewhere, a dog barks. Sun glares off the stones. It is hopeless. Settling back onto her haunches, she mops her brow with her sleeve. Her skin burns with pent-up frustration. If she knew more, if she had better training . . . She remembers visiting the Chelsea Physic Garden with her mother, being turned away by the man at the door who pointed them to a sign. Apothecarists Only. She remembers her mother muttering, casting looks of longing back at the high walls. What lay behind them? She could only imagine. Seeds more precious than silver, greenhouses flushed with gilded herbs, plants that could save a woman's life in childbed. But they were not allowed even a peek. It was the garden of paradise made real and it was guarded by men.

'We'll make our own door,' her mother said later.

But has she? Has she shared everything she knows, or has she kept her daughter away, held her at arm's length? A breeze trembles the flowerbeds. Too late, it whispers.

She wipes her palms on her apron, the dirt staining the cloth. The hole she has made is big enough to fit the body of a bird. She picks up the weedhook, ready to resume her digging but stops, blinking, unable to trust her own eyes.

Not a foot away from the hole, a tulip is growing, a green mast rising above the soil, white petals streaked with crimson strands. Triumphant, it absorbs the last of the day's sunlight, uncompromising in its delicate beauty and fragile strength.

26

'Pass me the hollyhock leaves, will you?' Bess gestures with her fingers, as impatient as Missus Clifton was when Bess first arrived to begin her training. Everything fades, eventually, she thinks; nerves, envy, the fear of not being good enough. All that remains of her ordeal with Piet is a plum-coloured bruise on her wrist.

'That's the last of them,' Susanna warns, thrusting the lobes into her hand.

Bess sprinkles them into the mortar. Water bubbles on the stove, releasing a sweet fug of steam.

'Mister Heath is coming by later with more,' Bess says.

'Did you remember –'

'Yes,' Bess sighs. 'I remembered.' Setting down the pestle, she touches her fingers together. 'Oil of violets, oil of almonds, quince kernels and a handful of mallow. Oh,' she adds, as Susanna opens her mouth to reply, 'and a pinch of saffron. Did I forget anything?'

'No.' Susanna purses her lips.

'Good.' Grinning, Bess pops a piece of candied ginger into her mouth. Susanna makes a sour face as she picks up the pile of freshly pressed clouts, ready for the linen cupboard. As she walks out, Bess resumes pounding the pestle into the bowl, the herbs liquefying into greenish water under the weight. A blister has burst and healed on her thumb, hardening to a callus, the kind of battle-scar which riddles her mother's hands. If she were home, she would ask Mam for some salve to rub on it, but Missus Clifton's supply cupboard holds all the ingredients she needs. She will make one herself, later, when this preparation has been decocted.

'Who's coming today?' she asks as Susanna returns.

Her friend rattles off the names of their clients; nobody new, many of them mothers three times over.

'Quiet then.' Bess drains the liquid, sieving it through the muslin. 'Although perhaps the mysterious Mister J will make his appearance.'

'Perhaps he will,' Susanna says and the two girls smile recalling last night's amusements. The room they share is papered with golden birds. At night, the birds come alive, flitting and swooping in the shadows cast by a glowing beeswax candle. It is a bewitching room that holds all their secrets, a life-size trinket box lined with the precious few years of their remaining girlhood. Later, when are they are grown midwives with children of their own, they will remember the room and the events which took place last night, with fondness. They will pause wherever they happen to be – at the bedside of a labouring woman or in the act of spooning pottage into their child's mouth – and nostalgia will rush in like an unstoppable tide. They will remember how Susanna ran a wooden comb through Bess's hair, her deft fingers unravelling the knots. How she took up her scissors and snipped a golden curl and placed it in Bess's palm where it glittered red and gold, shimmering like a coiled snake.

'Ready?' she said, her hand clenched around a gingery hank of her own tresses. 'On three.'

They tossed the hair over their shoulders, stifling their laughter.

Susanna was the first to drop to her knees. J. The girls had stared at each other, puzzled, chewing their lips. Did they know a J? All possibilities had to be considered and discussed. Bess's, of course, was easy. She'd cupped the gratifying C to her breast and when they lay down to sleep, slid it under the bolster. Last night she dreamed she was in the belly of a great leviathan, being rocked by the wave's gentle swell. Whale song filled her ears, haunting and lovely, but sweeter still was the sound of her name on Casper's lips, his voice calling to her across the oceans and hills that divide them.

Bess, Elisabeth Grace, Elisabeth Gulliver.

'Bess.' Susanna's voice recalls her. 'Your mam's here to see you. She's waiting in the parlour. She asked if you'd come out and speak to her.'

Bess pauses in her straining. 'I don't see why not,' she says at last. 'She can come and go as she pleases. She always does. Give this to Elinor, when she comes, for the store cupboard,' she says. 'With my compliments.' Then, wiping her hands on her apron, she goes out to the parlour to face her mother.

Marooned amidst the sea of trinkets in Missus Clifton's parlour, Mam looks like a pearl in her clean white dress. She has hung her mantle on the hook in the hallway next to Bess's, and without the crimson to brighten her cheeks, she looks paler than usual. She is beautiful, Bess realises, in a brittle sort of way. Odd, how you can see someone every day and never really look at them properly. It's only when they've gone and come back that their form reveals itself, rising through the murk to leap out at you.

She kisses her mother on the cheek and sits beside her, pretending not to notice the subtle application of handkin to cheek.

'How are you keeping?' her mother asks.

'Very well,' Bess says.

'I've been up to see Anne,' Mam says. 'How are you managing her? Her decline has been something dreadful. I cannot fathom she is the same woman who hired you.'

'Elinor thinks she was in a lot of pain but she didn't say anything until her leg got bad. She has a nurse now – Missus Everdeen.'

Bess describes the nurse in detail, relishing her mother's surprised gasp as she explains the arguments Elinor and Missus Everdeen have had over Missus Clifton's treatment.

'Elinor is convinced she's stealing from the tea caddy. She hides the key in a different place each day and keeps reminding us to keep a sharp eye on her. She would have liked to nurse Missus Clifton herself, but she has too much to do, taking on Missus Clifton's clients as well as her own. She's convinced that Missus Everdeen is only after being included in the will and that's why she's so accommodating.'

Mam rests her cheek in her hand. 'And what do you think?'

Bess hesitates. She cannot remember the last time the two of them sat this way, speaking without arguing. She cannot remember the last time Mam listened to her with such avid interest and wishes she had something more interesting to talk about than Missus Banks' complaints. 'I think Elinor likes to feel important and Missus Everdeen's presence upsets that.'

When she asks about her father, Mam's smile slips. She looks down at her gloved hands, rubbing at an invisible spot.

'I think he is doing well,' she says. 'Uncle Richard writes to say that he has been telling lots of stories. He is unburdening himself, although thankfully, not to those who might take advantage of him.'

'I wish I still had his map,' Bess says. 'I would send it back to him. Alas, it is far from these shores now. I hoped to disprove his theories. If the island is a true place, it could be claimed for Her Majesty, it could be overrun by people. And then he would know there are no such things as little horses or tiny sheep.'

Mam puts her hand into her pocket. 'If what you say is true, then perhaps I, too, can help him.' She holds up a doll's trinket. 'You see? I found it in his jacket pocket a few days ago. Richard has given me the address for a dollmaker. I'm to visit him this afternoon.'

Bess picks up the shoe. The heel is small and wooden, the fabric as golden yellow as an egg yolk.

Mam replaces it in her pocket. 'Perhaps if I can offer your father proof of its provenance, he might be convinced of the truth.'

'What if he does not believe you?'

Mam sighs. 'Then at least I will have tried.' She squeezes Bess's hand. 'We will both have tried.'

Above them, the ceiling creaks, heavy footsteps shifting the boards.

'That will be Missus Everdeen,' Bess says. 'She's regular as clockwork with her tonics.' She stands. 'I ought to start preparing supper. Do you know, I've discovered that I am not so awful at cooking as I once thought. There's an order to it that rather pleases me, odd as that sounds.'

Her mother stands, too. She lifts her fingers to her lips then lets them fall. Bess sees that they are chewed and ragged, the skin peeling away from the nailbeds. 'Bess,' she says, 'will you come home? Please? This has gone on long enough. You belong at home.'

Bess stiffens. 'Piet Willems. They have not yet caught him.'

'No,' her mother admits. 'But Mister Grape has redoubled his efforts and offered a reward for the man's capture. There is a rumour he has put to sea using a false name. Be assured, if he's still hiding they will find him. Mister Clements comes around each evening to make sure we're safe before we bolt the doors.'

Bess shakes her head, still unconvinced.

'But Johnny misses you.' Her mother's voice almost breaks. 'I miss you. Please, my dear, you must relent.'

'Do not ask it of me,' Bess says. 'I cannot. I am needed here.'

A look of dark pain crosses Mam's face. 'If you change your mind,' she says, 'you know you are always welcome. Things can go back to the way they were.'

'They cannot,' Bess says. 'Things are different now. I am different, I am free.'

Her mother releases a little choking sob and Bess, hating herself, goes back to the kitchen to prepare the broth.

27

The main street of St James is packed. Moving through the throngs of people, Mary searches above their heads for the dollmaker's board. She spies the barber's sign of hand and shears and the curled-up civet cat of the perfumer's store. Where can the dollmaker be? She halts, causing the men and women around her to grumble. I am distracted, she thinks miserably. Bess's refusal to come home has compounded an already difficult morning, deepening the anxiety she felt when a letter from the Bishop arrived before she'd even stepped out to do her rounds. The letter's contents left her shaken: *More evidence required. H. Chamberlen granted use of forceps for next hard delivery. Will send word.* Will send word. So there is no appeasing the Bishop or convincing him of an alternative. Hugh Chamberlen will be sent for and he will bring his forceps to a poor woman's bedside. Nothing she says can stop him, not a single word she has not already tried.

Shoppers drift around her, trailing valets and assistants. She sees the sign of a lock of hair hanging over a peruke maker's. The shorn snippet, tied neatly in this case with a ribbon, reminds her of Piet Willems and she has to stop in order to catch the breath that suddenly burns in her lungs like hot embers. She told Bess the truth: Jeremiah Grape believes Piet has given a false name and put out to sea. They have lifted the curfew, since there is no need to be afraid of every man, just one they are unable to find. Opportunistic, Jeremiah calls him, but to Mary that sounds as though he didn't plan to rape those women at all. It sounds almost like a defence that would fit well with the excuses she has heard men use during her time in court, when she testified against them. *I couldn't help it. I was out of my mind with lust. She was asking for it.* None of which the court clerics record. It is only she who remembers them, the way they wink at her or lick their gums, hoping she might withhold the dirty truth of their deeds.

As she walks along, Mary hears her name called faintly. She pauses, turns. A slight woman in a neat blue dress pushes through the crowd towards her. Mary frowns, puzzled, until the woman reaches her.

'Thea? By God's grace!' she says.

Thea beams at her. Her hair has started to grow back and curls softly around her ears. Before Mary can say anything else, Thea throws her arms around her. Mary's natural instinct is to stiffen but Thea only laughs and draws back.

'Bet you didn't think you'd see me again,' she says, her cheeks dimpling. 'Heard you were looking for me.'

'I was. Your friend Meg said you'd gone. She misses you. I think she was a little hurt you didn't tell her you were going.'

Thea sobers. 'I couldn't,' she says, softly. 'I am no longer in that line of work. An old friend, an acquaintance, found me a job in a house over the water. I help the cook, run to the market for him and fetch the victuals he wants. See?' She lifts a basket filled with root vegetables.

'I'm pleased to hear of your good fortune.'

'I'm going to find Meg something, too. And yourself, missus? Have things been well for you?'

'I'm afraid not,' she says.

Thea grimaces. 'Ah, well. That's rough, but chin up. You are not down and out yet. Some things are out of our control, aren't they? But the winds do change. Look at me.' She twirls around, showing off her clean dress. 'Meg – she's not so bad. She makes out she knows it all, but she's as lost as anyone. She cares about me, though. Was Meg who said to go to the constable about my hair. Did they ever catch the man?' she says. 'Did they ever find him?'

'I'm afraid they didn't,' Mary says. 'But they are hopeful.'

'Well, I hope he meets Mister Noose on his way to Hell,' Thea whispers, glancing around at the well-dressed crowd. Then, raising her voice, she says, 'I'd best be off. Good luck, missus.' She races across the street.

Mary watches her disappear into the throng before she moves on, stopping short at another signboard, wedged between two larger ones. The images etched upon the timber send a shiver down her spine. Doll parts: a leg, an arm, a tiny painted head, all dismembered. The timber steps leading down to the door have been recently cleaned, the sweet smell of varnish rising around her as she descends.

The shop is a glittering cave of wonders. Row upon row of dolls peer at her from the shelves, satin dresses shimmering in the flickering light of the wall sconces. The dolls regard her with more calm than she can muster. Reaching inside her skirt, she touches the little shoe and feels heartened.

'Yes, madame?' A short man steps out from behind a fluttering curtain. Through the gap, she glimpses a brightly lit workshop. 'Can I help you? You have an appointment?'

'Are you Monsieur Bernard? I was sent here by my husband's cousin, Mister Sympson. He is –'

'A lawyer. I know him. He helped me untangle a delicate situation last year – an unsatisfied customer. A rare occurrence but one, I sadly imagine, that will increase, now that France and England are again at arms.' He plucks a doll from its stand and cradles it like an infant. 'This is Mademoiselle Marie. She is my most recent creation. You can purchase her today and take her straight to your dressmaker.'

Marie's silk dress ripples under its lace netting and flowers bloom over her corset. Two serpentine garlands snake away from each other only to be reunited at the hem of her frilled skirt.

'She's very beautiful,' Mary says. 'Sadly, it's not fashion advice I have come for.'

'Then what have you come for?'

'I've something to show you. I think it belongs to a doll, but I'm uncertain.'

'Oh?' Monsieur Bernard fusses with Marie's skirt, smoothing the fabric with his big hands while he casts Mary a sidelong glance.

'My husband brought it back from the East. It seems like it might belong to a pair, but one remains missing.'

The shoe lies in her palm, the same size as a walnut.

Monsieur Bernard adjusts his half-moon spectacles. 'A doll's shoe?' he says.

'I believe so.'

He touches the shoe with the tip of his finger. 'May I?' Gently, he tips it upright so the leather tongue is exposed, the red stitches knotted either side to hold an invisible foot. 'Fine craftsmanship,' he mutters. 'Damask. And you see the heel? The sole is made of one piece, from breast to toe.' He straightens, holding out his hand. 'I would like to examine it more closely in my workshop. I need certain tools, equipment. You are welcome to join me.'

Flinging the curtains aside, he ushers her into a workshop filled with bolts of cloth and curling ribbons and tea chests disgorging an assortment of feathers and lace filigree. A bench running the length of the wall is home to the smaller items, limbs separated into their various parts, glittering needles and spindles of silk thread. The room is brilliantly lit, brighter than the display room – in order, she supposes, to banish shadows and aid his detailed work. Blinded by the glare, she takes refuge beside a cabinet that holds a rack of tiny stays. Pleated with whalebone, the garments are so fine and delicate, she is certain that if she pulls the front laces closed, the busk will cinch together like a concertina, as real as the one she is wearing.

Monsieur Bernard sits heavily on a cushioned stool and pulls a magnifying glass to him. After a few minutes, he clears his throat and beckons her over. Holding the shoe upturned between his fingers, he presses the glass into her hand.

'You see?' He points at the heel. Through the convex lens, she sees letters.

'D – I – N – G – L – E – Y,' she reads aloud. 'Dingley. Is that a name or a word?'

Monsieur Bernard frowns. 'I speak five languages, madame. I have never heard of it. Where did your husband say he found this?'

'On his travels.'

'It could be a Dutch dollmaker, or French. But the fashion is out of date and the name means nothing to me. Nobody wears shoes like this anywhere now.' His eyes flash and he lowers the shoe. 'Will you sell it to me?'

'I was under the impression I would be paying you.'

'My advice is free, madame. I collect, as well as sell. In this case, an unusual specimen, unknown origins . . .' His gaze returns to the little shoe, and he licks his lips hungrily as if it were a sweetmeat. 'Whoever crafted this must have the tiniest hands in the world.' He tapped a thread spindle next to his elbow. 'Sometimes, I hire children to help me make the dolls. Their fingers are so light they can construct the clothing much better than I. But this model. Fairies could not sew smaller stitches. Yet, somebody has. This Dingley, whoever he may be.' He claps his hands together, delighted. 'So, we are agreed? I will give you three pounds for it.'

Mary is tempted. But what will she do if Lem asks about the shoe? How can she justify selling it, when the whole reason for her visit was to disprove his theories about its origins?

'I'm sorry,' she hears herself say. 'I cannot.'

28

The twilight is cool as Mary kneels in her herb bed, unearthing handfuls of cress to serve with the supper she and Johnny will share. The first hint of autumn can be felt in the damp soil, a trace of cold creeping up through her shins. Alice has gone to have supper with her sister so the two of them are alone. Her limbs feel heavy, as though she is moving through honey. She thinks about her mother and how she always layered cool cress over her clients' breasts to ease the discomforting arrival of their milk. Dirt sticks to her fingers as she spreads the cress in her lap, picking off the clods.

'Mam?'

She looks up to find Johnny standing over her. Squinting up at him, she smiles and pats the earth near her feet. 'Come and sit with me, my little man.'

He obeys, dropping down onto his haunches so that they are the same height and she can look into his pale face and see the ghost of his grandmother staring back at her. Such wisdom the young possess and so much of it inherent, not what we teach them. When he is comfortably seated, she wraps her arms around him and basks in his soft skin, his curls brushing her jaw. Together, they watch dusk descend over Wapping's skyline. At least I have not lost him, she thinks, my little wonder, this star fallen from Heaven. But Bess – her chest squeezes painfully. Bess is gone. In the space of a few months, Bess has grown up and left her behind.

Johnny begins to wriggle in her arms. Laughing, she sets him free and watches him bound off to enjoy the last of the daylight in the safety of the garden. Birds dart across the sky and she tips back her head to watch their progress. In the peace and calm of the garden, it's almost possible to believe that things are not as bad as they truly are. Lemuel, gone again to a place nobody can follow him; the decision the Bishop will soon make about Chamberlen's forceps; the troubling prospect of how to continue paying the fees at Johnny's new school, now that she's withdrawn him from the old one and written to Uncle John to advise he will not return.

Her dark thoughts are interrupted by Johnny's return, his face pink-cheeked.

'I brought you a posy,' he says, proffering the blooms.

Taking them, she buries her nose in their fragrance, heartened by his spreading grin.

Settling beside her again, Johnny leans against her arm. 'Will Uncle Richard come back soon?' he says.

Mary closes her eyes, their last meeting lapping in her head like waves. 'Of course.'

'Can I tell you something?'

She looks at him. 'Anything you like.'

'I did something bad.' Johnny bites his lip. He pauses to gauge her reaction and when she nods encouragingly, he says, 'I made a wish, when I found out Pa had come back. I wished he would disappear and Uncle Richard was my father. Was that wrong?'

A lump lodges in her chest. 'Not at all,' she says. 'Sometimes, I wish that, too.'

His forehead clears. 'And Bess? She'll be back soon? I didn't wish she would disappear. Did you?'

Mary shakes her head, unable to speak.

'When Bess gets home, she can have her bedroom back,' he offers. 'Alice says I can stay with her. I like the attic; there are mice up there. Will you let me keep a mouse? As a pet?'

He continues to ramble and Mary, gazing towards Wapping, thinks how she misses the sight of them together. Bess, come home, she thinks miserably.

'I know a way to make Bess come back,' says Johnny, startling her. 'You can give her this.' He pulls his clenched fist from his pocket. 'Close your eyes,' he says and, obediently, Mary closes them. 'Now open.'

The child holds out his hand. Mary blinks, disbelieving. It cannot be.

'Where did you find this?' she says, taking the small shoe off her son's palm. It glows in the fading light, the yellow satin shot through with tiny stitches. An exact match for the one in her pocket, the one she carries everywhere, in an effort to convince herself it's a lucky talisman, a charm like the hare's foot her mother used to place upon a woman's belly, or the shrivelled heart of a female quail.

Johnny frowns. 'I can't remember. All I know is one day it was there, under my pillow. I looked everywhere for the other but I couldn't find it. Do you know where it is?'

In answer, she reaches into her pocket and pulls it out to show him.

'You found it,' he says, his face lighting up with happiness. 'I wonder which poppet they came from?'

Poppet. The word is so simple, full of childish reasoning and yet it seems to unlock something she could not, until this moment, fully believe. Studying the shoes, Mary can see quite clearly that they belong to a doll. They have never belonged to anything else. No matter that their provenance is mysterious; one shoe on its own is an enigma. Two is a revelation.

She stands up, the breeze tugging at her dress and loosening her hair. 'Let's go in,' she says. After supper, she thinks, I will take Johnny to the Clements' house and ask Missus Clement to watch over him. Then I will make my way to Anne's and ask for my daughter's forgiveness.

A pulse flares deep down in her womb, a ghostly contraction, an echo of the past.

29

'What did your mother want earlier?' Susanna says, taking Bess's elbow and steering her into the corridor.

Bess waits until Elinor's last client files out into the darkened street before she speaks. 'She wants me to go home.'

'You can't leave me here alone!' Susanna cries. 'What if she dies in her sleep? What if she –'

'That's what Missus Everdeen is here for.' Extracting her elbow, Bess goes into the parlour. Stooping, she picks up a poppet, old and faded, the features nearly rubbed away, and places it in the basket where the other toys live. The doll belonged to Elinor when she was a girl and now it is part of the arsenal they employ to entertain their clients' children.

'It won't be the same without you,' Susanna says. She hugs a toy horse to her chest. 'Please don't leave. I'll do your chores for a month if you stay.'

'I'm not going,' Bess says, but her voice wavers, as if she planned to give an altogether different answer. Will it be so bad? To go home? All this time, she has built it up as the worst possible scenario, but if she is honest, there are things she misses. The comforting domestic sound of Alice banging her skillet; watching Mam in her garden coaxing seeds into plants, transforming bare earth into flowering garden beds. Watching the lime tree drop its leaves as summer shivers into autumn. Bess even misses Puss, slow, indolent creature that she is. She misses her books, her atlases and nautical folios and Philomela's empty birdcage. I thought my home was a cage, she thinks. But I was wrong.

She drops into an armchair, hollowed out by what she has lost. It's not too late, is it? Mam will be delighted to see her. She will shower her with kisses and praise and together, they will rebuild their lives as best they can, until Pa is better. She can even help with the money. To have a salary is a thrill she cannot deny. There is power in knowing you can earn your own way.

Her thoughts are interrupted by Susanna rushing out to answer a sharp knock at the door. Bess hears it open and close and then Susanna returns, handing an envelope to her. Bess digs her fingernail under the flap.

'Wait.' Susanna goes out into the kitchen and comes back with a letter opener. 'Missus Clifton says that a lady never tears into her correspondence as if she were a beggar at a feast.'

Bess slices the envelope open, unfolding the contents. She jumps up.

'What's wrong?' Susanna tries to grab the letter out of her hands.

'I must go home,' Bess says. 'It's a message from Uncle Richard. He says he has news about Pa's condition that he needs to tell us and it would be better if I was home with Mam to hear it.'

She collects her mantle from the hook in the hallway, the letter burning a hole through her pocket. Uncle Richard has never sent her such an urgent note before. More often, it's questions about her health and spirit, enquiries about Mam, how her business fares and whether she has been resting in between stints at women's bedsides. Something drops suddenly into place about her mother and Uncle Richard. Uncle Richard, always a friend, a person she could rely on, just as she relies on Casper. She wonders why he sent the letter, whether Pa is gravely ill. How should she feel, if he is? He is still her father by blood, even if she can't defend the hurt he caused her. How will Mam feel? Free again, her widowhood restored? Mam respects the sanctity of life too much to wish for Pa's death. If only there was a way for them to all be happy.

When she hits the street, she breaks into a run, her cloak flying like wings. Wapping has shifted from day to night, the shops shuttered, the markets bare as she tears past. A big moon shines, casting its light over the puddles, helping her find her way.

At her own street, she slows down just enough to suck in another lungful of air. Then she is off again, the houses a blur of candlelight and clapboard.

At the Needle she hammers on the door, although nobody comes. Strange. The house has a deserted feel about it. Giving up, she pushes open the side gate and pounds past the hedgerows. The garden is awash with pale light, the plants and herbs cocooned in silence.

Nobody comes to the back door. Bess knocks again. Her skin prickles uneasily. Something is wrong.

'Mam?' she calls. 'Alice?'

No answer. Bess frowns, thinking of Mister Clement. She must go to the Clements' house and ask where everyone is. She tries to move, but her feet are stuck in something. Shifting the folds of her cloak out of the way, she looks down and wishes she hadn't. She is standing in a puddle of blood, Puss lying inert at her feet. The animal is almost unrecognisable; it is inside out, bones where there should be fur, glistening wet muscle raw and uncontained.

Bess jerks violently away. She's about to scream when a hand slips around her mouth. Lips brush her neck, sticky, slavering.

'I knew you would come,' he murmurs. 'I told your father I would take my payment, and now I shall.'

Bess tries to scream again but an elbow thumps into her back and she falls, knees buckling, all the breath leaving her body in one puff. Piet looms over her, a giant in dirt-stained clothing. Through the gloom, she makes out his unshaven cheeks, the glint of teeth. A shudder runs through her. She opens her mouth once more to scream but he grasps her hair, yanking her head back and exposing her neck with such force she cries out in shock and fear. A knife blade glints. Bess swallows convulsively, imagining the feel of it penetrating her throat. The hot smell of urine rises up through her skirts as he brings down the blade. To her surprise, she feels it shear through a clump of ringlets. They fall like writhing serpents to the earth around her. Piet grunts, releasing her to scoop them up and push them greedily into his pockets.

Bess's ears are filled with the terrible rhythm of her own breath. She tries to crawl to the side gate when light from the street lifts the gloom. Small stones and clods pierce her hands and knees. Herb tendrils brush her face, releasing their minty scent. She has almost reached the path when a hand seizes her neck, the fingers firm, relentless.

Bess screams.

'Did you think that was all?' Digging his hands into her shoulders, Piet pushes her roughly, face down into the earth.

Bess's mouth opens, tasting bitter soil. Legs astride her body, he is a mountain she cannot dislodge. She is helpless to stop his hand creeping under her waistband. The squirming coldness of his groping fingers on her bare skin causes something inside her to tear free. Mustering every bit of force, she bucks her body backwards. Piet topples off, and Bess springs up onto her heels. The movement spins her head, all that weight lifted. She scrabbles through the dirt, searching for a rock, a spade, something to protect herself. Behind her, Piet curses. Bess intensifies her search – she has only seconds, she knows, until he regains his equilibrium and seizes her again. A flat stone – too small to be useful. A gnarled root. Despair spreads, a tide gathering force. Then her fingers alight on something hard: the handle of her mother's weeding spade. She clutches it just as a thudding weight descends on her buttocks, pressing her flat against the ground.

'I thought you might object.' Forcing her over, Piet brings his fist down hard on the back of her head. Pain bursts. The sky above Piet's head is full of wheeling stars. Sensing the fight leave her body, Piet climbs slowly off her, leaving her sprawled in the dirt, staring up at the endless night. Dazed, Bess is only vaguely aware of his presence, only half-perceives the way he has climbed to his knees and is loosening his breeches. She feels like a midnight flower, unfurling its glossy petals. She is planted in this earth, this patch of soil, connected to the roots that travel deep under London, that lap the water of the Thames, that grow the cress and flowering horse chestnut on the riverbanks and nurture newborn babes. She is connected to Mam, their lives entwined. Something tugs at her mind – Mam. Mam is calling to her, instructing her. Something she must do. Bess's eyelids flutter; she clenches her hands. One is filled with soil, the other with a strange hardness, a shape she has to think hard to make sense of. The purpose shimmers over Piet's shoulders. Piet, who means to hurt her. Bess grips the handle of the tool tightly, afraid it will slip and fail her at the crucial moment. Very distantly, she feels the cool wind on her bare legs, a body over hers, blotting out the moon.

Summoning her courage, Bess brings her fist up. The spade flashes, once, twice, an iron fish writhing in her hand. She hears a grunt, a gurgle. Warm wetness spreads through her dress. Tasting salt, she pictures the tide coming in, blanketing the shoreline. She wriggles, tries to move more but something heavy pins her down. She cannot get free.

A few moments later, her mother's face appears, hovering over her, a teasing mirage.

'Mam,' she says, or thinks she says.

Her mother's fingers stroke her skin, her arms wrap around her body. She is held, safe enough to close her eyes and drift away.

30

'They think he was hiding in a warehouse.' Mam squeezes Bess's hand. It is late afternoon the day after Piet's attack. The sun throws dappled light against the white-washed walls of her room, twinkling on the surface of the drink Mam has brought her and placed on the bedside cabinet.

Mister Grape has come and gone. Bess has answered his questions as dutifully as she can. She licks her dry lips. Although she nodded along with Constable Grape's statements this morning, she's glad Mam was there to fill in the details. To describe the way she visited Missus Clifton's but, finding Bess gone, ran all the way home, arriving just moments after Bess had driven her spade into the man's neck in self-defence.

'Nobody knew he was there; he'd hidden himself in a crate and lived off the victuals in the barrels. Mister Grape says if he had not sent for you with that false letter, he might have stayed there longer. Waiting.'

Bess shudders. Cautious of her aching head, she tries to lift herself but her mother, ever vigilant, is there at once, shifting the bolsters to make her comfortable.

'I'm glad he's dead,' Bess says. 'It's un-Christian, but I am.'

Her mother leans in and kisses her cheek. 'I'm glad, too. For your father's sake and yours. I have a feeling Piet preyed upon him, feeding him stories, encouraging him to fall deeper and deeper into his own delusions. He supplied your father with opium until he could no longer distinguish fancy from reality. This may be the final proof he needs of Piet's stained character. But I would rather it had not come about in such a fashion.' She cups Bess's cheek, the sun bathing her in a rosy glow.

Alice stamps in, smiling brightly, a tray held in front of her. 'Here you are, my darling,' she says, setting it down on the edge of the bed. 'Gingerbread, waffles, marchpane, candied orange. I expect you to eat everything, on pain of death.' She holds out a bit of marchpane, and Bess opens her mouth, obedient. The maid pops it in, wiping her fingers on her sleeve.

'We must have a funeral for Puss,' Bess says, when she has gulped it down.

Alice frowns. 'Animals don't need funerals, Bess.'

'But then how can their souls get to Heaven?'

'Animals don't have souls. Do you ever listen at church or are you too busy daydreaming?'

Patting her shoulder, Alice walks out with the empty tray, humming to herself. Bess rolls marchpane between her fingers, making a sausage. Animals don't have souls? It seems unlikely. Why would God ignore them? They are better than some humans, she thinks. Better than Piet Willems.

'You had a visitor this morning,' her mother says. 'Susanna. I refused to wake you, though.'

'Good. She's angry with me,' Bess explains. 'For leaving her behind at Missus Clifton's. For wanting to come home.'

'Well, you had no choice.' Mam looks suddenly worried. 'You won't return to Missus Clifton's, will you? You're planning to stay, once you're healed?'

Bess hesitates. 'Of course,' she says. 'Susanna is only worried Missus Clifton might die and she won't know what to do alone.'

A shadow crosses her mother's face. 'You should know, Bess, that Missus Clifton is very close to the end. She may pass tonight or tomorrow.'

Bess sits up, immediately alert. 'We must go to her!' she cries. 'How can you just sit there? Help me dress.'

'Bess, no.' Her mother lays a firm hand on Bess's thigh. 'You need to rest.'

'Rest? How can I rest when Missus Clifton is dying?' Pushing her arm away, Bess throws her legs out of bed and stands up. Despite a dull ache throbbing at the back of her skull, she limps over to the drawers. Mam comes to help her, lacing up her stays, fixing the tabs on her skirt and blouse. When she's done, she takes the comb and runs it through Bess's hair, knotting it up with a few pins.

'Am I decent?' Bess says, her smile fading as her mother's eyes fill with tears.

'You are so grown up,' her mother says.

Bess cannot tell if this is a good thing or not.

They find a group of women gathered at Anne Clifton's house. Not just Susanna, but others Bess has never met before. The parlour is bursting with midwives from all over London who have come to pay their last respects and offer their assistance, wherever it is needed. Missus Elinor flits between them and her aunt's bedside, ferrying visitors in and out of the sickroom, her face etched with grief. As she enters with Mam, Bess notices the other women fall back in deference. The conversation lulls. Hanging up her mantle, Mam smiles benignly and, slowly, the talk resumes, but Bess cannot shake off her surprise at this new vision of her mother. Never before has she considered how respected she is.

Bess is swamped by women eager to hear about her brush with death. She tries to answer their questions as best she can. Once, she would have revelled in this, enjoyed the attention, but now she wants nothing more than to be left alone with Mam, for the two of them to go up together and say goodbye to Missus Clifton.

At last, the midwives drift away, their curiosity exhausted, and Bess joins her mother, who is handing around a salver of sweetmeats to sustain the women while they wait their turn.

'Let me,' she says, taking the platter from her mother and offering it to the nearest woman. These women are her peers now. They have come to their profession from different places, found their calling through the advice of friends or older mentors who could see their potential, but they are her sisters. She, who has never had a sister, now has dozens of them.

A man in black livery appears in the open doorway.

Mam, who is closest, asks him what he has come for, who he is after.

'Missus Clifton,' he says, puffing out his chest. 'She's a midwife. I've been sent to fetch her and escort her now to the Burroughs' residence in Limehouse. Lady Burroughs is in a delicate way and there has been some difficulty. I'm to ask Missus Clifton to assist with an urgent delivery.'

'I'm afraid you're too late,' Mam says. 'You must convey to her Ladyship the news that Missus Clifton is extremely unwell and not expected to last the night.'

The man frowns. 'That's unacceptable,' he says, shaking his head. 'The Burroughs will not like it.'

'I'm afraid it's the truth,' says Mam. 'But you may take your pick. Any one of these fine professionals will assist Lady Burroughs with her delivery.'

'It was to be Missus Clifton,' the man insists. 'She has the most experience, and the matter is extremely pressing. Missus Burroughs is at the end of her labour and is now in dire need of assistance. I cannot describe the particulars but suffice to say she is most unwell.'

'Has nobody assisted her?' Mam says. 'The birth . . . it was fast and unexpected?'

The man's frown deepens. 'She had assistance, madam. A surgeon. He used something, I cannot say for certain what. But he says it is unlikely the baby can be saved.'

Mam's jaw tightens. 'I will come. Bess?'

Bess steps forward, swallowing her nerves.

'You will be my deputy. Fetch your things,' Mam says. 'Quickly, now.'

The carriage deposits them in front of a wooden townhouse. A signboard over the door bears the shape of a grasshopper – the sign of wealth, prosperity. The husband must be a money lender, or else a merchant blessed with the ability to shift guineas from one place to the next, distracting his enemies with the flash of his brilliant wings.

The driver jumps down before the carriage has come to a stop and yanks open the door.

Mam turns to Bess and says, 'Listen, Bess. I know what these women are like. I want you to pay attention to what I say and to do only as I instruct you. There will be other women there, mothers, sisters, cousins. They will try to bend you, they think that they know better than us, better than you. Pay them no attention. They are not the ones on whom life and death hinges. They are not the ones who must endure the consequences of a bad decision for the rest of their lives. I am the only voice you listen to. Is that clear?'

Bess nods. Already she can sense the tension building, she can hear screaming coming from inside the house.

A woman in a starched cap waits in the hall to show them upstairs. She takes the stairs two at a time, urging them onwards. Upstairs the hall is filled with noise and women chatting quietly. They fall silent as Mary and Bess pass, and Bess feels the women's eyes linger on their red mantles. When they reach the next hallway, lined with portraits, Mam halts, forcing Bess to stop. Bess is about to ask why when she spies a tall man in a surgeon's frock coat standing outside the door from which the screaming issues. The surgeon, fair-haired and broad-shouldered, hands a box over to an assistant. 'Take that downstairs, boy,' he commands. His voice is timber and iron, tobacco and gilded plate. He seems vaguely familiar and Bess despises him but she can't readily think why. Perhaps it is the self-confidence with which he brushes past them, looking down his nose at her mother, as if he is the sun and Mam is just a piece of tripe tumbled off a fish cart. Or the way he cuffs his assistant across the head when the boy stumbles, almost dropping the case he carries. It's not until he has disappeared down the stairs after the lad that she realises who he reminds her of: Pa.

'Who was that?' she whispers as Mam, clearly shaken, grasps her kitbag and steadies herself against the wall.

'That was Mister Chamberlen,' Mam says. Closing her eyes, she draws air in through her nose and then hooks her arm through Bess's. 'Come on. We have a job to do.'

Inside the bedchamber, on a curtained bed, a girl hardly older than Bess is lying with her legs stretched wide apart. Bess's heart plummets at the sight of her. She hardly knows where to look first: the girl's ruptured privities or the blood trickling out of her or the overflowing pot next to the bed.

A woman strides forward. 'Are you the midwife?' she demands. The similarity between her and the young woman in the bed is striking but this woman is older, her hair streaked with white. Her eyes are strained, the whites glimmering as they flick desperately between Mam and the girl. The largest pearl Bess has ever seen sits over her throat.

'Yes,' Mam says. 'I'm the senior midwife, Missus Gulliver, and this is my assistant, Bess.'

'Good.' The older woman beckons them to the bed. 'This is my daughter, Lady Burroughs – Cecily. I cleared the room earlier, at Mister Chamberlen's insistence. I wish now I had not sent for him. He has done more damage than good.'

As they approach, a scream rips the air. It shudders through Bess like a knife rasping on bone. The girl on the bed writhes, her legs drawn up to her chest. When she slackens, Mam leans over and takes her hand, speaking quietly.

'Lady Burroughs? I'm Missus Gulliver. Mister Chamberlen examined you, I understand?'

Cecily nods, biting her chapped lips. 'He put something inside me,' she says, her voice quivering. 'Then I felt something give . . . and he said he couldn't help, and we'd better fetch a midwife to help. Oh, missus, it hurts so bad. I can feel it coming again.'

'Try to relax. We'll do what we can to help you,' Mam assures her. Commanding Bess to hold Cecily's hand, she examines the girl. Each wave of pain, Cecily grips Bess's hand so hard she thinks the bones will break.

At last, Mam straightens up and takes Bess aside. She has never seen her mother look so fierce nor so sad all at once.

'The child needs turning,' she says, quietly. 'His feet are facing the entrance of the womb. Mister Chamberlen's clamps have torn her insides badly. If the child continues down that path, it will go hard with her. We don't have much time.'

'Can we turn him?' Bess whispers.

Mam's expression clouds. 'We can try. First, we must make him uncomfortable.'

To Cecily, she says, 'We are going to turn the child so he is facing the right way. It may hurt, but it will pass soon enough, I promise you.'

Cecily whimpers, hair plastered to her face.

Mam rests her hands on either side of the girl's belly. Then she tilts her head. 'Bess? Come here. Press your hands where I show you.'

Aware of Cecily's mother watching her, Bess slips her hands under Mam's calloused ones until she can feel the child.

'When I give the word, you turn,' Mam says. 'Do not let go, not for anything, no matter how hard it hurts. Ready? Go.'

Bess does as she is told. Cecily screams, bucking her hips, wriggling to escape the pain. The child moves restlessly in Bess's hands, resisting her firm control. The muscles in her shoulders and arms cry out. Her arms ache in their sockets. She is tempted to let go, but Mam is there, as solid as a rock. Slowly, ever so slowly, their hands rotate the infant in his watery sack until at last Mam says hoarsely, 'You can let go.'

Bess's hands drop to her sides. 'Did it work?' she says, looking anxiously across at her mother. Mam frowns down at Cecily's figure, concentration knitting her brow.

'I think so,' Mam says. 'Time will tell.'

Bess never gave much thought to time before this year. At Missus Priest's, time was interminable and neverending. At home, time was never long enough when she snuck away to avoid her chores. Now she is standing here, watching a girl her own age push out a baby, Bess is certain time has expanded, swelling like a gibbous moon to hold them all in suspense.

As Cecily's screams intensify, Mam checks her privities again, dabbing at the damage the surgeon caused, applying salve and an ointment to soothe the scored flesh.

'You are making good progress,' she tells the girl. Although Cecily is too busy panting to reply, Bess acknowledges her mother's words.

'How much longer?' she says quietly, flexing her hand.

Mam eyes the girl on the bed. 'Soon.' A little frown mars her forehead and Bess's stomach clutches. Something is not right, although they have turned the babe. She wishes she could rub out the line with her thumb.

Cecily's mother hovers, talking to a woman with wide hips and thick ankles. The wet nurse, Mam says as she presses a clean clout against Cecily's wounds. Bess stares at the woman's stained pinafore, the breasts Cecily's baby will cling to once he has been checked over. It's astonishing, Bess thinks, the difference between women who can afford to pay for a wet nurse and the clients she has met who nurse their own children of necessity. She cannot draw her eyes away from the wet nurse until a sudden grunting gurgle at her elbow recalls Cecily's plight.

The energy alters. Mam drops to her knees by Bess's side, both of them staring while Cecily pants and strains. She hears her mother breathe deep. Bess feels afraid, a frisson of uncertainty spreading like a rash across her skin. What if she can't help? What if all their efforts to turn the child have failed, or Mam cannot stop the bleeding or –

Mam clutches her arm. Bess, leaning forward, sees the baby's crown appear. When the baby slips out, she catches it, heavier than she imagined, but lighter, too. She rubs the child with a cloth as it yelps and complains. She turns her face up to her mother's and finds it wreathed in smiles.

'You did it, Bess,' Mam says, squeezing her shoulder. Bess feels the warmth of her mother's pride flow through her.

Mam turns her attention to the baby. Frowning, she examines him, gently.

'His foot is broken,' she tells Cecily. 'The forceps snapped it. It may trouble him as he gets older. But he is alive, praise God.'

Passing the baby to his mother is like handing over a piece of herself. I did this, Bess thinks. Helped this little person to be born. No matter who he is, or what he becomes, today is the first day of life. And I was there. I fought for him and I won.

By the time they return to Missus Clifton's house, dusk has settled and the midwives have dispersed. As the carriage which brought them pulls away, Bess sees a landau rolling to a halt. A man is helped out, his dark robes and gleaming jewels a clear sign of his importance. It must be the Bishop. Bess lowers her eyes, trying to study him without being rude. Shown into the parlour, he ignores Elinor and Susanna, choosing to speak only to her mother.

'I've come to pay my respects to Missus Clifton,' he says. 'And to inform you that the trial is over. Lady Burroughs and her husband are honest, God-fearing citizens and the Queen's particular favourites. Lord Burroughs donated a substantial amount of money last year to rebuild the gardens at Fulham Palace. We can't risk displeasing him or his supporters.'

Mam shows the Bishop into the sickroom. He stays mere moments, reappearing in the parlour flanked by his attendants and dabbing his eyes.

'Thank you for coming,' Mam says formally and Bess wonders how her mother dares speak with such self-assurance to a man who holds the fate of all London's midwives in his bejewelled hands. After he leaves, Mam asks her to come into the sickroom with her, so that Missus Elinor and Susanna can rest. Bess's blood is still zinging around her body. She is so jittery, she can barely walk along the hallway without running. But as they enter the room together, all the excitement drains out of her, replaced by an aching sadness. Each breath is an effort for Missus Clifton. Even at this last hour, her body is fighting death off, holding onto everything that she was, reluctant to let go.

Mam reaches blindly for Bess's hand, her lovely eyes full of tears. Bess squeezes.

Missus Clifton's lips move.

'What's she saying?' Bess whispers.

Her mother strokes the old woman's knee. 'She is casting through her memories, like a fisherman examining his catch.'

'Diamonds and pearls,' Missus Clifton wheezes. 'Babies.'

'Hush,' Mam says, soothing.

As twilight steals into the chamber, Bess smiles and thinks, my mother is a wonder.

31

Lemuel finds her at the bottom of the garden. She would live there if she had a choice; she would use the soft daisies for a pillow and the stars for a blanket. When he appears around the corner of the hedgerows, she climbs to her feet, dusting off her smock. She scrubs her face and hands, trying to remove any traces of dirt.

They meet in the middle of the path, the crossroads where all paths lead and end.

'You look well,' she says.

'I am well.' He is wearing a new coat, dark blue, the fabric a little stiff.

'You should get Alice to soak that for you,' she says. 'Before you leave.'

His eyes widen. 'How did you know?'

She lifts a shoulder. 'You always leave when you're better. It's part of your story, part of you.' She taps his thumb. 'Do you remember that locket you once gave me? The little silver one? Shape of a heart?'

'Aye.'

'I found it. You'll never guess where it was. It was hidden at the back of our cupboard, as if it had always been there.'

'Fancy that,' he says.

'I thought I'd lost it, during the move from the Old Jewry.' She looks up at him, shading her face with her hand. 'Or that you sold it, the way you sold my wedding ring.'

His cheeks flush as she waits for him to deny the charge. 'I – I must confess . . . I did sell it.' He drops his chin to his chest, jowls quivering. 'I'm sorry.'

The sincerity of his apology eases something in her. Hard-won, but here it is; one true tale. 'Thank you.'

He pulls in a breath. 'About Piet –'

Her face darkens. 'I cannot forgive you,' she says. 'Do not ask it of me. You are weak, Lemuel. There is a weakness in you I have given up all hope of fixing.'

'I don't think that's –'

'It's true,' she says. 'But we will get on as best we can while you are gone.' She wipes her nose. 'And now, if you will excuse me, I have some planting to do.'

He looks at the neat rows of turned soil.

'Tulips,' she says. 'I am growing tulips. Bess has a friend who has gone to sea. I hope the flowers will make him feel welcome, when he returns.'

'You have never planted tulips for me,' he says.

She smiles. 'You were never really here.'

32

The funeral is a sea of red mantles. Crammed into St Paul's, the midwives of London stand together as the coffin bearing the body of Anne Clifton is carried in. Each woman wears a new pair of gloves, as Anne's will stipulates. United in their grief, they are consoled by the knowledge that Anne brought more children into this world than any other midwife. Her legacy is scattered across the city, visible in every rosy cheek and shining eye that graces these pews every other Sunday or clambers, wailing, onto its mother's lap, demanding to be taken outside. A less conspicuous legacy is the one that knocks on doors at any hour of the night or day, summoned by the call, women who absorbed the older woman's training and were lucky enough to be at her side during deliveries. The apprenticeships she licensed, sensing their deep desire to help the women of the parish birth their babies the way they wanted to rather than the way a man commanded.

Sitting in her pew, Mary imagines they are all flowers, red tulips straining towards the light. Anne has done everything she can for them and now they must grow on their own. They must band together, growing in the same direction, lifting themselves and each other.

The pallbearers lay the coffin on the slab. Bess jiggles her knee. She has always hated sitting still. Mary places a calming hand on her leg.

As the Bishop clears his throat and begins his sermon, Mary catches her daughter's eye and smiles.

'I am greatly in need of financial advice,' Mary says to Richard. They are sitting in her garden, on a flat bed of stone she has recently had installed at some considerable cost to act as a seat near the foxgloves. Johnny's laughter mingles with Bess's as they duck in and out of the house, playing a game of hide and seek. The day is warm, and a strong breeze blows, the same breeze that earlier returned her husband out to sea again, where he belongs.

'Well, I know a lawyer.' Richard pulls up a spear of grass and plays with the stalk.

Her lips curve into a smile. 'Is he experienced?' she says, teasing. 'Do you trust him?'

'I have known him all my life.'

'I have been left a little money by a good friend of mine, Anne Clifton. I would like Johnny to continue his schooling in London, if you can arrange it.'

He frowns. 'Uncle John –'

'I'm not afraid of him,' she says. 'I've enough now to pay the fees.'

His face breaks into a grin. 'Then you don't need my advice, Missus Gulliver. You seem determined to make your own way, just as you always have.'

'I always need your advice, Richard,' she says. She moves her hand until it covers his, warmth shifting between them. The air is awash with the last summer pollen which beads Richard's skin like golden sand.

'You aren't sniffling,' she says.

'I finally started drinking that tea,' Richard admits.

'So after all this time, we have misunderstood each other.'

'I understand you better than I understand myself,' he says. 'And I will always be here, if you need me. You need only say the word.'

She knows. They sit with their hands touching, nothing more than friendly contact, and yet she is filled with warm, glorious light. There are some friendships which cannot be defined by society's laws. There are good men and bad men, men who stay behind and men who go on ahead and do not look back. Richard is one of the good ones. And perhaps, one day, there will be more to share.

'I do have one job for you,' she says.

'Name it.'

'It's the purchase of a certain little jenny. Her name is Koko. Some people consider it a very sentimental dream, to own a pet, but I have it on good authority that a donkey is worth her weight in gold.'

He smiles.

'You may laugh,' she says. 'But a female donkey possesses more grit and backbone than many people I know. Hugh Chamberlen could learn a thing or two about humility from such a beast.'

Richard's expression sobers. 'I saw him at the club yesterday. Did I tell you? He is vowing to change the Bishop's mind. There will be other challenges,' he says. 'You know that.'

'I do. But I have faith. When the surgeon's guild comes after us, we will be meek. When they threaten us, we will submit. In public. In private, we will do what we have always done: we will share our knowledge and thrive.'

'Your courage still surprises me,' he says before looking away, embarrassed.

Does it? she thinks. Perhaps once, it might have surprised her too, but she knows herself better now. She has discovered that she is a woman who knows that winds can change. That things that are lost can be found. That children grow and find their feet. They make their own paths. They set off on glorious adventures, travelling to places we cannot even imagine.

And then, with luck, they come back.

Epilogue

The sea has given birth to a man.

He stands upon a bed of sand, dreaming of home. Not his home – the birthplace of the tulip – but the home he hopes to find waiting for him in London, with a family he has always dreamed about. A signboard, scrawled with a needle and thread. A girl with golden curls waiting behind a glass pane. Waiting for his letter, waiting for him to tell her that he has found nothing on the island. There was nothing to be found.

Locating the island demanded much of him, requiring tenacity, a firm belief in the improbable. As a child, in an orphanage in The Hague, he dreamed of drowned cities, submerged under channels of water. Islands that shimmered in the mind's eye, peopled with strange, exotic races. Casper bends to scoop up a handful of sand. He sifts the grains through his fingers, searching for something he cannot name. He has spent the afternoon walking. Circling the beach, keeping his ship in view the entire time. Now it is getting dark, the tide is coming in. He must row out soon, or risk being stuck.

There is nothing here. Nothing but sand and ocean and the longing for London. When he returns, he will go straight to her. He will not even send a letter. There is too much to say, and he cannot explain his feelings anyway, not in words.

He scoops up another handful of sand, thinking of her hair.

Raising his head, he looks back the way he has come, thinking he hears voices. But it's only gulls, wheeling overhead, cawing to each other in a language he cannot hope to understand.

GULLIVER'S
WIFE

Author's note

Gulliver's Wife draws its inspiration from Jonathan Swift's iconic 18th century satire *Travels into Several Remote Nations of the World In Four Parts By Lemuel Gulliver, First a Surgeon, and then a Captain of Several Ships*, better known as *Gulliver's Travels*. Swift's creation was an immediate publishing success, intended to be read as a parody of other popular travelogues of the time, such as Daniel Defoe's *The Adventures of Robinson Crusoe* (1719) and also, as an allegory for the relationship between government and monarchy. Swift's book opens with an introduction by Lemuel himself in which he gives an account of his early life before describing the fateful voyage to Lilliput. Thereafter, the text is divided into journeys to other 'lands' inhabited by fantastical creatures which serve to highlight the best and worst of the human condition. Of all Swift's creations, the Lilliputians (recognisable by their small stature of less than six inches) remain the most memorable, exposing the flaws of a society frequently caught between wars, both literal and figurative.

Driven onto the island of Lilliput by a storm, Gulliver is first imprisoned and then released after he agrees to help the Lilliputians defeat their enemies, the Blefuscudians. Eventually, he is charged with treason but escapes by hailing a passing ship which takes him back to England where he is reunited with his family. Gulliver's children are mentioned a handful of times, but it was mention of his wife, Mary Burton Gulliver, which captured my imagination when I re-read *Gulliver's Travels* as an adult.

Mary is an absent character throughout much of the story. A symbol of the domestic world, she exists on the fringes of Gulliver's adventures, never destined to travel further (as far as we are told) than the outskirts of London. Re-reading *Gulliver's Travels*, I found myself wanting to know more about this long-suffering spouse, left behind to pick up the pieces. If Mary had been a real woman living in the early 1700s she would, despite the considerable limitations imposed by society, have had her own dreams as well as responsibilities to her family and community. How would Mary have reacted to Gulliver's return and his claims of visiting an island of tiny people? Would she have believed him, or done her best to prevent his instability impacting her children? And what was the nature of their relationship, before he went to sea, and when he returned?

The decision to set my own novel between the first and second of Gulliver's journeys was driven by the desire to condense the action and highlight the drama around his possible madness and the impact it might have on his wife's life. In fact, in the original *Gulliver's Travels*, Mary's trials with her husband go on to become more intriguing and complex each time he returns home. The great genius of Swift's tale is that the more Gulliver sees of the wider world, the less he enjoys life in England with its myriad hypocrisies, yawning divide between rich and poor and dominance of powerful institutes like Church and monarchy over the 'small people'. Lemuel Gulliver never quite appreciates this irony, though. His name provides a telling clue about his nature: to gull someone in 18th century England was to convince them that something fake was true.

In order to fashion Mary with her own interior world, I turned to accounts written by women of the time, including the author Hannah Woolley (*The Gentlewomans Companion or, A Guide to the Female Sex*, 1673), the playwright Aphra Behn (*The Ten Pleasures of Marriage*, 1682), and the midwife Jane Sharp (*The Midwives Book or: the whole Art of Midwifery Discovered*, 1671). Through their words, Mary's character slowly took shape. Although the Mary Burton of *Gulliver's Travels* is the daughter of a London hosier, women were barred from inheriting property and the infrequency of Gulliver's salary meant she would have needed an alternative source of income. I chose to make her a midwife and herbalist, a woman with a strong sense of familial duty, a keen gardener with a passion for learning.

I am indebted to Dr Doreen Evenden's excellent book *The Midwives of Seventeenth-Century London* (2000) for illuminating the role of the midwife in English society and the hitherto undisclosed accomplishments of these extraordinary women. Contrary to stereotypes (reinforced by male practitioners) that the London midwives were 'ignorant, incompetent, and poor', they commanded immense respect within their close-knit communities and their commitment to the role, which included apprenticeships, licensing and oath-taking, meant they were often viewed as experts in the 'secret women's business' of childbirth. They also testified against criminals accused of rape and sexual assault and were considered 'expert witnesses' by the courts, since their work required extensive knowledge of female anatomy.

Not everyone approved. In the early 1700s, a movement aimed at discrediting female midwives to promote the interests of male practitioners began to gain momentum, supported by surgeons who favoured the medicalisation of birth via forceps and 'lying-in' hospitals which eventually led to devastatingly high mortality rates in the latter half of the 18th century. I have taken the liberty of positioning Mary at the forefront of this struggle and humbly defer to the wise words of Elizabeth Nihell, an 18th century midwife, who wrote: '. . . *where is the kingdom, where is the nation, where is the town, where in short, is the person who would prefer iron and steel to the hand of flesh, tender, soft, duly supple, dextrous and trusting to its own feeling for what it is about . . .*'

For gardening and herbal lore, I frequently consulted the beautifully illustrated manual *In a Unicorn's Garden* by Judyth A. McLeod (2008) as well as Nicholas Culpeper's *Complete Herbal* (1653) and Jenny Uglow's *A Little History of British Gardening* (2005). I was also fortunate to draw on the knowledge of contemporary herbalist Brodie Hearnden and the expertise of the staff at the Chelsea Physic Garden. To better understand the living conditions and politics of Stuart London, I recommend *Queen Anne: The Politics of Passion* by Anne Somerset (2012), as well as *Restoration London* by Liza Picard (2003), *1700: Scenes from London Life* by Maureen Waller (2000) and *Pasta for Nightingales: A 17th Century Handbook for Bird-Care and Folklore*, reprinted with a foreword by Helen Macdonald (2018). In researching the complex relationship between Holland and England, I am grateful to have discovered Lisa Jardine's *Going Dutch* (2008), with its excellent commentary and insights.

Book club questions

1. *Gulliver's Travels* is a classic work of fiction which has inspired countless movies and books. How much did you know (or remember) about the original story before you read *Gulliver's Wife* and did this knowledge affect your reading experience? Why or why not?
2. Mary Burton is an absent character in *Gulliver's Travels* but the events of *Gulliver's Wife* are told predominantly through her eyes. How does this change in perspective affect your opinion of Mary and her husband, Lemuel Gulliver? How would you have responded to Gulliver's remarkable return?
3. How does Mary's profession as a midwife affect her relationship with her Wapping neighbours? How has the role of midwives changed between the time the book is set and the present?
4. When the book opens, Bess Gulliver still clings to the impossible fantasy of becoming a sailor like her father. Who is more responsible for indulging this fantasy – Mary

or Gulliver? Does withholding the realities of life damage our children or set them free?

5. How is the idea of power and big people versus small people explored through the novel? Who has power over whom? How has this changed by the end of the story?

6. Contrast Bess's budding romance with Casper with Mary and Richard's relationship. How are they similar or different?

7. The tagline of *Gulliver's Wife* is 'Birth, death, wonder.' How are these themes woven through the story?

8. *Gulliver's Travels* was intended to be read as a parody of adventure tales like Daniel Defoe's *Robinson Crusoe*. Although Mary never actually leaves England, are the adventures we experience through her (and Bess's) eyes less engaging than those of Lemuel Gulliver or Robinson Crusoe? Why or why not?

9. Which of the women in Mary's history have had the most influence on her decisions about family and career? Do the women in the community support each other?

10. We know from *Gulliver's Travels* that Lemuel goes back to sea at the end of his first voyage and returns home again at least twice more with equally wild stories. Did you find the ending of *Gulliver's Wife* satisfying? How do you think Mary will react to Gulliver's return?

Acknowledgements

This book would not exist without the assistance of many people. Firstly, Bert Ivers, publisher extraordinaire, for believing in this story and in me and pushing me to write better; you have my eternal gratitude. Claire de Medici, Kylie Mason, Michelle Swainson and Vanessa Lanaway – thank you for your editing wisdom and professionalism. Thank you to the Simon & Schuster Australia dream team: Dan Ruffino, Fiona Henderson, Anna O'Grady, Kirsty Noffke, and all the wonderful sales and marketing staff who worked so tirelessly behind the scenes to get this book out into the world. Christa Moffitt – thank you for the beautiful cover.

Thank you to the staff at Tower Hamlets Library and Archives for your assistance with maps and resources related to historical Wapping and to my friend Helen Selvey, for walking me around the area and imagining what life might have been like for the seafaring families of that time. Two of my favourite London haunts – the London Museum and sister site Docklands Museum – provided answers to some tricky historical questions and Dennis Severs' House in Spitalfields was a sensory gift which conjured the sights and smells of 18th century London so effectively, I had trouble adjusting to the present.

My thanks to Emma Woods, Helen Selvey, Liang Lim, Sarah-Jane Burton, Mel Sargent, Pam Cook, Dasha Maiorova, David Beecroft, Wendy J. Dunn and Donna Cattana for all your support. Mum, thank you so much for your excellent midwifery advice and for minding the kids so I could write. Dad, thank you for inspiring my love of books and always believing. Michael, my greatest thanks for all your support. Thank you to my sister Annette for brainstorming sessions and early feedback. Lastly, a great big thank you to my smallest Lilliputians, Lachlan and Lily Mae – you are my world.

Lauren Chater

About the author

Lauren Chater is the author of the bestselling historical novel *The Lace Weaver* and the baking compendium *Well Read Cookies – Beautiful Biscuits Inspired by Great Literature*. She is currently working on her third novel, *The Winter Dress*, inspired by a real 17th century gown found off the Dutch coast in 2014. In her spare time, she loves baking and listening to her children tell their own stories. She lives in Sydney.

> For more about Lauren, see:
> www.laurenchater.com
> www.thewellreadcookie.com
> www.instagram.com/the_well_read_cookie
> www.facebook.com/LaurenChaterWriter
> www.twitter.com/WellReadCookie